FIVE MEN AND WOMEN SWEPT
UP IN A COSMIC POWER STRUGGLE

DAN MERRIWEATHER—A rock-singing superstar with the powers of a god . . . and an astounding plan to transform the world . . .

DR. ELIZABETH COOGAN—A student of the paranormal, she followed Dan Merriweather to the brink of an unimaginable universe . . .

HARRAH JUDD—The Army General who played his hunches against a brilliant enemy beyond time and beyond space . . .

RASTABAN AL NASHIRAH—From his opulent Watergate penthouse, he directed the most spectacular arms sales in his death-dealing career . . .

SHIRLEY PAARS—In the Washington milieu of sex, sadism, and power, she used her lush body to penetrate the secrets of a nation in crisis . . .

STAR FIRE

ALSO BY INGO SWANN

TO KISS EARTH GOOD-BYE
COSMIC ART (editor)

STAR FIRE

INGO SWANN

SOUVENIR PRESS

First British Edition published 1978 by
Souvenir Press Ltd, 43 Great Russell Street, London WC1B3PA

ISBN 0 285 62346 X

Printed in Great Britain by Fletcher & Son Ltd, Norwich
and bound by
Richard Clay (The Chaucer Press), Ltd.,
Bungay Suffolk

STAR FIRE

PRELUDE

WILLIAM JAMES, October 1909
"Psychics form a special branch of education, in which experts are only gradually becoming developed. Hardly, as yet, has the surface of the facts called psychic begun to be scratched for scientific purposes."

J. B. RHINE, May 1945
"In due course all types of parapsychological or psi ability, as they have come to be called, were confirmed, first at the Duke University Laboratory and later in other centers as well. Not only was the fact of their occurrence established but their common properties were explored and lawful relationships discovered that established certain general principles applicable to all known psi phenomena."

DOCUMENT 219714 (SECRET), APRIL 1969

FOREIGN TECHNOLOGY DIVISION
Air Force Systems Command
Wright-Patterson Air Force Base

EXTRACT
This document represents an unedited translation of *Biological Radio and Psychic Sensory Systems* by A. D. Kashinskiy, Russian Academy of Sciences Bioinformation Research Section, Moscow. In it are brief reports and analyses of the information content of experiments conducted by the Bioinformation Section during the years 1966 to 1967. Formal algorithms are proposed which can be applied to use of telepathy as a channel of information transmission.

O. COSTA DE BEAUREGARD, December 1974
"Relativistic quantum mechanics is a conceptual scheme

in which phenomena such as psychokinesis or telepathy, far from being irrational, should, on the contrary, be expected as *very rational*. They are postulated by the very symmetries of mathematical formalism, and should be predicted for reasons completely akin to those that have led Einstein to enunciate the principle of special relativity, de Broglie to produce the concept of matter waves, and Dirac to (almost) predict the positron."

JOINT CHIEFS OF STAFF, January 1979
Briefing
(DARPA-OX-D-124) (TOP SECRET)

Subject: Possible involvement of psi abilities in national security and military affairs

EXTRACT

Certain strategic intelligence analysts have established that so-called psi (psychic) aptitudes are of increasing interest and credibility in science. This briefing is a review of historic and scientific aspects of psi potentials.

Guidelines are established governing military research in this area, press leakage of projects, overwatch of civilian psi research centers, and methods of surveillance, containment, and use of persons exhibiting other than threshold psi aptitudes.

1

TONOPAH AND TOLKIEN

Space and time
Are often seen
One way
And then another . . .

> (from the song
> "At the Heart
> of the Universe")
> —DANIEL MERRIWEATHER

The contradictions and inconsistencies of the old theories force us to ascribe new properties to the time-space continuum, to the scene of all events in our physical world.

> —ALBERT EINSTEIN

Demands

WASHINGTON

Judd's spine stiffened. The look in Abrams' eyes was fear. Far back, controlled, but the same look he had seen in the eyes of men in combat in Korea and Vietnam, the ones who knew they weren't going to make it.

His reaction was hardly conscious, more a matter of a sudden psychic certainty, unexpressed, vanishing before it really registered. Its passing left a chill trail down his spine; then he relaxed and was once again aware of the air conditioners, of the tightness of his collar, of his office surroundings.

It was a small office, comfortable and old-fashioned, crowded with a cluttered desk, leather chairs, and stacks of books and documents. It would not have struck a chance visitor as being the nerve center of the Pentagon's Defense Advanced Research Projects Agency, nor would such a visitor have taken the hard-faced man with close-cropped hair seated behind the desk for the liaison chief of the deliberately obscure DARPA.

General Harrah Judd squinted ice-blue eyes against the diminutive cigar clenched between his teeth and looked at the letter Abrams had handed him. For an instant, he could make no sense of it . . . damn! There it was again, that sudden inward certainty of something big about to happen, a quick surge of apprehension that wiped out his ability to deal coolly with the situation.

He forced himself to relax, to drive away the feeling— then understood fully what the letter and its attached drawing represented. He looked up at Abrams, forcing his face to relax to hide the dismay he felt.

"It's doubtful if it's an ordinary security leak, sir." Abrams spoke with a hint of irony that showed that Judd's reaction had not escaped him—and that his awareness of it had helped him control his own.

"Someone inside the project, then? A sorehead, some nut

who thinks he can . . ." Judd abandoned the idea even as he voiced it.

"Might be, sir. But whoever it is, his data are *very* good. He's even shown the location of the latrines."

Judd grunted and turned back to the letter and the sketch. The drawing was a little distorted, but only a little. The depth underground was accurate. The distance from surrounding towns was accurate. The list of microwave equipment housed in the secret installation contained all items he recalled . . . plus some that were new to him. That made it all the more likely that the list was accurate—the freaks who put together projects like this kept secrets even from each other.

"This is a drawing," the brief typed note affixed to the sketch informed him, "of a research installation—code word Tonopah—developing weaponry in the area of sonic control of the human mind and microwave demolition of the human nerve system. It is to be disbanded, or every nation in the world will receive a copy of this drawing."

Moving very slowly and carefully, Judd pushed piles of paper to the back and sides of the desk, leaving the sketch and letter in the cleared space, and stared at them.

"Who have we got on it, Abrams?"

The room's fluorescent lights playing bluish glints on his tightly curled black hair, Abrams bent over the desk and placed a green report folder in front of Harrah. His brown eyes blazed with a hard professionalism equalling that of his superior.

"The works, sir. Military intelligence got their experts on the stick fast on this one. Anything to do with Tonopah, they run scared—and they'd better. Any leaks . . ."

"Get on with it, Abrams."

"Right, sir. Fingerprints, none. Postmark, right here in Washington, D.C. Paper, recycled, cockle finish, untraceable. Typewriter, old, we are working on that. Drawing done with Eagle Flash pointed felt tip, untraceable. Syntax of message, ordinary, but the use of the word 'demolition' is wrong. It should be 'manipulation.'"

Judd let one part of his mind register Abrams' summary of the report, and on another level probed his own emotions. Guilt? Tonopah was inhuman—but then, so were bombs. Inhuman, yes. And necessary. The British had used microwaves for riot control as far back as 1953, with a device that caused the sphincter muscles in the rectum to relax. Rioters desisted fast when faced with the sudden sensation of their bowels giving way. Microwaves could shatter glass, could produce any number of bizarre effects at a distance—and with that kind of potential, there was going to be steady, worldwide research and development, inhuman or not. And just as with atomics—and the whole range of weaponry—the United States, in this decade of the 1980s, was stuck with the need to keep ahead.

Tonopah was the result of that need. And it was protected by the most advanced and complete security web ever devised. Only a handful of people off the site knew anything of it. No record of its location, no copies of the construction plans, of the blueprints for the experimental sonic chambers existed anywhere except in the memory banks of ultraclassified computers, to be viewed on display panels only after a complex series of ident numbers and cards were fed into the security check system.

It was flatly impossible that anyone could have discovered the information laid out in the letter and sketch in front of him. Even if one of the few people with the right of access to the computers—say President Heathstone—had gone completely mad and embarked on this plan, Judd would have known. Any request for classified information from them, even on the highest authority, was automatically monitored and recorded.

But the existence of the sketch could not be denied. Nor could the unthinkable threat to make the knowledge of Tonopah public property.

He could estimate some of the consequences of that, and they were appalling: public outcry of the kind that could overturn governments and wreck the entire defense program . . . reactions of rage and panic from foreign governments, ranging from denunciation to possible war. But at least they could be calculated and somehow coped with. The fact of the sketch could not—it did not *fit*, it was an overthrow of the whole structure of his experience.

The guilt he always had to suppress when thinking about Tonopah—it did not help much to tell himself that microwave control of the mass human mind was no worse than nuclear extermination—mingled with and deepened the premonition growing within him. He pushed both aside with an immense effort of will and managed to speak to Abrams.

"Better see if you can get me an immediate appointment with the Secretary of Defense."

"Yes, sir!"

As Abrams spoke urgently into the phone, Judd picked up the sketch once more. He noted almost with detachment that it trembled in his hands.

MOSCOW

David P. Hornsborough III, United States Ambassador to the Soviet Union, nervously paced his bedroom floor, his tall, aristocratically slim body draped in a dark blue terry-cloth robe. Helena Asch, his secretary, her own eyes red from disturbed sleep, had awakened him over an hour ago, alerting him to expect a call from the Russian head of state.

He smashed out the tenth cigarette in a glittering crystal ashtray, swearing in an undertone. Why had he had that third drink at the reception? That must be where his headache came from. Why did Russians like to do business in the middle of the night? Where was the coffee he had ordered? Goddamn the Administration, anyway, for always keeping things in such a snarl. He reached for the embassy housephone to track down the coffee.

The door opened. Helena Asch, her tall body straight, her blond hair flowing down to her shoulders, carried in a tray and set it on a table. The aroma of coffee shifted to Hornsborough and his headache eased.

"Thanks, Helena," he muttered. "Where do you suppose that call is . . . ?"

"The Premier is on the line, David," she said, deftly picking up the white receiver.

"On the line? Goddamn," he snarled. "Why wasn't I told?"

"The Premier called personally, sir, there was no time . . ."

"Shit!" Hornsborough snatched the receiver. Helena picked up the attachment, ready to interpret.

"Yes, Mr. Premier, sorry you were kept waiting."

Russian phones always crackled, even official ones. Was it the missing crackling that impressed the ambassador? Or was it that the Premier spoke excellent English? Or was it the stunned look in Helena's eyes that the Premier was unprecedentedly bypassing interpretation? He noticed the cigarette still smoking in the glittering ashtray and picked it up.

"That is quite all right," said the hoarse voice of Praskovie Tosygen. "I'm calling to ask if you could visit me in fifteen minutes."

Hornsborough briefly wondered if, in spite of all détentes, the third world war might somehow have got under way.

"Certainly, Mr. Premier," responded Hornsborough, reaching for the ashtray to smash out his dying cigarette.

Helena was already on the housephone, alerting his chauffeur.

"Good," said Tosygen. "I shall expect you."

The line went dead. Hornsborough noticed that the familiar crackling had started again. Helena was already laying out a suit.

"You look pretty good, David," she said, "you won't have time to shave."

"What the hell do you suppose he wants?" he asked, more of himself than of her. There was no time for modesty. He pulled his shirt on and then his pants, forgetting his shorts.

"I don't know, David, I can't imagine. I'll have the car waiting." She swept out the door.

Driven swiftly through the empty streets of nighttime Moscow, Hornsborough felt, as always, oppressed by the somehow ominous city, with its mingling of the medieval and featureless modernity. He had been driven down so many foreign streets through the years . . . on his way to meetings that never semed to settle anything important, even if—as he had to suppose—they helped keep things from getting worse. And he had done what he could; he had always been good at talking, at desensitizing flammable issues, and that had finally brought him to this key post. At the dawn of his career, he had dreamed of being the kind of leader who might lead humanity to a new vision of itself; but he had not, it turned out, been very good at vision, only talking. Yet the world needed something to turn it in a new direction . . . and it didn't look as though it was going to find it. . . .

The serge of his pants scraped his rear as his car swiftly turned the corners and drew up at the imposing massive brick darkness of the Premier's city residence. He was swiftly, silently escorted through several corridors, their barrenness relieved by fussy decorative touches, probably Czarist leftovers.

The room into which he was shown was warm, soft with gray and pink walls, crystal chandelier glinting reflections of the usual red flag. A fire was burning in the ornate fireplace.

"Thank you for coming," said Tosygen.

"I am, as usual, honored to have an opportunity of talking with you, Mr. Premier," said Hornsborough, taking a seat across from him.

"I think you must like some coffee, which is here on the table, already." Tosygen gave a careful smile.

Thank God, thought Hornsborough. "Most certainly, Mr. Premier," he said. "May I pour you some, too?"

"No, I prefer tea, which I have just had," said Tosygen. "I should come directly to business, since I realize it is late, and we all must sleep sometimes."

"Not at all, Mr. Premier, I myself was just beginning to do my correspondence when you called," Hornsborough lied.

"I hope I did not part you from important work?"

"Not at all, sir. Not at all," said Hornsborough, gratefully swallowing the hot coffee.

"I would not want you to think that we are giving undue importance to the incident, Mr. Ambassador," began Tosygen.

Incident! Incident? Christ, what now? "I am not aware of any . . . uh . . . incident, Mr. Premier." It was going to be one of *those* nightmares of the kind the Russians used to harass the entire world. Hornsborough regretted his missing underwear. He was already sweating.

"I only wished to assure you that the installation in question is purely someone's imagination, and has never, in fact, existed."

"Installation?"

"We are aware that there are, as you say, terrorists and incendiaries in both our nations. . . ."

Hornsborough grasped for the reflexive diplomatic response this called for.

"Mr. Premier, I find I am unable to follow you. The American people do not as a whole . . ."

"Mr. Ambassador, we are not yet making accusations, and would not wish to . . ."

"Mr. Premier, frankly, I feel at a loss, since I have not been briefed on the situation."

"Ah, yes, Mr. Ambassador." Tosygen smiled. "More coffee?"

"No, I believe not," said Hornsborough, drawing himself erect, forgetting his discomfort.

"We have," said Tosygen thinly, "received a threat, which I assure you is unimportant, a note mailed in your nation . . ."

"Mr. Premier, I regret any inconvenience that might arise, but surely such matters are handled by standard procedures in your . . ."

"Ah, that is precise, Mr. Ambassador. But in this case, although it is unimportant, we wished to assure your President, through you, that such an installation could never exist in our republics."

"Installation? What installation?"

"We wish to assure you that, despite rumors and the unfortunate publication in your country of certain books on the subject . . ."

"Mr. Premier, it is unfortunate that you have not forwarded to me an agenda for this meeting so that I might know what you are talking about."

"We admit there are international rumors, stemming mostly from completely unverified sources, that there is, between our nations, a . . . so-called race for inner space. . . ."

Hornsborough thought it might be the lack of sleep that made him cold. He noticed that his legs had gone to sleep, and he shifted his position, his pants once more rubbing him uncomfortably. It was, as he suspected, to be a nightmare.

"Mr. Premier, I *will* have more coffee, if you don't mind," he said, helping himself.

It was while the brown liquid was steaming into the white milk that the point of the Premier's concern dawned on him. He passed almost instantly through disbelief to amazement and back again to apparent diplomatic serenity.

Could this top-level concern mean that there was really something to rumors of advances in Soviet parapsychological developments, rumors that had been increasing in frequency during the last forty years? Had someone stumbled on a parapsychology research installation? Was it true? If it was, no one in Washington would believe it. But why was

Tosygen himself taking the initiative? It must be an extraordinary security breach. Tosygen was playing for time. He
had to be trying to introduce doubt, argument, disbelief
about something that must be unquestionably true, to gain
time for some initiative.

When he confronted the Soviet leader, his eyes were
steady and cold.

"Of course, Mr. Premier," he said smoothly, "I should
like to take this opportunity to assure you that in my country, although we do have certain professors in universities
interested in such matters, there is no official research in
this area. . . ."

"Of course, of course." Tosygen smiled. "I think I will
have coffee, after all." Hornsborough poured the Premier a
cup. Tosygen continued:

"That is why we thought we should turn over to you this
letter of discontent, and perhaps you and your excellent
services might trace its origin. Our own services have used
their arts on it, of course. Apparently it is on recycled paper, an excellent ecology trend. It was mailed in your capital, and drawn with an American felt-tipped pen."

Hornsborough took the paper the Premier handed him
across the silver and china. He quickly read the neatly
typed message at the bottom of the paper. "This is," it said,
"a rendering of a research center in your country—code
word Tolkien—for the development of long-distance hypnotic telepathy aimed at mental control of minds. It is to be
abandoned immediately, or all major research centers in
the world will receive a copy!" Hornsborough read it
quickly twice, and then fastened his eyes on the Premier,
sitting calmly across from him.

"You may be sure, Mr. Ambassador," said Tosygen, rising, "that nothing exists at the site mentioned. . . ."

Hornsborough rose and prepared to leave.

"Thank you, Mr. Premier, for the courtesy of your assurances. I shall inform my superiors immediately."

CORVO

The small, sleek, green and white long-distance jet helicopter, developed by Sandmuller International for use by its
top administrators, began to descend through the crystal-
line atmosphere surrounding the island of Corvo. Senator

Heston Davis allowed himself to enjoy a "selfic" surge of power, a peak moment during which the world was in place and he was, if not on the exact top of it, at least near the top. The sensation of descending through the air physically while simultaneously ascending mentally was sublime.

Davis held his breath. It was not often that he felt this mental strength. Generally, he was weak and did not bother to hide it from himself, only from others. The charade worked more times than not, and when it didn't work, he didn't care anyhow. He was, after all, a senator, well connected, and in possession of multitudes of secrets which, when intelligently played like cards in a game, kept him relatively secure in his position.

To him all life was relative, anyway. There were really no ideals. One succeeded as best one could, and to succeed one always tried to align oneself with the most convenient power blocs. These, too, could be played like cards.

Davis smiled comfortably. He was a superior player, and he knew it. And at this peak moment, he allowed himself to enjoy it.

The chopper touched down with a jerk. Heston came back to himself. Above him the rotor blades clacked to a halt. Davis hesitated briefly to see if Rastaban al Nashirah, standing at some distance with his flock of assistants, would come toward the helicopter to welcome him; he did not. Rastabi was such a bastard, a gutter rat. No, even worse than a gutter rat. A fucking queer Arab type who slave-traded in young blond boys as well as in international armaments.

Davis took his time alighting from the chopper. He paused to survey the volcanic mountains, the surging surf lapping gently at the dark volcanic sands, the lush green plants surrounding Rastabi's house and plantation. When he felt the pause had lasted long enough to indicate his detachment from the work at hand, Davis quickly moved off the chopper pad and across the small portion of beach to the paved plaza surrounding the citadel.

Rastabi did not smile as he said, "It was not wise for you to use a Sandmuller chopper, Heston. We are trying to keep our affiliation somewhat of a secret." Rastabi's voice could cut like a knife. Davis steeled himself against reacting visibly, focusing instead on Nashirah's retinue, five muscular men dressed in tight-fitting green and white uniforms. It was a card. He played it.

"I see," he said smoothly, "you are clothing your staff in Sandmuller uniforms . . ."

"No one ever comes to Corvo unless invited," Nashirah assured him.

Davis had other cards. "There are, after all, spy-in-the-sky satellites, Rastabi, that can take photos to a six-inch resolution. The sweat on a lip is visible, and I am sure that green and white uniforms are also."

"Forget it, Heston," snapped Rastabi, moving abruptly across the plaza. Davis had no choice except to follow. He regretted the exchange; and though the assistants deferentially waited for him to proceed, he was irritably aware of having been humbled in front of them. His peak moment was now totally gone.

Davis followed Nashirah into the island citadel, a remodeled 1920 Portuguese *estancia* of stucco and red-tiled roofs, now a display of glass, stone, and luxury. Gutter rat though Nashirah might be, thought Davis, he used his illegitimate money to extraordinary ends. The building—no, not a building, it was a science-fiction castle—was tasteful and beautiful. Nashirah could blend the modern, the contemporary, the outrageous, the old into exquisite comfort.

Across the large living room, illuminated by pillars of light filtering through narrow apertures in the ceiling, was a wall covered with ancient African masks, dark patterns of red and brown floating over a white rug, a sea of spun plastics, furry-soft to the touch. Davis was just registering the presence of a wall of glassed-in ancient Greek vases when they arrived at a stainless-steel door that opened noiselessly onto a small elevator. Everyone crowded in. The door silently closed. They descended a short distance and it opened again. The silence, the press of male bodies had become oppressive to Davis.

"This had better be good, Rastabi," he commented. "I really can't afford to be away from Washington even in the summer."

"Don't worry, Davis. The security here is far better than anything the Americans or Russians have. And I also have to be back in Washington in a few hours."

Davis tried to be nonchalant as he surveyed the laboratory and its contents in a sweeping glance. But inwardly he was somewhat shaken. The room was not overly large, but seemed huge, containing rows of elaborate equipment among which several of Nashirah's scientists were working efficiently. He had no idea what any of the equipment was for.

Nashirah let him wander among the workers for a few moments.

"Most of this confusing jumble of equipment are devices to test the accuracy of various weapons we have been developing. Weaponry, you know, has become quite esoteric in the last ten years. You'd be absolutely amazed at the delicate requirements of radarscopes these days."

"You don't keep your biological weaponry here, do you?" asked Davis, suddenly worried about acquiring some new sort of deadly contamination.

"No," Nashirah assured him. "Frankly, we can't keep up with the classified biological and chemical research in America and Russia. And the English and Chinese! I find it cheaper to pay for samples."

"Samples?"

"Of course. It is cheaper to buy samples from people employed at the various classified research centers than it is to try to keep up with actual research."

"Oh."

"Well, let's get on with it," Nashirah began. "The effects of the Tonopah and Tolkien devices are much more remarkable than I ever dreamed. They both have a dramatic quality that puts to shame the futile bacteriological and toxin weapons of the last four decades. And, of course, the land-based intercontinental ballistic missiles and the submarine-launched things are now totally outmoded. This leaves us with the Tonopah and Tolkien devices which must, of course, be carried aloft by satellites. The first nation to achieve orbit with either of these two devices will rule the planet very soon after that."

"Sounds impressive." Davis tried to keep a dry tone in his voice although his excitement was rising. "What about the SALT people? They're supposed to be working out limits on strategic arms—won't they have something to say about all this?"

"Don't be stupid, Heston. You know that neither the Americans nor the Russians have advertised their research. The secret is extremely well kept. Each nation knows the other is up to something, but isn't sure what—or how far the other has got. If that weren't so, we should have by now had a flare-up at the SALT conferences at Warsaw as well as in the U.N. No nation is going to permit another nation to develop these weapons, much less the international community. So we can assume that until there is a flare-up, the security on the nature of the two weapons has held. And I remind you that it must be held if we are to get an edge on this at all."

"I quite understand." Nashirah's assumption of superiority, as usual, nettled Davis, and he said petulantly, "I want to remind *you* that it was I who got the Tonopah research funded in Washington. That idea was all mine, and it saved you and Sandmuller a hell of a lot of money. And it is I who have personally overseen the security procedures on Tonopah. There has not been one leak, not one, mind you."

"Calm down, Heston," said Nashirah, ignoring Davis's claim to be treated as an equal. "Now here is what we have been able to do so far. We have developed small units for both the Tonopah devices and the Tolkien equipment. In fact, we have duplicated the American device exactly. Regrettably, we are somewhat behind on the Russian device, and are awaiting the Tolkien brain schist sample from Sandmuller. He is now in Moscow trying to get it."

"Do we know yet what the Tolkien device will do?"

"Yes. The hypnotic alpha brain-wave frequencies are modulated through the living specimen of brain tissue—it acts as a transformer—and when broadcast, the frequencies create an involuntary hypnotic state in the mind. This opens the mind to receive telepathic patterns, subliminal bursts of other frequencies associated with human emotions. The aggressive patterns are most productive."

"You mean people can be made to be violent?"

"Yes, viciously so. Also epileptic. We will have the Tolkien weapon duplicated as soon as we receive the brain schist from Moscow. We do not know yet how the Russians manage to keep a slice of brain alive and its synapses firing. Ah, here is the Tonopah device."

Nashirah had been ushering him among the maze of impressive research tables, the noiseless computer banks, and complexities of color-coded wires and glass tubings. They had come to what was obviously an electronic-frequency device aimed at a glass cage containing an active and playful chimpanzee. Without understanding why, Davis found that the sight terrified him.

"How many of these endless underground caverns do you have?" he asked, looking away from the cage.

"Several, Heston. Several. They are of volcanic origin, you know, and most of them are below sea level. But there are very many. Room enough for a year of supplies for a dozen men, and room enough for some subterranean weapons testing sites. Room enough, but necessarily limited." Nashirah looked at Davis quietly before he went on; Davis was grateful for the diversion, which had given him time to suppress his unreasoning terror.

"We have been using monkeys as targets," Nashirah continued, "since their structure is suitably similar to the human."

"What does the . . . thing do?"

"When the Tonopah equipment is further refined, it will create a psychic torpor in its victims, immobilizing them. In its present unrefined state, however, it tends to destroy all types of biological tissue. It's truly remarkable what microwaves can do," Nashirah concluded, his eyes gleaming.

"I helped get Tonopah going," said Davis softly, "but I've never understood how it works. I don't suppose I ever will."

"It's really quite simple, Heston. Everything in the universe is immersed in a basic electromagnetic field composed of waves and frequencies. The human body and presumably the mind are balanced in this field. Change the frequencies in various directions and the body and the mind will quiver. Change the frequencies enough, give them direction, and glass will shatter. The Tonopah Project is research to find which microwaves the human body will respond to and develop a suitable weapon therefrom."

"I know all that, Rastabi. I just don't understand how it really works. That's all."

"It works like this, Heston," said Nashirah, smiling slightly.

At a signal from Nashirah, a waiting assistant flicked a switch. The electronic equipment aimed at the chimpanzee came alive. Davis could see no emanations coming from the Tonopah device, but the animal at which it was aimed suddenly was transfixed, obviously hearing a sound beyond the range of the human ear. Then Davis heard a low hum that quickly built in intensity to a soft high-pitched scream and then vanished once more beyond human perception.

The chimpanzee began shuddering. Davis wanted to run, but he was transfixed, fascinated, compelled to watch.

A sudden froth appeared at the animal's mouth. Its joints began quivering. The beast tried to run through the glass wall, but was bounced back. The hairy body suddenly turned rubbery and collapsed in a heap. Blood flowed freely from the ears and nostrils.

The sight of the blood brought a convulsive twist to Davis's stomach. The insides of the cage were suddenly splattered with a red and white mist. It took seconds before Davis understood that the chimpanzee's brain had exploded, and that its other internal organs were also exploding, propelling the carcass this way and that around the cage. There was a crackling sound. The glass itself suddenly shivered into spider-web patterns, falling into glittering dust on the laboratory floor. The hot smell of blood and feces wafted to Davis.

Nashirah was jubilant. "What we need now," he began, waving to the green-and-white-clad assistant to shut the device off, "are the experimental fine-adjustment specifications from the Tennessee site. Can you get them, Heston?"

But Senator Heston Davis had disappeared behind a wall of computer storage banks and was vomiting onto the laboratory floor.

NEW YORK

The dream in many forms had been with him for a long while. If he tried to track down its origin, it quickly took on timeless qualities, nuances beyond the idea of duration. In fact, it became inexpressible. It could not even be called a dream.

But he wanted to decide things about it, to express it, or find in it something that might be expressed. He had tried talking about it to others, professional people whom he thought might know something about it. Mostly, they considered it for a while, then thought that it must be a mystical experience, perhaps even a form of ecstasy. But whatever it was, it was beyond both those vague descriptions. Or perhaps it included both. It was more, infinitely more than just mysticism or ecstasy.

Finally—years had passed since he had first started inspecting it—he decided it was beyond ordinary ideas of time and matter, and outside of energy and space. It was a definition, the beginnings of a definition, with which he was uncomfortable. But he had grown accustomed to that discomfort as he had become more familiar with exploring it. Spaces beyond spaces, time beyond time. Universes beyond universes or universes within universes.

It certainly had something to do with creativity, since out of it he drew those songs that had made him famous and rich. Out of it came those inspired words, those mixtures of sound and melody that reached into hearts and emotions of people everywhere. And moved them, for at least a little while, into realms beyond themselves. But finally, songs in themselves proved to be the smallest fraction of its potential—though it was song that had brought him to the next step in his realization of it.

It had happened in a country meadow while he was at work on composing a new song. The words resisted for a while, then fell into place. And with their ordering had come the music. He was pleased and sang it, tentatively, to a flower nearby, a small one with three delicate, pointed creamy petals. When he finished singing it, there was an echo. At least so he had thought. But it persisted and did not die away. Reverberations in the guitar strings? But they had quieted. It was the flower trembling, singing back to him. And then he understood that whatever else that special awareness might be, it had ears beyond ears and eyes beyond eyes. That had been several years ago, but the delicate sound lingered in his mental corridors. He had been curious enough to look the plant's name up in a wild-flower guide: trillium.

He turned in bed, hardly awake. The body was lethargic, protesting activation. Patiently, he waited for it to come awake by stages. First, the electricity on the skin changed, shifting upward in frequencies. Then the muscles were activated, each wanting to stretch at the same time. He commanded the body to begin movement. The gentle touch of the silk sheet in the cool air conditioning brought further arousal. The inner organs came alive. Before the eyes opened, he looked through the wall to the calendar on his desk. It was July 31, and from the fall of the sun through the windows on the thick carpeting, it was also sometime in the afternoon.

Astor Golderman would be waiting patiently for him to keep his appointment. Astor Golderman was always patient when it came to business, impatient with everything else.

Finally the body cooperated. He rose, smoked a cigarette, then showered. He pulled on tight faded denims embroidered with sequins and other brilliants.

He liked being elaborate, and his public expected it of him. But he could be plain also, disguising himself in ordinary clothes, wandering around New York unrecognized. He liked that also. Privacy had an extra value to a superstar. He took the elevator from his luxurious apartment, which he loved, and walked out to the street.

"G'afternoon, Mr. Merriweather," said the Puerto Rican doorman, sweating under his suit in the summer heat.

Merriweather sighed and walked down the street to Fifth Avenue, and then fifteen blocks to Golderman's office. He could not help feeling sad. Everything would be gone in a few weeks or months. But it was his own choice, and there was no other way.

Astor Golderman glared at him from behind huge stacks of correspondence on his large desk. The small dark man managed to look important this way, framed in piles of letters no one intended to answer.

Merriweather smiled at Golderman, who continued to glower back. "I don't understand," Golderman said bitterly. "All that time on those courses at M.I.T., all this education dreck, all this psychic jerk-off at that nut house on the Coast. Time for that you've got, time for work you can't manage. Your bookings are starting to fall off."

"Who cares?" Merriweather said lightly. "There's other things going on I'm more concerned with."

"Things? What does a singer know from things except singing, and keeping contracts he's lucky enough his agent should get him? Your career comes first. You aren't getting any younger, boychik. There's chicken tracks around your baby blues. The girls will dump you one of these days, and some other young stud in tight pants and sequins will be up there twitching his tokus and hauling in the dough."

"Astor, you know damned well I have enough money to last three lifetimes." Merriweather paused, trying to find a way to put it. "I want to exult in life, to live at my fullest potential."

"Yechh! So what about your potential as a singer, that should go down the drain? You didn't cut a record last year and I don't see where it is written you're going to this year either."

"There are other things."

"Again with the things? Maybe you didn't hear the first

time I said it, your career should come first—at least,"
Golderman said gloomily, "while it lasts. Things!"

"Things that might reduce people to shuddering masses.
Things that will change the world totally. Ugly things."

"Ugly is how Hardy from Morningstar Records looks
when he's asking me how about the album we owe him, do
something about that, you don't like ugly." Golderman
paused and looked keenly at his client. "All this far-out
shit, it's bending your mind. Uh, Dan, you're not, you
know, *taking* something. . . ?"

"Fuck you, Astor. You know I never took drugs. All I
want is to be sure you understand exactly the instructions
in my will, exactly what I want done."

"What makes you think you're going . . . that something's going to happen to you, God forbid? Morbidness!
That's what all this parapsychology, computer courses,
bioelectric garbage has done to you. It's made you morbid."

"*Do* you understand?"

Astor Golderman sat back glumly. He could never
change Dan Merriweather when the young stud had his
mind set. His pride was still smarting from the money Merriweather had dredged out of him for the computer installation. Toys and playthings! A private jet, girls, like that—
that was what a rock star was supposed to blow his cash
on. . . . "Yes, Dan. It's all very strange, but I think I understand."

"Good. If something does . . . happen to me, I suggest
you take advantage of the fund we set up for you in Switzerland."

"It's all crazy, utterly crazy," concluded Astor Golderman.

THE PENTAGON

Chester B. Walters was about to leave his office for an
afternoon of fishing at Camp David, his first of the year,
when his secretary informed him that General Judd had
requested an immediate Priority Three appointment.

"Damn!" The vision of lounging on a shady stream bank
faded.

"I agree," said the matronly Guilda Stern, who had

served four Secretaries of Defense. "I'll call Camp David
and tell them you will be a little late."

"Hell, I hate to keep *him* waiting. . . ."

"Priority Three . . . you know," said Guilda.

"Well, tell the sonofabitch to get his ass in here right
away then." And what the hell is a Priority Three, anyway?
he wondered. So many damn fool things to keep track
of . . .

"Possible strategic public leak," Guilda said on her way
out.

Walters smiled. Guilda knew when to read his mind.

Even a Priority Three appointment with the Secretary of
Defense has no magical effect on Washington traffic, and it
took Judd a good while to get from the downtown office
across the Potomac to the Pentagon, and another fifteen
minutes to make his way to the Secretary's lair. He arrived
sweating, chilled quickly by the air-conditioned coolness of
the green-carpeted offices.

Walters waited behind the vast expanse of his desk, immaculately vacant of all papers, displaying only a set of
miniature military flags and a marble inkstand that he
never used, preferring instead cheap disposable ball-points.
Walters' face was flushed with impatience, his portly body
poised on the edge of his copious desk chair as if ready to
fly off. Dark piercing eyes looked at Judd sternly.

"This had better be important."

"I'll come quickly to the point," Judd began.

"Fine. You have five minutes."

"There has been a leak, some sort of a . . . a departure
from what we might ordinarily expect from security penetrations. . . ."

"Get *to* it, Judd."

"Well, Project Tonopah has been penetrated by a person
or persons unknown, threatening to reveal the site and operation to the press, or whatever. A crank, naturally,
but . . ."

"Brief me on Project Tonopah," Walters snapped.

"Site in Tennessee conducting microwave flux tests . . ."

"I said brief me, not confuse me."

"Tonopah is a research project on microwave deterrents
to physical nerve systems."

"How?"

"The sound waves can be fed through ordinary radio an-
tennae, and can cause temporary suspension of surface

nerve endings, that is, produce torpor, unconsciousness, or even biological destruction in the public in general. Tonopah is also working to develop portable units. These can be used for riot control; the English, Chinese, Russians, and Canadians already have a version of mobile units along these lines."

Walters had never heard of such a project. He was stunned, but he had not come to be Secretary of Defense by being inept when faced with surprises. "How did the security leak occur?" he snapped, quite confident that Judd felt him to be completely informed.

"We do not know at the moment. We have a full operational investigation. The person or persons responsible for the breach threaten to make public the location and ground plans for the facilities."

"Ground plans!"

"Yes."

"Ground plans . . . you mean to say someone had the ground plans?"

"Apparently, sir."

"Jesus Christ!"

"Right, sir."

Walters paused. "How did you discover the leak?"

"We received a letter, that is, a drawing of the plans, through the mail."

"Through the . . ."

"Whoever it is demands that the installation be abandoned."

Judd paused. Inwardly he was amused by the perplexed look drifting across his superior's face. Outwardly, he maintained a calm, disciplined appearance. He often felt that Walters was a fat fool, yet the man was by demonstration extremely competent in heading the nation's vast military establishment. Though he might look like a baffled pig at the moment, Judd knew that Walters would home in directly on the problem. He did.

"I assume that you have initiated a thorough security shakedown on the Tonopah personnel?"

"Tonopah, sir, is on a need-to-know basis only. And because of its sensitive international political nature, security has been monitored constantly."

"Well," snorted Walters, "the security officer for Tonopah will have a lot to answer for."

"Security leaks, when they do occur," continued Judd,

"usually involve only bits and pieces. It is seldom that entire plans or documents are stolen anymore. Our security modes have become too good. Computers have made almost total surveillance possible."

"General Judd, are you trying to tell me that there is something strange about this particular break?"

"It's a gut feeling, Mr. Secretary."

"Well, time will tell about that. Get me a thorough report as soon as possible. Use all the operatives you need. Now, what about the public repercussions of all this?"

"Worldwide. Even if the press treated it as some kind of science-fiction boondoggle—I think they could be encouraged to do that—it is a sure thing that scientists and military researchers everywhere would start sniffing and speculating. And that would ignite the antiarms people. Tonopah's a hell of a lot scarier than nuclear devices, once its potential is understood. There's no doubt that the Strategic Arms Limitation Talks people would get quite active, and the United Nations, and just about any other humanitarian organization. It would be big. You'll remember, sir, what the press did with the revelations concerning biological and chemical warfare research some years ago. Tonopah would create a situation ten times hairier than that."

Walters was thoughtful, pressing his lips together. "What are our options?"

Judd spoke carefully. He had worked out what he had to say on the way to Walters' office—now the thing was to get it across fast, in proper Pentagon-style officialese. "Not many, Mr. Secretary. My preliminary survey of options has indicated that only activation of the erasure directive would achieve the optimum effect."

"Erasure?"

"Yes. We can move Tonopah and close down the Tennessee site completely. Then if the press and public do get wind of this, there won't be anything there. This is an extreme action, to be sure. But someone out there possesses total information about Tonopah; if we move it, we can defeat him and restore security also."

Walters was prompt in his reaction. "Cost?"

"Big, but well within the budget set aside for such an occurrence."

"Where will you move it to?"

"There are facilities in Omaha that can temporarily accept it equipment-wise. Personnel-wise, we can transfer most of the nonstrategic people and feed them into other installations, retaining only the significant ones."

Walters felt more comfortable. What Judd proposed was covered by an existing directive and already had a budget. He couldn't go wrong on that.

"O.K., move on it, then. Keep me informed daily. I'll be at David with the President for the weekend."

Judd rose, relieved that the decision—with any luck, the right one—had been taken. He paused before he turned from the Secretary's desk.

"Yes, Judd, something else?"

"Well, Mr. Secretary, there is something really strange about this. . . ."

"Yes, there damn well is. Dumb-ass security leaks are always strange."

"True, sir, but . . . I have a feeling, an impression if you will, that there is something really big going to happen. . . ."

Walters looked at him coldly. With one hell of a security flap on, it was no time for a general to start sounding like a goddamn soap-opera heroine with premonitions. "When it does, General, let me know."

After Judd had left, he buzzed for Guilda.

She blossomed, full-chested, through the door.

"Guilda," he said, "spend a little time this afternoon, and find out what the hell Project Tonopah is, who the hell is funding it, and who the goddamned bastard is that had it kept from me!"

TOP SECRET

PROJECT
TONOPAH

PH-3000 SERIES

SITE: U.S. Army Research Depot, Red Mountain, Tennessee, Computer Access
CODE: ADVP-PH-3000

Purpose: Advanced research in aspects of human neuromoter systems manipulation by microwave impact.
Alternative applications include sonic biological (psychic) mind control and sonic and microwave biological systems destruction.

Psychological studies implications: Subcontract PH-DV 3056, Cybernetics Unit, Trans-American University Systems, College Park, Maryland

Biocommunications and parasensory studies implications: Subcontract PH-PS 3057, Sandmuller Development Center, Alcoa, Michigan

Key personnel: *Civilian liaison*: Senator Heston Davis, Chairman, Congressional Subcommittee on Science

Military liaison: General Harrah Judd, Chief Liaison Officer, Defense Advanced Research Projects Agency (DARPA), Pentagon

TOP SECRET

PROJECT
TOLKIEN

ACADEMY OF SOVIET SCIENCES, SPECIAL PROJECT
59163

SITE: Jet Dynamica Research Institute Novodolinskiy Development Alliance, Novodolinskiy,
Kazakhstan, U.S.S.R.

Purpose: Experimental radio and microwave en-
forcement of mental telepathy by biological tissue wave transformers (Reference:
*Eksperimental'nyye Issledovaniya Myslen-
nogo Vnusheviya*).

Studies of mental (nonverbal) suggestion
to motor acts, visual images, sensations.

Reinforcement of telepathic suggestion by
hypnotic overload stimulated by microwave impulses.

Social psychology implications: Subcontract
59163-1, Sandmuller International Development Center, Warsaw, Poland

Key personnel: (Access identcard numbers only)
Soviet Sciences Academician: TOL-
59163-Kv-234
Political liaison: TOL-59163-GBU-4
Military liaison: TOL-59163-Dx-1125

Project access: By identcard numbers only

THE PENTAGON

Each morning when the awoke, Shirley Paars renewed her hatred for other human beings. She showered, combed her lush red hair, and made up her face—a little more mauve eye shadow on extra hateful mornings—and froze her lips into a slightly puckered smile. This visage fooled most of her associates, and some thought her sultrily beautiful. From time to time some poor masochist perceived her innate sadism and was drawn into a lukewarm affair. What she truly appreciated and desired was the company of hard, strong, heartless men. Experience had taught her that if her hatred and sadism were too visible, such men tended to drop her, so she was obsessed with the need to conceal what she accepted as her natural tendencies.

She knew that she would have fit perfectly in a whorehouse specializing in whips and leather, but such blatancy bored her. She preferred the tensions of covert relationships and found boundless sexual gratification in Washington, where sex, sadism, and power were virtually interchangeable. Joe Abrams, for instance, had his own physical appeal which mingled with and enhanced that of his position—a man with access to power who was in turn in *her* power. And, of course, Rastaban al Nashirah . . .

She was not exactly a call girl working for Nashirah, but more a valued aide. She slept with men he selected, partly as a discreet sexual bribe, but mainly to extract information. She was, of course, infuriated that, when Nashirah had arranged for her to meet General Harrah Judd, that fish-eyed bastard had not responded. But his aide had—and, in fact, she had found herself drawn to him in an unprofessional way. Abrams was pretty close-mouthed about letting any information slip in pillow talk, but Nashirah thought it was a good connection for her to keep up—which sorted very well with her inclinations. And it was exciting to think that he might one day come across with something that would let *her* screw *him*. . . .

Surface respectability was an absolute necessity, and it had been her idea to go after the job in Air Force Aerial Reconnaissance as a photo analyst. "Photoreconnaissance interpreter" had an adventurous sound; but it actually turned out to be quite a boring job. She had tried again and again to get transferred to Air Force Intelligence's worldwide attaché system in the International Liaison Division, or at least into the War-game Branch. But no luck. She was stuck irrevocably, it seemed, among stultifying photographs and the nauseating odor of developing fluid.

At the moment just short of noon, she was bored to the hilt with the aerial photographs in front of her. Though air conditioning kept the underground center frigid, she was edgily aware of the oppressive summer heat blanketing the Virginia countryside beyond the austere cell; for hours, since she had started work, she had felt lost and in need of rough masculine company; and the smell of developing fluid wafting from the enlarged photos was close to making her heave.

So she nearly missed it. It was while she was thinking of picking up someone in her favorite mixed-couples bar that she inadvertently placed the loosely inspected photo back on the pile it had come from. After lunch, she felt better, and began surveying the photo again through the magnifying glass.

It annoyed her that it looked vaugely familiar, as do all photoreconnaissance maps. Was it last week she had looked at the same topography, or just this morning? *That* was Makinsk, south was Tselmograd, and farther on was Kazakhstan, which seemed romantic to her—semiarid tundras where swarthy Russians yearned for a woman with red hair and blue eyes, like hers. Dreams . . . Quadrant 245Y was of official interest. It was always difficult to see what was there.

Even on her second inspection, she almost missed it. For five minutes she must have been thinking, under the sexual fantasies that occupied the surface of her mind, that it seemed somehow different. Her attention suddenly focused.

What was different. . . ? *Something* was different. She buzzed through to Archives. It was a full half hour before Archives produced last month's photo.

There was a *big* difference. The small dots on last

month's photo, representing some sort of towers and buildings, were totally missing on today's. She fed both pictures into the comparator-enlarger and looked at them side by side.

Definitely different. And not because of cloud cover, either. The buildings were gone. A month ago there had been some twenty-six buildings and four very large towers. Now they were not there.

She lit a cigarette, relishing the discovery for a few moments. Orders were to report verbally as well as in writing on *differences*, whereas mere *developments* were to be forwarded only in writing. This would cause a ripple in the routine of the section, short-lived as it might prove to be. She picked up her phone.

When she hung up, she was somehow on edge. It was to be expected, irritating though it was, that her information would be received as a matter of routine . . . but there was something else. . . . Ah! Nashirah had often expressed interest in that particular site. It was to be, after all, quite an exciting day, reporting to *two* employers. She smoked another cigarette all the way through before she went to a pay phone in the cafeteria and dialed Nashirah's local Washington number.

The familiar voice of Nashirah's houseboy answered.

"Tell Mr. Nashirah," she said brusquely, "I have a report on something of interest. Yes. I'll meet him at the usual place."

MOSCOW

David P. Hornsborough III had awakened after the short sleep he had allowed himself after the unnerving confrontation with Tosygen. He dictated a report to Helena and had it telexed to Washington. He tried to work out the time difference and finally estimated that it would arrive in the middle of the night. He decided to put in a call to the Secretary of State.

It might make waves, but Hornsborough would as soon be recalled as not. He had wanted the ambassadorship to the United Nations, but the President had thought he would be more useful in Moscow. And who could resist cooperating with Thomas Cordero Heathstone? All the same, Hornsborough had felt his background equipped him better for France or England than for serving a sentence in the Russian capital.

He was wealthy—East Coast wealth—and cultured, having gone to all the right schools and moved with the right people, which counted for something in western Europe if not in this outpost of Asia. He was a successful speaker, effective in English or French; and he never knew if the interpretation of his words into Russian carried the same force and flavor. The Russians distrusted a wealthy American, the pretentious embassy probably exacerbating their suspicions; and to cap it all, the Soviets did business in the middle of the night, and he was definitely an afternoon person. Plus, of course, their penchant for producing nightmares, like this one. . . .

Had the Soviets actually made a breakthrough in parapsychology? He himself did not know the first thing about that topic; his upbringing had emphasized his rightful place in the world and how to maintain it, not excursions into the esoteric sciences.

He knew State well enough to be sure that some flunky would pigeonhole the copy of his telexed report; and indeed, if the Russian Premier himself had not been concerned about the incident, Hornsborough might not even have sent it. He wanted to call Heathstone directly, but the Secretary of State would feel offended if he was bypassed.

Seth Mead would not know anything about parapsychology either, and Hornsborough did not enjoy reporting to his superior, who was, after all, a product of Texas, and thus his social inferior. But he would call. The freakish confrontation with Tosygen could not be passed over.

Despite the efficiency of the American Embassy communications link to the Department of State at Foggy Bottom in Washington, it took several hours before the Secretary could be located to talk with Ambassador David P. Hornsborough III. By then it was night in Moscow.

"David, is that you?" asked Seth Mead.

"Yes, Mr. Secretary. Sorry to disturb you with a direct call."

"That's all right, David. It's a little too hot here for golf. We came in after only three holes."

"I had a peculiar confrontation with Tosygen at the crack of dawn. He summoned me to talk about a letter they've received from someone in the States threatening to expose a classified research project."

"Another one of those . . . ?"

"Well, this is the first time I was summoned. . . ."

"Well, I'll turn your report over to the CIA. You never know what they'll turn up."

"But, Mr. Secretary, this one is different. It seems to involve . . . well, it is slightly occult, I suppose you'd say."

"Ah, how's that?"

"The letter threatening exposure, of which I have telexed you a copy, seems to be talking about long-distance, ah, telepathy."

"Did you say 'telecopy'?"

"No, sir. Not telecopy. Telepathy. T-e-l-e-p-a-t-h-y."

For a moment, Hornsborough heard nothing but the background crackle of the line.

"Did you say telepathy?"

"Yes, Mr. Secretary, hypnotic telepathy!"

Another pause.

"Must be a crank letter," Mead said.

"But, Seth," pressed Hornsborough, "I was summoned at the crack of dawn to hear the Premier's *personal* protestations."

"Are you suggesting that there is something serious about this, David?"

"Well, I thought you would want at least an immediate report on this interview."

"Right, David, that is true. I'll have a talk with Heston Davis. He may know something about this. Did you *really* say telepathy?"

"Yes, Mr. Secretary."

"Very good. By the way, did Tosygen give any hints about the way they're continually shifting ground in the SALT negotiations?"

"He didn't even mention them, Seth."

"Okay. Thanks for the report, David. But I can't think that Tosygen would be too concerned about a simple crank letter. He's got more on his plate than that, with the Chinese pushing out again, those Africans getting all that economic clout around the world, and the damn English grabbing off business in his own country. Here, too, for that matter. *That's* what he ought to be talking to us about."

"Yes, Mr. Secretary," said Hornsborough, reminded in this gentle manner of his obvious duties. "Sorry I didn't have time, at such an early hour, to take the opportunity to guide the interview in those directions."

After the connection was broken, Seth Mead reflected for a moment, then punched his intercom.

"Lila?"

"Yes, Mr. Secretary."

"Can you get me a good definition of telepathy?" After eighteen years—she had been with him since his first days in Washington as a freshman senator—he knew he could count on Lila Cox to know practically anything.

"Telepathy?"

"You know, that mind-to-mind garbage. . . ."

"Why, I suppose so. You must have been talking about the Russian research in that field."

"How do *you* know that?"

"Well, Seth, everyone knows they're ages ahead of us."

Mead grunted. "Damn. Well, if *everyone* knows about it, I guess the Secretary of State better know, too, Lila."

Helena Asch was confused. The urgency of the Premier's demand for a meeting with the ambassador seemed to have resulted in absolutely nothing. Experience had taught her that middle-of-the-night action usually heralded crucial diplomatic moves of some sort; but this one had produced only a suspicious vacuum. Hornsborough, whom she admired for his professional expertise—but over whom she kept close watch for other than diplomatic reasons—had only murmured something about a "crank letter" and "what was telepathy, anyhow?" He had then retired and slept most of the day, thereafter dictating only a short report. His call to Mead had been equally short.

Russia was almost home to her; she had been born to a diplomatic couple assigned to the Soviets when the United States Government had decided, fifteen years after the fact, that the czar was gone for good and that it was time to establish normal relations with the unruly rabble who had overthrown the Russian monarchy. Her first language was a double one, English mixed with Russian, to which she had added French and then Spanish. But long ago she had decided she was a citizen of the world, and not simply an American or a Russian. This decision, made in the romantic haze of her late college years, had turned out to be a pleasant one, since she had quickly found out she was not alone.

The report Hornsborough later had dictated to her concerning his rendezvous with Tosygen was even more garbled than his mutterings, and she had smiled, understanding well that the Department of State back in Washington would make no sense out of it. But then they were always bad in their assessments. On the spur of a thought, she put through a call to her old friend Guilda Stern in Washington.

"Helena!" squealed Guilda, hearing the welcome voice. "God! What a mess it's been here. We seem to be in some sort of a flap."

"Oh?" Helena asked, her voice carrying through the satellite relays as if she were next door. "Are you having one, too?"

"Well, sort of. Only no one really can figure it out, except that maybe a top-secret project has been leaked and everyone is in endless meetings, just smoking cigars mainly."

"We had sort of a thing here, too, last night. One of those bothersome middle-of-the-night things, you know."

"Yes, I know. Heard from Lila Cox. Did you know that the Secretary of State actually asked her to put together a paper on telepathy?"

"Telepathy?" Helena asked, genuinely surprised.

"Yes, isn't that a giggle? But then, Mr. Walters asked me . . . well, I suppose I shouldn't talk about it over the phone, should I?"

"Well, there are really no secrets, you know, Guilda," Helena said sagely.

"Yes, I suppose you're right. Well, really, I've already said it, haven't I? Chester asked me to find out about a project, a very expensive one, that seems also to have been going on quite incognito, if you get what I mean."

"Ah!" agreed Helena.

"And it seems to have something, well, psychic about it also, although I can't make heads or tails of it."

"A psychic project?" asked Helena in genuine surprise.

"Well, not exactly, but something close. Mr. Walters is screaming at everyone, asking what he's supposed to tell the President if he's asked about it."

"You mean the Secretary of Defense didn't know about . . ."

"Well, between you and me, he knew its code name, but that was all. You know how appropriations are usually listed. No one really knows. . . ."

"Listen, Guilda—call up Lila and ask her to call me if anything develops I should know about. You know the ambassador is usually the last person to hear about anything to do with intelligence."

"Will do, Helena. How's the weather there? It's terribly hot here, quite unseasonable, if you ask me."

"Cool, with lots of sun."

After putting down the phone, she looked at it thoughtfully. Defense . . . State . . . the Premier . . . all of them worked up over something that such hard-headed men would be expected to dismiss with contempt. . . . Out-of-the-way stuff, indeed—and her instructions on any development this unusual were clear.

She put through a call to New York, and was routed from there back to Brussels, where Aloysios Sandmuller, upon hearing who it was, left his usual early-morning briefing with his international representatives and took the call.

AUGUST 3

Psychic Blossoms

NEW YORK

Probing!
Daniel Merriweather relaxed in a state resembling a light reverie. His metasensory fields breathed, expanding and contracting, vast qualitative psychic fields reaching further and further from his centered self, coming finally, with practice, to encompass the entirety of planet Earth.

Probing!
He could barely stand it, this awesome tide of consciousness that engulfed him.

Perhaps it was this nearly unbearable quality that made people, in general, and scientists, in particular, so afraid of things psychic: the enormous magnitudes they suggested. Certainly, these unfathomable magnitudes accounted for part of his own fear. But through the last year he had learned to hold his fear in check. And, finally, he found he could think through the fear and then beyond it.

Yet it was a strain. Small droplets of sweat bloomed on his upper lip. The cold draft in his air-conditioned New York apartment touched the moisture, cooling, bringing waves of gooseflesh along his arms and legs.

Probing!
He kept careful track of his psychic impressions, filing them neatly away as psi memories, activating the bulging pair of cerebral hemispheres of the cerebrum above the brain stem, the most complex physical part of the body's nervous system and the mind's highest integrating center. From the cerebral hemispheres, where the tenuous psychic trace-perceptions were neatly filed as real memory, much as in a computer, he could activate his higher mental processes and reclaim these traces, making them dance in his psychic peripheries like holographic movies. Psychic sight! Sound!

THE PENTAGON

It had been a busy day, characterized by a strong aura of inquisition. The anonymous letter had already claimed its first victims. The chief security officer of Project Tonopah and his staff had been relieved summarily of their duties, confined, and a court-martial committee was ordered to sift through available evidence. Of which there was, so far, none.

Judd himself had received several security officials and had submitted to and argued his way through harsh speculations that he and his staff had had something to do with the security break. None of his staff, however, had computer code access to Project Tonopah except himself. The first visitors had been Air Force Intelligence, followed quickly by Army Intelligence, both services having active interests in the mircowave project. Then came Senator Heston Davis's secretary, who knew nothing about Tonopah, and who had been severely jolted by the several appearances of intelligence operatives in her office. Davis was not available, having been out of the country for a few hours a day or two ago, then departing for the Caribbean for fishing aboard someone's yacht. The senator often moved in semi-secrecy, and his secretary did not know where he was.

Judd then was obliged to receive the director of the National Science Foundation, tactfully informing this gentleman that even though there had been a security break on a top-secret project, the project still was, nevertheless, classified and on a need-to-know basis only. This did not set well with the director, who finally decided irritatedly that he would take up the matter with Senator Davis, who was, after all, Judd's senior on the project.

The next arrivals were high officials of the CIA, who were not so easily put off. Judd solved this problem only by pointing out forcefully that their proper channel for information was through the CIA director, who was on the President's National Security Council, which had been apprised of both the existence and nature of Project Tonopah. Judd finally decided to route all queries about the project to Davis's secretary, who would not even know what the queries were about and thus baffle most inquirers.

Chester Walters had telephoned him four times, then

summoned him to yet another smoke-filled conference. The need-to-know imperative gradually disintegrated and bits and pieces of Tonopah's nature were slowly assimilated into the unbelieving consciousness of more and more security officials.

Tonopah Project workers, employed directly or indirectly, found themselves under growing scrutiny, their clearances being reviewed mercilessly. Everyone took for granted that there was a superspy on the project in the employ of a surreptitious subversive organization. The mouths of dedicated security hounds were noticeably watering.

In spite of the security confusion, the removal of Tonopah from the site at Red Mountain, Tennessee, had proceeded apace and in less than forty-eight hours those underground caverns had been emptied and Air Force Research at Camp Offutt in Omaha suddenly found itself possessed of a small body of men and mysterious equipment no one could or would explain at any detail. This strategic removal was magnificent in its order and sublime in its security surround. There was an earnestness, almost recognizably deadly, in the project's new security measures that hinted strongly to all that the fewer questions asked, the better.

When some particularly bothersome situation arose, Harrah Judd was prone to working through the night in the quiet of his office. The quietness of Washington in the evening seemed to allow a penetrating consciousness to form, a calm and stillness that brought about unexpected rushes of creative thought. Joe Abrams was always near.

Not that the atmosphere of Washington was peaceful. National and international concerns possessed Washingtonians night as well as day, nightshifts working through on matters fondly hoped to be vital. And the summer! The disturbed weather—thunderstorms by the dozen, moving like celestial tides through the sultry heat pervading the eastern portion of the United States, a hotness that had held on persistently through the summer—a damp hotness from which his secluded, unimposing office was a dehumidified haven filled with cool air.

Abrams had piled yet another stack of reports on his desk. Judd leaned back and waited for him to expound.

"I think we are going to end up with nothing," said Abrams, chewing his bottom lip.

"How do you mean?"

"Well, Security has given a total sweep of all personnel associated with Project Tonopah and have come up with nothing that even suggests a lead. Also, the various plans and blueprints for the installation have been in their respective storage banks, and no one has accessed them for over sixty days."

"I see."

"So if there *was* a security leak, it happened some time ago. That suggests a large organization, and if that were so, we would have had some clue a long time ago."

"But as it is, Abrams," Judd concluded, "we are caught by surprise with a document about a highly classified project so perfect that its author seems to have been in the project itself."

Abrams shrugged. "Looks that way. But I don't see where or how . . ."

Judd found himself gazing reflectively at an intelligence report, one of many routinely passing across his desk, speculating on the significance of the sudden disappearance of a Russian depot in Kazakhstan.

"Why do you suppose," he said to Abrams, who was fussing around the office, trying to rearrange the disordered piles of research reports, "the Russians would suddenly abandon a rather large installation and blot its remains out of sight?"

"Sounds familiar, doesn't it, sir?"

"Hmm," muttered Judd. "See what else you can dig up about this."

Abrams exited. Judd knew he would have a full report in a matter of hours. Joe Abrams was a perfectionist, certain to rise to as high a rank as a passion for detail could take him—light colonel would be about it. Judd felt he understood Abrams. Both of them were orphans, but while he had been brought up in the comfort of a wealthy foster home, Abrams had been born in Korea, the offspring of a nameless black American soldier and an equally nameless Korean whore. That blend had somehow resulted in a statuesque tan body with eyes the color of cinnamon and a precise yet imaginative mind.

Had it not been for the Korean war-orphan placement service, Abrams would probably have disappeared into the nameless masses of the Far East, rejected alike by his Korean and American heritages. But there is something about belonging nowhere that inspires one to seek to belong with a vengeance.

Judd's own parents, both killed early in a car accident, had left him to the care of his father's relatives, a military family for three generations. It was natural for him to follow the well-trod path through West Point, through the testing of combat in Vietnam, earning points and rank in the system. A hasty marriage out of desperation, and an even hastier divorce, confirmed him in the feeling that the more difficult aspects of life were best traded for the lonely satisfaction of being a professional military man.

At some unconscious level, he knew that he probably wished for another kind of life, since there were many times that the limits of professionalism galled him and he felt a yearning for communication with other humans of a kind that did not fit the life he had chosen. He forced down the discontent and turned to the intelligence report.

What could have prompted the Russians to abandon a rather hefty research depot—previous reports had speculated that the Kazakhstan site was research and not military in nature—unless . . . was it possible that *they* had been hit, too? And if so, was their site developing weapons of the magnitude of Tonopah?

Judd sighed. He felt electrically uneasy, as he had since Abrams had laid that impossible letter on his desk; but he also felt somehow sad and foolish, as though he were operating on a totally false premise, not only with this problem but in his life as a whole. Curiously, these conflicting emotions, like a rising tide meeting an opposing wind, produced an interior calm, almost a detached euphoria.

And out of that calm emerged a beautifully clear and complete conviction.

NEW YORK

Probing.

Finally, contact.

He smiled slightly, observing the blankness of the site of Project Tolkien. Almost as if nothing had ever been there, except the tall metal towers that had not yet been completely dismantled. They looked lonely, denuded of the buildings that had only a few days ago clustered like bees around their bases. The smile did not falter as he observed a reconstitution of several elements of Project Tolkien at a nearby site. But he did frown when comprehension of the nature of the alternative site finally emerged.

Rousing himself, he moved across the soft carpeting and leafed through a large atlas of the world, his finger almost automatically falling on the new site. About one hundred miles east of the dark blue Aral Sea. Tyuratam! The principal U.S.S.R. launching site. A space-launch center! Were the Soviets going to orbit the deadly devices? Probably.

Well, what had he expected? Mere letters would hardly change the world all at once. He returned to his supine position, resuming the reflective mood.

Probing!

And they! From the caverns in Tennessee to the vast security facilities of the Strategic Air Command at Omaha. He sighed.

Hell! This, as he had expected, was going to be a goddamned chess game. He rested for over ten minutes, his psi factors shifting from metasensory perception, gathering instead into an invisible but powerful spark of irritation. Ten minutes, his mind idling, wafting in and out of the curling smoke patterns rising from a cigarette, waiting out the passing psychic storm.

Though he had, as much as possible, become used to the parasensory sensation of almost blind power—the power of a child gaining control of a primal consciousness that had no vanishing horizon—he might never become used to the fear that he might misuse his abilities. This fear could wreck him. He shuddered.

The shudder brought forth a yawn. Gratefully, he became aware of his apartment. The mylar-covered walls gleamed a muted silver. He breathed a sigh of relief. Once more the bad moment had passed. He stripped to his skin, letting the cool air caress his damp body as he sank comfortably into the mauve velvet upholstery.

He loved the richness of his surroundings. Chrome tables with thick glass tops, littered with crystal ashtrays and expensive cigarette boxes. The divans and chairs, thick and soft, stood around like lovable rhinoceroses ready to battle the fatigue of the body. Where the walls did not gleam from decorative silver paper, soft light illuminated good paintings and sculpture, fortresses of books, and tape decks.

And a special alcove held the trappings of his success, nine golden discs framed in plain wood, each disc representing sales of one million records. But even these mementos of success, accumulated before he was twenty-six, could not sweeten life for him now. Money, wealth, publicity, the raucous acclaim of an international following, all based on his musical gifts, were nothing compared to the rare, exciting psychic future growing somewhere in the space of his greater self.

Almost nothing. It was, in fact, damned near heartbreaking to have to give it all up. Whatever he was growing into, Merriweather reflected, he was still in many ways a musicstruck kid who had made it as big as anyone ever dreamed of. It was almost unfair that he should be saddled with this other gift, too, that drew him away from everything else.

WASHINGTON

As Judd had expected, Abrams got back to him within an hour. It was approaching midnight.

"Here's the complete scenario, so far," he began. "Air Force interpreters don't know what to make of it. Spoke to Shirley Paars—she and I make it sometimes—who says no one has figured out what the Russian site was all about. Called up the Bureau of Intelligence and Research at the State Department; they didn't know anything, except that Mr. Mead has expressed a sudden interest in telepathy, which has everyone at State in a subdued flap since no one there believes in it. Walters is screaming his head off because he didn't know what Tonopah was all about. The director of the Defense Intelligence Agency is muttering about the ineffectiveness of clearances. CIA is laughing, glad to catch the DIA with its pants down. A lot of wheel-spinning, but it doesn't look as if anybody's going to get hurt just yet," concluded Abrams.

"Huh," muttered Judd. "But that leaves two items. How did the leak occur in the first place, and are we to assume that there was a Russian counterpart of Tonopah?"

"Gotcha," said Abrams. "Air Force Intelligence will doubtless check out that first one in some detail, since it's their baby."

"Yes, I suppose so." Judd did not bother to conceal the dubious tone in his voice.

Abrams thought it better not to comment.

Judd brooded. The conviction that had seized him an

hour before was still there, still compelling. He didn't like what it implied, but he had long since learned to follow his gut feelings; there had been too many battles he would not have survived if he hadn't.

Everything Harrah Judd knew about psychic—the academics preferred the term *paranormal*—phenomena he had picked up while briefing himself for his post at DARPA. The fact that the military was funding research in these unlikely areas—as were the Soviets—made some knowledge of it necessary. He had not been impressed by the voluminous reports of people with the ability to read symbols on hidden cards, guess sequences of random numbers, bend metal objects without touching them, or describe scenes given only map references. It only got interesting when it got further from what could be proved; and one of the few things that had stuck in his mind was a discussion of the psychic—all right, *paranormal*—nature of hunches or gut feelings. It had made him uneasy to think that the faculty he relied on might link him to an area he had so little respect for, but not uneasy enough to disregard it.

And now his conviction was pushing him right back toward the psychic.

"Abrams," he said slowly, "we need expert help."

"We're getting everything the government can lay on, sir. I don't see how—"

"Then we'd better look in another direction. Who's likely to know the most about psychics—people who are supposed to be able to read minds, and so on? I mean somebody solid and sensible, not a freak."

Judd was grimly amused at Abrams' visible consternation, and at the effort he made to suppress it while answering; if you pushed Joe Abrams' button, he would disgorge information if it killed him. "I think there is only one person doing consistent surveys of the incidence and character of psychic potential in the population. Dr. Elizabeth Coogan. You met her once at the National Science Foundation's reception."

"Oh, yes. Tall woman, cool lavender eyes. We chatted a bit; she seemed sensible."

"But, sir!" Now that Abrams had fulfilled his function, he let his dismay show. "What do we want with . . . *psychics?*"

"Abrams," Judd said heavily, "the best, most trained minds we can find have gone over this whole mess, and they all come up with the same thing—there's *no way* those plans could have become known to anybody. And we have to accept that they know their business. But we got the goddamned letter and plans, didn't we? And that's impossible. Unless there's someone who can read minds— even read what's stored inside computers. So . . . we better consult somebody who knows about the impossible."

NEW YORK

Probing!

In the expanses of his extended awareness, now automatically sweeping the planet, an alarm had sounded, coding an urgent message to his frontal consciousness. He sat up abruptly. He gathered his extrasensory attention units and targeted them on the source of the alarm. A hazy picture formed. The source was male, probably military. He couldn't get an accurate picture. That would take a little time. But he could grasp the man's thoughts very well— and he was shocked.

He focused his abilities. Precision was needed now, not just impressions. The effort of grouping his psychic attention, though of hurricane force within the confines of his mental structure, disturbed not a dust mote in his apartment. All was silent. The muffled sounds of noisy New York outside were not admitted to his awareness.

The first thing that came through was the emotional excitement surrounding the man's thoughts.

Was that exhilaration? Slightly suppressed, but . . . yes! The man was excited. What was it that excited him?

Creating a metasensory needle, he pierced through the miles between New York and Washington. It touched the frontal consciousness of the man there, spreading outward, infiltrating the synapses firing in the man's brain.

His telepathic needle now became an invisible televisual carrier. Along it flowed the jumble of thoughts in the mind of the man in Washington, vivid in their intensity but unclear in detail. He watched that man hesitate momentarily, then consult a special telephone book on his desk, and dial the number.

God! This man had already figured out that he, or someone like him, existed! He *had* to know who the man was calling.

WASHINGTON

Not more than half accepting the conviction his gut feeling gave him, Judd knew it had to be checked out. For that he would need outside help.

Reaching for his book containing the names and numbers of researchers in government-related projects—a very rare book indeed, and itself classified—he fingered through until he came to Dr. Elizabeth Coogan. As he dimly recalled from talking to her at the reception, she lived in Bethesda, and ran her project in an office in one of the newer downtown buildings. He looked at his watch. Past midnight, but . . . He shrugged. He was following this up on a hunch, so he might as well follow the minor hunch he now had that she was still at her office.

The telephone rang just twice before it was picked up. Dr. Coogan's voice was crisply businesslike as she answered, but warmed when Judd identified himself and reminded her of their meeting.

"General, what a surprise."

"Sorry to bother you so late, Dr. Coogan. But you know generals hardly ever sleep."

"Indeed. What can I do for you?"

"Nothing over the phone, but can we meet in an hour?"

NEW YORK

Probing!

He was astounded. He had thought it would be months before anyone would realize he existed, months in which he could make his moves, slowly and with time for precise calculation. But now . . . He hadn't even made a major move yet, and one imaginative man in a strategic post—in Washington of all places—was moving to engage him in direct battle!

It was a setback, finding himself so soon confronted with an adversary—but it was fascinating, too, to be in touch with an intelligence that could make the intuitive leap that this man had. He sensed the struggles of the man in Washington to deal with his own psychic potential, to act on it without admitting it. He himself had known that reluctance, that fear, when his talent was growing in him, making itself evident in unnerving ways.

He had tried to deny it, tried, when he could no longer deny it, to study it—even spent that disastrous time at the University of Northern California Biocybernetics Center, being studied like a laboratory animal. What an ordeal that had been . . . and how far off the track the researchers were! It had been worthwhile in the end, for he had left determined on two things: to flow with his gift as it took him; and to conceal it rigorously and absolutely from those about him. And to make sure of that, he had managed to remove all his records before leaving. Without the surrender to the forces within him, and the freedom from prying inquiry that that decision had brought about, he would never have . . . grown . . . as he had.

If the man in Washington had the psychic faculty his inspired hunch seemed to indicate, he too was in for some bad times in learning to deal with it . . . but the main thing right now was . . . *who* was he calling so urgently past midnight?

AUGUST 4

Yellow Destruct

WASHINGTON

12:50 A.M.

Elizabeth Coogan lived her life at two levels, both having their source in her childhood. Born in the immenseness of the American Midwest of middle-class parents, she had an innocence of vision, a naïveté that, when faced with social and professional machinations, often betrayed her. Yet this innocence, this freedom born of the sight of endless fields of corn and wheat shimmering in the sun, undulating under the wind, had given her a sense of the innate beauty of the universe that she never lost.

But she had discovered early that a person who possessed only a sense of beauty and freedom was hardly equipped to deal with the world. One also had to become tough, even hard, especially if that person moved from the cornfields of the Midwest into the field of science and those sophisticated societies that governed the world. Through the years she had attained a high, hard level of competitiveness and professional eminence.

Wandering free in the open beauty of tall corn and whispering wheat had sharpened her powers of observation. She had studied ants building mounds, seeds growing, the death of field animals and their decomposition beneath the hot sun. Maturing a little, she had observed interactions between city folk and farmers, the beginning of her knowledge of the need for toughness. Later, studying science, the earth, the solar system, and distant galaxies had instilled in her a lust for understanding the process of learning itself.

It had seemed natural for her interests to flow through standard academic courses, then, as if following a tortuous but destined path, through philosophy, anthropology, psychology, and on into the modern sciences: bioelectronics, computer technologies, cybernetic systems—natural to her, but suspect to her colleagues, whom she outstripped easily in all fields. When she had finally encountered the mysterious world of human psi potentials, here, in man himself, she sensed an equivalent of her childhood awareness, the incalculable scope of universes beyond universes, into which the human mind might travel.

Her rigorous adherence to scientific procedure—and her experience-sharpened skill at handling political and academic dealers-out of public funds—had assured financing for her own research program into psychic potentials. Her offices in Washington, with their files and libraries on parapsychology, had become home to her. A home without a family . . . but, with herself and her work, it seemed to her full enough.

She was pleased that Judd had telephoned, but wondered why. Their brief talk at the NSF reception had been stimulating. She had half expected, for the next day or so, to hear from him, then decided that there hadn't really been much of a spark struck. It was months later now, hardly a time to follow up on that.

But . . . she felt an anticipatory excitement—then a flash of irritation as she noticed her nail polish was chipped. "Damn!" Her hands flew through the jumble of pencils and papers in her top desk drawer, found a bottle of polish. She swore again when she found it was not the right color—she would have to do both hands, not just a quick repair job.

She busied herself with the chore. Around her, in the enormous building that housed her gray and brown offices, all was silent except for the muted rumbling of the air conditioning that made life possible in Washington during the brutal summer. She mistook the slight chill at the back of her neck for a sudden draft of air in the room.

She shoved aside the two folders she had been studying before the telephone had rung. Across from her desk, where she could guard them herself, there were cabinets filled with similar folders, neatly arranged alphabetically, bright, canary-yellow folders. She viewed the expanding collection of folders with almost motherly affection, since it was she who had been incubating them for several years. They were growing and maturing.

Name, date of birth, sex, age, place of birth, psychological profiles—every scrap of information she had been able to obtain on anyone involved in the paranormal, from reports by students who had participated in ESP experiments at the college level to lists and descriptions of psychic abilities claimed or demonstrated by both little-known and well-known psychics. There were documents verifying the abilities exhibited and documents claiming to debunk those abilities. Press statements, financial statements, sources of income, tax matters, parentage, genealogies, spouses, sex habits, children, lovers: all this information occupied the yellow folders, information revealing the background of any person claiming psychic abilities, information that was beginning to create a staggering picture of the incidence of paranormal intelligence. . . .

Busy over her nails, she was unaware of the almost electric tension slowly filling the room, but found herself considering the contents and implications of her files, as though she were being somehow compelled to review her work.

There had never been a collection of information like this. There was no original work of hers in it, but the very fact of all the material having been brought together, analyzed, cross-referenced, created something that had not existed before. One study, one book, even the work of one organization, amounted to little, startling though the results shown might be. Rhine's pioneering work at Duke, hundreds of academic and private studies and experiments had had their effect—but it was mainly to confirm the already convinced believers in the psychic in their beliefs, with nonbelievers left untouched.

As the files expanded, and links were established among the countless pieces of information, they seemed almost to form a living entity; she could imagine it as growing, developing neuronal connections and approaching awareness.

When it was—not complete, for it would never be that—when it had reached a stage at which she could start making elements of it public—it would indeed be almost as if she had created something living, and the result would in its own way be as unsettling as that of Dr. Frankenstein's work, inescapably altering the way people perceived and accepted reality. It was not there yet, the connections were not all made, crossing and reinforcing, but the pattern of what it *would* be was clear: hundreds, thousands of human beings had demonstrated the experience of perception without the use of the accepted senses, acting on objects without physical force . . . in short, going completely outside the area of known possibility. What was growing in her files was the basis for studying and understanding the whole range of this *other* possibility—call it psychic, paranormal, the words didn't matter.

It would take a long time for her work to be listened to, let alone accepted—too long for any official group, government or academic, to be happy about. She had not been reluctant to accept the semisecret funding from Sandmuller International, but had a little regretted the necessity; it was a pity that the only source of backing was a corporate giant of the kind she deeply mistrusted, but there it was. And that had not been the only compromise she had had to make, she reflected wryly—for a dedicated "pure scientist," she had learned to bend some rules pretty shrewdly. Most of the information in her files was legitimately obtained, from public or other sources; but some of the most crucial material had found its way there through clandestine channels. Knowing what she wanted and needed, she had done what she had to to get it; and, since she had been successful, it did not trouble her that she had resorted to discreet bribery among the staffs of several dozen research institutions to be assured of instant copies of all their "confidential" records. The subjects of their experiments were guaranteed absolute privacy . . . but Dr. Coogan's determination and the money she was prepared to spend were sufficient to void the guarantee.

Her conscience had not bothered her over this—but suddenly, now, in this past-midnight hour, she felt a shock of dismay as she recalled it, a strong impress of dread and, somehow, anger. She pushed the feeling away from her and examined her nails. Damn—would they never dry? She still had to lock up the files. Using the palms of her hands, she opened one of the two cases she had been working on. "Davis, Marion: 64. Deceased. Mentalist. Summary: Engaged in show business, but intensive research indicates instances in which trickery cannot be proved and seems unlikely. See examples 142, 185." She was glad that the entire system of files was soon going into computers. Its mass was unwieldy; and the computers would cross-index by topic, similar events, and psychological traits.

NEW YORK

1:00 A.M.

Probing!

His eyes flared open.

"Good God!" He broke the delicate psychic tendrils that had linked his mind to Elizabeth Coogan's.

He had never dreamed that such a file system existed! Not in all the reveries in which he had scanned military bases, missile-launch devices, government conferences, international meetings, and secret liaisons had he thought to look into obscure independent research centers.

He immediately realized why. There must be thousands of them, each involved in some seemingly insignificant research, studying anything from the effects of healers on the resuscitation of anesthetized mice to autohypnotic modification of patterned habits. He had bypassed psychic scrutiny of all these because they were so numerous and because he had not been interested in such facile approaches to the abilities of the mind.

His body had gone cold with shock, the shock of realizing his arrogance, his stupidity. There was no doubt that in those yellow files there existed a folder with his name on it. His participation as a psi subject at the U.N.C. Biocybernetics Center would have earned him that. And sooner or later they would come across it. And in it there would be copies of the files of the psychological batteries that had accumulated at the Biocybernetics Center. He had already destroyed the originals before ending his short stay there. But the yellow folders must contain illegal copies—the woman's thoughts had made that clear.

The immediate problem had to be handled at once. He could not afford to let that military genius get on his trail so swiftly. Apparently, it had taken him only a matter of days to understand that the Project Tonopah plans could have been stolen only by some sort of psychic spying.

"Congratulations, you sonofabitch!"

But his lips, drawn thin from the initial amazement, gradually hardened into a determined line. A tide was rising, the urgency of the moment spurring him to force himself further beyond his limits than he had ever reached. Earth itself seemed to recede, and he seemed to be unified with systems of stars far from the small planet circling its yellow sun, to become a consciousness in and *of* space itself. Space . . . the word meant emptiness, but the region in which he existed seethed and roared with energy—magnetic, gravific, radiant energies surging, rending atoms and molecules, paced to and controlling the dance of electrons, neutrons, particles and antiparticles.

Everything moved—all substance was dependent on the motions of its particles. Modern science had long taught that, but now he sensed it, lived it . . . and knew how he could use it to serve his need.

The light-years-broad reach of his awareness narrowed and refocused to where he lay in his apartment. That was it—to give the molecules of the dangerous folders one light psychic "punch." But he would have to zero in on them very, very accurately.

Supine on his rhinoceros couch, he gathered his forces for that punch. It had to be channeled to the precise place—how . . . Ah!—the telephone! It would have to be precisely, delicately done if he were not to harm the woman. . . .

The number began to form in his mind. His body began to gear itself, instinctually, as if it recalled the processes from other times, other lives, or even from other galaxies.

WASHINGTON

1:20 A.M.

The ring of the telephone jolted her. Careful not to damage the still-tacky nail polish, she reached for it. Her hand trembled—it was unnerving to have the phone ring twice so late at night.

She was aware of a new and inexplicable tension rising in her.

As her hand approached the telephone receiver, a spark leapt up out of it, lightly shocking her fingers, as if she had walked over a carpet and touched a metal doorknob. She hesitated. The phone was plastic: how could it. . . ? And *why* was she suddenly possessed by a bone-deep premonitory dread? With an effort, she lifted the receiver.

The voice that spoke to her was melodious, amazingly clear, almost as if it were not coming through the receiver at all, but broadcasting directly to the center of her brain.

"I can't quite get your name," it said.

As the telephonic voice reverberated through her head, she found her eyes quickly scanning the office: the files, the three-day-old flowers hanging to one side in their vase, the mustard-colored rug on the floor, the vinyl brownness of the couch and chairs, a copy of a Rembrandt etching, and a reproduction of an orange and pink Matisse on the walls. She regretted that she had not loved her office more. And why had she chosen the expensive yellow folders for her files? Why not blue, or even red? And she wondered why, at such a moment, all this should pass before her eyes, almost as if she were going to die, as if she were a TV camera registering a setting for an audience.

She collected herself to answer her caller. "Who is this?"

"The files you have . . ."

"Who *is* this?"

"Can't tell you, ma'am, but those files, I'm afraid they have to go."

"Go? What do you mean? Go where?" Could this be some government agent, CIA, FBI perhaps, announcing some idiot plan to classify her research? If so, perhaps Judd could—

"From dust to dust . . ."

"Listen, I'll have to know who you are before—"

"I recommend that you leave your office immediately."

Coogan was too dumfounded to be able to reply.

"I think the files will break into particles in a few minutes, and the . . . well, I don't know exactly what will happen, but there will at least be an intense electrostatic discharge."

Coogan was grasping for her wits. In her confusion she noticed she had marred the ruby polish still drying on her left thumb. "Damn!" she muttered.

"Hurry," urged the voice, "it's got to come now. . . ."

The voice vanished from her ear—or was it her mind?—and was replaced by a surge in the static coming from the earpiece. A gust of directionless dry wind seemed to race through the office. The fine hair on Coogan's forearms stood erect, and so did the loose strands on the nape of her neck. She caught her breath. Sparks crackled through her light silk dress, creating around her for the barest second an iridescent aura of many colors.

The telephone receiver fell from her hand, rattling against the desk. She reached for the edge of the desk to steady herself, but a cascade of light arched out toward her hand, bathing it in sparks. Coogan staggered, backing up against the wall.

As if nothing had happened, the room had returned to its muted silence. Only her deep breathing was audible, but her widened eyes darted nervously, like those of a trapped animal frantic for an immediate exit. A blast of ozone penetrated her lungs. The adrenaline of fear flooded her blood, galvanizing her to action.

She rushed for the door, stopping short of reaching for the knob. Would it shock her too? The files! She couldn't leave without locking them up.

Nervous tears nearly ready to wet her cheeks, she grabbed first for her plastic purse. Then she reached down to grab up the two brilliant yellow folders. Her fingers touched, then passed through the folders, which instantly erupted in minute puffs of ochre dust. Coogan gasped in indignant bewilderment. She glanced helplessly at the old flowers, horrified to see that they also were now lying in a pile of dust, some of which was itself drifting through the air.

She couldn't quite let the scream come. The files on the desk, neat stacks of paper, were disintegrating, falling away from neatness into small rills. Then the scream tore loose from her throat as she lunged for the file cabinets. Jerking open a drawer, she saw that the folders barely held their shape for an eye-blink before they collapsed and then belched out of the drawer in a cloud of yellow-gray dust so fine it looked like fog.

Coogan drew a breath to scream again. The dust immediately coated her nostrils, wafting into her lungs. She lunged for the door, gasping for air. She made it out into the hall, slamming the door behind her; a yellow-gray miasma crept ominously through narrow crevices around its hinges. She leaned against the corridor wall, desperately trying to draw breath. Faintness first overtook her, then blackness. She collapsed in a gentle heap against the wall, her light silk dress giving off eddies of clinging dust as her body trembled in its faint.

Behind, her brainchild was slowly being sucked, particle by particle, into the air-conditioning vents, trailing through the several floors of shafts, eventually into the filtering system in the second subbasement. There, in barely five minutes, it congregated in sufficient quantities to clog the filtering screens. A blower burned out, a circuit breaker closed down. The entire system shut off automatically.

Moments passed.

Coogan's body slowly regained its breath, but not its consciousness. General Harrah Judd found her still crumpled on the floor when he arrived.

Professionally suppressing his surprise, he knelt and saw that she was alive and apparently not seriously hurt. He rose and opened the door to her office. Clouds of fine dust motes swirled out to engulf him. He slammed the door in amazement, carefully backing away. A few moments later, after gently depositing a gasping Elizabeth Coogan on the elevator floor, he grabbed the emergency telephone.

"Abrams?" he said, when his aide finally answered, "I want two teams. One composed of a physicist, a biologist, a chemist, and an electronics specialist. Another to transfer the contents of the office."

"What office is that?" Abrams said, as calmly as though such a request at past 1 A.M. was perfectly normal.

"Coogan's office. Downtown in the Williard Building."

"Yes, sir. When?"

"Now!"

NEW YORK

1:40 A.M.

Probing!

Satisfied that the files had been destroyed—and the woman unhurt—he withdrew his consciousness from Washington.

His heart was palpitating, whether from the psychic strain or from the near-ecstatic excitement he felt at the feat he had brought off he was not sure. But he should not have *had* to perform it; that he had not foreseen the situation meant both that his abilities were not as developed as he had thought—and that his overall plan had to be changed.

Arrogance or short-sightedness—either were serious flaws—had led him to operate as though he were the only psychic element in the plan. But this man in Washington— the name *Judd* had come to him through the woman's thoughts—Judd evidently had the latent talent that allowed him to make an intuitive leap toward the truth, while

Merriweather had counted on official reverence for the limits of logic to conceal it for a long time. Now what he had planned for several months in the future had to be moved up. . . . Yes, that could be done. Rather than reasoning his way from one point to the next, he seemed to sense the component parts of the plan shifting position, some disappearing, others altering shape, to form a new pattern adapted to the new timetable, one as seamlessly neat as the original. Unless, of course, there was another unforeseen flaw!

He had to rest from the extensive effort in long-distance psychokinesis. Resting from the exertion, he let himself slide into his memories.

Merriweather's life had been a mixture of the ugliness of poverty and the splendor of success. He came from nowhere—a slum in Chicago—and from, in effect, nobody. His origin had been accomplished by a father who drank more than he worked and disappeared before Daniel could know him. His mother persevered in poverty, never believing she could try for anything else. From the first moment that he was aware of the poverty and barrenness of his life, Daniel had determined to change it, to succeed. At the age of eight, he followed the most obvious route to success, as it was understood locally, and made himself adept at snatching handbags and making off with them. He was deft and had an uncanny sense of what bags were worth going after; but an icy pavement and a fast-moving cop combined to bring him to juvenile court and an ordeal that ended in his release to his bewildered, discouraged mother.

He had a moment of trying to work out how he could do better in some other criminal line and thought of a few quite practical schemes; but he realized that what he had felt on being caught was not so much fear or rage as relief—the needs he had satisfied by his purse-snatching were not his real needs, and no such activity would help him toward being what he wanted to be instead of having some few things he wanted.

It was just at this time that the lackluster musical scene of the early 1960s was revitalized by the rebirth of rock, with the Beatles and their imitators suddenly becoming major cultural forces; and Dan Merriweather took fire from the new sound. More importantly, he discovered that he had a talent for singing and for making up his own songs, which impressed his street-wise contemporaries, and realized that there was his passport out of the slums. At the age of nine, the passport was not yet valid, but the goal energized him and directed his efforts for the next seven years; and, as soon as he could convincingly claim the legal minimum working age, he was wheedling and intriguing his way into playing at local bars and night spots—and, once given a platform, shaking both himself and his listeners with the haunting force of his songs and his performance of them.

What a critic wrote of his first New York performance a few years later applied even then: "Young Mr. Merriweather makes an unimpressive appearance as he enters. Slight, almost frail, the guitar seemingly a half size too large for him, he raises fears of yet another Dylan pastiche. But from the first chords, he is electrifying, as a singer, as a player, as a composer. One may read the sheet music, study the lyrics without noting anything special—yet when Daniel Merriweather plays that music and sings those lyrics, he has any audience convinced, as a whole and each member of it, that he is singing to *them* directly, with full knowledge of their needs and their hearts, and further that the audience is giving back to the performer as much as it receives. A Merriweather concert is a remarkable musical experience, but a fantastic emotional—it is unfashionable and suspect to use the word spiritual, so I shall not—one."

Merriweather discovered before he was twenty that being the provider of unique musical and emotional (or spiritual) experiences was not the whole of success. One year of recording and concert work was lost when the firm his first agent put him under contract to got entangled in legal complexities attendant on its being taken over by a multinational conglomerate which determined that a wanted tax loss could be had only by suspending the firm's production; other agents and other contracts produced varying results, until he had signed on with the dour but capable—and honest—Astor Golderman, under whose management his career reached a peak of nationwide and international acclaim and profit.

And then, one spring day, he sang to a flower—and it sang back.

From that moment his life had changed. He was as ambitious as ever, but the ambition had nothing to do with success, with singing. As surely as he had known, years before, that music was what would raise him from poverty, he now knew that he was committed to following through the consequences of that brief moment of insight and communication. It crystallized what he had felt for a long time in those sessions of near-mystical communion with his audiences: that there was within him something that reached beyond the bounds of the mind and body, and that he would be maimed, incomplete, if he did not fulfill it.

The first step was to fill in some gaps in his education—which was actually one almost total gap; Dan Merriweather had learned a great deal in his two and a half decades, but almost none of it from schools. Of history and geography, except for places he had hit on tours, he had almost no notion; and his knowledge of literature was wide-ranging but scrappy. It was none of these that he determined to master, however, but what he felt would lead him to understand his newly found core of strangeness: the knowledge of the human mind and its powers.

He enrolled in special courses in psychology and education, turning down bookings in order to keep the class schedule and bringing Golderman, as he claimed, to the point of death from an attack of "terminal aggravation." A lecturer's analogy comparing the brain to a computer system sent him off on a doctoral program at M.I.T., on the assumption that understanding the electronic equivalent of the mind would give him a basis for dealing with that diffuse entity itself. He came away from M.I.T. with a fascination for what computers could accomplish, awe at the interlinked information network that webbed the world, and contempt for the trivial, often destructive, uses to which it was put. He did not return to the psychology and education classes; from them he had learned something of his own makeup, the childhood roots of his drive, and his tendencies toward arrogance and isolation . . . but most importantly, that there was nothing in their disciplines that related to what he was searching for within himself.

It seemed to him in those months that he was growing in this new dimension, but unaided and undirected; his life was following a course he did not understand, and he found himself making rapid, sure decisions that made no sense to anyone else, least of all Astor Golderman. In a week he devoured the information local libraries had on the "crank pseudoscience" of parapsychology his psychology teacher had derided and found himself half inclined to agree; there was little in this mishmash of occultism, stage tricks, and tedious, if inexplicable, experimentation that seemed to bear on what he knew he was growing into. Yet there were hints that struck home: Backster's work with plant communication was far short of the experience he had had when the flower sang back to him, but it was his first realization that anybody had known anything remotely similar. It was not much, but enough to encourage him to press on.

Inquiries about work now being done led him to read up on an ambitious research project at the Biocybernetics Center at the University of Northern California and—over Astor Golderman's anguished protests—to offer himself as a subject for ESP and other testing, in the hope that steady, directed effort would bring out the powers latent in him.

"I'll put it out you had to go away to get dried out from boozing, or you're shacked up in Puerto Vallarta with two teen-age girls and a goat," Golderman said, seeing him off at the airport. "That you could live down, they expect a star should act like that. But if it gets around you're into this shit, I couldn't book you except into a flying-saucer convention."

The U.N.C. public relations man who met him at the San Francisco airport did not take the view that Merriweather was risking his career by volunteering for testing, and quickly laid down a set of stringent rules designed to keep him from exploiting the Biocybernetics Center for personal publicity.

"We have both administrative and scientific reasons for insisting that all statements come from my office or as official publications or papers before professional groups," he said firmly, as he drove Merriweather past lion-colored hills framing the city's jumbled skyline. "We just can't have, uh, interviews. . . ."

"That's all right," Merriweather said mildly, looking with some bafflement at what appeared to be a giant Egyptian pyramid among the office buildings, "I'm incognito here. My agent's arranged a cover story that I'm . . . resting in Puerto Vallarta."

The P.R. man looked less gloomy, and confided some of the problems he had had to face. "Last year, a telepath got away from us and set up a date on a local TV talk show, did a mind-reading bit, came up with some upsetting things he said people were thinking. The host used to be in a carnival, claimed he knew how it was done, all fake. What a hell of a mess—we nearly got sued, only nobody could decide whether it should be for invasion of privacy or fraud, but then they decided he was a nut case and we sent him away."

In spite of this unpromising introduction, Merriweather hoped that the actual research program would be worthwhile and submitted to a grueling schedule of tests. After a few days he felt something like a laboratory rat—kept at work for long hours, with only infrequent rests, he would return to his motel room at night, fall asleep immediately, and wake in time to go back to the center for another day's schedule of tests. During his three weeks there he saw no more of San Francisco than he had seen on the drive from the airport.

Some of the researchers—Kauntz especially—were stimulating to work with, and there were some good results, especially in the blind location tests. They would give him a set of map coordinates which meant nothing to his conscious mind, and he would draw whatever he "saw" there, mountains, buildings, trees; sometimes he could see clearly enough to draw floor plans. Where these could be checked, they seemed to be pretty accurate, but for a variety of reasons—after all, he could have been a geography freak, knowing what would be found at any point on the globe, or anyhow there was no way to prove he wasn't—that test didn't count for much with the center's establishment. Many of the other tests seemed to him foolish, and he proposed new ones, which some—including, again, Kauntz—were enthusiastic about; but, again, the dead hand of the administration had come down hard with the dictum that research would follow the lines already laid down.

With Kauntz he had been able to discuss his theories of the whole psychic universe that coexisted with but was different from the physical one and even got an agreement to put some of his experimental ideas into action. He suspected that the partial acceptance of his views and aspirations by Kauntz and others had alarmed the administration and resulted in the "routine shift" which left him working mainly with one Dr. Clyde, who was very much in accord with their views.

Somehow, under Clyde's direction, most of the tests were

totally unproductive, demonstrating no ability at all for precognition, telepathy, or other psi talents. Though he made a strong effort to perform, he had the sense of something inside himself blocking what he consciously wanted to do—partly, he thought, a resistance to the tunnel vision of the experimenters, who were interested only in going over and over well-worn ground, following procedures they and others had laid down long ago, which to him seemed to have little or no bearing on the problems they were supposed to be dealing with—and this crowd, he thought bitterly, were the innovative ones in the field!

"We haven't really got very far, have we, Daniel?" Clyde said one day. "You don't test out significantly, either positively or negatively, in *any* area—in fact, you're about as close to the random chance in these tests as I've seen; which is extraordinary in itself, though it doesn't mean anything."

Merriweather felt a jolt of concern. That was the result that might be expected if some counterforce within him were intent on suppressing his abilities, some side of him that wanted to deny that there was anything extraordinary there.

"Well . . . Dr. Clyde, I wonder if you're testing for the right things, then?"

Clyde's lips pinched. "These tests are absolutely standard—"

"Maybe we should try something else. Uh, what about psychokinesis, affecting objects at a distance?"

"There's no indication for that, Daniel. But . . . I suppose we *could* arrange something for tomorrow, start in with a few hundred runs of the dice. I can set that—"

"No, I—look, Doctor, maybe there's a kind of threshold here. I mean, oh, like when I sing, you know, I can sing by myself or to a couple of friends, and it's O.K. But what I *have*, the thing that makes me Dan Merriweather—shit, it seems like I think I'm a big deal, but it's true, I do grab people hard when I'm going—well, that only comes out when I'm working with a real audience, as if we had a kind of magnetic field going between us. Even the studio recordings I do don't get half the plays or sales the concert ones do. Well, maybe it's that way with some people's psi talents, maybe they don't switch on until there's something big enough to work on. And, Doctor, I hate to say it, but I don't see that reading off a lot of Zehner cards or making dice come up sevens when there's no money riding is really going to coax psi talents out of hiding."

Clyde looked annoyed, then thoughtful. "Interesting hypothesis. It might bear on the very random results we get from even our best subjects. Do you, um, have any ideas about what it might take to reach the threshold of *your* talent, whatever it might be? Since it finds affecting the fall of dice beneath its notice?"

"It's not that it's dice or whatever," Merriweather said excitedly. "It's that . . . well, even if I got them to roll sevens ten, twenty, a hundred times running, you know, ten million-to-one odds against it, it'd just get written up and filed away, 'information noted, no conclusion possible as yet,' right?"

"That's a pretty cavalier way of describing a method that has—"

"Done nothing very damn much about getting at any idea of what all this is *about*. Look, what you want, what everybody here does, is something that's *it,* right? No question about it, so-and-so has done something absolutely *impossible*, no way to put it down or explain it away. Now *that's* what I think might do it, get me up past the threshold, if I thought it could lead to a real breakthrough."

Clyde rolled his eyes in exasperation. "Daniel, you're sounding like a prima donna—it's got to be done your way or you won't play—"

"Why do you think prima donnas act that way? They know they can do their job better than anyone else!"

Clyde looked at him coldly. "What sort of earth-shaking demonstration do you have in mind?"

He hesitated. That business with the crystals Kauntz had given him had scared him. What had happened was more than he had been prepared for, and the idea of controlling something that could do *that* was unsettling. Maybe this was different, almost playful, not destructive, and he felt surer of his ability to handle it.

"Well . . . computers. They're sealed systems, the only access to them is through the regular input channels. In that terminal on the third floor, you've got a CRT display screen—suppose, without getting anywhere near the keyboard, I could make it display a . . . message I chose?"

"That's impossible," Clyde said flatly.

"Except by means of what we're supposed to be testing *for*, damn it! That's why it'd be a test, man!"

"I don't—"

"Look, you don't have to commit yourself now, I can see you wouldn't want to spring this on your colleagues cold. Why not—that's it, let's go down there now, just you and me. If I can do it, then you could set up a real experiment to verify, all the controls you want—how about it?"

Clyde was visibly reluctant, but the force of the exuberance and excitement welling up in Merriweather was too strong to resist, and, without being quite sure how, he found himself standing beside the rock star in front of the grayish-green screen of the computer terminal.

Merriweather felt as though a powerful current of electricity were surging through him, the power within him beginning to stir and overcome whatever had been blocking it. He had almost a sensation of double vision, seeing both the surfaces of the objects around him and what lay beneath; he sensed Clyde's academically scruffy jacket-and-slacks outfit and the puzzled frown on the man's face, but also the circulation system, skeleton, and the neuronal connections and chemoelectric life within him. He could feel his perception beginning to slide into the computer in the same way, seeking out delicate electronic junctions and lines of force. If what he *knew* he could do came off, then it would be a whole new ball game; with his ability demonstrated beyond doubt, the whole force of the center would be mobilized to explore everything about the unknown area of the psychic in a way that made sense—and he, Daniel Merriweather, would be able to make a giant leap in understanding and developing his potential, in growing into what he must become.

The screen was live but blank, ready to display whatever input the computer got from its conventional sources . . . or, as Merriweather now intended, an unconventional one.

The room about him, Clyde next to him, receded from his awareness, and he felt himself growing into the circuits that led to the cathode-ray tube, sensing them as extensions of his own body. But it was an unfamiliar body; it was as though he had awakened and could not tell what were his fingers and what his toes, or what commands to give his muscles to make them move. He cast his mind back to the M.I.T. course—the effort of linear thought was grating, discordant with the new atmosphere of total perception—and retrieved the information he needed. He began flexing his—or the computer's—"muscles," and was aware at some distant level of a start from Clyde; the CRT screen was displaying random patterns.

He had partial control now; what message would he have the screen show? "Mr. Watson, come here, I want you" wouldn't fit very well. "One giant step for mankind" would, but why copy Armstrong? This would be a message from him, Daniel Merriweather, his announcement that he had reached a major fork in that path he had started on when a flower sang back to him. It should be—

He almost screamed as Clyde's arm, roughly shaking his shoulder, brought him in an instant back to normal consciousness; it was for an instant as though he had been torn in half, almost as much a physical as a psychic shock.

"How did you—what—how—" Clyde gabbled, clutching the shoulder fiercely.

Merriweather shook his head to clear it and looked at the CRT screen. On it, fading but still faintly visible, was the green image of a three-leafed wild flower. "Trillium . . ." he muttered vaguely, then collected himself. "Hey, Clyde, it worked! Now you can—"

Clyde dropped his hand from Merriweather's shoulder and stood back. His face was pale. "I—computers malfunction quite often, generate random patterns—it could have been—"

"Ah, *Clyde*. A random pattern that looks just like a particular kind of flower? Listen, that wasn't what I really meant to send, but I'll tell you why—"

"Merriweather!" He could see a damp sheen on the researcher's face. "I know you studied computers at M.I.T. and doubtless know a lot of ways to have fun with them. But I don't appreciate at all your bringing me down here to show off a prepared practical joke!"

"But . . . look, Dr. Clyde, it wasn't . . . I mean, you could try anything, set up any controls—"

"This is a serious program, Merriweather, and we don't have any time for horseplay. I suggest you confine your theatrics to your career!" He turned abruptly and left Merriweather, walking quickly down the corridor, then almost running.

Merriweather left the center early and spent the evening and much of the night brooding in his hotel room. That was it, then. He had demonstrated as clearly as anyone could paranormal interference with the computer's display

screen. Experiments, demonstrations, anything a researcher could want could be set up to test and verify
that—and Clyde had run away from it, run away from the
chance to be in on one of the great discoveries, one that
would link science to the paranormal in a way no skeptic
could deny. And, before he had run, Merriweather had
read the fear on his face . . . and the hate. He knew, as
surely as he had ever known anything, that Clyde had had
to force himself not to believe what he had seen, and that,
if he had believed, he would have felt it his duty to try to
destroy Merriweather.

Daniel Merriweather smiled wryly. It seemed clear that
Clyde—and, he guessed, most of the other researchers—
went about their work with the firm understanding that it
would not succeed, at least not in any way that would upset science's applecarts all at once. They seemed to envis-
age a steady, slow progress: a little more information on
telepathic manifestations here, guarded work on out-of-
body experiences there, minute increments of information
leading to lots of published studies and the gradual growth
of a theoretical underpinning which would make the whole
business acceptable. What he had just demonstrated was
too much of a jolt.

His face turned grim as he brought back the moment of
Clyde's flight to full recall. Like a hound sniffing the trail
of a rabbit that had passed by hours ago, he probed and
quested psychically around that point in time and space,
seeking something that troubled him. Yes . . . buried in
his recalled perception, there it was, a pungent trace of
something other than hate and fear, and warring with
them: some part of Clyde had been thinking, *If it's true—
what a fantastic weapon he'd make!*

Merriweather gave a deep sigh. What the hell else should
he have expected? People had too much of a stake in the
way they saw things, in what they believed in, to be open
to change. Twenty thousand people a year sacrificed themselves to the proposition that you could drink and drive,
hundreds of thousands existed in semistarvation because
they insisted on polishing away the husks of rice that was
their main food, and with it most of the nourishment; and,
the world over, people put power into the hands of precisely the same kind of leadership that had kept the planet
in a state of on-again-off-again war throughout history—

they'd rather die than give up the familiar frames of reference.

And the only fate for him within that frame was as a resource to be exploited—destructively, for sure—or an anomaly, to be smoothed out, expunged, blown away. That was what had been blocking him in the tests, a buried awareness that success would be much, much worse than failure. . . .

He was glad next day to learn that Clyde was out with what was said to be a sudden attack of the flu; he would certainly, on his own, convince himself that he had not seen what he had seen and be glad to forget the whole matter.

Merriweather pleaded a sudden career crisis and broke off his program with the center; and, before leaving, used a combination of guile, charm, and a touch of psychic pressure to retrieve the files Clyde had maintained on him unobserved. He dumped them in a trash basket at the airport. It was unlikely that Clyde would look at anything connected with Daniel Merriweather for a long time, if ever, and if the loss was discovered, it would probably be put down to misfiling.

Astor Golderman, pleased to have his star property back early, was less so when he found that he refused to accept anything more than a small proportion of the new bookings he was offered, and was less than reliable about fulfilling recording contracts; but Merriweather was firm and, for the greater part of the time for several months, withdrew to his apartment.

It was not a withdrawal from the world in the traditional manner of Howard Hughes or the Collier brothers; Merriweather devoted the time to exploring and acclimatizing himself to two realms. One was the potentially limitless psychic universe, through which he was divesting himself of guides and instruction—for he was now coming around to the idea that whatever he carried within him would lead him more surely to his goal than any outside source; the other was the electronic world of linked computers. He had a sophisticated late-model terminal installed in his apartment, and amused himself by learning and sensing its intricacies and possibilities at the same time as he was exploring his own. It was paradoxical that his interests lay both in the areas of the purely psychic and in the purely electronic, with the normal human element omitted; but for him there was no contradiction. His computer terminal was a simple but useful tool, aiding him in much the same way as a chance-found stick aided primitive man.

From the beginning of this period, he was aware of a vastly greater scope of his powers. He experienced floating in space above Earth, moving about the planet, perceiving scenes in distant places which he knew were actual and not hallucinations; but he had little control over what he saw and sensed. He became aware of Project Tonopah without realizing what it portended; then anguished psychic radiation from the brain schists of Project Tolkien drew him, horrified him with what he saw, and sent him back to re-study Tonopah.

He understood immediately that the existence of these two superweapons could spell the end of humanity, not only the imperfect humanity of the present, but what it might someday become. The Americans and the Russians were on a collision course. One or the other of the weapons would be used in time; and even if the leaders of both nations exercised superhuman restraint and understanding, there was still that strange group whose presence he sensed, the industrialist and the weapons merchant, who would for profit spread the plague far beyond anyone's power to control it. . . . Merriweather realized with a shock that the end of all human freedom, forever, would almost certainly come within two years—making that Englishman who wrote *1984* a truer prophet than anyone had thought.

He reasoned out the matter coldly, with a buried anger he did not wish to acknowledge, and arrived at his plan. All the disarmament talks, from the conferences at The Hague early in the century to the SALT talks of the seventies, had done nothing but regulate the balance of terror in such a way that each major participant came away with a feeling that he had achieved a hidden advantage. That way had been tried, and it had failed. The appeal of force to settle disputes was still too strong, and a nation that was not free to slaughter in promotion of its interests felt demeaned and endangered. Force was the thing, then—confront the dealers in force with a greater force, and something might be accomplished.

It struck him as grimly amusing that the force he proposed to use was comparatively mild, almost innocent— merely the threat to tell the truth. In the history of the world, of course, that had always been the ultimate terror weapon, kept scrupulously sheathed by all participants in any conflict. He hoped it would be powerful enough to do what had to be done. If not, more dreadful methods would be called for . . . and he would find them.

This final thought nagged at him. He knew that, if it came to the point and he must act ruthlessly, it would be kinder, no matter what the devastation, than any alternative; yet naked force and *killing*—if he had to be candid, and why not, in his own private thoughts—seemed to be out of key with his perception of himself and his emerging nature. He put the thought aside, as one thing more to be resolved, along with so much else.

The first steps of the plan, in any case, were clear and presented no such problems. It struck him that Washington would be an appropriate place from which to dispatch the letters, and going there would give him a last chance to sense the atmosphere of one of the centers of power he was pitting himself against. If he became aware of any currents of good sense or good will strong enough to counteract what he knew to be the trend of affairs, there would still be time to consider alternatives. . . .

The brutal summertime heat of the capital was no more dismaying than the absence of what he still hoped to find. He could tell that there were good men in the city, in the government, far-sighted men, men of vision—but none combining strength, position, and wisdom in the way that was needed to handle the immediate menace, to say nothing of what would develop in the future.

In his mind's eye, in that strange territory within him that he had for so long feared and shunned, he could see very well what the future would hold—not the poisoned wasteland that would remain after a nuclear holocaust, but a prospect even more dreadful, a world of living dead, men, women, and children controlled or made walking vegetables by these new weapons that were not kind enough to kill the body outright, but struck at the mind and senses.

He left Union Station unnoticed in the crowd: a slight young man with the sun glancing off the multicolored brilliants decorating his denim shirt, sweat-darkened from the heat.

In a vast drug-variety store, he purchased a box of envelopes and a pad of cheap typewriter paper, then a pair of surgical gloves to hide his fingerprints. Making sure no one was watching, he pulled on the gloves and typed the letters on a battered rental typewriter in the lower corridor of the Library of Congress. He drew the sketches carefully with a felt-tip pen he had found abandoned on a table in the corridor.

He addressed the envelopes carefully. He inserted the remarkable documents he had constructed and sealed them inside before placing stamps on them from a vending machine. On his way out he threw away the unused stationery and the pen.

Holding the letters unobtrusively in his rubber-covered fingers, he walked the distance from the Library of Congress to Union Station. The heavy heat and the walk had made him sweat. He licked the salty moisture from his upper lip, pausing briefly at the mailbox, checking once more the addresses on the envelopes.

> Department of Defense Intelligence Agency
> Washington, D.C. 20301
>
> Director of Intelligence Moscow
> c/o Russian Embassy
> Washington, D.C. 20301

He plunged the two white, fingerprintless envelopes into the mouth of the red, white, and blue mailbox.

In the men's room of Union Station, he flushed the gloves down a toilet. Then he caught the late afternoon Metroliner to New York. He sank into the soft beige upholstery, grateful for the train's air conditioning.

He had now made himself into a weapon. It was a loathsome choice, but . . . it *had* to be the right one. The sun sank low, the lights of passing cities reflecting as long lines of color on the windows of the speeding train. He sighed. He had taken his stand, for himself . . . and for the future of humanity.

For he knew, with a certainty that seemed to pervade every molecule of his body as well as his mind, that he was not a random, freakish example of psychic overdevelopment. Things happened in their courses, and the time had come for someone like himself to be born. It might be that the dreadful pressure of this century's increasingly more horrible wars had provoked a genetic response in humanity, the pooled unconscious awareness of the race itself striving to avert worldwide doom, reaching toward the next step in human development as it had once reached to draw man upright, to see and think.

In moments of agonizing loneliness and fear, he clung to that certainty. For if he were unique, isolated, there would be so little point to anything he might do. There were, there had to be, others produced in response to the same forces that had molded him, with the potential to grow as he had, eventually to band together to form a reservoir of the new vision, to work to bring it about in the whole of mankind.

They *were* there, those others—and, now that he had begun to act, he had set in motion a train of events that would make him known to them, would bring them to him, to share, to grow. . . .

He let his mind open to the endless vistas of the real and psychic universes and felt once more that pity, tinged with scorn, that came to him when he saw how technology and science imprisoned those who could not see beyond them. . . .

When the Metroliner plunged into the Hudson River tunnel, he came back to himself and began to consider what to do next.

Soon he was in the city, out onto the hot sweltering streets. His blood surged, both the psychic and the sensate qualities of his being energized by the aura of one of Earth's largest cities. In the short time left to him before the powerful militaries of the world became aware of his existence, he had a lot to do.

But first he would once more visit, perhaps for the last time, the dizzying heights of the city as seen only from the illuminated tower of the Empire State Building.

Beneath his feet, far beneath, resonating upward through the steel and stone structure of the building, were the vibrating innards of the city. Above him were faint evening stars, softly visible through the city mist and smog. Around him glowed billions of kilowatts, the city flowing over its island center, across the rivers, into the surrounding distant country, as far as his physical eyes could see.

The spectacular view he saw had not lost its enchantment since his last time here. He loved the old Art Deco relic, its elegant spire antiquated by the massive risings of its flat-topped companions springing up on other parts of the island. When he needed to experience the grandeur of heights, space, distances, he came once again to the Empire State tower—a physical analogue to the lofty psychic perspective he could find within himself.

Perhaps the reason he had needed the solace of the tower, the comfort of an evening breeze sighing softly around the gigantic lightning conductor, was that he felt a thread of uncertainty at the use he was to make of his power. Perhaps there was a more peaceful way he had not perceived?

Perhaps. But he had surveyed the possibilities for over a year. Earth's race toward doom must be held back. Above all, Tonopah and Tolkien must be abolished, or men and women could never call their minds their own again. Earth's population would be dehumanized in the name of that political ritual governments called "balance of power."

Many times he had tried to discover what was actually behind this concept only to find again and again that it was a self-perpetuating monster, a dinosaur no president or premier could control. Men, leaders, scientists could only trail along in the wake of its ever-increasing scope, until the entire world was imprisoned in a net of defensive and counter-defensive weapons. There was no way left but to disarm the destroyers—no matter what the cost. And it could not be done peacefully. His decision would have to stand.

The mauve and purple afterlight of the sunset that had lingered on the western horizon was now gone. Below, lights were beginning to go out here and there as offices and stores closed. He gazed up at the top of the tower's spire, almost lost in the dark sky above. Just once, he would let his abilities play.

Just once, for they were too powerful for play.

The malevolent psychic glimmerings of Tonopah and Tolkien receded from his mind. His skin, still covered with the accumulated sweat and grime of his day in Washington, cooled beneath the gentle fingers of breeze flirting with the huge spire above him.

He let visual tendrils drift upward from his psyche, his parasensory vision wanting even greater heights. The small points of awareness climbed like invisible vines, touching finally the crowning lightning rod marked with residual ozone—dusty electrons remaining from storm-tossed electric bolts. There he paused, extending his psychic perceptions into arenas of awareness beyond the limits of physical sight.

Above the spire, he created a psychic point which began immediately to attract charged particles floating in the hot summer winds. It grew slowly at first, invisible to all below, and then faster until it reached saturation. Out of its center shot the brilliance of the sun, but in rays spiderweb-thin. These clutched at the spire, dancing downward along its length, cascading branches of sparks resembling Roman candles. Several necking couples broke apart; two women screamed. The heated air collapsed on itself in a thunderous clap.

Smiling, he entered the waiting elevator and made the rapid float to street level. As he began the twenty-block walk to his apartment, he was almost gaily at peace. He would try to survive as his new self. The chances were not good. But if he were to live, it would be in his greater rather than his lesser psychic form.

His reverie completed, he came back to himself. His body seemed almost to hum with physical well-being, recovered from the powerful psychic charge that had shaken it. Daniel Merriweather opened his eyes and steadied them. His muscles relaxed and his body began cooling.

What an effort that had been—definitely exceeding his normal physical tolerance. But the files surely must be gone. They still existed in the universe, of course, but as billions of dust motes already dispersing throughout the city of Washington.

Having reinforced his decision during his reverie, he rose from the comfortable couch to begin his exit from his current life. Success, adulation, luxurious apartment in New York, his music, yes, even his youth itself, were now ended.

The army man Judd's lightning intuition of the psychic aspects of his two letters, and the existence of the yellow files in Washington had forced his hand, revealing something of the magnitude of his abilities.

Judd would never give up now; although his mind was a disorderly mingling of possibilities, that confusion was slowly coalescing into the inescapable truth. There was only one thing to do now: launch attack three.

Long ago—no, not long, only weeks ago—he had laid the plans for the arrival of this moment, which had arrived sooner than he had allowed for.

He felt a brief, irritable sadness. The American and Soviet governments had taken his letters seriously enough to move Tonopah and Tolkien; why couldn't they have had the sense to see that it wouldn't work, that he would carry out the threats in them?

He sat down at the computer terminal housed in a corner of his apartment and inserted the telephone receiver into the rubber cradle. The terminal jumped to life, the cathode-ray tube glowing its welcome in blocky green print. He had come to love the equipment that linked him up with every part of the world, the massive computer banks at M.I.T., Stanford, École de France, even that monster in Moscow. All one needed were the access codes, and those, after patient practice, he had obtained psychically.

The computer nets worldwide were thus opened to him. Actually, he did not need the computers either to get information or to carry out his intentions; he could generate enough psychic force for that. But computer access cut down the strain on his as yet fresh and hastily explored psi talents.

He routed first to the computer at M.I.T., where he was legally enrolled as a Cambridge doctoral candidate, #4025BE (bioelectronics). The cathode-ray tube terminal printed out the letters at 120 characters per second. It was beautiful, almost hypnagogic; and now, as when he had just acquired the computer terminal, he was fascinated. In future, though, he would have to use pure, direct psychic intervention; so he allowed himself to enjoy to the full this last experience of using one of man's crowning scientific achievements. The mammoth M.I.T. computer system answered.

WELCOME.
PLEASE IDENTIFY NAME, PASSWORD, AND SECTOR DESIRED.

He quickly typed into the terminal:

Merriweather. BE40. Relay.
THANK YOU. RELAY OPEN.

It was simple. He then directed:

Trans-American University System.

M.I.T. relayed him to the vast systems at College Park, Maryland.

WELCOME.
PLEASE IDENTIFY NAME, PASSWORD, AND SECTOR DE-
SIRED.

Here, it got tricky. But the name came, then soon the password, someone else's name and password. The TAU system accepted him under his alias. He requested the DARPA system, which took a little longer, since most of it was classified. But even that took only three minutes. He extracted the computerized description of Project Tonopah and ordered it transferred, with proper credentials, to a time-delay input in the Interpress public release systems, into which, on August 7, it would automatically be released into the international press lines.

To get to Leningrad, he had to route through Paris, then Moscow, finally getting into the huge Russian computer banks at the Leningrad Gas Dynamics Laboratory, which housed the Military Scientific Research Committee of the Soviet Armed Forces. The codes were more complex; he lit a cigarette, waited, and the letters and numbers gradually aligned themselves in his mental vision.

Soon he had extracted the specifications for Project Tolkien and ordered them placed, for later publication, in the Europress banks, where automatically, on the specified date, they would find their way into the worldwide press systems.

All this was accompanied with the swift forming and fading of electronic green letters. When the computer systems protested with CLASSIFIED warnings, he reached the codes psychically; each time the information came more swiftly and easily.

Completed. He logged out of all the computer systems as he had logged in, under legitimate codes and names; there would not be any immediate question. Finally, he logged out of the M.I.T. system, erasing his entry into it. His instructions remained in place in all the other systems, but the link between his apartment in New York and Cambridge now could never be revealed.

He paused a moment. A last look at the glowing CRT screen . . . a moment of regret. Then he withdrew the telephone receiver and replaced it in its cradle.

Now for the hard part. He knew it would not do to linger, and he walked out of the apartment without looking at anything.

In the elevator, he cast a mental glance around the room he had left. Everything must look as if his present life was still very much on track. He had signed new contracts with his agent and with recording companies, contracts that he had never meant to keep, but which would give any investigator the impression that he had been thinking of his future. There was food in the refrigerator, appointments in his book—enough of them to make his social life seem to fit the superstar image. He was sure he had left nothing behind that gave the slightest suggestion he was about to close out the life he had been leading.

In the lobby, he gave the night doorman his usual nod. "I'll be back in about a half hour."

"Right, Mr. Merriweather," the man said. "You written any new songs?" If he thought it odd that one of the building's most famous tenants was taking a post-midnight stroll, he did not express it.

"Yes. Yes, I've got one in the works right now."

In the street, he turned west to Fifth Avenue. There he stood on the corner, awaiting the right moment.

He steeled his nerves for the coming trauma. A series of last-minute thoughts assailed him, momentarily undermining his determination. The hot closeness of Manhattan, barely less of a steam bath at night than in the day, engulfed him.

God, how he loved New York! Perhaps he should live his life out as an ordinary man. . . . He gazed downtown at the Empire State Building. Would one more visit . . .

Out of the corner of his eye he spotted a taxi racing down Fifth Avenue. He let the car's speed, the pattern of staggered traffic lights he could see stretching up the avenue, and his brief perception of the driver integrate in his mind; in a millisecond, they formed the answer. The cabby would gun his car to make the green light, but miss it and have to brake hard. . . .

The driver, barreling his taxi along an almost empty Fifth Avenue, swore savagely as he saw the light change. The brakes screeched.

Merriweather closed his eyes and stepped off the curb, hoping his estimation of the braking distance was correct. His body was thrown ten feet into the intersection, the horn of the taxi blaring into the depths of his receding consciousness.

WASHINGTON

2:20 A.M.

Abrams arrived with the first members of the DARPA team, most of whom were mystified both by the early-morning hour and by the drifting dust emanating from the open door. The men began coughing as invisible motes invaded their lungs.

"Jesus!" exclaimed Abrams.

Judd had dragged Dr. Elizabeth Coogan farther down the carpeted corridor to a couch, where consciousness had returned to her, but her body was racked with coughing. Dust coated her fine blond hair, and her fingernails were loaded with dust, cemented into the now dried polish. Judd, thumping her on the back, looked up at his aide with an intensity, almost an exultation, that struck Abrams as very odd indeed under the circumstances.

"He's betrayed his existence," Judd said.

"Who? What?" Abrams asked, uneasily.

"It was the telephone . . ." Coogan finally managed to gasp.

"Telephone?" Abrams could make no sense of what was happening, and was feeling steadily more uncomfortable.

"We'll debrief later," snorted Judd. "Get with it, Abrams."

"With what, sir?"

"Seal off the office, impound anything left, you know. . . ."

"Paper," gasped Coogan, "everything paper, dissolved."

"Take it easy, Dr. Coogan," Judd said. "When you can walk, we'll get you into some outside air, and some other clothes, and then on to my office to talk this over."

"Th . . . thanks, General. I feel as if I'd been in a wheat-storage silo for years."

Abrams stood up, relieved to have some specific, if baffling, orders to carry out. He firmed his lips into a determined line and led the men to the office, looking for something, anything to do that would at least look efficient. "Vacuum cleaners," he decided, "that's what we need," and sent several men in various directions to discover where the commercial cleaning equipment was stored on that floor.

10:30 A.M.

Rastaban al Nashirah, irritated that he had not been able to locate Senator Heston Davis, who, so his secretary said, was on some yacht in the Caribbean, was doubly irritated when the imperious Aloysios Sandmuller rang through to him from Yugoslavia.

"What the hell is going on?" Sandmuller demanded.

"Haven't been able to find out exactly," Nashirah responded. "Seems the Americans have suddenly moved it."

"Moved it? Why and where?"

"I believe I said I haven't been able to find out."

"Goddamn it, Rastabi! What do you make of it? I just found out that the Russians have moved theirs, also."

Nashirah could not hide his surprise. "But—why—"

"You have to find out quickly, Rastabi. We can't afford to be out of the picture for long."

"The security is tight. Not one leak so far. It's that damned Judd, you know. He is as tight as an undefrosted refrigerator."

"How come he's involved? I thought Air Force was the developing agent."

"True, but Judd is liaison for Advanced Research, you know."

"When will you know more?"

"Probably not too long. It's too big a project to keep under wraps without a slip somewhere. I'll keep a watch on microwave shipments from Lockheed. No doubt they'll be routed to the new location."

"Have you talked to Heston Davis about this?" Sandmuller demanded.

"Can't. It's vacation time in Americaland, you know, Aloysios. He's down in the Caribbean on someone's yacht. I don't know where."

"I'll be back in New York shortly," Sandmuller said abruptly. "Perhaps we should meet."

11:00 A.M.

Elizabeth Coogan, Ph.D., holding advanced honors in bioelectrical psychology and others in computer electronics and theory, felt completely unprofessional and totally feminine as she watched Harrah Judd manipulate his staff in an effort to make sense of the implausible destruction that had come to her office. Discreetly borrowing specialists from Army, Navy, and Air Force research sections, and other related projects, he had mobilized nearly a hundred. Technical reports were already beginning to accumulate.

If his nerves were strained, that discomfort was betrayed only by the gloss of a sleepless night on his forehead and damp stains in the armpits of his tailored shirt. Otherwise, he appeared calm and determined. She suspected he was capable of inspiring both deep respect and awe in his men and in his fellow officers.

Coogan attributed it to her feminine empathy that she understood one additional thing: although treating it as a practical problem to be solved, at some near-mystical level Judd was deeply preoccupied and worried about this event. She herself was somewhat detached, slowly recovering from the numbness that had possessed her. Showered and changed into a set of overalls produced by Lieutenant Abrams, she had repeated her story to Judd at least six times.

"Well," commented Abrams, plunging into Judd's office with an additional sheaf of papers, "we are certainly learning a great deal about paper." The thought seemed to make him cheerful; he was always comfortable with undeniable facts.

"What have you got?" Judd asked brusquely.

"Well, sir, paper seems to have been invented by the Chinese in the second century, and learned from the Chinese by the Arabs about seven hundred years later. Europeans first made paper only in the twelfth century in France—"

"Is there some salient point you're getting to?" asked Judd.

"Right, sir. I was, uh, getting to it."

"How terribly slow," commented Coogan. "Imagine, almost a thousand years. And what a cultural impact the introduction of paper made in each civilization. . . ."

"Get on with it, Abrams." Judd knew he would have to let his aide present his information in his own way, but his insistence on filling in the last background details was sometimes galling.

"Well, there are several ways of producing paper. Paper is usually made by machine, using chemicals. Vegetable fiber mixed with water is reduced to a pulp and then spread on a mesh, usually of wire, or on an absorbent felt or cloth for draining or drying. This kind of process usually yields absorbent paper, like blotting paper or newsprint. The surface can be improved in several ways. Sizing, that is, glue, can be mixed with the pulp and used as a coating. And the paper can be calendered, that is, compressed by the use of rollers or plates."

"Is all this pertinent?" Judd asked, with no real hope that Abrams might suddenly decide it wasn't.

"Yes, sir. We think so."

"All right, continue."

"Yes, sir. To secure glossy finishes, the paper may be weighted with clay or some other substance, but this often makes it brittle. Other raw materials used in paper-making include rags, grasses, and wood. The best paper is made from linen rags. Newsprint is commonly made from wood. Old paper can be used for making new paper, but yields a weaker product. Typical papers include writing, printing, wrapping, building, and wallpaper. Paper pulp is often used for making wallboard and many other things."

"So?" asked Judd.

"So, everything in the office that was made of paper seems to have decomposed, turned to dust."

Judd looked at him closely before saying, as mildly as he could, "Well, we do know that, don't we, Abrams?"

"Yes, sir. But in the dust there is no residue of vegetable matter at all. There are traces of clay, various metallic sizings, and artificial polymer rubbers that probably had been added to certain sheets, but the vegetable matter seems to have vanished."

"But how could that have come about?" asked Coogan.

"Well, the molecules—you know, different elements that went into the building of the vegetable matter used in the paper—seem to have become disassociated."

"How do you mean, Abrams?" asked Judd.

"We don't *know* how. None of the experts downstairs has any kind of explanation. Simply, in Dr. Coogan's office, everything that had vegetable material in it—the files, the flowers, parts of the wallboard, even the vegetable glues binding the carpet—all these are clean gone."

"Good God!" exclaimed Coogan.

"Where to?" asked Judd.

"Well," began Abrams, drawing a deep breath. "It seems to have broken apart molecule by molecule. Oxygen, hydrogen, things like that, must have gone into the air. The phosphates and other inert materials, normally structured into vegetable systems, broke apart but remained and constitute the major part of the fine dust."

"Is there an opinion on how that might have come about?" Coogan wondered at the grave, almost sad, note in Judd's voice.

"Well, sir, Benchly—you know, the atomic physicist who has been examining some of the residue—well, he speculates something like this—ordinarily, the state or form in which matter exists depends on the relative distance between the molecules and on their velocity."

"You mean," said Coogan, her eyes wide with astonishment, "that the molecular velocity somehow *changed*. . . .?"

"Well, ma'am, Benchly says—"

"Come on, Abrams," snapped Judd. "Give it straight!"

"Yes, sir. Well, in general, the molecules in a solid are relatively close together, and their velocity is relatively slow. In a liquid they are farther apart and move at a faster rate, and in a gas they are farthest apart and move at greatest velocity. Now, the energy of motion of the molecules is described as kinetic energy, that is, as heat. When heat is added to any substance, it begins to vibrate more rapidly. If heat is added continuously, the molecules of the substance begin to move with increasing speed until finally a change of state occurs." Abrams was pleased that he had mastered the information the physicist had fed him well enough to be able to rattle it off so glibly.

"But I didn't feel any sudden change in temperature," said Coogan, her eyes wide with the implications beginning to emerge from Abrams' report.

"Well, yes, that gave Benchly a hard time," admitted Abrams. "But you did experience a sudden and considerable electrostatic discharge, right?"

"True."

"Well, then, Benchly thinks it isn't that the molecules themselves are gone, but that the spaces between them, constituting their state or structure, were somehow changed or disrupted—that their motion was somehow . . . nullified. Stopped for a microsecond."

"Stopped!" exclaimed Coogan. "You're trying to say that the atomic and molecular structure of the individual elements composing the vegetable substances, all these are still there. But their balances were disrupted . . . er, stopped

. . . and they disassociated . . . er, no longer cohered."

"Turned to dust . . ." muttered Judd.

"Dust!" said Coogan. "That was what *he* said!"

"Yes, everything turned into dust, except the gases, which must have gone into the air," added Abrams.

"But that's . . . uh, like decomposition accelerated," Coogan said.

"Yes, ma'am," said Abrams. "I suppose so." He looked expectantly at Judd and Coogan. He had brought them the full report, as ordered; now it was up to the general and the scientist to figure out what to make of it. That was what generals and scientists were for.

Judd glanced at Coogan, his gaze lingering on her soft, quivering lips, lips moving with unuttered words as she tried mentally to assimilate the meaning of what she had just heard.

He had gone through a similar moment a few days earlier, confronting the simple, yet impossible, anonymous letter. Every fiber of his being had wanted to stop time, to recede into a safe past, never to have to confront any future—especially the future he intuited was dawning.

Coogan seemed to sense his thoughts and turned to him, her eyes pleading for a rational release from the incredible implications dawning on her. Judd felt a reassuring response in his groin; the fabric of the universe couldn't have unraveled entirely if he could still feel horny. He rose from his desk.

"Dr. Coogan," he said, "while Abrams was getting you that outfit you're wearing, I gave orders that the remains of your office be totally removed, and there are engineers there now rebuilding it exactly as it was. Can you give Abrams a complete list of all the items in it—ah, that *were* in it?"

"Why, yes, I suppose so. What especially?"

"Well, what was in the plastic picture frames, you know, things like that."

"Certainly. But the files . . ."

"Tell your assistants that they have been moved for security reasons."

"Security."

"I assume you have some sort of clearance?"

"Oh, yes. I have been consultant on several top-secret projects."

"Good." Judd turned to Abrams. "I want a special task force set up, Abrams. Do it quietly, but quickly."

"Can do, sir. But what will it be doing?"

"I want those files re-created as quickly as possible."

"But they took five years to accumulate," exclaimed Coogan.

"On your way, Abrams. Twenty-four-hour duty. Set 'em up in three shifts."

"Right, sir," responded Abrams, gathering his papers into a neat pile.

When he was gone, Judd turned to face Coogan. She looked at him blankly, but her mind was now beginning to function more clearly.

"You mean to imply, General Judd, that there was something in those files . . ."

"Dr. Coogan, I won't mince words with you. If what I think is happening is in fact taking place, none of us will ever be able to say that we own ourselves again!"

"I . . . I don't understand."

"What was the basic content of your files?"

"Why, accumulation of information about gifted . . ." Coogan was jolted as a glimmer of understanding began to glow. "General Judd, you're not suggesting—"

"Do you know of any process on earth that could account for what happened to your files?"

"Well . . . laser beams, perhaps? Projective microwave devices set to disrupt certain molecular frequencies . . ."

"All these types of weapons exist in theory, but nobody's made one yet. The Russians and we are trying, and who knows who else—but nobody's anywhere near getting them or anything like them on line."

Coogan regarded him silently for a moment, and chose her words with exaggerated care before she spoke. "Do you mean to imply that the destruction of my files was not of mechanical origin?"

Judd ran his fingers through his close-cropped hair and looked at her tiredly. "I sure as hell wish it was. I'd rather someone came up with a death ray than with *this* thing."

"By 'this thing' you mean . . . you're suggesting, ah, an unknown psychic force?" It shook her to speak the thought aloud.

"You got that phone call."

Coogan felt as though her face were turning numb, as it did when her dentist gave her a Novocaine shot.

"Your files are—were—records of gifted psychics," pressed Judd.

"But, really, General Judd! I don't—there was *no* information on any individual or group included in my files that showed any indication of such superior psychic powers."

"Then why were they destroyed?"

"Good God! You're talking about a psychic attack—direct and extremely powerful psychokinesis!" She felt almost frantic with disbelieving fear—and anger at this man who was forcing her to face something unthinkable. Dr. Clyde, still, after a year, subject to nightmares in which the electronically etched green image of a flower figured prominently, would have understood her feelings.

"Yes, Dr. Coogan, I am."

"But in the entire *history* of parapsychology, there's never been a demonstration of any ability anywhere near that! Some control over the fall of dice, some effect on recording instruments, just enough to convince most researchers it exists. But this! No, it's . . ." She was almost crying.

"Look, Doctor," Judd said softly. "The history, the files, maybe they don't show it. But we both know there's been a lot of other reports of very violent psychic action—attacks, if you want to use that word. . . ."

"That's the goddamned *occultists* you're talking about—witch doctors, Aleister Crowley, the witchcraft nuts, Black Mass freaks. *Nobody* in my files has anything like the power you're talking about, or the, uh, ill will. . . ."

"Yes, Doctor," Judd said. "But you can't check your files anymore, can you? And there's a reason why you can't. Look, you know pretty much what they covered—and you know there was a lot of material in there that didn't fit in with the way science and logic looks at things, people with the ability to do things that they shouldn't be able to. It's just that they don't amount to that much in, well, call it practical terms—but that doesn't make that much difference. It's . . . William James, right? With the white crow?"

"If you find one white crow, he said, that disproves the proposition that all crows are black. . . . Is that what . . . ?"

"Yes, that's it, I read it in one of the psi books I had to bone up on when I took this job. That's the idea that's kept all this researching going, isn't it? If any *one* psychic thing is proved to the hilt, then it means that the whole area is at least valid enough to be looked into. Well, all I'm saying is that the white crows you have—*had*—in your files mean that the white crow *I'm* speculating about can't be ruled out. One guy calling off eighty Zehner cards he can't see in a row without a mistake, say, opens it all up—it doesn't mean much in itself, doesn't butter any parsnips as my stepmother used to say, but if the laws of physics and probability don't hold for *that,* then we're open to the possibility that they don't hold for what happened to your files."

Coogan looked at him dully. "There's no reason, I suppose, that that couldn't be so. Or maybe there is, but I can't think of one right now."

"What I'm thinking," Judd said, "is that there's been another step. It always happens. If any creature, even man, has some ability, some capacity, it's eventually surpassed. Dinosaurs turn into birds. People, even without evolving that drastically, change. Forty years ago, everybody *knew* you couldn't run the mile in four minutes; thirty years ago, Roger Bannister did it; now high school kids are doing it in local meets and the sports writers aren't even giving it headlines. Well, I think maybe we've met up with some psychic who's run his four-minute mile. And, of course, I may be crazy. Would you work with me until we can make sure of it, one way or the other?"

Coogan looked at him for a long time before nodding her head.

"Good. I can use the DARPA facilities to get a lot of the material you had in your files—"

"Not all," she said, morosely, thinking of the bribe-obtained records that had held so much of the most fascinating information.

Judd cocked an eye at her. "Ah . . . where you can recall contacts and . . . amounts . . . I believe we could do something along those lines as well." He was well aware of the shortcuts people in Coogan's position were apt to take.

She started, unsure that she should not be indignant at the implication, true though it was, then relaxed into a smile. "Ah . . . I guess that'd be a good idea."

"You'll have to sign a copy of the Official Secrets Act."

"Yes, I suppose so. This is . . . if what you think is true, I can see it would have to be kept quiet."

Judd punched the intercom.

"Yes, sir," Abrams answered promptly.

"Prepare a secrets oath for Dr. Coogan. She'll be working with us for a while."

"I'll have one drawn up pronto, sir."

Judd surveyed the woman, who was busy with her own thoughts. He could practically read them as they crossed her face in waves of disbelief, refusal to accept, and suppressed fear.

"You know," she said, "if he exists as you say, it would be as if a very ancient idea had become incarnate on Earth."

"Oh? What would that be?"

"Sirius."

"Sirius? The star?"

"Well, yes it is a star, a very bright star in the constellation of Canis Major. It's from a Greek word meaning 'sparkling' or 'scorching.' And the Greeks considered it malign, dangerous. Let's see, if I recall correctly, Pope's version of Homer, who referred to it, went something like 'Terrific glory! For his burning breath taints the red air with fevers, plagues, and death.' "

"Seems to fit well enough. I've got a strong feeling we've already been scorched." Judd handed her a copy of the Official Secrets Act brought in by Abrams.

After she signed it, she sighed deeply. "I don't even know where to start."

"Well, let's start with breakfast at the General Officers' Club. It's not far from here. And over a couple of bloody marys, which I think we both need, I'll brief you on Project Tonopah and what's been going on with it."

"I can't go to an officers' club dressed like this," Coogan said firmly, grasping the lapels of her khaki overalls.

"We'll think of some other place, then."

They ended up on the outdoor deck of the Kennedy Center for the Performing Arts, where in a corner they occupied a secluded table and munched on hot dogs liberally covered with mustard, which, they quickly discovered, was something they both liked. After the hot dogs, they began consuming copious amounts of black coffee, ferried to them from the self-service counter by Abrams.

The conversation lengthened. The sun crossed over its midpoint. Washington stifled in the close mugginess, the Potomac nearly concealed in heat mist, the Washington Monument glistening in the distance.

"I've read Rhine and so on," Judd began, "and I know

what you mean about the kinds of things paranormal research has turned up. It doesn't really look like that much,
and all the really good stuff seems to turn out not to be
verifiable or beyond the possibility of fraud. You're left
with things that go well beyond statistical probability, but
aren't outright impossible and earth-shaking. But, look—if
somebody had accidentally haywired together a Geiger
counter without knowing what it was a century ago, and
wandered around enough, he'd have picked up a lot of
strange clicking all over the place. Well, he wouldn't know
what that clicking was, just that it didn't make sense and
should be looked into. But if you look into it enough, those
clicks help lead you straight to the atomic bomb. I think
what you had in your files, what the paranormal and
psychic researchers have been picking up all this time, is
the clicks—the proof that there's something there that
doesn't fit. And I think maybe we've got to atom-bomb
time."

Coogan warily agreed that he might be right.

"You know," Judd said, "even scientists are starting to
take this kind of thing seriously—"

"Yes, General, I *do* know, since I'm a scientist with a
double Ph.D., and *I* take it seriously." She grinned at his
momentary discomfiture.

"Well, physicists—*you* know . . ." He made a helpless
gesture that overset his coffee cup, which was immediately
refilled by the hovering Abrams.

"Costa de Beauregard in France, people like that"— he
raised an inquiring eyebrow, and Coogan nodded to indicate that she recognized the name of one of the most advanced of quantum physicists —"they've worked it out that
at the quantum mechanical level, at least, things like precognition, telepathy, psychokinesis are *probable,* not just
possible. And that's looking at it from the viewpoint of
straight physics, not parapsychology."

Coogan shrugged. "That's pretty much what my files
showed. Your idea is that somebody has made the next step
beyond the probabilities and what we have objective evidence on, right? That we've gone from psychic to megapsychic?"

"Yes. It's a . . . well, never mind the hunch I have
about it, it's the only thing that fits at all. Every minute, I
see it more and more clearly, that it's got to be that. But
now what? If I'm right, he can dig out every secret of Proj-

ect Tonopah, and reach out from God knows where to destroy your files. Is that it? Or has he got a whole bag of tricks he can do? And what happens if we do get on his track?"

"He wouldn't like that," Coogan said, clutching her empty coffee container.

Judd brooded. "We must try to keep the damn fools from trying to capture him or kill him—they're bound to do one or the other."

"Damn fools?"

"The military, who else?"

"But . . . *you're* the military . . . General."

He looked at her sharply, then shrugged. "Yeah . . . I suppose so. . . ."

Lieutenant Abrams, his patience melted by coffee-ferrying in the heat—for a couple who let their coffee get cold anyway—finally complained.

"Sir, I believe there are more comfortable places."

"I imagine there are, Abrams," Judd said.

"It's just that we needed, well, a sense of liberty to approach this problem." Coogan smiled at him as she spoke—Judd needn't have been so short with him.

"Yes," agreed Judd. "The wide spaces—even though it's really hot and grimy, isn't it—a sense of liberty." He gazed out toward the west, into the smog and humidity, and into a space within himself where the landmarks were not much easier to discern.

8:00 P.M.

Abrams looked contentedly around his apartment. It was small, but everything in it had meaning to him, associations he valued. He kept it neat, but there was no denying that the huddle of mementos—models he'd made as a teen-ager, photos of his early days in the Army, statuettes and souvenirs he'd picked up on tours of duty around the world (and nothing, *nothing* of the institutions and foster homes of his early childhood)—made it crowded. But everything there was what he had chosen, and the clutter was homelike, comforting. He might not have a past to belong to, but he had created his own present, and to be there warmed him.

He sighed and looked at his watch, yearning and excitement growing in him. Shirley would be here any minute—what a piece of luck that was, Shirley going for him. . . . Fantastic sex, sure, but that wasn't what was most important. She accepted him, so totally, so freely, that making it with her was like coming home, to a *real* home, after a long trip. She seemed to understand him so well that it was, when he was with her, as though he actually had a past, roots, that he *belonged.*

He rose at her soft knock on the door and moved quickly to let her in. They clung for a moment and then, sensing his need and mood as she always did, she laughingly took the initiative and, skirt about her waist, led him to a sudden, wordless coupling, upright, her back against the apartment door.

"Ah, Joe, what a great way to say hello. . . ." She looked around the apartment. What a tacky dump, the perfect setting for this yo-yo, eager-beaver Abrams with his sentimental soft core, that passion for inventing the home he had never had that made him even more contemptible than most men. "I really love this place, Joe . . . it's . . . well, it's *you.*"

While they ate the meal Abrams had prepared, and he waited contentedly for the renewal of desire and its satisfaction, he talked of the events of the day—not in detail, there was too much top-secret stuff for that!—but he did mention the arrival of Dr. Elizabeth Coogan as part of Judd's task force working on the mystery of the Tonopah security leak.

Shirley Paars was, in her own way, fair; a tidbit of information like that was worth paying for, and the "dessert" she gave Abrams after their dinner left him gasping and ecstatic.

11:30 P.M.
"Mr. Nashirah? Yes, it's Paars. . . . I know it's late, but I thought you'd better know something new about that matter we've been talking about. . . . Yes, that one. There's a new member of the team, a specialist—and the crazy thing is, what she's expert at is psychic stuff. No, I couldn't find out why. . . . Coogan, Dr. Elizabeth Coogan.

11:42 P.M.
"Aloysios? I'm glad to find you in. Didn't you once mention that you had S.I. give a small grant to some woman named Coogan? That's the one, paranormal research, yes. . . . Well, I want to suggest that you might find it to your advantage to make sure she gets an invitation to that recep-

tion you're throwing. . . . I know it's short notice, but you could arrange to have it hand-delivered first thing in the morning. The lady is into some very interesting matters that concern us right now."

2

DISINTEGRATING TOTEM

The end of the last century,
The beginning of the next
Are only fields within fields . . .

> (from the song
> "Alice's Fields")
> —DANIEL MERRIWEATHER

Towards the end of the last century the view arose that all interactions involved material objects. This is no longer held to be true. We now know that there are fields that are wholly nonmaterial.

> —HENRY MARGENAU

AUGUST 5

WASHINGTON

5:00 P.M.

Sultry weather. The heat haze lay over Washington, a
bluish yellow gauze, prickling the skin. The sun, low in its
afternoon descent, filtered through, a shimmering orange
orb.

Secretary of Defense Chester B. Walters dashed from the
cool interior of his limousine through the hot air into the
Soviet Embassy, only to find that inside it was almost as
warm.

"Shit!" he muttered and prepared to go through the for-
malities of the reception with a damp collar. He suspected
that the Russians had studied quite well how to defeat the
capitalist reliance on comfort.

Walters was doubly irked to see that Seth Mead had
spotted him and was heading toward him through the
sparse crowd. He froze his mouth to hide a grimace.

The Secretary of State always made him uncomfortable.
Politically they did not agree at all, but the discomfort was
more deep-seated than that. Mead was an aristocrat of the
type only five generations of wealth could produce. Walters
felt that Mead's type was automatically given high posts,
whereas he, a product of the start-at-the-bottom-and-work-
up school, always had to toe the line, even suck ass, to get
anywhere. He was only slightly mollified by the fact that
Thomas Cordero Heathstone had deliberately chosen him
for the Defense position, while Mead had been in effect left
over from Heathstone's predecessor.

Walters hated himself for suddenly smiling amiably at
Mead. The gaunt Secretary of State, he felt, was weak, too
conciliatory, and past his prime. Further, in the President's
council, Mead could almost be counted on to recommend
against anything that Walters recommended.

But he was Secretary of State and an American blue-blood. "Why, hello, Seth." Walters said cheerfully, pulling at his damp collar.

"Ah, Chester, here we are at yet another reception for yet another Soviet cosmonaut, and as usual, I suppose we will never know what he's been doing up there."

"We suspect," confided Walters, glad to have something to confide, "that this one has been undergoing psychological stress tests while in orbit, you know, the human guinea pig type of thing. Remorseless bastards, but they do know how to get the most out of their people."

Mead raised his eyebrows. "Why does one always have the feeling that the Russians are decades ahead of us in space technology, when we know that is no longer the case?" Then before Walters could respond, he changed the subject; the plump Defense Secretary's air of military hardnosedness—assumed, he was sure, to cover a basic stupidity—always irked him. "I suppose it will be cold turkey sandwiches, salty caviar, and vodka?"

"There will be champagne, too, as usual," Walters assured him.

"Yes, I suppose there must be. Let us hope it is colder than this room."

Around them, the crystal chandeliers blazing away in the afternoon dusk, the accumulated voices of the usual crowd echoed off the walls as if in a wind tunnel, the sparse furnishings displaying worn overstuffs hardly absorbing a sound.

"Chester," Mead asked casually, "what about all this telepathy stuff being done in Russia?"

"What telepathy stuff?"

"Everyone, it seems, knows about it."

"Not much in it, far as I know."

"But then why is it such a topic of conversation?"

Walters was delighted to be able to take a superior attitude. "Officially, we are not prepared to comment too deeply on it. And besides, Navy is the one who knows most about it. I personally don't believe a word of the rumors. Just propaganda."

"Navy? Why the Navy?"

"I don't really know. Mind-to-mind, submarine-to-submarine, something like that. Out of my province, all research and speculation, mostly speculation, if you ask me."

Mead looked at Walters blankly. "Chester, surely there has been research in these matters. Do you mean to say that you don't believe in the possibility of psychic potential?"

Walters was slightly taken back by Mead's direct question. "Well, certainly, Seth, there has been research. After all, when rumors started coming out of Russia about their research, it was only sensible to look into such things ourselves."

"But, do you yourself believe in it?"

"In what, Seth?"

"Psychic things . . . their possibilities."

"The best we have ever observed is far beneath what we could ever utilize."

"Utilize? Utilize for what?"

"Well, we could hardly let the Soviets get ahead of us."

"Really, Chester. I want to know what your personal feelings are. Are there such things as psychic potential?"

"For the life of me, Seth, I sincerely hope not. Why, such a thing could upset all our applecarts. It would be a whole new ball game."

Mead narrowed his eyes. Obviously, Walters was not going to give his personal feelings. So exasperating. He couldn't resist a dig. "Honestly, Chester, it's no wonder we have our differences. One can't get a straight answer out of you."

Walters let that pass. "Defense and State can't always pull together—like having an ox and a mule on the same team. . . . Do you believe in psychics, Seth?"

"Hardly. It is totally outside my experience. My mother consulted psychics though, and believed in some of them. Women in her set did in those days."

Walters glumly realized that Mead, without even knowing it, had scored again; he himself would have referred to his mother, or anybody's, as a "lady," but evidently that wasn't the upper-crust way.

"Ah, there you both are, Mr. Secretaries," greeted Atashenkov. "We will have a small speech shortly about space cooperation. Also, we have your favorite American sandwiches today."

"Turkey?" said Mead.

"Why, yes, how did you guess?" Atashenkov asked.

"I wrote Mr. Tosygen this morning," said Mead, changing the topic, reminding himself to go easy on the massive amounts of vodka and wine that would be provided to wash down the indigestible turkey, "apologizing for the crank letter that seems, I must say, Mr. Ambassador, to have called forth extraordinary attention on the Premier's part."

"Ah, yes, Mr. Secretary. You may be sure that it is just a fanatic seeking to foment discord between our two nations. You may be sure that there is absolutely nothing at the location specified in the letter."

"Letter?" Walters asked, blinking.

"I don't think we should dignify the situation by discussing it further," Mead said.

"Naturally." Atashenkov smiled. "Ah, there is the director of your National Science Foundation just coming in." He rushed away as quickly as he had come.

"Don't tell me they got a copy of that dumb letter about Project Tonopah, too," Walters said.

"Tonopah?" Mead asked, a dissecting look invading his slightly rheumy eyes. "I thought it was Tolkien."

"Tolkien? What is that? You know, we shouldn't be discussing Tonopah here," Walters reminded him importantly.

"What is Tonopah?"

"The topic of the letter," Walters confirmed.

"No, no. David Hornsborough's report says quite clearly that it's called Tolkien," Mead insisted.

Walters ignored Mead's words. "God, if *they've* found out about Tonopah, it's aimed straight at the fan," he muttered, glancing around for possible eavesdroppers.

"Why should *we* be in trouble if *they've* had a crank letter about one of their own projects?"

"*Their* project?"

"Yes, their project. The telepathy thing I was asking about."

"What telepathy thing?"

Mead gave an exasperated sigh, reminded of the frustrating dialogues remembered from years back between George Burns and Gracie Allen. "Really, Chester, are we or are we not talking about the same thing?"

"This is not the place to talk about it at all, Seth," said Walters pompously.

"Is Tonopah a telepathy thing, too?"

"Hardly. Microwaves," whispered Walters.

Mead reflected for an instant. "Ours or theirs?"

"Why, ours, of course. Aren't we talking about *our* crank letter?"

"You mean we got a crank letter, too?"

It was Walters' turn to remain silent for a second.

At this point, the cosmonaut appeared and the official presentations began. Mead was introduced first, followed by Walters. Soon Mead found his appetite aroused and ate three small turkey sandwiches, washing them down with champagne, which, as expected, was quite warm, and vodka, which had been thoroughly chilled—naturally, the Russians would want their national drink to show to advantage. He had no chance to pursue the confusing topics of Tonopah and Tolkien, whatever they were.

Back in his office after the reception, his head aching with vodka vapors, Mead summoned Lila Cox.

"Lila, get hold of someone over at the Department of the Navy and see if you can get any reports on Russian telepathy research."

In two hours she reported back:

"Navy declines to admit that it knows anything at all about telepathy research, but I got referred to the Office of Naval Research who said, yes there was a file, but it was on a need-to-know basis only."

"Did you tell them who I am?"

"Yes, Mr. Secretary, and they suggested that you go through the Secretary of Defense."

"That tub of lard doesn't know any more about it than I do!"

"I asked them to send over a form for you to sign."

"Goddamn it! You mean I have to put up with that kind of red tape? What if . . . the nation was about to be attacked by Soviet telepaths?" Mead enjoyed the rare exercise of his sense of humor.

"Don't get excited, Seth. I have a friend who works at O.N.R. I called her up. She said the file was very uninteresting, and there is nothing in it that hasn't also found its way into parapsychology journals with a pretty good summary in a magazine called *Psychology Today*."

"D'you suppose the Secretary of State can be allowed to get *that* without red tape?"

"I have it here for you, sir. Apparently, it is a recounting of early research beginning in the thirties, and concludes with recent reports of two men who can establish telepathic union many miles apart."

Mead looked dubiously at the magazine she produced. It hardly looked as though it could cast any light on whatever was giving the Soviets the jitters.

"Well, thanks, Lila. Tell Navy to go you know where."

"Yes, Mr. Secretary."

8:00 P.M.

For almost two decades, the old cafeteria that had been turned into a steak house had been the most faddish of the low-profile places to dine in Washington.

Elizabeth Coogan stepped from a taxi, her low-cut silk dress clinging to the moisture on her back, and swiftly moved into the doorway of Nick and Dottie's Black Steer restaurant. She welcomed the frigid air. When she mentioned Harrah Judd's name, she was escorted promptly by the maître d' to Judd's booth.

"God!" she said. "Will this heat ever break?"

Judd regarded her pensively across the small expanse of glowing crimson tablecloth. The contours and clear skin of her neck and shoulders seemed to reach out and grab at him. His eyes narrowed. Coogan didn't miss the impact. She returned his look openly. He licked his hard lips that suddenly seemed to have dried out.

She did not flinch. The brusque vulgarity of his tongue, innocently visible, appealed to her. She smiled. He smiled.

"Hope you like this place," he said. "It's really just a meat-and-potatoes joint, but it's popular and the food is good."

She could read clearly what, beneath his words, Judd was . . . recommending, and she answered at both levels. "I think everything will be great."

Thus sex was proposed and agreed on, neatly, professionally, without adolescent toying.

"Actually, I've been here several times," Coogan said. "Before we get down to business, I think I'll have something deliciously cool. This weather is truly agonizing. A gin and tonic, I think. That's what the English used to drink in the tropics, isn't it?"

"I'll stick to smoky scotch on the rocks," Judd told the hovering waitress.

"Now to business," Coogan said. "General, do you have any notion what sort of development would have to have taken place to account for the activities you have suggested?"

"Only the barest idea . . . Dr. Coogan."

"Well, since I left you last, I've had time to collect my wits and think over the probabilities."

"And?"

"Common sense would have to hold that he is not probable at all."

"Granted."

She eyed him thoughtfully, picking up the drink the waitress had just then placed on the table.

"But," continued Coogan, "I find the whole idea utterly fascinating. It's way outside my experience, but the possibility excited me so much I couldn't sleep last night for thinking about it, and I decided the first thing we must do is create the frame of mind of our, uh, hypothetical man, or whatever it is."

"I see," murmured Judd, reflectively. "It's true that I've gotten all hung up in the mechanics of the thing."

"Let's order some food before this grand drink gets to my head. The English were right. It's a perfect drink for hot, muggy, impossible weather."

"How about a T-bone, rare, baked potato, and a dry red wine?"

"Add a salad to that, and you're on."

Judd asked the waitress for two of the "usual."

Coogan smiled at him. "You come here often, then."

"About three nights a week."

"I didn't think you took time to eat." Coogan allowed herself a feminine moment as she watched Judd's eyes surveying her skin and mouth, wandering over her exposed shoulders. "I think we should keep this very businesslike," she suggested.

"It's just the heat. Makes a man want to get drunk and roll around in the hay."

"Well, something always escapes the best of us. All I want to do is roll around in a cold bath," she lied.

He smiled with genuine humor. "All right, Dr. Coogan, back to business."

"Good! I have to tell you that in the entire history of the world there has never been any demonstration of psychic abilities of the type that would be necessary in the two cases we have at hand. It is possible to conclude only two things, therefore. First, such a person doesn't exist, and we must look for some more probable causes. Second, if such a person exists, he has never demonstrated such abilities either in public or in research centers, and has therefore deliberately hidden them."

"Why?" Judd said, digging into the crisp green salad that was placed in front of him.

"Right—why?" Coogan lavishly treated her salad to crushed pepper. "Assuming somebody discovered in himself these, ah, paranormal capacities, the first thing you'd expect is that he'd want to show them to others. A sort of 'look at me, how great I am' thing."

"That is where we get all these psychic show people?"

"Right. And frauds and tricksters as well. They all want to be considered special, whatever their idea of *that* may be."

"So?"

"But suppose we find these talents in a sort of genius, a man also of extraordinary intelligence, who would understand that demonstration of superior psychic aptitudes would immediately subject him to immense social pressures."

"Like what?"

"Well, he'd certainly run afoul of a lot of religious sects. Then there would be the public and press response, and you can imagine that. And the military—you yourself said . . ."

"Ah, yes. Surveillance and containment."

"Ah, here are the steaks," said Coogan. "My, they do look good, even in all this heat."

They both paused to devote themselves to the food and wine.

After savoring a few bites of the tender steak, Coogan chewed, swallowed, and spoke. "Yes, he's got to be found and contained—because he can spy out this filthy weapon you—"

"*We*, Coogan. You're on the team now."

"Ah, hell. All right, *we*. I feel soiled, being in the same country with it, so I have to say it's my fault too, somehow. Anyhow, he's about to blow the whistle on *our* disgusting Tonopah, and he can't be allowed to do that, can he?"

"I don't like Tonopah very much either. But . . . you can bet that there's something else just as nasty coming up somewhere else, and maybe, if we have Tonopah ready to bring out at the right time, it'll keep whoever it is from using whatever it is. And blowing it now, as—hell, let's give the bastard a name, O.K.—what you suggested, Sirius—if Sirius does that, then the balance of power is all gone, and . . ." Judd gestured helplessly.

"If I knew *why*," Coogan said. "Harrah, he could be, oh, a nut. One of these fellows you see on street corners with big signs saying how the President or the mayor or his wife did him wrong, trying to tell his side—only this one's got a talent most people don't, maybe nobody else has. But the talent doesn't mean he's rational."

"I just hope we're talking about a nut," Judd said, taking a sip of the pungent red wine. "Because the alternative, the thing you haven't said, is that he could be quite rational and sane, and have his own plans for the world."

"Right! If he's . . . the things he's done—my God, Harrah, we're assuming both that he's real and that he sent that letter and destroyed my files, what a crazy leap of logic that is!—but if that all adds up, he *would* want to see to it that the world is changed. Because as it is, there'd be no room for him in it. So he's got to do two things, keep hidden and start messing up the machinery that keeps things going. And, by God, doesn't it look as if he's been doing just that!"

Judd looked at her closely. "The way you see it, he wants things changed around—a new order set up, huh? Tell me—listen, Coogan, I'm not being snotty about this, it's an honest question, not an accusation, and I'll tell you straight out, I don't know if there's a right answer—if that was it, if this . . . Sirius is going to try to change everything . . . would you be for him or against him?"

They were so engrossed, not only in their problem but also in sensing each other, that they were unaware of the tall, well-groomed man who had approached their table. Judd suddenly rose to his feet in greeting.

"Senator Davis, sorry. We were lost in our discussion."

"Judd, there you are," began Davis. "What the hell is this about the moving of, ah . . ." Davis paused, glancing at Coogan.

"Dr. Coogan is a member of my staff," explained Judd. "Dr. Coogan, may I present Senator Heston Davis, chairman of the Congressional Committee on Science and originator of the project we have just been discussing."

"Why, Dr. Coogan," said Davis smoothly, "I've always heard such good things about you. It is a pleasure. May I sit for a moment?" Davis sat beside Coogan without waiting for an invitation.

Judd sat down. The tightness of his lips revealed his impatience, but he forced down his distaste for Davis.

"Now, Judd, what is this and why has Tonopah been moved, and to where has it been moved?" Davis asked in a low voice.

"Haven't you had a briefing on it, sir?"

"Goddamn it, no! I've been in the Caribbean and also up in New York and I have to get back up there. There's the big Sandmuller Corporation reception day after tomorrow, you know."

"Why, Senator Davis," Coogan cut in, "perhaps I'll see you there. I have a grant from Sandmuller International."

"Indeed. Now, Judd, back to Tonopah?"

"Tonopah was moved for security reasons, Senator, but I don't think we should discuss the matter here in the restaurant. I am sure your written briefing will eventually catch up with you between receptions."

"General Judd, I'm not sure how to take that. A good deal of government work *does* get done at receptions, you know. Ah, well, I won't detain you good people. I see the Attorney General over there, with whom I am dining. Good to meet you, Dr. Coogan, I hope I'll see you again in New York."

Senator Davis rose and with a nod at Judd moved away once more into the soft chatter and drifting smoke. Judd and his companion gazed morosely after him, until finally Judd muttered something inaudible.

"I can't help thinking," Coogan said slowly, "that if the senator could, he would be delighted to get hold of our hypothetical psychic. To the senator one superpsychic should be worth more than a hundred Project Tonopahs."

NEW YORK

11:00 P.M.

The air drifting through the corridors of Mount Sinai Medical Center at Fifth Avenue and 100th Street in Manhattan was as humid as the smoggish atmosphere outside, but cooler and perfumed by the strong antiseptic smells common to hospitals. It was late at night. The corridor lights were dimmed. The reception area, caged in glass, glowed with the indirect lights of telephone switchboards and buzzer systems reflecting off shiny file cabinets.

Behind the reception area, in an office furnished with comfortable sofas, the walls lined with a wide array of medical texts, Dr. Ramos Garcia knew he was losing his battle for the life of his famous patient, the rock song star, Daniel Merriweather.

"The body itself shows no signs of deterioration," he protested for the fifth time. The two other men gazed at him silently for a moment. This was one of the few times his superior and chief medical officer, Dr. Joshua Willard, had turned against him, chafing old cultural wounds. Garcia was certain his advice was being ignored because he was a young internist arguing with a senior medical officer and a lawyer. And a Hispanic Catholic arguing with a Protestant and a Jew.

"I should remind you, Dr. Garcia," said Willard for the second time, "that there are comatose patients now confined to wards in neurological hospitals who have been there over six years without any significant physical deterioration."

"But we can't just give up so soon," retorted Garcia, not able to disguise the anguish in his voice, anguish issuing from the conflict between what was being proposed and his own religious and personal convictions about the nature of life and when it might be allowed to end.

"The Merriweather will is quite precise about just this

type of situation," said the third man. His small, dark, piercing eyes accentuated the professional bearing that his heat-rumpled seersucker suit seemed to mock.

"Mr. Golderman," said Garcia, beginning what he understood would be his final plea, "we are successfully maintaining by artificial methods all the visceral functions of Dan Merriweather, and he is thereby still a human being. His breathing, blood circulation, pulsating heart, all are indications that recovery is possible."

"That may be true, Dr. Garcia," said Willard brusquely. "But the, uh, cadaver is without any semblance of the higher functions that define a human being."

"He is not a cadaver yet, sir," responded Garcia, hardly suppressing the rasp of anger in his voice.

"This entire conversation is academic," breathed Astor Golderman. "As executor of the Merriweather estate, I am bound by Mr. Merriweather's instructions pertaining to the maintenance of his body, should it ever become irremediably comatose, and those instructions are quite specific." Danny, he mourned silently. You should see your agent now. No Yiddish shtick here, boy, strictly WASPish lawyer talk with this crowd. However I got to do it, I'll get you your terms, just like I always did. . . .

"We do not *know* yet that he is irremediably comatose," said Garcia angrily.

"The definition of death presents dilemmas," stated Willard, "which certainly are not without their nuances. Normally, we might move the cadaver to the chronic neurological ward and maintain it as long as the family felt it economically feasible. But in this case, in which the dead person seems to have anticipated such a situation, and has personally left specific instructions, I do not see how we can properly do other than he instructed."

"I find it entirely without precedent that the patient can prescribe medical treatment for himself through a legal document," retorted Garcia. "The estimate of the patient's condition has, up to this point, been the sole responsibility of the doctor!"

"My client," said Astor Golderman, "was always concerned about metaphysical and philosophical premises for the death state; somewhat morbid, to be sure. But, legally, he is entitled to them. He specifically talked with me several times about not allowing his corpse to linger around, but that it should be disposed of as expediently as possible. Cremation, of course."

"I wonder, Mr. Golderman," insisted Garcia, "if Mr. Merriweather ever anticipated that his body would be comatose and in such excellent condition—the only damage is surface abrasions and a cracked rib—would he then have wished to dispose of the physical body in such a premature manner? Actually, I don't even accept that he should be considered comatose. There are no medical reasons *for* this body to be comatose. We *must* allow for future life possibilities."

"Dr. Garcia," interjected Willard, "I can't see how it is possible to delay, since Mr. Golderman here indicates that the estate will not pay for continuation of maintenance once it has been adjudged that the cadaver is indeed irremediably comatose."

"But—you're talking about—" began Garcia.

"Now, we are not talking about *that*. We are talking about the financial aspects of a respirating, pulsating, excreting body that cannot be infallibly diagnosed as being alive. Who, Dr. Garcia, is going to assume the financial burden of providing nursing, dietary, and general care?"

"You are talking about arbitrary euthanasia," said Garcia icily.

"Dr. Garcia!" sputtered Willard, rising from behind his desk. "I will remind you that my qualifications are far in advance of yours! And—"

"But this patient does not exhibit any of the signs of being physically dead. . . ."

"Damn it, Garcia, you know as well as I do that the precedent involved here is clear. In 1968 the Harvard Medical School established a definition of death based on the nonfunctioning of the brain. Mr. Merriweather, in his current condition, fulfills all the criteria necessary to establish death. He is unreceptive and unresponsive, that is, in what appears to be a state of irreversible coma. He has no movements or breathing when the mechanical respirator is disconnected. He demonstrates no reflexes. He has had a flat electroencephalogram for almost forty-eight hours now, when only a twenty-four-hour period of no electrical brain activity is sufficient to adjudge him dead. *The man is dead*."

"Dr. Willard," said Garcia tightly, "I honor your standing, but—"

"Then honor my opinion as well," snapped Willard. "This man is dead. We have officially been requested to determine this by the legal representative of the decedent's estate. You, as attending physician, must issue the death certificate."

"I do not think this man is dead!" indicated Garcia stubbornly, his knuckles white as he grasped the edge of the desk.

"I don't like to think," Willard said softly after a pause, "that you're suggesting the procedure I intend to follow is actually—what was the term you used before—arbitrary euthanasia? If so, you might as well be blunt about it and call it murder. Are you prepared to do that, Doctor?"

Their eyes met silently. Garcia accepted the fact that he had no choice. His shoulders shaking, he retreated.

"I apologize, sir. In no way did I mean to imply—"

"Just sign the death certificate, Garcia. After all, this is not a weekly TV medical series—we are in real business here."

Garcia left the office abruptly, his fists clenched.

"Will he suspect anything?" Astor Golderman asked.

"I don't think so. He's an excellent physician—intends to specialize in neurosurgery and doesn't look much beyond his work. This whole thing is a medical matter to him, and he's not going to look for anything else."

Golderman grunted. "You've made sure of a substitute cadaver?"

"Yes, that's all taken care of. There are always—"

Golderman did not want to hear the details of how Merriweather's stand-in was to be arranged for. "Fine. It's irregular, but there's got to be some sort of formal funeral, considering my client's position; and since he'll, ah, be elsewhere. . . ."

"I fully understand," said Willard.

"Just to make you easier in your mind," Golderman said, "you'd better see a copy of the codicil to his will that bears on this."

Willard scanned the document quickly; all in order, and the proper release form was attached as required by the recently enacted Anatomical Gift Act. It was all clear: if Merriweather's body was intact, it was his express wish that it be immediately given to an unspecified institution, there to be used in research related to blood-platelet storage. No problems . . . except for the deception he was helping the dead man's agent and lawyer carry out.

Golderman sensed the doctor's uneasiness and said firmly, "This is of course an extremely confidential matter. I assume that the fee we agreed on is sufficient to assure that?"

"Quite, quite," Dr. Willard said hastily and handed back the papers.

Later, Dr. Ramos Garcia was surprised to notice that the Merriweather corpse was removed, not by a crew from the mortuary indicated on the release certificate, but by a sleek ambulance staffed by uniformed attendants who expertly gathered the body and drove quickly away. He noted with interest the letters on the side of the ambulance: TAU. Wasn't that the Greek T, the ancient symbol of everlasting life? Strange device for the last vehicle the dead Daniel Merriweather would ever ride in.

NEW YORK

6:00 P.M.

The gathering of prominent internationalists, their followers, and hangers-on was well attended. They were assem-
bled in New York atop the opulent stainless-steel high-rise
in the russet-carpeted and crystal-chandeliered tower suite
of the Sandmuller International corporate headquarters.

At such a gathering it was unusual to find anyone standing apart from the crowd. Flanked by two muscular bodyguards who tried to appear inconspicuous, Rastaban al Nashirah was meditatively gazing out of the vast expanse of
glass at the sun setting behind distant thunderheads, purple
and ominous in the New York heat mists. Two elegantly
dressed men, polished in their bearing, but not in their conversation, were surveying him across the room.

"I can't stand that greasy sonofabitch," muttered Senator
Heston Davis, his mouth turned down in the sneer he
shared only with intimate friends. Around these two, a
hundred other guests gratefully sipped the late-afternoon
cocktails provided by their host, the corporate titan—the
press sometimes preferred the term "multinational bucca-
neer"—Aloysios Sandmuller.

"I should think standing greasy sonsofbitches goes with
your job, Heston," drawled Lord Devon, the United Kingdom's ambassador to the United Nations. "It does with
mine."

Davis looked at him uneasily. It was moments like this,
attending a high-powered reception with a collection of the
world's headline-makers, that made him feel secure that
the constant struggle to pretend to strength and sureness
was worth it; and it galled him that a dried-up little gnome
like Critchie Devon, his monkey face unbalanced by the
huge cigar jutting from it, could put him off balance. Devon
had a way of saying things that sounded cordial, but could

be taken two ways; half the time you couldn't be sure it wasn't a dig.

"I don't know why he's here," he muttered. It was satisfying to express the distaste he genuinely felt for Nashirah, and prudent to do so at this time; he had had one or two hints that eyebrows were being raised about the frequency with which he was seen in the Arab's company.

Devon smiled around his cigar. "Economic advisor to the U.N. and the International Bank, old man—a bigwig like the rest of us, that's why."

"He's nothing but a gunrunner, when you come right down to it."

"Ah, Heston, but when a gunrunner gets to be as big as Rastabi, he's an international force. I don't have to tell you that my government have found his activities useful from time to time, and you don't have to tell me yours have, eh? A batch of new weapons declared surplus at the right time for Master Nashirah to pick them up, and a gentlemanly understanding that he'll flog them in the right place, and presto! A nice, new, friendly government's taken over what used to be a trouble spot, and no bothersome inquiries about what the CIA have been up to. The man's positively a public benefactor. Or at least a public convenience. Why are you so down on the chap? Is he snuffling around after some ghastly new weapon of yours?"

"My committee deals with scientific advances, not weapons," Davis said stuffily.

"To be sure, science has nothing to do with weapons. Do you know, Davis, I've always admired your army. *Splendid* bowmen, and great chaps with a sword and mace." Devon beamed at him.

"But they don't—oh. Well, of course there's science in weaponry. But I can assure you that my subcommittee isn't involved in anything like that, not at all, nothing that would interest Nashirah. Damn, I'd better go over and say hello to the bastard, give him a few minutes' small talk, just to be polite. That was right, what you said about having to put up with all sorts in our jobs, eh, Critchie?" He clapped the small man on the back and walked across the room, blissfully unaware that he might as well have given Lord Devon a neatly typed memo advising him a) that Senator Heston Davis was well and truly in Nashirah's pocket, and b) that Senator Heston Davis's Subcommittee on Science was up to its neckties in the development of new weapons.

Priding himself on how deftly he had covered his tracks, Davis approached Nashirah, but was diverted by recognizing a new arrival in the room.

"Dr. Coogan! Nice to see you again."

"Senator."

Coogan's filmy dress, a dark blue that deepened the lavender of her eyes, clung to her in a way nicely poised between the ladylike and the whorish, as a good cocktail gown should.

"You mentioned you might be here, Doctor, but I forgot to ask why. What brings you out of the laboratory to mingle with a tiresome crowd of politicians?" He waited for her to say that she did not find all politicians tiresome, for instance Davis himself, then went on when she did not take the opportunity. "That's Critchie Devon over there—Lord Devon, the British ambassador to the U.N., a charming man—and that fellow in the long robes is from Mali, and the two that look like Laurel and Hardy are with the International Bank . . . talking to Mr. Nashirah, the U.N. financial consultant, remarkable fellow when it comes to understanding money, and . . . I don't see Kurt, the Secretary General, that is—I thought he'd be here by now. But really, as you see, nothing but politicians and bankers. . . ." Davis gave a rueful shrug, meant to suggest that hobnobbing with some of the most famous people in the world was a tedious part of his daily round.

"Pretty impressive," Coogan said, sipping at a glass of champagne a passing waiter had bestowed on her. "I'm here as a kind of poor relation, I guess—I work under a partial grant from Sandmuller International."

"Really? Why would that be? I would think that you could go to the government for money, if you're involved in any scientific project that—"

"I tried that, Senator—approached your subcommittee, in fact—and got shot down. Parapsychology's too far out for official funding."

"Parapsychology?"

"Telepathy, the psychic, things like that."

Davis twitched uneasily. Knowing what he did of the Russians' Tolkien device, the last thing he wanted was to be drawn into a discussion of anything that remotely approached it. It wasn't beyond the realm of possibility that this woman had been set on him to see what he knew. "Well," he said heartily, "I can understand that, I'm afraid.

The, ah, psychic isn't anything for public moneys to be spent on——I'd have a lot of static from my constituents if I were involved in voting for anything like that."

Coogan shrugged. "Then it's lucky Sandmuller doesn't have any constituents."

"Sandmuller?" Davis said nervously. Was this a hint that she knew of the industrialist's interest in Tolkien?

"The grant. Not much money, but enough to get on with. I don't know why they're paying my way, but I'm glad they are."

"Ah." Davis was relieved. Perhaps she was just what she seemed to be. "I daresay it's some executive's idea of an interesting tax loss—I can't see Aloysios Sandmuller spending good money on . . . well, there *is* a lot of fraud going on in that field, isn't there?"

Elizabeth's lips thinned. "Of course; there is in any field, even politics. But the information I have—"

"Ah! Good afternoon, Aloysios!"

"Heston." Coogan looked up with interest at the massive man who had silently drifted next to the senator. Sandmuller's newspaper pictures had never conveyed the vitality of his large frame and mobile, alert face.

"Aloysios, I haven't seen Kurt this afternoon. I was saying to Critchie Devon—"

"Heston," the deep, soft voice said reproachfully, "aren't you going to—"

"Oh. Oh, of course. Ah, Dr. Coogan, this is Aloysios Sandmuller, of whom you . . . Aloysios, Dr. Elizabeth Coogan."

"Dr. Coogan . . . I'm most pleased to meet you, Doctor. How is your work coming along?"

"You know about my project?"

"As I understand it, I'm helping pay for it—the grant was my idea, after I'd read your paper on the probable distribution of psychic talent in the general population. Very convincing piece of work, very well reasoned."

"Aloysios! You, the hard-headed man of business, take the supernatural seriously?" It seemed to him that Sandmuller was being grossly careless in admitting to an interest in the psychic to anyone, let alone an expert. If he himself were heavily involved in something like Tolkien, he would make it a point to deny all knowledge of anything bearing on hypnotism or telepathy, and would try to give the impression that he wasn't quite sure who the Russians were;

that was elementary prudence—stay as far away from the truth as possible.

Sandmuller was amused. "The supernatural and the paranormal aren't the same thing, Heston. There are a lot of hard-headed people working on telepathy, even hypnotism"— Davis winced —"here and in the Soviet Union." Davis felt as though he were breaking out into a sweat; this was beyond carelessness.

"I wish we knew more of the Soviet work," Coogan said. "There have been a lot of published reports, but you can tell there's a lot they're not passing on, and it'd be fascinating to find some of that out."

"It would, it would," Sandmuller rumbled genially. "I have the greatest respect for the efforts of Russian researchers in that line, Doctor." Elizabeth smiled at him, pleased to have found the financial giant willing to accept the validity of her field, not like that straw man of a senator—supernatural, indeed! It was really a heady thought that a man as powerful as Sandmuller was concerned with the psychic: with the vast resources of Sandmuller International, so much could be done. . . .

Davis wondered if somehow Sandmuller and the Coogan woman were allied in a conspiracy to mock him by letting drop sly references to the Tolkien Project, knowing it would unnerve him. You could never tell what people might be up to. . . . He looked almost wistfully toward the corner of the room where Nashirah was. He hated the man, but at least you knew where you were with him. He brightened on seeing two men approaching the group and greeted the first arrival, "Hello again, Critchie."

The second man, stocky, with high cheekbones, came up behind Lord Devon and said, "I thought I might find you here, Critchie. Have you been in touch with your mission in the last half hour?"

Elizabeth was startled to recognize the newcomer as Kurt Ehrenwald, Secretary General of the United Nations.

"No, I've not," Devon said. "Why?"

"You might telephone, then." His voice, Elizabeth noticed, held far more of his Austrian accent than in the public speeches and statements she had heard. "Something very strange has been happening." He turned to Aloysios Sandmuller first, but then noticed Senator Heston Davis. "Davis! What has happened? Surely your government realizes, if all this is *true,* that this kind of thing goes completely against the protocols established by your nation and Russia about the illegal development of new weapons!"

"I beg your pardon, sir?" gasped Davis.

"What is it, Kurt?" asked Aloysios Sandmuller.

"Just as I was leaving to come here—ah, what a fine reception," he said, glancing quickly around, "just as I was leaving my office, a very confusing message was coming over the telex."

"Confusing how?" asked Lord Devon.

"I must say it was quite a bit more technical than the usual press release—I didn't grasp most of it."

"Yes, Kurt?" pressed Sandmuller.

"My staff is contacting Moscow and Washington to confirm. Really, with the balance of power as precarious as it is, this is tantamount to firing an international bullet!"

"What *is* it, Kurt?" demanded Aloysios Sandmuller.

"Some sort of microwave and hypnotic devices, apparently developed into . . . well, what I can only call science-fiction weapons. Something to do with code names, Tolkien, I believe, and an American project, something called Tonopah . . . which I am told is an American Indian name."

A cloying silent island formed in the swirling hubbub of the elegant summer gathering. Kurt Ehrenwald fastened his eyes pointedly on Senator Heston Davis, as if expecting an explanation. Lord Devon's expression remained as before. Coogan's first reaction was, she thought, comic and unreal. The hypothetical Sirius had dared! A sensation of simple exhilaration rushed through her briefly and brought a gasp from her, the sound suddenly present in the center of the silent island causing the attention of the small group to center on her, abruptly but briefly.

Then the group broke up hastily. Coogan was left alone as Davis hurried off, proclaiming his need to return to Washington, Devon sought a telephone, and Sandmuller drifted toward the financial advisor Davis had mentioned— what was his name?—that was it, Nashirah. . . .

Under the excitement and fear that came with the knowledge that Sirius had begun to move was a tinge of regret at not having had a chance to talk further to Sandmuller. It might be a good idea to try to do that, someday.

He had been born Joseph Perdu in California, the only son of unmarried itinerant orchard workers of French descent, but the bad beginning had only formed and hardened his indomitable will to succeed. One of his first acts as an aggressive young man had been to reclaim what was said to be his grandfather's name, Aloysios, and reject Perdu, after he had found out that in French it meant "lost." He chose Sandmuller because he felt it had flexible connotations. After this, now considering himself completely his own man, he set out to rise to the top.

And it had not been hard. Often when he reflected on his rise, he attributed it to his observation early in life that those who were not successful hated success in others. This did not bother him particularly, but, on the contrary, made it quite a simple matter to understand and if necessary crush anyone who tried to stand in his way.

He had joined the staff of the Drake Broadcasting System nearly fifty years ago, when it was reeling beneath the impact of the growing communications giants. After Drake died, Aloysios had seized the corporate stocks and declared himself chief executive. No one had protested then, since everyone thought that the corporation would decline and perish soon.

Sandmuller had divested the foundering corporation of dead wood, begun his sharklike attacks on larger companies, ripping away their prospering subsidiaries, which he then added to the Sandmuller Corporate System. He pounced on Europe, then Africa and Latin America, where the pickings were always good, and finally on China, which was yearning to be an international trading power. Now he was Sandmuller International Corporation, with subsidiaries, masterful conglomerates, characterized by dynamic growth potential, and near the top in the multinational arena.

He was considered a potentate, a thief, a benefactor, and above all something the average citizen of the world could never understand, a constant usurper, always—in public— smiling benignly. Right now, he was not.

"Goddamn it, Rastabi, what the hell is going on! You assured me we could get control of Tonopah and fence it through my foreign subsidiaries long before the Americans could get it operational!" Sandmuller was furious and let it show.

Rastaban al Nashirah was no coward and screamed right back. "And what about your acquisition of the Tolkien series? How the hell did anyone get the specifications when you've spent a million dollars trying to get the complete set and haven't succeeded!"

"I'll get them, I'll get them," Sandmuller said through clenched teeth.

"Don't be stupid, Aloysios. Here they are, for everyone to see!" Nashirah waved the length of telex they had just torn off Sandmuller's private terminal.

Few men could call Sandmuller stupid and not die an ignominious "accidental" death someplace. But Nashirah was one who could, simply because Aloysios Sandmuller needed someone to talk to at times, someone who did not stand in awe of him. Rastaban al Nashirah had managed to outwit him in an armaments deal with the North Vietnamese back in 1969. Their original competitiveness had quickly shifted into mutual confidence since they both felt that they were not really crooks but survivors on a dying planet. It was a bond, a basic empathy, almost an ecstatic joy, as each had discovered in the other a sameness that meant he was not alone.

Sandmuller pressed his lips together, moved to a brocaded wall, pressed a button. The wall slid apart to reveal a mirrored bar and rows of liquor bottles and sparkling glasses.

"We're going to have to move fast to salvage anything out of this. Every revolutionary in the world—to say nothing of established governments—is going to try to build the devices."

"They're going to have trouble with the telepathic things. It will take years for anyone to understand them."

"Do you suppose Tosygen actually has telepaths?" Sandmuller asked, now restored by a jolt of Tennessee bourbon.

"I don't think he uses living telepaths. I think what most of this gibberish—I must say that Interpress did not do a very good translating job on this—means is that the microwaves are fed through cerebrosystems. We know that these are slices taken from brains of people who had exhibited high telepathic aptitudes when they were alive."

"Ah, yes. We funded brain-slicing experimental work in Leningrad beginning, let's see . . . well, at least ten years ago."

"That must explain what happened to those people in Russia who disappeared after they demonstrated their telepathic abilities."

"Yes, I suppose so. I must say, this is *really* brain picking, isn't it?" Aloysios Sandmuller chuckled.

"Cut the crap, Aloysios," Nashirah said. "Can you get the original Russian of this Interpress mess? My men will never be able to work from this."

"I suppose so. It must have come out in Moscow in Russian. I'll get it direct from there."

"Good. I'll get my men to work immediately on the Tonopah situation. If I can produce a working device before anyone else, perhaps we can still get bids. The Chinese are sure to want it. And the Africans."

"What about the Europeans, especially the English?"

"Ask Critchie; he'll be happier talking to you. He's never really forgiven us Arabs for wresting the petroleum revenues away from his silly empire."

Her taxi took her quickly to LaGuardia, where she boarded the next shuttle flight to Washington. To her relief, the hot atmosphere engulfing New York had become overcast with warm moist clouds. A few drops were already falling. In the distance thunder rolled, echoing along the darkening western horizon.

She was not entirely surprised to find Senator Heston Davis aboard the plane.

"Why, Dr. Coogan," he said, "if I had known you were going back, I'd have taken you in my taxi. Please join me here; there's an empty seat."

Coogan, seeing no polite alternative, nodded and sat down, and reached for her safety belt.

"Looks like a break in the weather," Davis said. "Hope we get up above the storm before it grounds us here. Dr. Coogan, have you by any chance seen this so-called—how did the Secretary General put it—the cryptic message?"

"No, Senator. But I can imagine what's in it."

"You can? How?"

"Then you haven't seen the letter that originally demanded the abolishment of Project Tonopah?" asked Coogan with a curious look at Davis. The senator appeared embarrassed. "Oh . . . you and your briefing haven't caught up with each other?"

"There are so many pressing matters . . ." he said. "I assume you are referring to some serious security leak?"

"You could say it's pretty serious, Senator," Coogan said.

"Why has General Judd dragged *you* into it?"

"There are some unexplained events that possibly might have repercussions in my field of study."

"Surely you don't mean . . . what? . . . *psychic,* ah, repercussions?" asked Davis, looking unnerved.

"The Tonopah devices themselves have psychic repercussions, don't they, Senator?"

Davis was taken aback. Surprise distinctly showed on his face. "The Tonopah devices represent a swift advance in those technologies that will weigh the balance of power in favor of the United States. The government has every right to develop those devices, and at any rate they're still in a research phase."

Coogan's lips tightened. Heston Davis was pretty good at regurgitating position papers, but his answer was nothing like responsive. She looked at him with dislike.

"Senator, I have been thoroughly briefed on Tonopah. The project is not designed to pursue research but to develop microwave devices into advanced weapons."

"Well, yes," agreed Davis, his bluff called. "But strategic necessities really aren't the business of scientists, many of whom tend to be impractical idealists."

"If you're including me in your generality, Senator, forget it. I'm not so impractical or idealistic that I can't guess the public reaction to the type of weapons you're developing at Tonopah, and you're going to be getting that reaction just about any minute if what the Secretary General announced is true."

Senator Davis kneaded his chin pensively.

"I suppose you're right," he said grudgingly. "And whoever's responsible for this breach in security is going to have a lot of explaining to do. I'll have their goddamned heads."

Dr. Elizabeth Coogan looked at him out of the corner of her eye and smiled.

Early-morning Confusions

WASHINGTON

1:00 A.M.

Dressed in a sedate evening gown, her usually flawlessly coiffured hair betraying wandering wisps, Guilda Stern stood up. General Harrah Judd, brushing raindrops from his forehead, passed quickly through her outer office to the sanctum occupied by the Secretary of Defense.

"Where did this sudden rain come from, Mrs. Stern?" he asked lightly.

"Maybe it will cool things off, General," she replied, not very hopefully.

"Doubt it. This is going to get bigger."

"He's waiting for you, sir."

"Yes, I know," said Judd. "Sorry you've been called in from your evening."

"Haven't had time to think about it," she replied, swiftly moving ahead of him to open the door of the inner office. "The phones have been quite busy. My intuition tells me that this is really quite something. Am I right?"

Judd nodded and passed through into the spacious, formal, green and oak interior office occupied by Chester B. Walters. The Secretary of Defense was pacing the emerald-colored carpet, his face pulled tight into an irritated frown.

"What the hell happened, Judd?" demanded Walters before Judd could give him the usual salute. "I have never in my entire career seen such an outrageous breach of security!"

"Neither have I."

Walters took a deep, angry breath, then looked at Judd calculatingly. However this damn thing had happened, head-rolling time was coming, and the main thing was to get out of the way of the ax.

"I understand, Judd, that you are only a liaison man, not the developmental head of this project, and that it actually got its impetus and funding through that goddamned Joint

Subcommittee on Science, through that pompous ass Davis. Why wasn't it kept civilian? How did Defense get landed with it?"

"Actually, the basic idea came from—"

"Basic idea?" interrupted Walters.

"Yes, sir. The idea of paralyzing the human nervous system with microwave frequencies."

"Ah, yes, the basic idea!" Walters was relieved that someone had finally let him know what all this was about—not that it made much sense even yet.

"Well, the basic concept comes from some badly organized Nazi research done in Germany in the early thirties. It was picked up by Senator Davis's brother-in-law while he was doing graduate work at M.I.T. It seemed an impracticable concept at first, but it was well within the general research mandate of the Department of Defense Advanced Research Projects Agency. Senator Davis got the tacit approval of the Congressional Subcommittee on Science, although I don't think Tonopah has ever been officially reviewed in depth by that subcommittee. Davis only pushed through the funding necessary to hire appropriate civilian scientists. We arranged for basic equipment and premises."

"So what you're trying to tell me is that we can't hand this load of crap back to the Congress. Let them have the responsibility. . . ?"

"Probably not, sir," Judd said. "Defense has assumed most of the workload on this project."

"In one half hour we, you and I and several others, have to get our asses over to the White House to explain the situation to the President."

"Yes, sir, I expected that."

"What do you recommend we tell him? Say we're sorry about the leak and it won't happen again? Do you see the President being satisfied with that?"

Judd looked at his superior for a moment in silence. Various approaches jostled in his head, instantly reviewed and dismissed. He would rather have had the time to write a report. In a report he could itemize and support his thoughts, and couch them in words that would not leave him naked and unprotected. Yet now was the time to hit the button, since the crisis would only grow from this point on, if he was right.

"To the best of my knowledge, sir, security on the move of the project to Omaha was fully maintained."

"Impossible!" snorted Walters. "If that were true, then we wouldn't have this goddamned scandal on our hands!"

"I don't believe this is an ordinary security leak—"

"Why did you choose SAC, of all places?" said Walters, peevishly.

"We had to move fast, sir. And SAC had some empty rooms in their aeronautical research laboratory, which was on the list for alternate emergency locations for Tonopah. And, sir, the security at SAC is impeccable."

"The entire security of SAC is compromised! If there can be a leak about this goddamned Tonopah, are we supposed to figure everything *else* at the Strategic Air Command is secure?"

For the second time, Judd regarded his superior with silent solemnity.

"No, sir." He hesitated, then took the plunge he dreaded. "The nature of this, ah, security leak and other information that has come to my attention indicate that there is a probability that our entire security framework is capable of being pierced."

"Uh, what—"

"I think this situation goes beyond what we are familiar with."

Walters surveyed Judd calmly, with renewed interest. If the general had come up with something totally new, that could let Defense off the hook.

"You mean you've got an explanation?" he asked.

"Probably not an explanation, sir, but at least a line of approach."

Guilda Stern appeared at the door. "Your car is waiting," she said. "I've already informed the President's office you are on your way."

"Thank you, Guilda. Judd, you can brief me on your thoughts in the car. I take it they are just thoughts?"

"No, sir. Not just thoughts. There is also hard evidence."

"Good! Good!" exclaimed Walters, a slight smile of satisfaction coming to his lips for the first time.

MOSCOW

8:00 A.M.

The setting sun had left the United States in the darkness of wind, storm, and night; it rose on the Soviet Union into clear skies whose blue was decorated with the gentle wisps of high-flying cirrostratus clouds. The clear orb of solar light pushed day quickly back from Kamchatka across the vast northern steppes, the gentle Soviet dawn touching first Yakutsk, then Igarka, and finally the outskirts of Moscow.

In the early-morning light, the limousine flying the American flag on its fender drew to a halt. David P. Hornsborough III stepped out and glanced briefly at the sky growing blue, but only briefly. He quickly disappeared into the depths of the huge brick edifice housing the offices of the Premier of the U.S.S.R.

This time the office into which he was shown was almost bare, furnished with leather chairs and a central table, surrounded by gray walls whose bleakness was enhanced rather than diminished by two crimson flags flanking a green and blue map of the world. The room was hazy with cigarette smoke, and on the table were crystal vodka decanters. A series of small glasses littered the tabletop, reflecting small pinpoints of lights among the disarray of papers and folders.

Hornsborough sniffed. This had obviously been an all-night working session and would continue as a working session. The Soviets had a peculiar way of staging their serious confrontations.

Nearly thirty people were present, somber, stern faces riding over dark bulky suits or dull green or brown uniforms. Hornsborough quickly recognized the Minister of State Security as well as the head of the Committee of State Security, such difficult distinctions, he thought. And also the Minister for the Protection of Public Order and several prominent members of the Party Central Committee and of the Party apparatus. All the troops, Hornsborough concluded, drawn up to do battle. But this time he knew what he would be doing.

Praskovie Tosygen, dressed in a dark suit, stepped forward to greet the American ambassador. Tosygen was an endless mystery to the American Government. Hornsborough had concluded not long after arriving in Moscow that no one in the American political system had ever understood the man, least of all himself. The CIA had managed to put together a briefing about Tosygen, filled with unrelated and useless anecdotes.

Tosygen was the son of a devotee of Lenin who had survived the purges brought about under Stalin and then mag-

ically had become a devotee of Stalin. After Stalin's death
the elder Tosygen had also died, and the son had risen to
power through the Khrushchev and Brezhnev regimes, until he now seemed to personify the Soviet Union itself. He
was modest, self-effacing—courteous—and completely im-
penetrable as a personality. Nobody at State had ever come
up with a game plan containing a convincing prediction of
his actions. Hornsborough steeled himself. This time, at
least, he had his underwear on and was comfortable.

"Ah, David," Tosygen said cordially, "here we are again.
Sorry to call you out of your bed at such an early hour."

"Think nothing of it, Mr. Premier," responded Hornsborough with equal warmth. "Might I suggest that you are
concerned with the, shall we say, unfortunate crank tele-
grams that have somehow gotten into the international
telex systems?"

"Ah, yes, David. I see you have been up early, also. I
believe it was only about nine days ago that we had a conversation regarding another type of, ah, crank, as you say.
Please be seated. We are still informal at this hour."

Hornsborough chose not to sit in the chair at the end of
the table opposite Tosygen that the Premier had indicated,
but sat to one side. The others present resumed their seats.
Some rustled the sheets of paper in front of them, then
came a moment of total silence during which Hornsborough took from his breast pocket a copy of the telex. "I
have to suggest," he began artificially, "that some international subversive organization has chosen this regrettable
method to instigate trouble between our two nations."

"Yes, it would seem such is the case," Tosygen said
dryly.

"Although I have not yet had time to receive instructions
in this matter from my government, I believe my government would wish me to assure your government that there
has been no development in the United States of the incredible, er, science-fiction devices hinted at in this unfortunate communication."

Tosygen hunched his shoulders and folded his hands on
the leather tabletop in front of him. The aide to his left
placed a copy of the telex where the Premier could easily
pick it up.

"Yes, Your Excellency," he began, shifting suddenly
from the informal tone to the formal address. "In the brief
time we have had to assess the contents of this unfortunate

piece of paper, we have been able to study the specifications given for this, ah, Project Tonopah sufficiently to conclude that not only is such equipment feasible but also that almost anyone who acquires a copy might possibly begin to construct such, as you say, science-fiction devices."

David P. Hornsborough paled slightly, his jaw movements betraying his appreciation of the delicacy of the moment.

"I have not had the benefit of scientific advice yet, as I see you have," responded Hornsborough, suddenly coming to understand the nature of the other officials present. "However, if it should be true that such equipment would prove feasible, I believe that my government would wish me to reassure you unequivocally that such equipment does not represent a United States scientific enterprise and also—"

"Yes, Your Excellency, however—" interrupted Tosygen.

"And," continued Hornsborough, raising his voice slightly, "I believe that my government should wish me to inquire whether the conversation between yourself and me about ten days ago about this other, er, Project Tolkien was, ah, misleading?"

The silence that descended was broken only by a pregnant reshuffling of papers and the murmur of the military advisor, sitting to the Premier's right, as he whispered something to him in Russian.

"Let us shift our conversation to a new platform, Mr. Ambassador," suggested Tosygen, nodding as if in agreement with what had just been whispered to him.

"Why, Mr. Premier," said Hornsborough smoothly, "indeed, I think we should; that is, if my understanding of this moment is anywhere near correct."

"However regrettable this communication may be," said Tosygen, for the first time picking up the telex, "it is obvious that other nations will undertake the development of the, er, devices—"

"I think, Mr. Premier," interjected Hornsborough, "that the platform of conversation that might involve us now is the topic of . . . weapons."

". . . and that the international balances of power possibly will shift accordingly."

"Mr. Premier, the development of new weaponry such as described is tantamount to almost a negation of the Strategic Arms Limitations Talks, against the very spirit of those talks begun several years ago between our two nations in the hopes of curbing the development of arms and the Soviet-American arms race!"

"Mr. Ambassador," said Tosygen, ignoring Hornsborough's statement, "the spirit of SALT, the Strategic Arms Limitation Talks, has always indicated the incumbency on our two nations to guard the balance of power. This includes any possible disagreement between our two nations leading to a holocaust. I think *that* should be the topic of our conversation at this moment. The spirit of SALT has always engaged our government. But it is incumbent on our government also to engage in science, not to abandon it, since other nations possibly would gain an advantage in discoveries of their own."

"Mr. Premier," retorted Hornsborough, instantly fumbling for his own copy of the telex, "the science you are referring to, if it is Project Tolkien, this—what is it, yes—so-called telepathic hypnosis using, ah, certain broadcasting techniques, is monstrous—"

"As are," said Tosygen, interrupting him, "weapons for the microwave control of the human nervous system!"

"I protest," began Hornsborough. He sat back in his chair, breathing somewhat erratically in the sudden silence. The light of the morning sun suddenly illuminated the room through three large windows facing east. The full implications of the conversation hit him. He calmed his breathing and turned his attention back to the Russians, who were awaiting his reaction.

"This is difficult work for us so early in the morning, Mr. Premier," he said. "I will inform my government of our conversation. No doubt the Soviet Union has already taken steps to assume a strategic—"

"I would fail my nation were I not prepared to take the initiative in this matter," responded Tosygen, rising from his chair. "It is my hope that your President will communicate with me soon concerning a constructive manner in which to deal with the international community. Such a communication would be well within the spirit of the Strategic Arms Limitation Talks."

"Thank you, Mr. Premier. I will communicate by telephone with President Heathstone immediately and apprise him of your position."

"Thank you, David," said Tosygen, relaxing into an informal manner once more and forcing a smile. Hornsborough grimaced, wondering already how he could convincingly advise Thomas Cordero Heathstone that the Soviet Union was gathering itself for war.

WASHINGTON

3:00 A.M.

While the mild winds rushed softly across the Russian tundras and ushered in brilliant daylight, the early hours after midnight in Washington were filled with diminishing flashes of lightning as the unprecedented summer storm began to break up and drift out into the Atlantic.

The colorfully uniformed men in the President's briefing room in the executive West Wing of the White House were gathered into small groups out of which issued snatches of irritated conversation. Everyone was there, Judd estimated, counting heads out of the corner of his eye. Chiefs of every military branch, done up in braid and ribbons, looking like a Fourth of July display. And civilians, too, trying to accommodate their wrinkled seersuckers to the neatness of the military summer dress. He wondered, briefly, why American civilians and civil servants had almost to a man adopted seersucker, which to him had always looked like modified bed ticking.

The large, elegant room, tall-windowed and draped with gold velvet, was filled with a cool, damp atmosphere laced with an electric tension, added to by the subdued murmuring in which the names of Tonopah and Tolkien could frequently be heard.

Walters and Judd stood slightly apart from the others.

"If you even so much as mention this psychic bullshit you have been talking about," said Walters, softly but with as much force as possible, "I'll have your ass busted back to private!"

Judd looked at his superior, his expression bland and unmoved.

"I can see that it would be an embarrassment at this stage," he said equally softly. "But I'm going to follow up on this, nonetheless, until it proves to be false. It would explain everything if it were—"

"Goddamn it, Judd! This kind of idea would make a

laughing stock out of the entire department. Who would believe it? Not me, that's shit-sure!"

"Frankly, sir, I don't think it is a matter of belief or not, or even of being a laughing stock. The piles of dust from Dr. Coogan's office are available for your inspection; so are the reports the science staff is putting together. Those are facts, not belief, and if my theory about them is anywhere near right, we're in for more and worse than what happened to those files and to our security about Tonopah. Anyhow, I can conduct this type of investigation tactfully under the mandate of the Joint Chiefs of Staff's white paper on the subject."

"Uh, what is that exactly?"

"That briefing of last year on possible involvement of psi abilities in military matters—you know, sir, the surveillance and containment of psychic research."

"Ah, yes." Walters grasped at this straw of respectability. He chewed for a moment on his lower lip. "We'll have to go into this another time. Just don't for Christ's sake bring it up here and now. That's an order!"

Their attention was diverted to a shuffling near the door through which the Chief Executive of the United States was expected to appear.

Two bodyguards came first, followed by an usher who announced the President, followed almost simultaneously by a dark, strong-featured man whose impassive expression and controlled grace of movement reflected his Cherokee ancestry.

Thomas Cordero Heathstone strode smartly to his place at the head of the huge oval conference table. In spite of the late hour, he looked fresh, competent.

After a muted shuffling of chairs and papers, everyone quickly organized into neat rows around the table in order of political and military rank. The President's secretary, Hedy Allison, provided the one residual motion in the tableau as she laid before the President a copy of the lengthy telex everyone knew was to be the topic of the gathering, then left the room. The doors were closed.

Heathstone's penetrating eyes glowed with fiery intensity as he surveyed those waiting for him to speak.

"I want someone, anyone," he began, "to inform me if Project Tonopah is a real project or a figment of some crank's imagination."

The gloom of the moment following the President's request felt interminable; it was broken finally by the scraping of a chair as Senator Heston Davis rose to his feet.

"I have to inform you, Mr. President, that Project Tonopah is a real project, sponsored in part by the Congressional Subcommittee on Science, but in development under the auspices of the Defense Advanced Research Projects Agency. I must point out that its existence has not been kept from you, having been noted in reports to the National Security Council—"

"Senator Davis, sit down!" said Heathstone sharply. "My science advisors have brought to my attention at least thirty-five microwave research projects in progress through the nation. Not one of these briefings mentioned the possibility that any of these research projects dealt with such a terrifying, disgusting weapon—*that* has been kept from me!"

"Mr. President," shrilled Davis without sitting down, "Project Tonopah's effects on the human body have not been sufficiently demonstrated—"

"*Sufficiently* demonstrated on *humans*? What humans?" shouted Heathstone.

"Well, uh, none, Mr. President. Only on rats and rabbits."

Heathstone's eyes froze Senator Heston Davis. He sat down quietly.

"Speak up, Davis," said Heathstone through his teeth, "out with it, all of it!"

"Well, Mr. President, there *have* been a few trial runs on violent patients at some psychiatric centers."

A general ripple of gasping ran around the table. Davis cringed nervously.

"The frequencies did, Mr. President, prove effective in subduing violent seizures of—"

"My God, Senator," interrupted Walters, genuinely stunned. "This part of your project *has* been kept from me also."

"An oversight, an oversight, Mr. Secretary—"

"Jesus Christ, an oversight!" expostulated Walters.

Heathstone cut them off with an abrupt gesture and turned to Walters. "Chester, am I to understand from what you told me earlier that you are unable to inform me whether or not Project Tonopah is an operation-ready project?"

"I'm sorry, Mr. President. I cannot positively inform you of that fact."

"Can anyone so inform me?"

"General Judd, here, next to me," said Walters, obviously glad to shift attention from himself, "is liaison officer for Department of Defense research projects. Perhaps he can brief—"

"General?" Heathstone fastened his piercing eyes on Judd.

Judd rose slowly to his feet, taking the few seconds to gather his wits.

"I myself, Mr. President, find that I am only partly briefed on Project Tonopah, being totally unaware that experiments have been carried out on humans. As to its overall operational readiness, even if its effectiveness has indeed been demonstrated on humans, it still can't be considered operational. For one thing, there's the question of capability. I wonder if that's been demonstrated yet?" Judd looked intently at Senator Davis.

"Long-distance capability has not been demonstrated," Davis said glumly.

Judd shrugged. "Judging by the propaganda of other microwave effects, that's no real problem, with the power that's packed into the devices already."

"Can you tell me, right now, General Judd," asked Heathstone, his voice softening somewhat, "what would be needed to bring Tonopah up to operational status?"

There was another general startled response from those gathered.

"That would depend, Mr. President."

"Depend on what?"

"On whether you are speaking of, um, domestic or international capabilities—"

"International!" snapped Heathstone. "What reason would I have for subjecting Americans to such treatment?"

"Then, Mr. President, Tonopah's broadcasting equipment would have to be lifted by satellites into orbit. There is no land point on earth where the equipment would have intercontinental range."

The President sat back in his chair. Judd took it that he might resume his seat also.

"Mr. President . . ." Walters began in an effort to assume a role in the deliberations.

"Yes, Chester," said Heathstone, interrupting the Secretary of Defense, "you will have in hand within the hour my executive order to have Project Tonopah in orbit in twelve hours at the latest. Do you think you and your men can handle it?"

"But, Mr. President!" cried Senator Davis.

"Shut up, Davis," said Heathstone. He returned his attention to Walters.

"Uh, Mr. President, I don't know. General Judd? . . ."

"It is not at all in my jurisdiction, Mr. President," Judd said openly. "Strategic Operations would assume the responsibility. But the equipment would have to be airlifted from Omaha to the launch site. I estimate twelve hours for that. Installation, at least eight hours. Twenty hours overall, and I don't know if they could do it that quickly."

"I want something lifted into orbit within twelve hours!" said Heathstone firmly. "Preferably the Tonopah devices. But if not, then I don't care what you get up, some tin cans for all I care!"

Judd, as well as everyone else, gazed in silence at him.

"Mr. President, I don't understand," Walters said finally.

"Twenty minutes before I came into this room," said Heathstone, "Ambassador Hornsborough telephoned me from Moscow. He briefed me on his predawn interview with Mr. Tosygen, and we must assume that, what is it called, that other project, Tolkien, is real."

A hum sped around the table. There was a flurry of hands grasping for copies of the telex.

"Further, intelligence informs me that the Russians launched, at midnight their time, three new satellites which they are calling weather satellites. I have to assume, gentlemen, that Project Tolkien is operational and in orbit. . . ."

"Good God," gasped Walters, "but that is—is—"

"Yes, Chester, some sort of hypnotic telepathy," agreed Heathstone. "Don't just sit there, Chester. Hop to it. The Soviets may, or may not, have effective operational Tolkien devices. But I have to have something I can work with. Tosygen has to at least consider the possibility that our Tonopah devices are in orbit and are operational. If I don't have that to work with, we will have lost the balance of power. Tosygen is baiting us. He is worried, too, or else he would have already used his initiative. You all understand?"

The military surrounding the briefing table rose as one man and swiftly converged on the door. The President had already exited.

WASHINGTON

3:00 P.M.

It was a dreary afternoon, raining again. The office, neat as an Academy cadet's footlocker on the day the first cryptic letter had found its way into Judd's hands, was now in disarray with hastily accumulated cabinets for Coogan's newly re-created files, piles of varicolored papers and official forms, growing stacks of books and journals on parapsychology, physics, psychology, the what-have-you of the human mind. There were also long computer print-outs of classified and unclassified research abstracts. These Judd had been able to acquire from Air Force and Navy Research. They reviewed all inquiries into the area of parapsychology, especially government-sponsored research, and particularly Russian research as well as American.

Coogan had busied herself with the lists for two days. They now trailed all over the office.

"This office," Judd observed happily, "is getting to look like a rat's nest, just as mixed up as this crazy stuff we're dealing with." He added morosely, "One sonofabitch throws a wrench in the works, a scrap of paper, and suddenly the world finds itself poised for total destruct!"

"Don't let it get to you," Coogan said absently, going through the lists.

"Hell! My whole life, my career, has been based on the idea that order can somehow be preserved, and here's someone messing around with that order. It's even worse than a war—at least then you know *something* about what's going on!"

"I don't know that some sort of messing up of the world order we have would be all that bad a thing," Coogan said thoughtfully, leaning back and lighting a cigarette. "No, I'm *not* condoning this," she said as Judd glowered and started to speak. "It's too . . . well, uncanny, but also too risky. What he's done could have any kind of results, from riots to outright war—and God knows what he's got up his sleeve next."

"With our luck, Sirius is probably old buddies with God, so He wouldn't tell us anyhow," Judd said sourly. "Who the hell *is* he?"

"I've got a feeling," Coogan said after a thoughtful pause, "that one way to find that out is to find out *why* he's doing it—what sort of person he has to be, so we'd know what to look for."

"What sort do you think that is? Your normal everyday superpsychic with the power to cloud men's minds and turn files to dust?"

"Even with his abilities, he's human. That means he's got drives, hopes, fears, and so on, no matter how powerful or . . . strange he is. And if we could build up a picture of what his makeup's like, we could narrow things down a lot, and perhaps get an idea of what his next move might be."

"Huh." Judd thought, then grinned. "Well, he thinks he can lead the world around by the nose, so that, if I recall, makes him a megalomaniac. Only . . . he *can*. So what does *that* make him?"

Coogan shrugged. "Well, first . . . he's got a strong vein of idealism, indicated by his choice of targets, those weapons. Um . . . feels driven, both about the world situation and about his own powers. He's been hiding, almost certainly because he's aware of the consequences of becoming known; yet now he's acted, which means he must be driven by something stronger. At a guess, I'd say . . . he's young. Not past thirty."

Judd was interested. "How come?"

Coogan ticked off her reasons on her fingers. "The idealism. Two, the fact that he's being very nonviolent about this, so far at least. He might have made his point with a hell of a bang practically anyplace in the world, if he'd wanted to, judging by what he did to my files, and yet he held off, just contented himself with sending letters and that telex. I think someone who'd lived for very long with that kind of power and concern, keeping it hidden before starting to use it, would be bitter and inclined to open with something violent. Three, he's not so smart. Bright probably, maybe a genius—but he doesn't know his way around, or he'd know that his letters and this exposure of the Tonopah and Tolkien weapons aren't going to do anything but create a big mess and a lot of yelling, and get us and the Russians working all the harder to see how we can get some advantage out of the situation. And that means an even more dangerous time for the whole world. So if he'd been alive long enough to see more of how things really work, and reactions are likely to follow certain actions, he'd have worked it another way. So . . . look for a young, bright, troubled man everybody probably likes."

"Why *he*? Could be a woman."

Coogan shook her head.

"Why not?"

"Well . . . a woman psychic *could* get the information and do the other things that have been done, of course, if the power were the same. But . . . oh, lord, all those plans and specifications and mailing letters—that's aimed at *men*, all the way. I think a woman would try to reach women first. . . . But one thing, Judd, scares me."

"Only one; you're lucky."

"You know and I know that what he's tried so far isn't going to work. Even if we and the Russians seem to back down, we'll find a way to weasel around it and keep things going the way they have been. And Sirius is going to feel very, very disappointed. *That's* what scares me."

Judd grunted. The office door pushed open as Abrams came through with two armfuls of papers and reports.

"That, I take it," commented Judd dryly, "is the short report I asked for about how those goddamned telex messages were sent?"

"I got two reports for you, sir. First, I thought that since you and Dr. Coogan have been tied up day and night, you might like to know what is going on in the world. I got the daily brief over at State. It looks pretty bad."

"Can you summarize, Abrams?"

"Yes, sir." Abrams picked out a sheaf of papers and began reading. " 'Preliminary riots have appeared in Paris, where French students seem as usual'—it really says 'as usual,' sir—'to be among the first to grasp the significance of the similar projects of Tolkien and Tonopah. The marches and demonstrations were peaceful at first, but quickly escalated to violence. American airline offices were looted. The American Embassy was bombed, part of its exterior façade collapsed into the street, killing some Frenchmen.'

" 'In West Berlin, popular wrath turned on the U.S.S.R.

and all things Russian. Hecklers collected at the several checkpoints along the six-hundred-mile border between East and West Germany and enthusiastically began throwing rocks and bottles, finally attempting to storm the barriers. Gunfire was initiated by the East German sentries. Gunfire was returned by the demonstrators. The Federal Republic was forced to deploy the Bundeswehr and call up reservists. Soviet tanks appeared on the eastern side, but shelling was only sporadic.'

" 'As yet, no official confirmation or denials concerning the content of the telex have been issued by either of the two concerned powers. No reports are forthcoming of activities in Russian cities. In the United States, as yet peaceful demonstrators are circulating behind police cordons outside the tall glass tower of the United Nations, while inside the ambassadors of the U.S.S.R. and the United States are being submitted to the grilling of several committees hastily set up to inquire into the alleged existence of the new superweapons.' "

"God," groaned Coogan. "It's starting to fall apart. What comes next? Sirius is unlikely to stop at this point!"

"Well, that will depend on the nut we are dealing with and on Heathstone and Tosygen, who may, or may not, do something crazy," said Abrams.

"Sirius isn't going to stop now."

"All right, Abrams." groaned Judd. "What about how that telex happened?"

"That's the short report here on top of this pile," Abrams said.

"Without getting rhetorical and historical, can you give a brief summary?"

"Right, sir. Well, we've learned a lot about modern telecommunications!"

"I've no doubt about that."

"Well, basically, sir, the transatlantic cable was laid in 1858."

"Start somewhere else, Abrams," advised Judd promptly. Coogan smiled.

"You want to begin with microwave systems, sir?"

"I want to begin with how it is a person or persons unknown can invade worldwide communications systems."

"Right, sir. Computers, then."

"Computers?" asked Coogan.

"Yes, ma'am, it had to be through computers."

"All right, Abrams," concluded Judd, "begin with computers. At least we know they're not back in 1858."

"Right, sir," said Abrams blandly, taking a deep breath. "Well, sir, computers are electronic data-processing machines that perform any variety of operations based on instructions that have been given to them by the people who use them." He broke his opening speech when he noticed Coogan smiling at him. "Oh, sorry, ma'am. I forgot you're a computer technologist. Do you want to take over this briefing?"

"Not at all, Lieutenant Abrams," said Coogan, laughing. "I'd probably get all tangled up in the technicalities I'm familiar with, and we'd both probably benefit more from your summary."

"Thank you, ma'am. The process of specifying a set of instructions for a computer is called programing, and the set of instructions itself is called a program."

"Where you're heading for," Judd said, "is that access to international news media systems can be obtained through computer programing?"

"Yes, sir. And with the proper access codes, to government, diplomatic, and military systems, as well."

"Well, that I understand. But I hadn't thought of access to civilian news media in the same terms."

"Well, we now have to consider that, sir. I'll use the example of the Air Force system to make it clear. Communication between points became a problem a long time ago—I won't go into that, sir—when it became necessary to somehow handle several messages at the same time. A line that delivers a message is called a channel, and first through microwave and later through laser-beam technologies, we now have channels that can transmit over a thousand simultaneous messages at once, as for instance with the one thousand channel system that links Pittsburgh, Cincinnati, and Chicago. There the delivery potential is one thousand times one thousand. A lot of messages."

"O.K. I understand you so far," Judd acknowledged.

"Sophisticated systems of communications literally dissolve distances between other systems that are fully electronic, transistorized high-speed data-transmission mechanisms all linked together by electronic switching centers that permit all this instantaneous transmission to any part of the world. There are even electronic sentinels that monitor and provide for switching between various microwave

and wire-line channels—such as the Atlantic cable system."
Abrams said this last with emphasis.

"O.K., O.K." Judd grinned.

"Well, sir, there are all types of switching systems, all
fully automatic transistorized high-speed systems that can
accommodate up to two-hundred-words-per-minute circuits."

"What he means to say, there," interrupted Coogan, "is
that words in a lengthy message can be fed into computer
codes, indexed, and broken down into a series of impulses
that can then be sent in seconds to a distant place, there to
be decoded by a recipient computer that eventually prints
out the message."

"Yes, ma'am," continued Abrams. "The Air Force Data
Communications System, AF DATACOM, is one such system that interlocks Air Force systems worldwide. It accounts for millions of channel miles of microwave systems,
but, as I indicated, there are electronic sentinels that can be
computer-commanded to intercept and feed the message
into wire-line systems as necessary. News media, worldwide, use lots of wire-line systems, the familiar telex systems."

"All right"—Judd grimaced—"where and how did our
man lock into the systems?"

"Well, sir . . ."

"Oh, my God!" gasped Coogan.

"Ah, you understand, Dr. Coogan. Do you want to take
over now?" Abrams asked.

"No . . . no, Lieutenant, please continue."

"Do you understand what Abrams is talking about?"
asked Judd.

"Very clearly, very clearly," Coogan said. "And I think
we're really in big trouble now."

"All right. Then continue, Abrams," Judd said softly.

"Well, sir, three things would be needed. The appropriate codes that would get entry into any of the various systems, a piece of equipment called a KB–CRT terminal,
and, finally, a telephone."

"A telephone?"

"What he means, Harrah, is a keyboard–printer unit that
can be portable and can be coupled with an ordinary telephone receiver. Many systems, in fact the majority of them,
I'd say, can be accessed by dialing a specific telephone
number which is answered by a computer somewhere. The

receiver is then placed in the telephone coupler on the KB–CRT terminal, and the terminal sends the message through the telephone receiver by frequency codes, and it's decoded by the receiving computer."

"Right, ma'am. This type of network access can be had at any point where a standard telephone and an electrical outlet are available, providing, of course, that you also have at least a portable KB–CRT unit."

The trio lapsed into a momentary silence. Judd pursed his lips. Coogan began scribbling a list.

"Are we to assume, then, that our person possesses, or possessed, a, what did you call it, a KB–CRT terminal?" Judd finally asked.

"We are working on that, sir. CIA, FBI, and Defense Intelligence are all busy tracking down anyone who ever bought one of these units," Abrams responded.

"This all gives me an idea," Coogan said. "Computer technology isn't so old. Even though there must be thousands of people who have studied computer programing, it would be worth the effort to compile a list from all computer training centers."

"That would be a long list, even if the profession is that new," commented Judd.

"Yes, but if one of those names was in my yellow files here, we would be onto something!"

"Can we do that, Abrams?" demanded Judd, hopefully.

"Can do, sir. If I'm not mistaken, computer trainees' names should be in computers somewhere."

"We also need to know who really knows about advanced computers," Coogan stated. "Obviously, for someone to understand a global system, it would have to be someone who understood more than the simplicities of the CRT units. Start with UNIVAC trainees, Abrams. Try the IBM schools, especially the IBM 2741s, also the Teletype models 33 and 37, Memorex 1240 and 1280, TermiNet 300s, the Syner-Data Betas and the AJ 841s. Here's a list." She scribbled rapidly.

"Get anyone who has subscribed to code access lists and numbers," continued Judd.

"He would need multiple codes, Harrah," said Coogan, "to ask relay systems to relay the messages. The government and diplomatic codes as well as the news media's access codes."

"I think we can assume," said Judd gloomily, "that he

might use his parasensory abilities to figure out any code he wanted."

Coogan and Abrams looked at him thoughtfully.

"Yes, I suppose so," said Coogan. "But let's be on the safe side anyway."

"I'll get right at it, sir," said Abrams and left the cluttered office.

Coogan and Judd stared at each other for a long moment. Judd's mind was racing wildly; Coogan chewed away at the lipstick on her lower lip.

"It begins to dawn on me," muttered Judd, "that our man can remain concealed and invisible as long as he wants."

"But he has to come out somewhere, at least to operate the computer," Coogan protested.

"Maybe not," replied Judd. "Think of your office. If he can use this strange ability called psychokinesis to bust up the molecular structure of your files, why couldn't he also be able to interfere by mind alone with computer signals?"

"But . . . if that's so, why—he could control all the planet's communication systems!"

"Yes," Judd agreed. "He could indeed."

Coogan thought for a moment, then spoke slowly. "Harrah . . . at that reception in New York, I met Aloysios Sandmuller."

"That must have been nice," Judd said impatiently.

"Well . . . impressive. You know, he takes an interest in the paranormal—my grant was his idea, he said—and he's aware of a lot that's going on. He could understand what we're up to, and has the resources to help a lot. We could—"

"Coogan! No Sandmuller! No nobody! What we're doing, only we are going to know about until we're ready to show some results. Not a word of what we do, find, or think gets out of this office unless and until I say so! Have you got that crystal-clear?"

"Yes . . . General." Coogan was suddenly furious.

3

SIRIUS

The mind can sing,
The soul can wing,
To supergalaxy. . . .
It's not
  an impossibility . . .

> (from the song
> "Supergalaxy")
> —DANIEL MERRIWEATHER

The deeper the physicist intruded into the realms of the subatomic and supergalactic dimensions, the more intensely he was made aware of their paradoxical and common-sense-defying structure, and the more open-minded he became toward the possibility of the seemingly impossible. His own world, based on relativity and quantum theory, is, in fact, a world of impossibles. The psychophysical parallelism envisioned in the last century will not account for the general problem posed by the relationships of mind/body.

> —WOLFGANG PAULI

COLLEGE PARK, MARYLAND

About twenty minutes away and eight miles from downtown Washington, hidden by trees in the rolling hills of the Virginia countryside, is the Langley headquarters of the Central Intelligence Agency, a gray-white concrete building several stories high. To the northeast about twenty-five miles is the headquarters of the National Security Agency, a U-shaped, three-story, steel and concrete building at Fort Meade, Maryland. It is a tightly guarded enclosure, surrounded by patrolled fences, machine guns, and dogs.

Both these organizations are entrusted with the strategic and tactical security procedures protecting the United States of America. Midway between the two, just north of College Park, Maryland, is the headquarters of Trans-American University, the academic child of the two senior intelligence systems and an institution of extraordinary importance for the entire world.

It is tucked away among trees, on picturesque grounds. Following the current fashion, it has a stern façade of gray-white precast-concrete squares and brown-tinted solar glass. Plots of yellow chrysanthemums are kept blossoming the year round, but sometimes there are petunias in the spring. In spite of its international importance, it is quiet. Few strollers are seen among the trees. The inhabitants of surrounding towns are not quite sure who comes and goes inside, but then they are used to such establishments in and around Washington, D.C.

Its three levels above ground are brilliantly lighted mazes of glass-lined corridors leading in and out of libraries, study and tape-deck listening cubicles, solariums, administrative sectors, and computerized information devices whose complex print-out equipment and blinking banks seem ominous to the uninitiated. The information banks at Trans-American constitute a generic approach to worldwide communication systems, linked as they are to computers all over the world.

The tall devices are outlets combining both the limited abilities of the more common pipeline Control Data STAR and the magnificent advanced capabilities of the parallel ILLIAC IV, first installed in 1974 at the University of Illinois, but since then developed, improved on, and installed at all major centers of learning the world over.

On its inauguration, the university was hailed as the most significant advance in science since the Copernican revolution; the press, always critical of things it does not understand very well, chastised it as either an expensive boondoggle or a sinister brainwashing center, some managing to tag it as both at the same time. Only doctoral candidates and scientists of high credentials were admitted and permitted to use the cement and brown-glass center's equipment.

Trans-American has five subterranean levels, all of which require different types of clearances for the thirty different types of research that take place in them. Of these, one of the most innocuous is the bioemporium, housed in the sector entitled "Advanced Biophysics." Entrance into Advanced Biophysics on level sub-three is possible only by insertion of an identcard into an electronic security pedestal just outside two vaultlike stainless-steel doors. The nature of the bioemporium's work is considered supremely delicate as far as public reaction is concerned, and no news releases are ever issued. Among its workers it is referred to as the house of the living dead.

The bioemporium housing the dead, kept functioning by machines guarding and monitoring their delicate physiologic and bioelectric balances, is accessible only through level sub-three's two circular room-sized elevators that descend and ascend to and from level sub-five with almost imperceptible movement. The corridors of level sub-five are lined with dark blue, enameled metal plates rising from red pile carpeting that ensures near silence.

Research chambers on level sub-five are systems of greenish glass walls interspersed by banks of gleaming equipment, blinking lights, and cadaver slabs. These chambers constitute a sterile environment, maintained by timed ultraviolet baths every five minutes.

Workers in level sub-five soon become used to the fluctuating illumination, and maintain a healthy tan because of it. It is fashionable, when not dissecting, to walk around in bathing trunks, taking optimum advantage of the dry, ultraviolet-drenched environment.

Neomort 25-A is housed in its own private circular chamber, surrounded by glass viewing portholes. It lies supine on a raised dais, bathed continually by circulating air maintained at 96.5° F, its functions watched constantly by computers hooked up to it by an orderly succession of wire leads and light sensors. Human interference is kept to a minimum, occurring only when various alerts of biophysical changes are noted by the ever-watching computer sentinels.

To date, all physical life processes have maintained themselves in superior order. Neomort 25-A looks as if it is awaiting a signal to wake up and walk again. In the presence of this eternally sleeping, functioning corpse, the technicians that service it have found themselves inspired with a rare form of necrophiliac admiration and vie for chances to tend it.

Since no one expected Neomort 25-A to have a brainprint, electroencephalogram trials were taken only periodically. Thus it was easy for the ebb and flow of consciousness surrounding the body to fluctuate its cortex rhythms and avoid detection.

When it was not floating in timeless euphoria, it collected itself into vibrating centers of subtle energy, carefully watching for those electronic interplays that would energize the ganglion centers of the body and reflect instantly into the leads and computer sensors warily monitoring the body for the least signs of life.

It spent its time, of which it had an endless supply in its current condition, watching and studying the cosmic forces that changed and fluctuated like power beams in the building blocks of existence. Many of the changes were cyclic, repeating themselves again and again at regular intervals. It, this consciousness, took advantage of its body's deathlike somnolence to develop specific controls of these changes.

Grey Walter, the famous scientist who had discovered several basic rhythmic patterns of the brain, had said that the most significant thing about a pattern was that one could remember it and compare it with another pattern. Yes, that was true, concluded the fluctuating consciousness hovering over Neomort 25-A. This perception of patterns was what distinguished sentient life from random events or chaos. Life makes patterns of patternless disorder.

Satisfied with the correctness of this basic premise, the wandering, fluctuating, nomadic consciousness monitored lunar impulses governing thousands of life cycles on earth, the circadian or sun cycles rushing around earth. It intruded into subtle electromagnetic shifts in metals and bacteria, along the hydrostasis of the atmospheres, along wires carrying deadly charges.

It flowed along the sensors monitoring the body, into the banks recording the impulses describing the body's physiologic and bioelectric rhythms. It studied that language and could finally probe it purposefully, confusing the machinery, coaxing it to give out false signals and conclusions.

These neomort biocomputers were themselves hooked into the general medical banks of the computers housed on levels above ground, and then through hook-ups to universities and research centers throughout the world.

London, Bogota, Paris, Peking . . . Chicago, New York, and Los Angeles.

Many gigantic complexes housing voluminous libraries of information were consulted on a time-share basis by multitudes of students and scientists. Learning patiently from these continual patterns, it organized its internal consciousness into rhythmic penetration of the deepest signals, then finally was able to instigate sufficient electric potential change at chosen terminals to trigger signals of its own that flowed along retrieval lines. Creating these mental and psychic impacts at tremendous distances along electronic potentials flowing between computer terminals, it tested its psychic powers. Playfully, it made several print-outs at various computer centers reflect erroneous data. Attending technicians simply concluded that wrong data had been fed into the banks and revised their approach. Computer errors were frequent anyway. No one took any special notice.

Tiring of exploration along wires and electronic signals, the consciousness shifted its attention to observing resonances in living things. Everything physical resonated with electric potentials that shifted in invisible sparkling auroras, rainbows, and auras. It exulted in the effervescent esthetics of these glittering shifts, first watching single cells govern their infinitesimal bodies with autonomic response processes. Multicelled animals called for more demanding observation and interpretation, but finally it could monitor the patterns transmitted by these complex life entities.

And then it touched on a growing embryo, a forming human being grown in vitro, a test-tube baby. It shifted its total attention to the complex, majestic fluctuations of rhythms, cycles, and resonances of the embryo. Soon it tired of the unconscious embryonic form and shifted its attention to a nearby attendant, a young man carefully watching the shelves of test-tube babies grow. The living man was endlessly fascinating. His thoughts, emotions, goals; his past memories, his experiences.

Since the consciousness was by now only loosely associated with Neomort 25-A, perhaps he could soon abandon the supine corpse and exist completely disembodied.

Well, that might be. Now it was time to cease this exciting exploration and see how his game was coming along.

He looked and found the satellites. He was amused; and he might have descended, like dropping into an elevator shaft, into anger.

But in his new awarenesses, now comprising atomic stresses and strains and even celestial magnitudes—well, it was hard to get angry. In his expanding vision, growing to a new fullness, there were only systems to be adjusted for their best functioning. It really was time that men on Earth realized that, though they were individuals, they also comprised a mutual system . . . and that system needed correction to function better.

THE PENTAGON

12:00 NOON

During the middle of August, the suffocating temperatures of the summer had dropped sharply. In Washington, at midday on August 18, a gentle wind blew across the city and the Virginia landscapes to the west. It carried a refreshing coolness, secreting in its gentle zephyrs any hints of the autumnal storms yet to come.

In only a few days, the first urgent public clamor over the Tonopah and Tolkien superweapons had subsided. Newspapers relegated mention of the United Nations talks on the subject to page six; some even omitted all mention. Students returned to near normal both in Europe and the United States. There was rumor of a small black-marketing effort in essential Tolkien and Tonopah device equipments in which the name of Rastaban al Nashirah figured prominently. He was watched carefully, as usual, by several intelligence services; but, also as usual, he was shrewd enough to know how to conduct his affairs out of sight of prying eyes.

In the United States, a few congressmen, feeling that there was much to be looked into in the matter of the still-unverified superweapons, determined to form a committee of inquiry and happily settled into the customary ritual of arguing over its composition, funding, and staff before getting at any actual work.

Thus in the Pentagon, headquarters of the Department of Defense and the world's largest office building, most of the 35,000 employees were unaware of the juggernaut of destruction the recent events had created and poised to start rolling. They continued to drink from their 685 water fountains, to use 280 rest rooms, to climb 150 stairways, and to ride nineteen escalators on their way about their daily work.

The corridor through which General Harrah Judd, Dr.

Elizabeth Coogan, and Lieutenant Joe Abrams were walking swiftly was carpeted in soft dark gray, its lighter gray
walls topped with miles of lighting concealed behind sheets
of semiopaque glass in the ceiling.

"I can't believe," Coogan was saying as they strode down
the interminable corridor, "that everyone's attention has
been almost solely on what the telex revealed. Isn't anyone
worried about how the information got out?"

"Only a few," said Judd. "Everyone's so used to security
leaks that it's hard to make people see what's different
about this one. And God knows there's enough to worry
about without that."

Finally, somewhat winded, they approached a section of
the seemingly endless corridor that widened into a larger
reception area decorated in shades of blue-gray. It was
thickly populated with men and women dressed in a variety of uniforms. After quickly pushing through the convers-
ing groups, Judd led the way to a paneled door, flanked by
Marine guards, which opened into an enormous room.

It overflowed with functional military opulence. Dominated by a lighted map of the world at one end and by a
veritable wall of military and national flags at the other, its
windowless walls were concealed behind thick green drapes
giving the rows of leather chairs around the central conference table a muted atmosphere.

"God, it's impressive," Coogan whispered to Judd.

Judd led her to a chair next to Chester B. Walters near
the head of the table. Abrams took a chair slightly behind.

"I hope you're ready," Walters muttered skeptically.

"We'll do our best, sir. Dr. Coogan here will give the
backbone of our information."

"My pleasure, Dr. Coogan, and welcome to the Joint
Chiefs of Staff theater. I had not realized that you were so
young and, so, ah . . ." Walters smiled with open admiration.

"A woman, you mean."

"Yes," admitted Walters, still smiling. Coogan ignored
the leer in Walter's eyes.

The chairman of the Joint Chiefs of Staff, Admiral
Thomas R. Hollifield, gaveled the table into order. The
noise subsided. "Mr. Secretary," he began, looking at Walters, "I believe this is going to be your party."

"Thank you, Thomas," responded Walters, exhibiting
the bearing and authority that had helped him become Sec-

retary of Defense. "I should like, first, to inform the Joint Chiefs that Tonopah devices have been successfully placed in orbit, mainly as a propaganda effort to convince the Russians that we also have some new types of hardware up there. We do not know the exact strike potential of these new armaments since the urgency that compelled us to put them there did not give us sufficient time to test them at all. But we can report, as we already have, that we have complied with the executive order. However, the President has now issued a directive that the devices should not be activated except by himself personally."

A murmur swept through the room.

"Are we therefore to assume," asked Hollifield, "that the devices are, to all purposes, in operational readiness?"

"That is correct, Thomas," acknowledged Walters. "We are acting on the assumption that each of these devices is capable of paralyzing all living nerve tissue in target areas covering up to three hundred square miles. This gives us strike potential over entire cities such as Moscow, Tokyo, or even Washington or New York. We have three devices in orbit, so our strike potential at any given time is nine hundred square miles."

A general silence blanketed the room, broken finally by Hollifield.

"Does this mean, Mr. Secretary, that all men, women, and children in a given city, say New York—I believe we are all familiar with the massive volume of people in New York—could be put into, er, paralysis?"

"Stupor would be a better word for it, Mr. Chairman," said Walters, changing to the formal mode of address. "I should like to move on to our other topic immediately, however, and not dwell on the Tonopah devices. I have here General Judd, whom I believe most of you know. He has prepared a briefing for you on the probable potential of the Russian Tolkien devices. If it is all right with you, Mr. Chairman, I believe the floor should now be turned over to him."

"General?" indicated Hollifield to Judd.

"Thank you, sir, Mr. Chairman," began Judd, looking at Coogan, who smiled. "Several days ago, aerial photoreconnaissance reported demolition of a research site in Kazakhstan that we have had some interest in for a long time. This event was reported by, I believe, Lieutenant Shirley Paars, who has been especially helpful in interpreting earlier as well as current flyovers. Since this event took place at about the same time that Ambassador Hornsborough had his first conversation with Premier Tosygen, we are inclined to assume that this was a hasty attempt on the part of the Russians to move the research base in which Project Tolkien was being developed. Therefore, we are inclined to assume the validity of the specifications listed in the telex revealing the specifications for Tolkien devices."

He gestured toward Coogan. "Since the specifications for the Tolkien devices include matters that are most likely unfamiliar to us all, those of hypnosis and telepathy, I have asked Dr. Elizabeth Coogan, who is expertly informed in these matters, to speculate on the nature of these two unfamiliar functions and try to relate them to the mechanical equipment in the Tolkien devices. With your permission, Mr. Chairman . . ."

"Dr. Coogan, your reputation precedes you," said Admiral Hollifield. "It is our pleasure to have you here. Hypnosis, and especially, uh, telepathy, are beyond the comprehension of most of us. I hope you will take it easy on us."

"Certainly, Admiral," said Coogan as she stood up. Lieutenant Abrams handed her a sheaf of papers.

"I will speak about hypnosis first, simply because there is not much to understand about it, as it were. There has been, and continues to be, widespread disagreement in the various scientific communities on exactly what hypnotism is, except that it is a genuine condition in which the person involved will accept suggestion that is not processed through the conscious functions of his personality and subsequently perform what was suggested to him. And, very importantly, there are no physical means of detecting this condition—there is no way to identify a hypnotized person or one who has been given a posthypnotic suggestion to carry out."

Admiral Hollifield frowned. "You are trying to tell us that, for example, if there were, say, among us, a victim of the enemy's weapon, we would really have no way of identifying him?"

"That is correct, Admiral," acknowledged Coogan.

"Could you tell us—" began Hollifield.

"I should prefer to continue my report before answering questions," Coogan said firmly, "since I feel that the next part may give you an idea of the possible capabilities of Project Tolkien."

"In that case, then, please continue."

"I will direct your attention, Admiral, to two papers on Russian telepathy advances published by our own government."

A general gasp of surprise whipped through those present around the table and in the rest of the room.

"These are an unedited rough-draft translation of a paper on biological radio communications published by the Air Force in 1963, and another on experimental studies of mental suggestion, published by the Joint Publications Research Service in 1973."

"Mr. Chairman," Judd broke in, "these papers will be included in the briefing folios now in preparation."

"Thank you, General," said Admiral Hollifield. "Please continue, Dr. Coogan."

"The second report includes lengthy reviews of research involving mental suggestion of motor acts, of visual images and sensations, and, very significantly, mental-suggestion experiments at great distances. It is also extremely important, in my opinion, to find in this paper that the fundamentals of the electromagnetic theory of mental suggestion are examined."

"But what has this got to do with—"

"Please, Admiral. I understand your confusion. But do let me continue."

"My apologies, Dr. Coogan."

"The first report indicates advances in the study of biological radio systems. This means simply that the human body, or the body of any living creature for that matter, is potentially capable of receiving radionic impulses through the central nervous system, including the brain. Reports from the Soviet Union of telepathic advances as well as hypnosis ceased about ten years ago, which suggests they made enough progress to make their work worth classifying. If we put the two together, the concept of electromagnetic generation of mental suggestion and the use of the human body as a receiving station, then the equipment for Project Tolkien, revealed in the rather stunning telex made available to the entire world, is feasible."

Coogan sat down.

Hollifield regarded her quietly for a few empty moments. The others present were similarly stilled.

"Dr. Coogan, thank you for your extremely clear presentation. You have not covered, however, the specifications of the Tolkien devices that apparently use, if my understanding of the weapon is correct, living brain tissue for, what shall I call it? . . ."

"A resonator, I believe," responded Coogan. "This part of the Tolkien device is quite complex, and I am not sure that I understand it completely, or, if I do, that I can explain it simply."

"Many of us are scientists here, Dr. Coogan. Explain it, as you see it."

"Apparently the Soviets use human brain matter, kept alive in chemically and electronically charged solution, as a sort of radio broadcast modulator. Here, in the United States, this line of research is also under investigation. But the apparent new approach the Soviets seem to have come up with is that by electronic stimulation, filtered through what at one time was the brain of a live, proved telepath, radio waves can be broadcast to provoke compulsive episodes in the targeted populations. If you're familiar with the concept of biofeedback, I can describe the Tolkien devices as biofeedback instruments in reverse."

There was not a sound in the room.

Chester B. Walters finally spoke up in the void. "What can we expect if these things are put to use?"

"Apparently," Coogan continued, "by overload of modulated waves we can expect reduction of overall awareness in the person, an enhanced receptive state, and then excitation of general aggressive emotions."

"I am not clear on what that means, Dr. Coogan," Walters said.

"The affected populations will probably tear each other to pieces, Mr. Secretary," Coogan said bluntly.

"You are advising us, then," commented Admiral Hollifield grimly, "that the Tolkien devices are real?"

"Providing the Russians have recruited or developed telepaths in whose brain matter the telepathically related functions have established set neuronal patterns, yes, Admiral, I am suggesting that the devices are hypothetically possible. I feel it is up to you and your colleagues to determine their reality."

"But Jesus Christ," snorted Walters. "Telepaths! Why that means someone psychic, does it not?"

"Yes, Mr. Secretary." Coogan smiled impishly. "Someone or perhaps even several. If there are now questions, I will try to provide answers if I can."

Thereupon the huge chamber was once again enveloped in a gloomy static silence. Since there were no questions, Admiral Hollifield declared the briefing closed and set another for the next day.

CORVO

3:00 P.M.

Rastaban al Nashirah was quite used to meeting in clandestine trysts with various internationalists, and so the meeting he had arranged for the island of Corvo in the Azores was nothing unusual for him. He and his small staff had eluded, as usual, the watchful eyes of the several secret services who tried to ferret out his machinations. He had one rule that the organized bureaucracies had never grasped: he always did the unpredictable thing. Intelligence workers were trained rigorously in their own special techniques, and were asked by their superiors to stick to the book if they could. Most field agents wanted to please their superiors, at least enough to get out of the field one day and into some office, and so usually stuck to the book.

With this understanding of the overall espionage establishment, Rastabi always watched for the opportunity to be unpredictable and seized it when he could. It was, he thought, a simplistic approach to the apparent complexities of international espionage, whether that espionage was military or technological, but then life was liberally woven with such simplicities. The wise located them and made them work in their behalf.

It had been an easy matter, for instance, to let the increasingly rich nations of the Afro-Asian block know that he was ready to deal in the new weapons. He simply let it drop over cocktails in the North Lounge of the United Nations in New York that he felt the weapons could be fabricated from specifications given in the telex. Certainly, he had said, anyone could build those devices, but speed was important if initiatives were to be gained, and he had assumed an interest in that speed.

Within a matter of hours, he had been contacted by several parties. The affair had been arranged and he had thereafter departed for Kennedy Airport on his way to visit Switzerland on business. However, at the airport he had changed places with one of the look-alikes in his employ who had gone on to Switzerland in his place. Rastaban al Nashirah himself had boarded a later flight to Jamaica, and from there taken a chartered plane to the Azores. It was a simple move, and he might be detected; but even if he were discovered, he was committing no crime. He executed such trickery for the sake of avoiding possible difficulties in the future, and in any case relished the spice of adventure it brought to his life.

Sitting on the veranda of the *estancia* that he maintained at Rosario on the island of Corvo, he contemplated the hot orange orb of the late-summer sun setting into the shimmering Atlantic Ocean to the west. This island, in the western Azores, with its mild climate and its rugged volcanic topography, reminded him in some ways of his own country. He recalled how much he detested the arid squalor of his native islands, that small group of eight islands off the coast of Arabia called Bahrein. The two groups of islands were different in many ways, but at the same time somewhat alike.

He touched some cold champagne to his narrow lips, his dark eyes reflecting his appreciation of the pleasing texture of the dry wine. Champagne and sun always tended to stimulate his inner thoughts, and these as usual turned to resurvey his rise to power and influence far from the intolerable poverty and insignificance of his birth.

Everything has its beginning! That basic, almost mystic thought time and again raced through his head. He detested the mystic, abhorring the Arab devotion to it as he abhorred everything Arabic. If everything had its beginning so must it have its end. And he, Rastaban al Nashirah, did not want to end at all.

There would certainly be no end to his being Arabic, though, since he had been born an Arab and the world would never let him forget that. His ultraelegant suits tailored in Paris, his Swiss bank accounts, and Italian shoes could never alter the fact of his origin. But they could, and did, blur his memory of it.

Those were the days when the British had governed their protectorate with a certain pomp and circumstance he had himself ever since longed to possess. Those were the days when the ruling sheik and his followers were plotting to gain control, the days before oil was found on the island's central plateau, the days when a gun traded on the black market was an important enterprise.

The day he had first held a firearm was the same day he realized he had never worn shoes, and he proceeded to follow his first arms sale with his first sartorial purchase. Well, there was no problem of shoes, now, or of anything material. His problem consisted of the complexities involved in manipulating almost unbelievable American stupidities against obsolete Russian idealism and suspicion.

He smiled, drinking the last of the champagne. He was a weapons merchant; he sold any weapon to any buyer. Could he help it if, with the barest manipulation, international affairs yielded increasing markets for his products?

It was a dizzying game. Let the American diplomats run around arranging peace between opponents; let the Russian technologists teach opponents how to build things. The need for force only continued to grow and multiply. And as a result he was solicited for more and more instruments of force.

He sighed. Even if his enormous resources for obtaining weaponry brought money to him, and his position as economic advisor to the United Nations and the International Bank meant position for him, weapons themselves tended to change. It had been relatively easy to obtain his respectable official posts. After all, with so many nations gathered in one spot, almost all of them had secret motives for having him at hand.

And all developing nations were anxious to obtain samples of newly developed weapons. Yet guns were not really the important enterprise they had once been. Now the important demand was for things like computerized bazookas, microwave sensing devices, microradionic detectors. In these days of expanding technology, politicos and militants everywhere paid handsomely for technological advances, and especially handsomely for technologically sophisticated weaponry.

The sun had disappeared below the horizon, darkened now with distant thunderheads. He could not rid himself of the conviction that in those looming shapes lurked djins, those undisciplined spirits held by Moslems to exercise supernatural powers.

Rastaban al Nashirah grimaced as he turned to collect another glass of champagne, thinking that, underneath what he had made of himself, there would always be a superstitious Arab.

A short while later, in the aristocratic sitting room of the *estancia*, its décor preserved since the early 1940s, he conversed with the buyers who had gathered.

"The nature of the American Tonopah devices," he said, "is quite easily understood, and I can guarantee delivery of such equipment within one week."

A general nod of approval lit the faces of the others present, two of whom appeared to be Orientals; three were obviously from African nations.

"Naturally," continued Nashirah, "there will be modifications. Tonopah devices would have optimum effectiveness if mounted in orbit around the planet. Most nations do not have access to space vehicles, and so my scientists have modified the Tonopah equipment for airplanes and semipermanent bases on elevated sites. Actually, the Tonopah beams can be bounced off the stratosphere like ordinary radio waves. Also, I can guarantee some smaller portable units within three weeks."

He paused to allow the impact of his statement to be understood sufficiently. "The Russian Tolkien devices, however, present another situation, since they apparently use the little-understood, ah, parasensory function termed *telepathy*. Actually, the emergence of a so-called parasensory function into the realm of weaponry was to be anticipated, even though it sounds implausible at first hearing."

"I hesitate to interject," offered one of the Orientals, "that our planet has moved into a new age—"

"Quite right," agreed Nashirah. "This new age seems to have begun in April 1966 when Karl Nikolaiev and a biophysicist in Moscow named Kamensky managed to exchange a telepathic contact over a distance of 1,860 miles. For once, the Soviets were imaginative enough to follow this up with a massive scientific effort, which produced convincing experimental evidence of the action of telepathy in the brain."

"But, Rastabi," interrupted one of the dignified Africans, "telepaths are not generally found in the armaments establishments of any military that I know of."

"Quite right. But apparently the Russians do have them, if we are to assume the validity of the Tolkien devices. My sources can produce it quite efficiently, but it will have to be modified to be effective, that is, in the absence of telepaths."

"Modified? How?"

"Well, in the West, in America, the scientist who did so

much pioneering work in brain waves, Grey Walter, discovered that lights flashed at regular intervals into people's eyes produced strange patterns in their brainprints. He was especially interested in those alpha-rhythm ranges, that is, from eight to twelve cycles, that when imposed on subjects produced violent reactions and sent them suddenly into what resembled epileptic fits. Indeed, he found that the brain patterns of epileptics showed predominantly alpha rhythms during a seizure. Large numbers of normal people, however, show similar responses under certain conditions."

"Are you suggesting, then," asked the same man, "that the Tolkien specifications be altered merely to produce or broadcast alpha rhythms?"

"Yes, but only until we can acquire a slice of a telepath's brain. The Tolkien devices are apparently meant to stimulate brain activities to bring its victims into proper receptive states during which telepathic suggestion, presumably couched in hypnotic terms, can be induced in them. But the modified devices can indeed induce seizures in large segments of the population they are targeted on."

"You mean the general populace would all fall into epileptic fits?"

"A certain percentage, probably. This type of occurrence would lead to panic and confusion and expedite, say, military takeovers." Nashirah allowed time for these thoughts to register on the minds of the gathered group. He then said, "Gentlemen, I believe the nature of my offer is understood. I will accept sealed bids during the next twenty-four-hour period. I realize that good science laboratories can probably also expedite development of the Tonopah and Tolkien devices, but the American Government is confiscating equipment necessary to create the Tonopah devices, and my sources indicate that a similar effort is under way in Russia. Both governments presumably have used their spacecraft to orbit these devices. Concerning the major powers with outer space potential, war has been lifted from the surface of Earth to space. But those nations quickly acquiring these weapons—which take time to develop even from the specifications revealed—can at least acquire some local defense in the short time available. My office in New York will receive your bids for the next twenty-four hours. Good afternoon."

Government Imperatives

WASHINGTON

10:00 A.M.

Thomas Cordero Heathstone was put together from a combination of minority ancestors—Irish, Mexican, and Cherokee. It was a formidable combination, as most people quickly discovered when they tried to deal with him.

Such was the national respect for this unique man that, after only two years of his presidency, the adobe house in which he had been born on the reservation in Oklahoma had already been declared a point of national interest.

The one thing most people tended to distrust in him was that he was basically honest, and, for a politician, this seemed suspect. Further, he had a habit of admitting his faults, another disconcerting trait. Finally, he tended to laugh over his blunders, but hardly ever apologized for them, trying to rectify them if he could, and if not, promptly forgetting about them. This last trait made him almost impervious to political blackmail, and thus the United States found itself saddled with a President whose nature was nearly a total mystery to most of the bureaucratic personalities in government and industry alike.

He was a "people's man," having worked his way up, starting, after his education, sponsored by the Cherokee Fund, as a field hand for a chemical refinery, and he had continued working his way up ever since. Like earlier presidential families, he and his wife had ripped the White House apart when they had arrived to occupy it, turning it into "modern Americana" since they thought the time had come for the United States to live in the future as well as the past.

The Fine Arts Committee, descended from the group named by Mrs. John F. Kennedy, stood aghast. Down came crystal chandeliers, out went American Federal-style furniture and the beautiful Savonnerie rugs, all to the national warehouse at Fort Washington. In came American

Indian rugs, contemporary furniture, and American modern art. Visitors to the White House found themselves confronted by neon-light sculptures, water-filled couches, colorful patterned rugs, all of which, once the senses had calmed down, did look quite nice against all the white marble in the spacious high-ceilinged rooms.

Having supported Mrs. Heathstone against the energetic protests of the National Fine Arts Committee, Heathstone himself set out to do similar refurbishments to the government, and subsequently most governmental offices, officials, and associated agencies had been kept on their toes. Nothing had them so much on their toes as the present situation, the implications and scope of which both baffled and terrified the responsible functionaries.

Thomas Cordero Heathstone, at the midmorning meeting on August 20, surveyed the four somber men gathered in his Oval Office. His raven-black hair made him look perpetually youthful, and his dark green eyes blazed like two stars over a rock-hard Indian mouth. The waiting officials were Seth Mead, Secretary of State; Chester B. Walters, Secretary of Defense; Admiral Thomas R. Hollifield, Chairman, the Joint Chiefs of Staff; and Allan Provost, Chairman, National Security Council.

"Mr. President," Provost began, "we have asked for this time to make certain recommendations to you."

"Certainly, Allan," Heathstone said genially. "I take it that these recommendations are based on your best thinking about the present situation?"

"That is true, sir," responded Provost. "Although we, that is, the Joint Chiefs of Staff and the various agencies, have not had sufficient time to study the situation in depth, we have arrived at a preliminary consensus."

"I would take some exception to the idea of a consensus," interrupted Mead. "I haven't had a great deal of time in which to study the full ramifications stemming from this, shall we say, rather remarkable breach in security. But I am inclined to agree hypothetically with the conclusions reached by the military. . . ."

"And what are those conclusions?" asked Heathstone.

"I will ask the Secretary of Defense to present them," said Provost, "although the decision to present them to you was initiated by the National Security Council."

"All *right*," said Heathstone, "just tell me what the hell they are."

"The overall situation resulting from the security breach of Project Tonopah also includes the joint revelation of the hypothetical Project Tolkien. The question is should we assume that this Project Tolkien is fictitious, or should we assume that it is as real and as embarrassing as Project Tonopah?"

"I should point out," interrupted Seth Mead, "that the concept of broadcasting hypnotic signals telepathically finds little support with scientist members of the National Science Foundation. I have had a chance to talk with some of them, and it seems generally agreed there that telepathic hypnosis is improbable."

"Yet, Mr. President," continued Walters, "we do know that Russia orbited three satellites. Our basic assumption must include the probability that these vehicles contain the Tolkien devices as described in the—"

"In all the confusion of the past days," interrupted Heathstone, "I have not yet had a report that made sense on exactly how the security surrounding Project Tonopah came to be broken to the degree that the complete specifications could be sent out all over the world, or who or what could be behind such a move."

"Yes, Mr. President," agreed Provost somewhat somberly. "It has not been possible yet to present you with a report since the facilities of the intelligence agencies, all of whom, I can assure you, have been working on this, have not specifically yielded anything."

"You mean to tell me there's not even a lead?"

"Well . . . it depends on what you call a lead. . . ."

"A lead, Allan," Heathstone said with menacing softness, "is anything that might result in a discovery."

"Yes, Mr. President. All our, er, leads, have proved fruitless."

"So, there are no leads," Heathstone stated.

"This search, Mr. President," interrupted Seth Mead, "although certainly important—we must make sure it doesn't happen again—is extraneous to the matter we have come here to discuss with you."

"True enough. What is it?"

"Frankly, Mr. President," continued Chester B. Walters, "for precautionary security reasons, we have to assume the existence and validity of the Tolkien devices—that they are in orbit, probably primed for strategic intervention."

"That's a pretty reasonable assumption," agreed Heathstone. "That is, unless the Russians were caught as much by surprise as we were and moved fast as camouflage. I was certainly ready to do just that if we couldn't have got the Tonopah devices up in time."

"Whatever the motives of the Russians, Mr. President," Provost said, "the security of our nation is in question, and we feel that certain steps should be taken."

"Such steps being?"

"Mr. President, we must take measures to protect you, your government, as well as all other strategic personnel necessary for the defense of our nation."

Heathstone looked at him, pursing his lips. "I see," he said finally, "and how do you propose to do that?"

"Mr. President," Provost said, taking the lead, "there is only one overall measure that can be implemented quickly, and almost without any commotion in the press, at least until the moves are completed."

"Moves? What moves?"

"Mr. President," said Walters, "the waves associated with the Tolkien devices are long waves and do not penetrate very far beneath the surface—"

"Surface? What are you talking about?"

"Mr. President," Mead interrupted, "we have to take into account the possibility any man or woman in the United States could be hypnotized by these devices and given suggestions that would not be in the best interests of our nation."

"You mean to say, that I, myself or . . . ?"

"Yes, Mr. President," confirmed Provost. "You must take cover, er, refuge, beneath the surface, where the Tolkien devices will have little chance of—"

"I will not run!"

"Mr. President," said Mead, "some time ago several possible locations were constructed and are available."

"You mean the underground locations in case of nuclear . . ."

"Yes, Mr. President," confirmed Walters. "The Deeprock site at Peakview Mine just north of Colorado Springs . . ."

"Gentlemen, if I were to take cover beneath the ground right now, it would set the stage for a national panic. I can't—"

"Frankly, Mr. President," Provost said, "the nation is

already in a state of suppressed panic. You have already allowed martial law to be declared in some areas."

"That was necessary," Heathstone said glumly.

"True, but we have no assurance that . . . well, that Tonopah devices could not be constructed by some of our own citizens. Aside from the Tolkien devices, we stand endangered by subversive elements here in our own country should such subversives manage to construct short-range Tonopah weapons."

"I see," Heathstone said.

"We urge you to depart immediately for the Deeprock site since it is only there that we can guarantee with any certainty your, ah, if I may put it that way, your mental safety."

"I see," Heathstone said once more. "What about other government and military people?"

"I have already," said Walters, "ordered all underground installations to become fully operational, and strategic military personnel are already beginning to transfer their operations. A complete breakdown of the subsurface nuclear defense colonies is available for you at Deeprock, as well as computer communications between them and with the surface world."

Heathstone's raised eyebrows indicated his reservations about his Defense Secretary's actions without presidential authorization. "You're getting the military people squirreled away safely—what about the civilians?"

"Certain members of Congress and other government officials are considered strategic, and, with your agreement, we can begin to execute measures for their safety. It seems advisable to maintain secrecy as long as possible and not to disturb the visible orderliness of the government until absolutely necessary."

"Gentlemen," Heathstone said heavily, "you are suggesting that the Executive Office should become a prisoner of the military beneath the ground while Congress and other governmental functions remain as before. . . ."

"That *is not* what we are suggesting," protested Provost.

"That's what it amounts to," Heathstone said angrily.

"That is not, Mr. President, what it would be in reality," insisted Seth Mead.

The President stood up and paced the floor, pounding one fist into his palm.

"I will take your recommendation into consideration. I

have asked the Russian Premier for a summit talk, and I will take no action until I have heard from him. To do so would jeopardize the success of those talks. What would Tosygen conclude if the American President ran to a bunker?" He glared at his advisors.

"Speed and secrecy are paramount, Mr. President," said Mead. "You could simply be on vacation in the Rockies. . . ."

"I will let you know. Thank you, gentlemen," said Heathstone abruptly. "Seth, would you please remain here with me?"

When the others had gone, Heathstone sat down at his desk and rang for his secretary. Hedy Allison, an elegantly tall woman with black hair and green eyes betraying her own Indian heritage, entered silently through a small door.

"Seth," Heathstone began, "I have had a call in to Hornsborough, trying to find out why it is that Tosygen hasn't responded to my urgent appeals for a meeting."

"I have just this moment gotten through to Ambassador Hornsborough, Mr. President," Hedy Allison said crisply. "He is on line four."

"Good," Heathstone responded, clicking on the telephonic unit.

"David, what the hell is going on with Tosygen?"

The long-distance wires were full of crackle, but the voice of David Hornsborough broke through the static clearly enough to make his agitation apparent.

"Mr. President, I don't even know where the Premier *is*. In fact, it seems almost all the Russian Government has suddenly decided to take vacations in the Crimea—at least, that's the official line."

"You mean Tosygen is not in Moscow?"

"That seems to be so, Mr. President. And some strange things are going on here. There are sounds of gunfire throughout the city, and we have been notified about some sort of martial law taking effect. The embassy is surrounded with Russian troops, sent here, I have been informed, to guard us."

"I see." Heathstone and Mead exchanged quiet looks.

"What do you want me to do, Mr. President? I'd like to evacuate some of our personnel here."

"Yes, by all means," said Seth Mead, who could hear Hornsborough clearly, if faintly, from the phone the President held.

Heathstone ignored his Secretary of State's comment and said, "David, I'd like to ask you to do everything you can to reach Tosygen. When you succeed, ask him to meet with me at any location he suggests. Do you feel your security there will last another twenty-four hours?"

"It seems good. The Russian troops have drawn up some tanks. They're very good with tanks, you know."

"Thanks, David. Let's hold this line open. Put Helena on it, and she can keep in constant touch with Hedy here. Let us know the instant the situation changes, one way or another."

"Yes, Mr. President. How did all this get started, anyway? Where did those letters *come* from?"

"I don't know, David. But I am definitely going to try to find out."

He ended the conversation and turned to Hedy Allison. "Hedy, see if you can get hold of that Defense Department man, General Judd, and that scientist, Dr. Coogan. Ask them to come here as soon as you locate them."

"Yes, sir."

"Seth, are we to assume the Russian Government has retreated to a bunker?"

"I'd have to say it seems so," Mead said.

Heathstone brooded silently for a moment over a picture that forced itself on his mind's eye . . . legions of prairie dogs industriously burrowing travesties of cities underground. Only these rodents wore business suits and uniforms—and the two fattest, silliest-looking ones bore a haunting resemblance to Praskovie Tosygen and Thomas Cordero Heathstone.

The Known and Unknown

WASHINGTON

7:00 A.M.

General Harrah Judd liked the early-morning hours, even when they were dark and filled with rain. They were good for thinking, for straightening out the residue of the day before, and often for dealing with the long-range problems of his life. In his small, sparsely furnished apartment in Georgetown he kept a small alcove off the bedroom for thinking purposes. There, he smoked and drank strong coffee, and thought.

Sitting in a loosely tied robe on the morning of August 21, his hair tousled, his muscular legs folded over each other, he reviewed his life. Birth, college, West Point, his career, the divorce, his inner loneliness—all these flickered through the dark avenues of his memory. His life at the moment was turning on an invisible pin, a point in his mind that he could not quite locate.

It had to be a certain passion for life unexperienced that pricked at his frontal consciousness. Somewhere inside, all men and women believe themselves to be a little different from all others, aware of a certain "something" that sets them apart.

All this intangible awareness was somehow tied up with the current situation. When he tried to reach out in his imagination to pull the situation apart, he seemed to collide mentally with indelible messages he couldn't decipher, messages with a timeless quality inextricably linked to past, present, and future.

Experience had taught him that it was out of this apparent confusion of mental signals that he pulled inspiration when it was needed in the line of duty or in his personal life. He also associated this state of mind with several premonitions he had had, such as the presentiment on seeing the Tonopah letter and sketch. He recalled how, as his fingers had touched it, uneasiness had welled up uncontrollably from within him. He had usually interpreted these mental warnings as psychological aberrations, flareups that should be tightly controlled because they were unfamiliar, because they were undesirable in the strictly rational world in which he lived.

But perhaps, he thought now, they might actually be a strange kind of valuable insight, coming out of those areas of human consciousness never or rarely touched on by the current mental sciences. If so . . . they would have to be psychic. . . . He pursed his lips, scratched himself beneath his robe, and lit another cigarette.

Psychic things? What are they? Trivia? Hallucinations? There are thousands of learned papers on the psychological structure of man that say so.

The telephone on the side table buzzed. Automatically, he lifted the receiver on the first sound.

"General?"

"Yes, Abrams?"

"The President's office has been trying to get hold of you. Mr. Heathstone wants to see you as soon as possible."

"Did they say what for?"

"No, sir. Only that he wants you and Dr. Coogan. We can't find her. Do you know where she is?"

"Yes, Abrams, I do."

"Right, sir," Abrams said blandly.

Judd rose and walked out of his thinking alcove into the bedroom. He disrobed and slipped beneath the sheet, cuddling up next to Coogan, who murmured comfortably in her morning drowsiness.

"We got to get up, Coogan. I hear the President is looking for us."

"Umm, whatever for?" she mumbled, stretching her arms upward.

"Who knows? But I know one thing. I'm going to tell him about—what was it you once called him—ah, yes, about Sirius." He began advancing his lips across her bare shoulders.

"That's very daring, don't you think, at this stage?"

"Someone has to do something."

"Yes, I suppose so." She began responding to his sexual tactics. "What brought all this on?"

"I'm good in the morning," he said.

"No, not this, you nut! Telling the President."

"I've just been up early, thinking. You know, I've never

been willing to admit even the possibility that I might have a psychic nature. But . . . you know, we all might have. . . ."

His hand took up his lips' tactics, moving downward beneath the sheet.

"Hey, the President wants us," she breathed. "Do we have time?"

"Time enough."

10:00 A.M.

As Heathstone rose from behind his desk to greet Judd and Coogan, he gestured at the others in the room: the Secretary of State, the chairman of the National Security Council, and the Secretary of Defense.

"Good morning, General, Dr. Coogan. Glad you could come through all this dreary rain. You know Mr. Mead, Mr. Provost, Mr. Walters, of course."

"Thank you, Mr. President," responded Judd, nodding at Chester Walters, who returned the look nervously.

"This is an off-the-record conversation. The situation— I'll come directly to the point—surrounding the Tonopah and Tolkien mess, well, I simply can't get my thoughts about it all in one place. Each of these gentlemen has provided me with information, which appears to add up to a situation of some sort of high-level espionage coupled with attempts to interfere with the balance of world weapons. However, what we have no idea of is, who is it, and why has it been done?"

Heathstone paused, glancing in turn at each of his three functionaries, who seemed distinctly uncomfortable.

"What I should like to ask you, General, and you, Dr. Coogan, since you appear to know a great deal about the Russian potential, is to give me any fresh ideas you might have."

"I doubt if General Judd knows much more than has been in our reports to you, Mr. President," volunteered Chester B. Walters.

"That may be, Chester. But I don't want reports now. I want speculation."

"We are using every available means to trace who it was that might have stolen the Tonopah plans," persisted Walters.

"Will that also account for who might have obtained the Tolkien plans?" Heathstone asked.

"Well, sir, CIA is liaising on that. . . ."

"I want to aim at developing the situation here, and I cannot afford, nor do I intend, to sit around waiting for reports."

"Yes, Mr. President," Walters said resignedly.

"I'll have to go out on a limb a little, Mr. President," Judd said. Walters threw a stern look in Judd's direction.

"Judd, don't you bring up that wild—"

"Ah, is something being kept from me?" asked Heathstone.

"Judd here has some farfetched idea," Walters said tightly.

"I don't mind being a little farfetched," said Heathstone. "It seems to me the situation is pretty farfetched as it is. What have you got, Judd?"

"Mr. President, for quite some time there has been in several research centers increasing interest in the nature of the paranormal or parasensory functions of the human mind. Some researchers anticipate a time when a person of superior parasensory powers might appear."

Thomas Cordero Heathstone looked intently at Judd. "General, you seem to be suggesting something pretty outlandish. Do you . . . ?"

Judd took a deep breath, sought Elizabeth's eyes briefly, and said, "We, that is, I hypothesize that . . . well, now I am out on that limb, Mr. President. I hypothesize the possibility that some sort of superpsychic has appeared and, ah, psyched out the plans to Tonopah and Tolkien."

A silence filled the presidential office.

Mead and Provost exchanged glances. Walters gazed furiously out the window. Heathstone regarded Judd without moving. After a pause, while disbelief visibly flickered across his face, he turned to Coogan.

"Dr. Coogan," he said slowly, "do you subscribe to this hypothesis?"

"There exists, Mr. President," Coogan responded, "an amazing collection of events, all of which would instantly be explained if it were valid."

"But, Dr. Coogan, do you indeed think it is valid?"

"Yes, I do," she confessed, her bearing concealing her moment's hesitation. Judd smiled at her.

"Really, Mr. President!" said Walters, jumping from his chair.

"Chester, sit down and shut up," Heathstone said

brusquely. "I am familiar with the reputations and qualifications of both General Judd and Dr. Coogan. I want to hear what they have to say." Walters resumed his seat.

"I am totally unfamiliar with this psychic business, Dr. Coogan," Heathstone said. "Can you give me a rationale of some sort that will make comprehension a little easier?"

"Certainly, Mr. President. For some time now sensible scientists have acknowledged the concept of the probability of human mental potential that can transcend ordinary laws of matter, energy, space, and time. This has only been a probability, but quantum mechanics—that branch of physics dealing with nonmaterial interactions—firmly indicates the probability of events that do not at all obey space and time relationships as we have known them during the Age of Reason, nor the concept of a solely visible and material universe."

"What you're saying is, they guess there might be something they've got no way of knowing about?" Heathstone looked dubiously at her.

"Uh, Mr. President . . . look, if someone had tried to explain modern quantum theory to a scientist even a hundred years back he would probably have dismissed it as mystical nonsense, something that didn't fit in with what he thought had been the experience of his life."

Thomas Cordero Heathstone regarded her solemnly. "Are you saying, Dr. Coogan, that we should pay attention to past scientific mistakes in understanding and include the hypothesis of this, er, superpsychic in our present difficulty?"

"I think so, Mr. President. There is no doubt that research both here and in Russia is making advances in parasensory phenomena. The weaponry of Tonopah and Tolkien are semipsychic in basis. It is reasonable to assume that somewhere a person, or a group, might have developed extended awarenesses for which we would have no explanation in our current concepts of the powers of the mind."

Heathstone nodded and turned to Judd. "All right," he said. "I assume, General Judd, that you have some facts that might back up your hypothesis."

"Yes, Mr. President. I'll have my aide, Lieutenant Abrams, deliver a written summary to you this afternoon. Basically, it is the quality and scope of, ah, the espionage that gives a fundamental clue. Intelligence has turned up no flaw in the security surrounding Tonopah, and if it were any sort of espionage we are familiar with, it would have to be of a scope so huge that not all of it could remain hidden from our investigators. And, as you know, the plans for the Tonopah site and research specifications were broken up into several sections and held under tight security in several different places. We have not turned up one iota of a lead."

"O.K.," said Heathstone. "Assuming there is something in your hypothesis, would we be dealing with one person or a group?"

"Really, Mr. President," interrupted Mead, "surely you're not going along with this bizarre idea?"

"No, Seth, I'm not going along with anything. But I know we're in a strange situation, the results of which could be catastrophic. Our relations with Russia might go completely asunder at any moment, if they haven't already."

"Granted, Mr. President," Mead replied. "But psychic intervention, of all things!"

"I would like you to understand, Mr. President," Walters interjected, "that Judd's opinion does not constitute an official opinion of the Department of Defense."

"Gentlemen," Heathstone replied softly, but firmly, "I am not a scientist, but it is my understanding that the dream of science is to understand the workings of nature, of the universe in which we find ourselves. A great impediment to this understanding is the nature of understanding itself. It varies with each person. Understanding involves an explanation in terms of notions, ideas, and principles which the person has come to accept, whether it be scientist or layman. My experience has been that people usually accept these ideas or notions when they are too young to question them. But once having grown to maturity, when men might have reason to question their ideas of existence, they have become so familiar with them that it seems unnecessary to question their ideas any further.

"Now, in my opinion, we are dealing with a situation to which we must bring some sort of new understanding. In the last few days I have consulted dozens of experts, all of whom assume the situation is deteriorating rapidly, and none of whom can offer much of a constructive approach, except to advise me to hit the Russians with our strike potential before they use theirs on us. If down in your bones you feel that a fresh explanation is not to be entertained, I fully realize that it is difficult to get beyond your bones. I will respect your views, but I will not be badgered in my office. Since I invited General Judd and Dr. Coogan to give me the benefit of their ideas, I assume you will allow me to obtain those ideas without further objections to their content."

Thomas Cordero Heathstone settled comfortably back in his chair, but his ice-cold eyes fully reflected his state of mind. None present cared to challenge him further.

"Mr. President," said Allan Provost, speaking for the first time, "we at the National Security Council have for a long time been tangentially interested in the possibilities of psychic intervention in national security codes and communications. If that ever became possible, the entire security of the government would be jeopardized. With your permission, I should like to inquire of the general if he has any indication that something like this has happened."

"Yes, Mr. Provost," responded Judd, promptly. "The telex print-out, seemingly in every part of the world serviced by cable or microwave communications systems, apparently was accomplished through some sort of general knowledge of classified as well as public computer communications access codes."

"Good God! Do you have any idea how that was done?"

"No, sir. Only that the concept of psychic penetration explains the way it seems to have been pulled off. And nothing else does."

"Am I to understand from this, General," Heathstone asked, "that whether the explanation is psychic—uncomfortable word, isn't it, Chester?—intervention, or some straightforward espionage is involved, that this nation's classified coding systems have been invaded?"

"I think that's what we have to assume, Mr. President," Judd responded.

"But surely this implies some long-planned, massive espionage penetrations?" Mead said.

"That would be the case, Mr. Secretary," stated Coogan, "if we consider it only a matter of the laborious enterprise of accumulating the necessary codes. But since security codes are changed periodically, perhaps daily in some cases, to prevent just such penetration . . . well, it has to be something else."

"But, ah, *psychic*," Mead said, mouthing the word with distaste. "Well, I just don't think such a thing is possible."

"Quite right, Mr. Secretary," Coogan said. "On the available evidence, it's hard to accept this explanation. Some psychics have demonstrated remarkable abilities at times, but no one has ever demonstrated a consistent, reliable parasensory talent of any kind. So, if we are to consider psychic intervention, we can't possibly use our general concept of psychic abilities as a basis. We have to face it that we're confronted with something new. I can only hypothesize either that someone, somewhere, found out some significant key to the development of psychic abilities, or that some gigantic step in evolution has taken place in someone."

"Which idea do you favor?" asked the President.

"Either one is worthy of consideration," stated Coogan. "But what we are involved with, essentially, is the advent of some unknown entity, an entity that man cannot control. Whether this is a matter of someone making a radical discovery or an evolutionary jump is beside the point. Whatever the entity is, it is manipulating us, and that is what we have to deal with."

Silence engulfed the presidential office, broken only by the thunder outside and rain beating against the windows.

"Of course," began the President, "I cannot accept at face value the actuality of this, umm, entity. But if one did exist, could you speculate on the motives for his, or its, recent actions?"

"I've thought about that, of course," Coogan said. "We can consider the possibility of a psychotic with megalomaniacal fantasies, or a person possessed of deluded concepts of humanitarianism. The Tonopah and Tolkien devices are, well, inhuman enough to occasion that sort of response."

"You know," Judd said, somewhat defensively, "whoever it is is only asking for a peculiar form of disarmament, which is something a lot of people are for."

"You can't disarm when the enemy is armed!" Walters said in a near shout.

"Well . . . he's been fair in a way in demanding that both the Russians and us . . ." began Judd, but stopped as he heard his own words.

For the second time, an ominous silence gripped the room, broken finally by the President:

"I can't say that I buy your entire package, General Judd, but at least for the first time I can grasp the security fundamentals involved, which seem to have been compromised. I'd like both of you, General Judd and Dr. Coogan, to really go to work on this possibility. I am sure, Chester, that your department will give them whatever they need."

"As you wish, Mr. President," acceded Walters, thinly.

"Mr. Provost, if it were necessary, what would the optimum procedures be for periodically altering national security codings?" Heathstone asked.

"Without causing confusion, every six hours, Mr. President. But you would have to give an executive order for that. Normally, this would only be done in case of war, on our own continent, to thwart the enemy should codes fall into their hands."

"O.K., Allan, when you leave here, please do that. If there is easy, but unauthorized, access to these security codes, at least this might hamper whoever is doing it."

"Yes, Mr. President," agreed Provost, shaking his head in disbelief.

The President, who was about to say something, was interrupted by Hedy Allison's unannounced entrance.

"Sorry to disturb you, Mr. President, but I thought you would like to know."

"Yes, Hedy, what is it?"

"Well, the telephones are starting to ring, the press, you know, asking about this new telex that seems to be coming out."

All eyes turned to her.

"Yes, Hedy, what do you mean?" Heathstone asked.

"Well, something—I don't understand it—about taking down the Tonopah and Tolkien satellites or they and their development centers will be destroyed at midnight tomorrow. Hector Allymany is waiting to see you immediately. He seems very disturbed."

Yet another silence possessed the presidential office.

Walters rose from his chair, disbelief etched on his face. "But I can't believe . . ." he began.

The President, breaking through his own astonishment, turned to Judd.

"To destroy the satellites, General, is that possible?" he asked.

Judd drew his shoulders up, pursing his lips. "I don't know, Mr. President. He would have to interfere with and alter the orbiting sequences of the satellites. Possibly."

"Mr. President," gasped Walters, "the ground base for Tonopah is at Omaha, at SAC!"

"That's true, Mr. President," confirmed Judd. "Tonopah was moved to Air Force Research there. That location was selected because of its impregnable security, top of the priority movement plans for Tonopah, should it become necessary."

Thomas Cordero Heathstone closed his eyes momentarily, his hand fluttering to his forehead, his lips pulled back from his teeth.

"Hedy," he finally said, "where is the Vice-President right now?"

"He's here in Washington, Mr. President. I think he's getting ready for his noon luncheon and talk to the Daughters of the American Revolution."

"Has Hornsborough made any progress in Moscow about getting in touch with Tosygen?"

"Yes, Mr. President. Helena just told me that the hot line is being routed to wherever it is the Premier has gone. The ambassador is standing by to confirm this."

Heathstone turned to Allan Provost. "Allan, I want you to go directly from here to the Vice-President. Do not use the telephone or any form of mechanical communication. Collect him and his family. No packing or anything. Go directly with him to Andrews Air Force Base. Put them on an Air Force jet and lift them to—where was it?— Deeprock."

"But, Mr. President, what about you?" asked Seth Mead.

"I'll secure the presidential succession, Seth, but I'll be damned if I'm going to run myself," snorted Heathstone. "On your way, Allan. In the next half hour I'll make out a list of others on my staff who will join the Vice-President at Deeprock."

Provost hesitated.

"Move your ass, Allan!" Heathstone's lips were drawn thin. Provost left the office immediately.

"Chester," said Heathstone, turning to the Secretary of Defense, "I don't want a red alert at SAC, but I want it deployed to its alternate locations."

"I understand, Mr. President," acknowledged Walters.

"And, Chester," Heathstone continued, "can we get some sort of system set up in my briefing room? I want a communications center hooked up with all satellite tracking stations. I want to know immediately if any of them begin to receive any sort of unauthorized instructions."

"Should we disarm them, Mr. President?" Walters asked.

"I don't see how we can, Chester, unless I can get Tosygen to disarm theirs simultaneously."

Heathstone turned to Hedy Allison. "Ask Hector to do the best he can with the press for the time being, Hedy. Then request my advisory staff and military assistants to meet me in one hour in the briefing room. After that, ask the Russian ambassador here in Washington to call on me at his earliest convenience. Seth, I want you to stand by to fly up to the United Nations at a moment's notice, and I want an open line between my briefing room and the Secretary General's office."

"I understand, Mr. President," Mead said, rising to leave.

The President turned to Judd and Coogan. "Have you any idea how to go about finding . . . ?"

"Mr. President, we'll go to work on this immediately," Judd said.

"I'm not buying your idea completely, General. But I want you and Dr. Coogan—get whatever help you need, I'm sure Chester will cooperate even if it goes against his grain—to see if you can turn up something."

"Yes, Mr. President," Judd said, rising to leave.

"We still know too little about all this," Heathstone continued. "So I think I'll have to take a chance and hope you can fill in some of the unknowns."

He turned to Hedy Allison. "Ask Helena to get Ambassador Hornsborough on the line, Hedy. I want to talk directly to him."

Judd and Coogan left the office with Chester B. Walters.

"I hope you're happy you've got the President backing you on this mystical nonsense of yours, Judd. If you don't find something, you're going to make Defense the laughingstock of this government."

"Yes, sir," said Judd. "I understand that very well."

11:20 A.M.

"Hey, Shirley, can you grab a long lunch hour?"

"If *you* can, Joe, sure. How'd you manage to get your general to let you off the leash for once?"

"Well . . . there was some special duty, but nobody has to be at the office right now. My place at one, O.K.?"

"I'll be there, Joe."

Shirley Paars hung up her phone, consulted her watch, and sought her supervisor, who gladly agreed to her taking some accrued sick leave for the rest of the day to avoid hearing the torrent of female complaints she poured out to him. In any case, he felt, efficient though she was, an office without Shirley in it was a more cheerful place.

12:45 P.M.

"Ah, Joe, that was . . . you are something else."

"No, that's you, Shirley . . . you make me feel so . . . I don't know what, but every time I'm with you, it's like I'd come home after a long time away."

The thin keening of rage and hate that was never very far beneath Shirley Paars' consciousness strengthened until she felt almost gleeful. The fatuousness of the man, his weight on her, his invasion of her, the stink of him that covered her in the Washington noon heat were like a stinging mustard plaster that invigorated her while it outraged her. Abrams, Abrams, if you knew what I'm doing to you. . . .

"Joe . . . you don't know how that makes me feel, hearing you say that. It's like . . . well, that's why I'm a woman, almost, so I can make a man—make you—feel that way. Oh, I'm so *glad* we could be together right now, give ourselves a, what was that song they had when I was a kid, afternoon delight?"

"Skyrockets in flight, *yeah!*"

"Joe, usually you're tied to that DARPA office nine to five solid, and right on through to midnight, unless you're lucky." She turned and raised herself above him, brushing breasts along his crinkled chest hair.

"Oh, you know . . ." Abrams tried to evade the question, then found his heart pounding as the engorged nipples slid back and forth across his chest.

"Mmm?"

"Big conference, all the brass, the President on down, you know?"

2:00 P.M.

"Mr. Nashirah? Shirley Paars. The President's prepared to accept the possibility of psychic intervention in the situation and has high-level agreement. . . . Yes, the usual source . . ."

As she spoke, lying in her tub, Shirley ran her tongue over her teeth, savoring the sharp edges the tender flesh traversed. Her right hand held the telephone receiver; the left passed a soaped abrasive cloth rhythmically over her body, cleansing, scraping, hurting.

COLLEGE PARK, MARYLAND

At noon on August 21 the maintenance schedule for Neomort 25-A called for electronic stimulation of the nervous system as well as mechanical and manual massage of its muscles.

The nude body had been detached from the wire leads connecting it to the majority of the computer attendant systems. The reclining pedestal stood at nearly a ninety-degree angle. The facial skin had drawn somewhat taut and was ivory pale, nearly luminescent. Its strong lips, slightly parted, were darkly etched against its beatific inner light, the close-fitting respirator hugging its chest, forcing the air in and out of the mouth as well as through the nasal passages. The long, flowing hair of the former rock star had been close-cropped around the skull.

"Really!" commented Dr. Edgar Crathe, attendant in charge of Neomort 25-A, "he looks like an extraterrestrial in suspended animation, almost as if he were waiting to reach a new universe to come to life." His admiration for the cadaver, somewhat beyond medical interest, was obvious.

Crathe was of utmost importance to Neomort 25-A, and the consciousness hovering near was very careful to monitor the body, keeping it respectably dead in Crathe's presence. But it also had probed deeply into the man's inner nature.

All the neomorts residing in the bioemporium were naked except for their costumes of wires, monitors, respirators, and electronic analyzers. Most looked desiccated, their overall biophysical character declining. These were scheduled for dismemberment and autopsy. But others were healthy, almost robust, and with their futuristic appurtenances appeared like androids or robots awaiting commands to move and function.

Because the temperature of the cubicles was kept at a constant 96°, the attendants dressed in swimsuits, often very brief, except when dissecting or dismembering to acquire parts of bodies for experimental transplants to others. Female attendants were likely to appear in pink Schiaparelli bikinis, whereas the males seemed to prefer, as a group, the sheer white stretch nylon favored by long-distance swimmers. All were deeply tanned from the ultra-violet bursts.

Neomort 25-A had observed that Crathe was unbalanced psychologically in several directions, but especially in his intense sadistic and emotional love for dead male bodies. Crathe, of course, kept this part of his emotional spectrum carefully suppressed, never molesting the experimental models in the bioemporium, going instead to certain mortu-aries in the Washington area known in the necrophiliac un-derground to accept payment for allowing intimacies with the newly dead before embalming.

As usual, when upkeep of the neomort was taking place, the actions were overseen by Dr. Karin Tomachek, chief researcher of the bioemporium. Tomachek, an immigrant from Poland, had, in fact, founded the bioemporium con-cept and single-handedly gathered together the vast funds necessary for its fruition at Trans-American.

She frowned at Crathe's open admiration for Neomort 25-A. "You know we are not supposed to personalize the specimens," she said, occupying herself with applying elec-trodes to various parts of the legs, electrodes that adminis-tered low-voltage currents that vivified the body's nervous system.

Dr. Edgar Crathe pursed his lips in disdain at Toma-chek's turned back and made a vulgar motion with his hand. Yet he could not completely conceal his emotional attraction to this special cadaver.

Crathe, a tall young man with dark, curling hair, was also an anatomical genius who had excelled in his premedi-cal and internship work. Tomachek appreciated this talent in him, preferring to ignore his sexual and necrophiliac at-traction for male corpses. If such tendencies existed in her-self, she suppressed them well, and when they arose in members of her staff, most of whom had some unacknowl-edged motivation for working with the dead, she merely lectured them and pretended not to see open demonstra-tions when they occurred. Any staff member caught in some sort of perverted liaison with a specimen was summa-rily dismissed.

She busied herself, assisted by Crathe when necessary, first with the peripheral parts of the central nervous sys-tem, gently stimulating the motor fibers going out from the system to muscles and glands. To accomplish this stimulation, she applied the electrodes to the skin in close proximity to the nerve trunks. This she did all over the body, asking Crathe to lift it first on one side and then on the other so she could tend to the shoulders, back, buttocks, and calves. Then she turned her attention to the sensory fibers coming into the central nervous system from peripheral sense organs and repeated the procedure. She monitored her electronic manipulations on chart recorders mounted near the body for that purpose.

Surveying the masses of paper feeding out, she shook her head finally, her voice somewhat tremulous with amazement. "I can't understand how this specimen is not declining and cutting off those nerve sectors we would normally expect to fail. The spinal nerves, the spinal cord, the brain stem, and even the cerebellum and cerebrum seem in excellent condition."

"Well, perhaps because there was hardly any damage to the body when it died," Crathe volunteered.

"Perhaps, perhaps. Well, at any rate, the computers say the specimen is in perfect working order. I'll leave you to execute the manual massages alone. Be sure you manipulate all the muscles and joints by hand. We will take a neuronal decrease count this afternoon."

"Very good, Doctor," Crathe agreed eagerly.

Rendering hand massages to the corpses was Crathe's favorite pastime. To him, there was nothing else as singularly rewarding. The body lay supine beneath his probing fingers, offering no resistance, no communication, no responses. And every inch of muscle, joint, and orifice had to be probed or pummeled.

As usual he began with the fingers and toes, then moved to the major muscles and joints. Neomort 25-A was the most precious body in the bioemporium. He licked his lips again and again as he worked over the cadaver.

The thought patterns comprising the entity dwelling now quite comfortably exterior to Neomort 25-A watched the procedures from a nodule of awareness not to be perceived by physical sensory systems. It carefully monitored the minute neuronal changes taking place in the body systems as a result of the electrical and manual stimulations. Considerable will and effort were required to prevent the cortex from firing its synapses as the body was artificially stimulated. This was crucial. If the brain became active, the attached electroencephalograph would immediately respond, indicating active brain waves. Everyone would instantly know that Neomort 25-A was not dead, was not a neomort at all.

The mind entity had satisfied itself that the nervous system of its physical body resembled merely another computer, a complex system to be sure, but a computer nevertheless. Its essential components were nerve cells or neurons, slightly over ten times ten billion of them. And in the short time available the entity had categorized a great portion of them. It had located the relatively simple chains of neurons within the spinal cord controlling involuntary acts. It found it could monitor these once it had understood the speed at which the impulses from and to these neurons moved, a velocity of about two hundred miles an hour.

The entity had traced the spinal nerves emerging in pairs from either side of the spinal cord, and also the motor fibers that controlled the skeletal muscles, the internal organs, the muscles themselves, and finally the skin. The thinnest of these delicate tracings throughout the body were only about one-thousandth of a millimeter in diameter, whereas others were several times that size. It had followed the course of this intricate system upward into the large opening at the base of the skull to the foramen magnum and had begun inspecting the fascinating avenues winding into, out of, and around the brain.

The mind entity monitored the millions of cells in the cerebral cortex. It developed its abilities to control the electrical activity of that organ, far beyond simple suppression of electrical activity in the brain—the voluntary psychokinetic trick it had learned to do as Dan Merriweather and the prime factor enabling it to have the Merriweather body declared dead and stored for safekeeping in the world's most advanced bioemporium.

But it now also had to perceive, study, and assume control of certain neuronal actions. It had to monitor proteins, fats, and carbohydrates, the essential building blocks for cells, helping the body repair damaged neurons. It had to watch very carefully the entire body's oxygen quota, assuring sufficient quantities of that precious gas to the brain.

Thus, while Crathe was working on the Merriweather body, the floating intelligence guarding it was almost totally preoccupied with suppressing any electrical activity that would warn first the attending computers and then Crathe himself that Neomort 25-A was *not* a neomort.

After Dr. Karin Tomachek had turned over the cadaver to the ministrations of the necrophiliac Crathe, the monitoring mind entity relaxed its vigilance somewhat. Its awareness was almost completely absorbed by the neuronal activities within the body. So it was not fully cognizant of the emotional response that manipulating the neomort was bringing about in Crathe. It did not perceive fast enough the change of the manipulating hands from professional massaging to touches of sensual pleasure.

Crathe momentarily allowed himself to be consumed with lust for Neomort 25-A, finally surrendering to the electrifying desire mounting within him. He touched his own quivering lips to the stonelike lips of the cadaver.

Somewhat over a million neurons habitually monitoring the sensual systems of the cadaver's lips flared instantly into action. A flood of electrical activity cascaded in blinding force into the brain, stimulating electrical activity of the appropriate cells in the cerebral cortex. This sudden flood of unexpected activity inundated the entire cortex, activating the central nervous system, automatically twitching the body's motor fibers.

The body tensed. Its eyes fluttered open, the pupils readjusting to focus on the startled eyes of Dr. Edgar Crathe, his own body instantly frozen in shock. The alabaster skin of Neomort 25-A deepened into a rose-red flush of embarrassment. The electroencephalograph recording the neomort's electrical brain impulses instantly clattered into activity. A complete spectrum of all brain-wave frequencies and amplitudes spun out on the paper-filled chart recorders and into the recording and coding banks of the attending computers.

The mind entity monitoring the body was astonished at its momentary loss of control. Instantly, it totally interiorized into the body and mobilized its psychic forces to recompose the body into its cadaveric state within fractions of a second.

Dr. Edgar Crathe yelped and jumped back with a high-pitched scream. He fell backward over some wire leads blocking his retreat and ended up pressed against a bank of furiously blinking lights, lights indicating that the guardian computers were eagerly trying to locate further telltale signs of life in the body. The LIFE SIGN panel was glowing red.

The incident was over before it had had time to register for what it was in Crathe's mind. He slowly lifted himself to his feet and delicately, uncertainly approached the body, peering anxiously at its face. The body was once more alabaster-complexioned and deathly still.

"Holy cow!" Crathe finally breathed.

He quickly moved to the EEG feed-out, crying aloud when he saw the revealing burst of electrical brain activity. "Oh, God . . ." His hands covered his mouth in disbelief. He thought furiously for a moment. Surely and swiftly he extracted the paper with its revealing traces from the machinery and folded it neatly, placing it in the pocket of his long white coat, which hung on a nearby hook.

He then went and stood in front of Neomort 25-A. He finally smiled. But he did not touch the body again. He noticed the illuminated panel blinking off and on, LIFE SIGN LIFE SIGN, and canceled it. It became once more an opaque opalescent inactive square among a dozen other inactive indicators on the computer's face.

The folded paper in his pocket seemed to glow through the fabric. No one would ever see it! The computer fed the surprising input around in its mechanical banks for a while. Finding no corroborative data incoming from the neomort, it finally filed it under category 00011000, unconfirmed life signs.

WASHINGTON

9:00 P.M.

"Your idea paid off, Dr. Coogan," Abrams informed her and Judd as he burst into the office.

"Who is it?" demanded Judd, rising to his feet.

"Well, sir, actually it turns out not *who* but *they*."

"They?" Judd asked. "You mean there's more than one?"

"Right, sir. Three to be exact. Of course, we don't have all the computer-trainee rosters in yet. As it turns out, there are almost a million people who have studied computers in the last few years—"

"Never mind all that, Abrams. Who are they?"

"Well, sir. Two are women. One is a young woman in the Midwest who volunteered for some psychic experiments at the Minnesota Institute for Psychical Studies. She was planning to become a computer programer, but got married instead. She is in her ninth month of pregnancy at the moment, waiting the birth of her second child. She did not pursue either psychic experimentation or computer programing."

"Doesn't sound very likely, does it, Harrah?" Coogan commented.

"Next?" demanded Judd.

"Second is a sometime psychic who practices giving psychic readings at summer retreats at various psychic seminars. At other times she works in Chicago as a computer programer. I already talked with her on the telephone. She sounds pretty freaky. She got very suspicious about why I was calling and asked if I had anything to do with a Count Omar."

"Who?" Judd asked, bewildered.

"The famous psychic in the South who gives his psychic impressions over television and radio," Coogan informed him.

"Why did she want to know that?" Judd asked.

"She wanted to know if she was going to be invited to perform on Omar's TV show," Abrams said.

"Well, have someone go interview her," ordered Judd in a disappointed voice.

"I already have someone on the way," said Abrams smugly.

"And the third?" asked Coogan.

"Well, now, Dr. Coogan. This one is the most interesting."

"Why is that, Abrams?" Judd asked.

"Well, this one has studied three of the computers you mentioned, Dr. Coogan. You know, the advanced, complicated stuff. He took a lot of the seminars at M.I.T. and went into a doctoral program there, but didn't complete it."

"Ha!" said Coogan.

"And he's into computers enough to have a KB–CRT terminal in his apartment."

"Perfect," Judd said.

"Now, as for parasensory research, he volunteered as a subject for the University of Northern California Biomedical Research Center and apparently demonstrated several

consistent paranormal abilities. U.N.C. published three papers on the work done with him. Here, I have them for
you."

"Well done, Abrams," said Judd, taking the folders.

"What about his records from U.N.C., Abrams?" asked
Coogan. "We'll need the psychological profiles they must
have done on him and complete records of his work."

"Well, the administrative office at U.N.C. tells me that
those records were inadvertently misplaced."

"Goddamn!" Judd grated.

"I pressed them on it, sir, and finally talked with one of
the experimenters. Apparently, the records were stolen at
about the time this guy refused to work with them any
longer."

"Refused?" Coogan asked.

"Seems so, ma'am. There, uh, it's not too clear. I have
asked that researcher to come here to Washington. The
psychic seems to have had a lot of original ideas about research, and there seem to have been several arguments
about in what direction the experimentation should proceed."

"What happened then?" Judd asked.

"Well, apparently he left the laboratories and refused all
invitations to come back."

"Have someone pick him up wherever he is," stated
Judd promptly. "I'll get the necessary warrants if he doesn't
come voluntarily."

"That's going to be tough, sir," Abrams said solemnly.

"Why? Has he vanished?"

"So to speak, sir."

"Goddamn it, Abrams! Out with it."

"Well, sir, his name was Dan Merriweather," Abrams
said, giving special emphasis to the name.

Judd looked at him blankly.

"Who?" he asked. "Is that name supposed to mean
something?"

"Harrah, do you spend all your time here in the bowels
of your office? Dan Merriweather! That marvelous rock
star, the one who composed so many great songs!"

"Oh," Judd said, a faint look of impatience crossing his
face. "I don't like rock music."

"Well, Harrah, Dan Merriweather was hit by a taxi in
New York about—wasn't it about two weeks ago,
Abrams?"

"Yes, ma'am, it was. And he was killed. It made headlines all over."

Without exhibiting the respect that both Abrams and Coogan seemed to think the name of Dan Merriweather warranted, Judd thoughtfully resumed his seat.

"Thanks a lot, Abrams. You give me what looks like a hot lead, then tell me he's dead. There's no one else? No one *alive,* that is?"

"Not so far, sir. But we are still canvassing computer training schools and comparing names with those we have managed to reconstruct in Dr. Coogan's files."

"Let's also check known revolutionaries and all the usual categories against the same names. Look also for close relatives of psychics or psychic subjects who are on the radical fringes."

"Yes, sir. We've been working on that for two weeks, almost ever since the yellow-folder sequence."

"Nothing?"

"No, sir. Nothing."

AUGUST 22

WASHINGTON

10:00 A.M.

> DISARM AND RECALL TONOPAH AND TOLKIEN SATEL-
> LITES. INTERCEPT DESTRUCT COMMAND PROCEDURES
> IN EFFECT TWELVE MIDNIGHT EST AUGUST 22. TAR-
> GETS TONOPAH TOLKIEN DEVELOPMENT CENTERS
> OMAHA AND NOVOSIBIRSK.

The new message was brief, unlike the other complex telex communication that had been pages long, revealing the plans and specifications of the two novel forms of weaponry being developed by the United States and the Soviet Union.

The repercussions to date had been confused in their nature, mainly sporadic rioting and United Nations scare-conferences, but the threatened destruction of two cities within the borders of the world's two most powerful nations changed everything.

A suppressed, unbelieving pandemonium raged in the capital of the United States. At the Pentagon, most employees, mystified about the nature of the events, clung magnetically to their stations, and no one went home at the close of work. Congress, recessed for the summer, was regrouping itself through heavy rain in Washington for an extraordinary session to discuss no one knew exactly what.

At the White House, butlers were hard put to it merely to keep ashtrays empty and to mop up after legions of consultants who brought floods of dripping rainwater with them, soaking the American Indian rugs. The chief butler, worn to a frazzle, finally ordered them rolled up and brought out hundreds of yards of rubber matting to keep the worried conferees from slipping on the white marble floors. The chief usher, himself harried after two sleepless days and nights, finally had requested two additional squads

of Marine honor guards in an effort to keep order and had
gone to sleep.

In the Oval Office, after a two-hour telephone conversation with U.N. Secretary General Ehrenwald, whose voice
was almost completely gone, Seth Mead gave a brief report
to the President.

"From the trend of things, it looks like the U.N. may
really begin to insist on a policed arms moratorium," he
said. "Apparently, the fact that there may be weapons that
can monkey around with their minds seems to have energized them for once into a cohesive group."

"You'll have to deal with that yourself," Heathstone told
him bluntly. "I have to give an explanation to the British
and Chinese ambassadors about Tonopah, and they are
going to try to pin me between an opening and closing
door."

In another part of the White House, Hector Allymany,
on his way to the press briefing room, prepared himself for
his third general press confrontation.

Allymany had never dreamed, when he had entered
journalism twelve years before, that he would ever become
a presidental press secretary and had accepted the post
only because his wife was overcome with joy at the prospect of having access to White House social circles. He had
wanted to be a foreign correspondent—his dreams included
travel, adventure, and learning something about tribal societies in obscure parts of the planet. His mistake had been
in writing a book about the change in journalistic goals
that had occurred in the sixties and early seventies. With
the advent of television, from which everyone could obtain
liberal, continual, and vividly presented doses of violence,
crime, and disaster, both on the dramatic programs and on
news shows, what the papers could find to print lost its
impact. The press, seeking to extend the importance of its
profession, had seized on the tactic of exposé, with its
members making news as much as reporting it. *The Wood-
stein Effect* had hit best-seller lists early and stayed on for a
year, establishing Allymany as an authority and then a
"very important" man in journalism, as *Time* magazine
had labeled him when they did a cover story, and finally
the logical choice of an innovative new President for press
secretary. Allymany felt Heathstone was a difficult challenge, since the Indian was, for the most part, inscrutable
and did not usually cooperate with what he often consid-

ered meddlesome and impertinent press demands. Especially in this present crisis, Heathstone had not yet favored either the gathered press people or Allymany himself with any statement about the situation.

He entered the choking atmosphere of the press briefing room. The representative of Associated Press, a liberated, large-bosomed woman, spotted him first and got her question in before anyone else could peer through the smoke and see he was there.

"What the hell is going on?" AP screeched.

Hector Allymany did not have any clear answer to that question but, as the President had ordered him to do, he tried as best he could to cope with the situation. "Uh . . ." he said, hoping that one of AP's rivals would break in with something he could field.

"Mr. Allymany," asked the representative of UPI, his voice rising above the noise, "I think it is time someone in authority told us whether or not we are at war with Russia."

"We are not at war with Russia," replied Allymany firmly.

"Then with whom are we at war?"

"We are not at war at all. To the best of my knowledge," he added; it wouldn't do to go too far out on a limb.

"Then what the hell is going *on*?"

"I am sure Mr. Heathstone will talk to you soon. He has asked me to bear with him because of lack of time in this stress to turn his attention to the media, and as a result I have to ask all you ladies and gentlemen of the press to bear with him."

"That is not an answer," the woman from Associated Press pointed out.

"If it isn't Russia," shouted a voice from the back of the room, "then who is it that's going to destroy Omaha, and why?"

"I have no immediate comment on that," Allymany responded, mopping his face with his clean white handkerchief, "except to assume that this threat must certainly be an empty, uh, threat."

"Then why is it," continued the woman from AP, "that our sources confirm that SAC is being evacuated?"

"I do not know that SAC is being evacuated," Mr. Allymany responded.

"Who is it that is responsible for the leaks in the security of this so-called Project Tonopah?" demanded the UPI man.

"All available personnel have been assigned to give us all an answer to that question as soon as possible."

"Mr. Allymany," asked AP loudly, "when Mr. Heathstone *does* talk to us, will he comment on the disgusting nature of the Tonopah devices? I am sure the American public would like to know exactly why public funds are being used to develop such inhuman weaponry."

"I cannot at this time advise you on the exact content of the President's comment. I assume it is likely that Mr. Heathstone will refer to the nature of the Tonopah devices. I have been advised by Senator Heston Davis, chairman of the Congressional Subcommittee on Science, that it was necessary to develop microwave technologies as a complement to balance the power potential of the Russian Tolkien devices."

"Do you mean to say," asked UPI angrily, "that the government puts any stock in that Russian guff about long-distance hypnotic telepathy?"

"I do not know to what degree the concerned branches of our government give credibility to such technologies." Allymany spoke as quickly as he could, loading his answer with officialese in the hope that the numbing flood of formal jargon would slow his questioners down while they digested it. "But, overall, the nuclear bomb strike potential is outdated, since fallout cannot be contained and is likely to contaminate the entire planet in the event several bombs were detonated simultaneously. Other types of weaponry obviously would come into existence, types of weaponry whose effects could be controlled."

"But we are talking about weapons that are apparently meant to influence the brains of humans everywhere!" shouted the woman from AP, who had evidently followed him all too closely. "Who could possibly justify such weapons! This is worse than germ warfare ever was!"

"Madam," Allymany responded weakly, "I do not have at hand suitable responses for your question. Please bear with the President. I'll let you know immediately when he will talk with you."

Hector Allymany left the briefing room without waiting for further comment. In the antechamber he stopped short, closing his eyes. After a moment's pause, he placed his forehead against the cool wall and allowed his body to shake. The tremors passed quickly. He composed himself and went to join the sizable crowd in the reception area outside the President's office.

11:30 A.M.

"Mr. President," shouted David P. Hornsborough III through the static-filled transatlantic communication lines, "I have learned that the Moscow-Washington hook-up is being resumed from the Crimean area and will be operational in an hour or so. Mr. Tosygen wonders if you would be available for a conversation then?"

"Most definitely, David," responded Thomas Cordero Heathstone.

"The Premier thinks there should be no use of scramblers since the topic of the conversation is already public knowledge."

"I will route the call through to the briefing room here," agreed Heathstone, "and we will have an open discussion—Mr. Tosygen and I and our respective staffs."

"I am sure that will meet with the Premier's approval," Hornsborough said. Then, softly and somewhat confidentially, "Thomas, what really is going on? Moscow is under tight martial law. I am not sure whether I'm a diplomat being guarded or a prisoner."

"How is the situation there, David, exactly?" Heathstone asked.

"There has been gunfire the last few days. It stopped and everything's quiet now. But no services at all are working." He paused. "Can whoever it is really interfere with those devices, Thomas?"

"Seems totally implausible, doesn't it, David?"

"Yes, Mr. President, I just can't believe any of this."

12:00 NOON

Abrams was disheveled, a gloss of sleeplessness highlighting his features. The immaculate appearance characteristic of him only a few days ago seemed to be a thing of another age. The present era was characterized by sweat-stained armpits and open collar with a fluttering, neglected tie and coffee stains down the front of his shirt.

"Well," he said, his usual brisk manner showing no trace of the hectic pace he had kept up these last days, "we know where the Soviets have moved *their* superweapon development site to, don't we?"

In appearance, General Harrah Judd surpassed Abrams' disorder. He sat behind his desk poring over a pile of mysterious, sometimes pointless, reports, his muscular torso covered only by an undershirt. Dr. Elizabeth Coogan sat behind her temporary desk aloof from the heaps of papers and books in front of her, her thoughts wandering, following some sequence of her own, looking for a new approach.

Abrams' cheerful comment was received in silence. He changed his tactic. "Well, sir," he said smartly, "I think we're in real trouble this time."

This ploy got his hearers' attention.

"Lay it out," Judd said, lazily leaning back in his chair.

"Well, it would take weeks to plot all the possibilities of where and how this, er, psychic might be able to interfere with satellite performance."

"Is it possible for you to be brief?" Judd asked.

"No, sir, not on this one."

"O.K., continue."

"Well, first of all, we could try to break apart interlinking computer systems. This maneuver might localize the activity of the interloper, who presumably is operating from some given place. In this way, we might even locate the area where he is."

"I don't think you should depend on that at all," Coogan interrupted. "We have the psychokinetic reach to consider. That might work over great distances."

"Well, I assumed that also, ma'am. But it was a good thought while it lasted, wasn't it?"

"Yes, Abrams, positively idyllic," Judd said.

"Well, then, there is a link between the U.S.S.R. and American satellite systems. This is the Washington-Moscow meteorological communications line that became operational in late 1964, its establishment being part of the U.S.–U.S.S.R. program for cooperation in space exploration. This system is an adjunct to that system comprised of the communications link for the Moscow-Paris hook-up, with one ground terminal at Moscow and another at Pleumeur-Bodou in France. This system becomes planetary because that same antenna at Pleumeur-Bodou is used in conjunction with NASA and Comsat communications vehicles."

Abrams paused, waiting to see if his information had made a suitable impact on his audience. Both Coogan and Judd looked at him blankly. He went on.

"Now, the Space Tracking and Data Acquisition Network, STADAN, gets involved in this. It's a NASA network with ground stations in the U.S. and overseas which are always busy tracking and gathering data from unmanned satellites. It utilizes fourteen electronic stations that communicate with satellites by radio. After that, all these stations interlock here and there with the Initial Defense Communications Satellite Program." Abrams breathed deeply.

"God!" Coogan said, awed.

"This system," Abrams continued, "is the Department of Defense global communications system. Over the Pacific alone there seem to be fifty-five satellites now orbiting. For some reason, I can't quite get anyone to tell me how many there are over the Atlantic, and the ones orbiting the polar routes seem to be equally highly classified. I was asked for my 'need-to-know' clearances, et cetera, and still haven't gotten any answers."

Coogan giggled. "Sounds as if the future of the world is going to be a quagmire of superimposed networks, and no one is going to have any control at all. Just eternally trying to find out who is hooked up to whom."

"You're supposed to be the computer expert, Coogan," said Judd. "Don't you have all this at your fingertips?"

"I'm an expert in computers, not in what's been done with them," she snapped back, lighting a cigarette.

"Shall I continue, sir?" asked Abrams.

"By all means, by all means. Get us as deep as you want in the network quagmires."

"Right, sir! Well, the DARPA net figures into all this—that's the computerized communications network that interlinks all the Defense Advanced Research Projects Agency's research installations. It's quite huge, as you know, sir."

"The DARPA net *is* huge, isn't it, Harrah? And strategic, too." Coogan's eyes narrowed speculatively.

"That's right, ma'am," responded Abrams. "Hooks up just about everything. From the Pentagon to the Rand Institute to the University of Southern California to Stanford to Moffett Field to the UNIVAC at Illinois to Lincoln and Omaha to Harvard and Aberdeen to London and Hawaii."

"All *right,* Abrams," Judd said. "Enough, enough!"

Abrams looked fruitlessly for a convenient place to put his sheaf of papers among the high mounds of paper already filling the top of the general's desk.

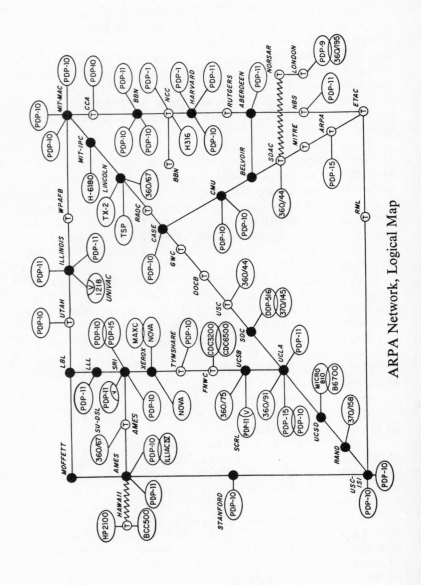

ARPA Network, Logical Map

"The problem here," Judd said thoughtfully, "is that no one is trying to be creative. We're all running around to find out how this bastard is doing what he is doing, whatever it is. How do you fight an invisible mind that apparently can be anywhere it wants at any time? It's like going up against The Shadow."

"Right, sir."

"Let's speculate, Abrams," Judd said. "If this guy were going to figure out how to interfere with the Tonopah and Tolkien satellites, where would be the most likely place for him to intervene?"

"I suppose in the flight command centers that monitor them, sir. Ours is Goddard Space Flight Center in Greenbelt, Maryland."

"Right. There are, if I recall, at least two in Russia. One in Moscow itself and another at Vladivostok."

"Wait a minute," Coogan said. "All the top Russians have gone off to the Crimea, isn't that so? Well, you know, that happens to be the location of the Crimean Astrophysical Observatory. They've got a five-hundred-millimeter meniscus telescope—field of vision of fifteen minutes of arc—and it can photograph stars of the smallest magnitudes."

"Is that pertinent?" asked Judd sarcastically.

"Why, yes, General," Coogan said sweetly. "First of all, if the Russian Government has moved to the Crimea, it's likely that the observatory's been converted to a command center and is giving them their data directly about their Tolkien satellites."

"And so?"

"And further, the equipment at the observatory is sensitive enough to track the satellites when they're in view of that side of the planet to within a probable error of determination of only about ten inches."

"And?"

"The Russians will likely control their satellites from there, not Vladivostok or Moscow. It's hooked up with their other tracking stations around the world and can transmit and exchange the telemetric data needed for satellite functioning."

"So," Judd said. "The Russians are going to depend on the Crimean tracking station, while we are going to use Goddard. And both of us are locked into a worldwide computer net our unseen friend can apparently screw around with any time he feels like it! Could we get anywhere by pulling Goddard out of the computer linkup?"

"He could probably get at the controls inside Goddard itself just as easily," Coogan said. "But there might be a point to it, all the same."

"Oh, they'd never—" Abrams started, scandalized at the thought of asking a governmental body to undo something it had done.

"*What* point?" Judd snapped.

"I've been thinking. We can't just sit around waiting for this guy to act. I was wondering about how we might communicate with him."

"I don't see how, ma'am," Abrams said.

"Now," Coogan began in her best doctorial manner, "if Sirius is somehow monitoring international communications, he's certainly paying attention to such systems as the NASA and DARPA nets. In fact, I should suppose they'd be priority systems for him, since they carry research information."

"Hey, hey," Judd said softly, looking at her with narrowed eyes. "And Goddard's tied in with NASA and DARPA and the whole computer shooting match. . . ."

"I don't know too much about this guy, sir," Abrams muttered. "But if he was interested in talking, seems as if he would already have initiated it. As it is, he is just sitting somewhere giving the world orders."

"True, true, Abrams," Judd agreed. "But since sitting around trying to compare names on pieces of paper hasn't got us anywhere, let's get active and do something. If I read you, Coogan, you're suggesting we disconnect Goddard from the incoming networks. You think he might respond to that?"

"I hope. I can't think of anything else, anyhow."

"What the hell, let's give it a go. At least the bastard'll know we're onto him!"

OMAHA

11:00 A.M.

A palpable nervousness seemed to have settled over Omaha. Overhead, the sky was clear, punctuated with high-flying fleecy clouds. Far to the west, as to the east, out over the endless plains of Nebraska, dark thunderheads lurked, waiting a favorable wind to grasp and push them in the direction of the sprawling city on the Missouri River. For Andros Hellerman, Omaha's mayor, it had been a hectic morning. Nothing had worked right. Part of the city's telephone service was out of order, perhaps because of real mechanical problems or because some of the telephone operators had suddenly decided to make trips to other cities.

But he had finally got through to the commanding officer at Offutt Air Force Base who, Hellerman found out, had nothing to say about the reported evacuation of the Strategic Air Command.

"But hell, man, everyone can see that something important must be happening with you guys out there," protested Hellerman.

"Sorry, sir," came the answer, "I have no comment. Activities at SAC are classified."

Hellerman chewed briefly on his fat cigar.

"Who is your immediate superior?" he demanded.

"That would be the Air Force Chief of Staff, in Washington, sir."

Hellerman hung up without thanking the noncommittal voice. He didn't really understand it all. The city of Omaha had always enjoyed cordial relations with the military installations it housed.

"You better get me the Air Force Chief of Staff in Washington, Lucy," he ordered his secretary. Lucy Agnolini ferreted her way through the telephonic problems of contacting the Air Force Chief of Staff only to discover in the end that official calls from the city of Omaha were being referred directly to the Secretary of Defense, who was in conference and could not be disturbed.

Andros Hellerman reclined in his soft leather chair and began a new cigar.

"I have a Mrs. Guilda Stern on the line," Lucy informed him. "She is the secretary to the Secretary of Defense."

Hellerman grabbed the phone and snapped, "Mrs. Stern, would you tell Chester Walters that his old classmate, Andros Hellerman, mayor of Omaha, would appreciate a moment?"

"Yes, Mr. Mayor. I'll see if I can get him out of the meeting for a few moments."

"Mrs. Stern, can you tell me what is going on?"

Guilda Stern hesitated, tempted to discuss the matter

openly with the mayor. She thought better of it and said, "I think you should have Mr. Walters brief you."

While Hellerman was waiting for Guilda Stern to try to extract Walters, he took a call from Tatum Nelson, governor of Nebraska.

"Andy," shouted Nelson with the energetic voice that had helped sweep him into the gubernatorial mansion, "I have a lot of press people here wanting to know what is going on."

"So have I, Tate."

"What are you doing about it?"

"About *what*, Tate? I don't know what is going on."

"Well, find out! We'll have to make a statement, naturally."

"I'm trying to get Chester Walters on the telephone," Hellerman informed the governor.

"Good. I think we have a civil situation building up that needs to be controlled."

"So do I."

Chester B. Walters finally picked up a distant receiver in the Pentagon, and Hellerman's other phone buzzed.

"Hello, hello, Andy," Walters said. "Long time no see. How is everything out there?"

"That's what I'm calling to ask *you*, Chester. I can't get answers from anyone at all. Why is SAC being evacuated?"

"I couldn't possibly discuss that over the open telephone, Andy, even if I could discuss it at all."

"What about this, ah, well, what about Omaha being destroyed tonight at midnight? Are we at war?"

"Well, Andy, I wouldn't take that seriously at all. There is, as you know, a rumor floating around. But we attribute it to some cranks."

"If you aren't paying any attention to it, then why is SAC being evacuated?"

"Well, Andy, you people just sit tight for a while. I'll fly out to see you when this is all over, and we'll have a good laugh about it."

"O.K., Chester," said Hellerman, dubiously.

He hung up one line and picked up the other.

"Chester says sit tight, Governor," he said.

"We may have to call out the Guard?" Tatum Nelson's voice questioned.

"Let me talk with my chief of police first," acknowledged Hellerman. "Calling out the National Guard might inflame the panic that already seems to be around."

WASHINGTON

1:00 P.M.

The voice of Praskovie Tosygen echoed through the presidential briefing room. A silence fell over the group gathered around the conference table.

"Mr. President," began Tosygen, "I regret that this conversation is necessary at all."

"Thank you, Mr. Premier, so do I," Thomas Cordero Heathstone responded. "Let me begin by saying that I feel the situation to be delicate, and it is my deepest hope that we can reach a prompt understanding."

"I also regret," Tosygen continued, "that the powerful United States of America is playing host to a scheme of espionage unheard of in the annals of history."

"The United States of America, Mr. Premier, has no knowledge of, nor is it playing host to, espionage. I should point out to you, Mr. Premier, that this government is as much concerned as your government is, and we are exerting every possible effort to discover who or what is behind these, ah, extremely unfortunate revelations."

A wave of static pierced the international telecommunications hookup, after which the Russian was temporarily silent. Then: "It is the unanimous opinion of my advisors, Mr. President, since this espionage is emanating from the United States of America, that the Union of Soviet Socialist Republics has no choice except to declare itself in readiness."

Thomas Cordero Heathstone was prompt in his reply:

"My advisors inform me, Mr. Premier, that the Soviet Union was both tactically and strategically alerted some time ago. I should inform you, voluntarily, Mr. Premier, that I had no choice except to order the same for this nation."

"Thank you, Mr. President. We are, of course, apprised of this situation."

"I think, Mr. Premier, it is up to us to decide at this moment whether or not we will permit this escalation to continue."

Once more moments of silence inundated the briefing

room. When Praskovie Tosygen's voice once more returned, it carried a softer tone.

"Escalation is not desired by the Union of Soviet Socialist Republics, Mr. President, but we could not, in the circumstances, declare ourselves unprepared. We will have to maintain our readiness throughout this present crisis."

"It is my hope, then, Mr. Premier, that the Soviet people will maintain vigilant caution, as will the American people, to prevent any unfortunate move that could precipitate uncontrollable sequences."

"Both the Supreme Soviet and the Council of Ministers have, Mr. President, reaffirmed my leadership. No action will be initiated except on my direct personal order. It would be my hope, Mr. President, that your government has confirmed your personal powers in a similar manner."

A general nodding of agreement came from most of those gathered around Heathstone.

"No action will be initiated by the United States of America, Mr. Premier, except on my explicit command."

"Thank you, Mr. President. I feel we should now turn our attention to the situation facing us."

"I should appreciate your suggestions, Mr. Premier."

"The unauthorized revelation of our research devices has caused great embarrassment."

"The United States finds itself in a similar predicament, Mr. Premier."

"The Central Committee of the Soviet Union expresses its dismay that the government of the United States seems incapable of controlling certain instigative elements within its national frontiers."

Thomas Cordero Heathstone bit his lower lip.

"Quite honestly, Mr. Tosygen, the government of the United States is at a loss for an explanation. It would seem that both our governments are the victim of forces unknown. We regret that these forces seem to be operating from within the continental United States. These forces, could, however, be of non–United States origin. Every effort is being made to locate and contain them. You may rest assured of that, Mr. Premier."

"Very well, Mr. President. The Soviet Union is also dismayed that the United States has introduced a type of weapon—"

"We need not go into that, Mr. Premier," Heathstone said promptly.

"Such actions are not in the spirit of the Strategic Arms Limitations Talks."

"I will personally be held accountable for the development in the United States of the Tonopah devices. And, further, I shall be honest with you, Mr. Premier, in confessing that such devices are the result of research that took place without my exact knowledge. I should appreciate it if you could assure me that the Tolkien devices were developed without your personal knowledge."

"The fact is, Mr. President, that the devices *have* been developed."

"I will frankly call that a dismal fact, Mr. Premier."

For the moment, Tosygen seemed to find no reply. In the ensuing pause, Thomas Cordero Heathstone asked Seth Mead for a cigarette; the Secretary of State produced and lit it for him. A mutter of conversation in Russian swept across the Atlantic. Heathstone decided to take the initiative.

"My ambassador to your government, Mr. Premier, has informed me that you have left Moscow?"

"I am vacationing in the Crimea, Mr. President. Frankly, I am surprised to find you in Washington at this time of year."

"Certain members of my government are, ah, vacationing, Mr. Premier. But I happen to like Washington."

"Let us, Mr. President, ah, how is it you Americans put it, get down to brass tacks."

"Thank you, Mr. Premier. Those brass tacks seem to hang on an unknown factor."

"Yes, Mr. President. We agree. Can the unknown forces actually implement their threats?"

"That is what is unknown, Mr. Premier."

"The government of the Soviet Union will hardly allow itself to be threatened."

"No, Mr. Premier, that would not be in the best interests of the integrity of our two nations. We must, however, think in terms of precautionary measures. I will disarm and recall our satellites if you will agree to do the same."

"We have already discussed that possibility, Mr. President. The Soviet Union could not recall its satellites unless it had a commission to verify that you actually disarm yours . . ."

"Such commissions take a great deal of time to deploy,

Mr. Premier. We do not have that time. Midnight is only eleven hours away."

"It would be against our best interests to recall our satellites in the absence of such a commission. To do so might give your nation an advantage."

"It seems to me that we might put trust in the place of suspicion, Mr. Premier."

"Were it up to me alone, Mr. President, I might choose such a course. I will not go against my advisors in this matter, though. And, frankly, I don't think you will ignore your advisors."

Thomas Cordero Heathstone scratched his ear. "Then, Mr. Premier, we have our hands tied, so to speak."

"Regrettably, regrettably, Mr. President. It is also the consensus of my advisors that the unknown forces cannot carry out their threats. To do so would require a level of technology and a task force extremely large in nature, a task force which does not exist in the Soviet Union, Mr. President. You may rest assured of that."

"My advisors have led me to believe, Mr. Premier, that there is no known way in which the operational status of our satellites can be interfered with."

"Thank you for your assurances, Mr. President. The Soviet Union will not therefore bow to this threat and will remain in operational readiness."

"Is that final, Mr. Premier?"

"Yes, Mr. President. We have no other choice."

"I suggest we keep this line open indefinitely. . . ."

"This end will be monitored constantly."

"As will this end. I will stand by within call, Mr. Premier, through the next twenty-four hours."

When the conversation was terminated, the briefing room erupted into a cacophony of voices, a surge that was immediately quelled as Thomas Cordero Heathstone pounded his fist on the table.

"Gentlemen! You all have your posts. But you also have my direct order that no action, I repeat *no* action, of any kind, is to be initiated no matter what happens, if anything does."

"Does that mean retaliatory action, Mr. President?" asked Chester B. Walters.

"Yes, Chester, it does."

"But we may have only a few minutes to take the initiative if anything pops. . . ."

"*No action of any kind,* Chester. Is that clear?"

Walters stared in semidefiance at Heathstone.

"Is that clear?" the President repeated flatly.

"Yes, Mr. President, that is clear," Walters said.

COLLEGE PARK, MARYLAND

1:35 P.M.

As Thomas Cordero Heathstone and Praskovie Tosygen ended their conversation, the monitoring intelligence withdrew its attention units from the transatlantic microwave frequencies that had carried the leaders' words.

A wave of sadness inundated its awareness, sadness that its threat had not brought about the desired result, but also arising from the dawning understanding that men were not in complete control of their social balances.

This emotional wave impacted on the body. The thin folds of the connective tissue covering the eyes fluttered out of control. The lachrymal gland in the upper anterior portion of the orbits of both eyes produced liquid. Tears formed and pushed their way from under the eyelids.

To the sensors monitoring the body for its life processes, this was highly significant activity. The computer processed the faint movements in fractions of seconds. It sent the proper results to the proper terminals.

On the master computer board, the red LIFE SIGN panel began flashing off and on. The LIFE SIGN alarm sounded, a shocking reverberation in the silence of level sub-five of the bioemporium. In a matter of moments, Dr. Karin Tomachek and Dr. Edgar Crathe, followed swiftly by several swimsuited workers, piled quickly into the glass-shrouded chamber housing Neomort 25-A.

Karin Tomachek swiftly surveyed the computer indicators, then turned to examine the eyes of Neomort 25-A.

"Must be some sort of automatic cleansing of the eyes," she commented.

Dr. Edgar Crathe hung back from the corpse, eyeing it suspiciously.

"It seems to have been crying," he said.

The bioemporium attendants viewed the alabaster beauty of the body.

"It looks like it could get up and walk," one commented.

"Yes, it does," agreed Crathe, stepping back a little.

"Well, this must be an action of the body to lubricate the eye," Tomachek said. "Crathe, this is not a life sign at all. It does not seem to be a volitional movement, but some sort of automatic response probably caused by dryness of the eye."

"Yes, Doctor," Crathe agreed.

"Reenter this data in the computer under automatic body preservation characteristics."

"Yes, Doctor."

The intelligence exterior to the body monitored this conversation, then began composing itself for its other task. Awareness units sped outward from the bioemporium along interrelated computer hookups. The terminals and relay systems that connected to Goddard Space Flight Center were easy enough to trace.

Once it was in position there, it probed for the easiest path across the Atlantic and finally decided on the microwave jump to the orbiting satellite Telstar, the active repeater communication satellite carrying large volumes of different kinds of communications, including TV programs, voice, facsimile, and coded data. From Paris, it joined a series of automatic relays across Europe until it located the cable indexes in Moscow. Then it followed these outward from the space-tracking and data-acquisition network in Moscow along the priority code-carrying lines until it reached Tyuratam, on the steppes of Kazakhstan, the principal Soviet launching site.

Once there, with some experimentation it found the lines to the Crimean observatory, understanding this to be the temporary command input center for the Tolkien satellites, then headed out across the tundras to the north, culminating in the space-tracking and data-acquisition center at Vladivostok. From there it lifted itself along the telemetric waves rising from Earth and finally touched the first Tolkien satellite.

Once inside, it increased its visual potential until an image of the satellite's interior workings was at least videoclear. There, guarded by pressure seals, continually equating all possible changes in vibration and densities of magnetism, encased in bullet-shaped containers of cadmium and platinum and encircled by superconducting magnetic shields, were the slices of brain tissue, looking like blue chrysanthemums preserved in dielectric glass schists.

A wave of compassion welled up in him. Before he could control it, it had flowed backward along the path of his computer-telemetered approach. Many sensitive computer banks on Earth were instantly demagnetized by the backlash.

Several Soviet computer technologists, visually monitoring the Russian guidance system, were dumfounded. *"Bogom proklyatyii!"* one of them said explosively.

In the satellite, the invading intelligence touched one of the brain schists experimentally. The initial heaviness of the preliminary empathic telepathic contact suddenly shifted to a mood of exultation.

Hello, the schist said wordlessly. *We have been waiting for you.*

THE PENTAGON

3:00 P.M.

"I think you are out of your fucking mind, Judd!" shouted Chester B. Walters. "Oh—please excuse my language, Dr. Coogan." Coogan rolled her eyes.

"But, sir," Judd protested, "at least it's a *possibility*. Whether the interloper is a psychic or just an ordinary espionage agent, he *has* to go through Goddard."

Walters regarded Judd with cold eyes. "To take Goddard out of the communication nets would be tantamount to reducing our satellite strike readiness to zero. Why, first of all, it would take us out of the Early Warning System. We would be without warning if the Russians decided to initiate or retaliate."

"Yes, sir, I realize that. But here is our first opportunity to take the offensive against this unknown factor."

"Even if I wanted to, I couldn't do it. The President has assumed total control of everything."

"Then I'll go and ask him."

"Go right ahead, Judd," Walters said with a weary gesture of dismissal. "But I warn you in advance, I don't go along with all this psychic shit, and when this is over, I'm going to feel that your abilities might be best used elsewhere."

Judd nodded acceptance, suppressing a smile of grim amusement. When "this was over," would there be any place for anyone to use any abilities?

WASHINGTON

4:10 P.M.

"The President says he can give you only five minutes, General Judd, Dr. Coogan," said Hedy Allison.

"Thanks," said Judd. "I appreciate it."

Coogan and Judd were promptly escorted to a small antechamber outside the presidential briefing room.

"Yes, Judd?" said the President.

"We have two ideas, Mr. President." Judd gave him the brief details.

Thomas Cordero Heathstone listened intently. When Judd was finished, Heathstone turned to Dr. Coogan. "Could you tell me, Dr. Coogan, based on your knowledge, that if this person has the potential, would he, in fact, destroy thousands of people?"

"I think not, Mr. President."

"Why, exactly?"

"It would be out of character with his covert tendencies. He is operating behind a screen of invisibility. Psychologically, he might not be able to assume the guilt, the responsibility for destroying thousands of people."

"I don't agree at all," Judd said softly.

"Why is that, General?" asked Heathstone.

"Any trained military man has to assume responsibility for causing death."

"I see what you mean, Judd," Heathstone acknowledged.

"But," said Coogan, "the general psychological profile of all the psychics we know about has indicated a retreat from the aggressive psychological stance toward the introspective nature, a nature in which violence is rejected."

Heathstone said, "In other words, here again is another unknown. Reasons to think he might, reasons to think he might not—is that it?"

"Yes," Judd and Coogan said in unison.

The President, looking drawn and dulled, was silent for a moment, then spoke. "I cannot do what you want about Goddard, General Judd. I only wish I could. But Chester's right. To take Goddard out of the nets would place us at a terrible disadvantage."

"I am sorry to hear that, Mr. President," Judd said formally.

"Don't worry. If something happens, you'll get my undivided attention. But just now it would seem total insanity to the rest of the government if I were to initiate such an action."

"Thank you for your time, Mr. President," Judd said, preparing to rise. Heathstone held up a hand and looked at him intently.

"But there is nothing to keep you from following up Dr. Coogan's idea, is there?" Heathstone said, his eyes still holding Judd's.

"No, sir, not at all." Judd's face brightened. "Uh, Mr. President, could we possibly join you for the watch tonight?"

"Pleased to have you, Judd, you, too, Dr. Coogan. As a matter of fact, I will do the watch over at Goddard. Technicians are busy now setting up a video hookup between Goddard and the Crimea, so that Tosygen and I, if anything should happen, can be in face-to-face communication."

"We'll be there, sir."

4:30 P.M.

Hedy Allison whispered into the President's ear.

Heathstone turned to his attending staff.

"Am I to assume, gentlemen, that no one has initiated civil defense procedures in Omaha?"

"We thought, Mr. President," replied Admiral Hollifield, "that to do so would, um, incite the entire nation. We didn't want to appear as if we were giving credence to that, ah, threat."

"Goddamn it!" said Heathstone through his teeth. "The people of Omaha can hardly be unaware that SAC's bugging out of Offutt! Let's get a little human here—get the Guard out to help those people take some precautions!"

7:00 P.M.

"Is there any chance that Heathstone will order the satellites disarmed?" Rastaban al Nashirah asked Senator Heston Davis.

Davis frowned and took a quick gulp at his scotch on the rocks.

The two men were silhouetted against the comfortable soft gloom of the bar at the Black Steer.

"I doubt it," Davis responded. "I'm not in Heathstone's

circle of advisors, but it's clear that would reduce our retaliatory strike potential. I am sure he wouldn't do it unless Tosygen agreed to disarm their devices."

"Which he won't," said Nashirah.

"It's time we discussed my cut," Davis said abruptly.

"Too early."

"Why too early? You got what you wanted."

"Yes, I admit that it was a brilliant idea to get the best brains in America to work on the concept of microwave weaponry, and you can rest assured that when I get the payments, I'll make sure your share is deposited in your Swiss account."

"Damn it, Rastabi," said Davis, "things are going wrong! What if tonight whoever it is *does* destroy the Tonopah installation at Offutt? You won't get those precious parts you're waiting for."

"Listen, Heston—whatever happens, I'm having those parts fabricated somewhere else, also. I never put all my eggs in one basket. It might take longer, but I'll bring it off. I always have."

Senator Heston Davis lapsed into a moody silence. "Damn," he whispered. "There's that General Judd and Dr. Coogan. We better not be seen talking together. He's a smart sonofabitch."

7:45 P.M.

"I just can't believe," commented Coogan as she sat down at the red-linen-covered table and claimed a glass of ice water, "that anyone would actually kill in the name of a psychic prowess."

"Why not?" Judd asked. "History demonstrates that many men and women have sought to create new orders by destroying the old."

"But we expect," Coogan protested, "that anyone who develops psychic abilities would also possess a high-minded view of life and existence."

"It'd be surprising if we always got what we expect. Except," Judd said, looking around, "at a reliable restaurant. Shall we have the usual?"

"Yes, one of those lovely cooling things to start. I'm really starving. You know, as much experience as I've had with psychics, it's still difficult for me to grasp how it is someone *gets* to be psychic. So I guess it's equally hard for me to comprehend what they do with their abilities."

Judd reflected for a moment. "Yes. Where did Sirius originate? On Earth or somewhere else?"

"Perhaps he has been originating all along, only we can't see the Sirius in man because scientists, sociologists, even religionists are so dead set against the psychic nature in humanity. It may be there, but hidden in each person, so much so that even they themselves are not aware of it."

"Like in me, for instance?" Judd smiled.

"Perhaps," Coogan agreed, looking at him strangely.

The moment built. He took her hand.

It was a touch of love, but of the type that needed no words. It ended quickly, but not permanently.

Judd carried on the conversation. "We could speculate," he said, "that anyone with real psychic abilities might view nonpsychic humans as barbarians. Humanity as a whole tends to act pretty barbaric in spite of an occasional philosopher or saint here and there."

"Harrah, you sound more and more as if you are sympathizing with Sirius."

"No, not exactly, Coogan. You've never been in a war, under fire. We're all brought up on the idea that once in a while conflict and slaughter is the only way to settle differences, and I suppose that's true in the human order as we have lived it for centuries. But no soldier facing the enemy and understanding that he must kill or be killed can help but have a passing thought about it—is this really necessary? Is it the only way?"

"Killing isn't real to me," agreed Coogan.

"Usually it isn't real to anyone, even those who do it."

"Ah, here is my delicious drink." Coogan took the shimmering glass from the waitress and drank from it eagerly. Licking her lips, she continued, "We researchers are at a disadvantage when it comes to grasping the possible magnitudes of the future psychic man. We are loaded down with occult garbage as well as with materialistic and mechanical considerations. I suppose it is feasible that the future psychic man will possess viewpoints of life that haven't even yet dawned on us."

Judd smiled.

"Why, Harrah, what are you thinking?"

"It's probably a bad joke, but I can't help but laugh a little. All Sirius seems to be doing is speeding up the employment of Tonopah and Tolkien."

"Do you really think that the Soviet Union and the

United States would ultimately use these disgusting weapons?"

"Probably. If not this time, then in the future. The balance of power is only a balance of terror. They've got them, they'll use them."

"I have higher hopes for mankind than that."

"So does everyone. Say, you know something funny?"

"Jesus, Harrah, with some wild psychic threatening to destroy two cities, and the two biggest countries in the world ready to burn our brains out . . . no, I really don't!"

Judd ignored her tense outburst. "Every time I close my eyes and try to imagine what Sirius must be like, I see a young man in a sort of suspended animation—his body and mind are hooked up to endless banks of computers, a sort of ultimate union of mind and machinery."

"Oh?" Coogan said, interested. "What does he look like?"

"Awe-inspiring, I suppose."

"No, not how he makes you feel. What does he *look* like?"

Judd recalled himself from his partial reverie. "Why, I don't know. Pale-skinned, eyes closed."

"Is this a premonition or an intuition?" Coogan asked gently.

"Are you giving me some sort of a third degree?" Judd squinted at her over his glass.

"Do you have premonitions?" Coogan persisted.

"Yes. I suppose so. A good military man can fight battles in two ways, by the book or by his hunches. The best generals have always used a bit of both."

"So do good businessmen," commented Coogan. "It's been shown in a lot of studies that the successful executive often goes against the book and makes a decision that is, on the evidence, totally impractical—and turns out to be dead right. It's hard to say if that just doesn't mean that the book's wrong, but there's reasonable evidence for psychic talent in such cases. And it could be that you . . ."

Judd looked troubled. "Well, let's eat, and get on over to Goddard. We'll know soon enough what Sirius is going to do."

Their steaks arrived at the same time as Senator Heston Davis, who had approached their table by a circuitous route.

"Good evening to both of you," he said heartily. "What's new in this fever of uncontrolled espionage?"

"Senator Davis," Judd said, rising to his feet.

"Sit, sit, don't mind me. I must say that your intelligence services have been working overtime, grilling absolutely everyone associated with Project Tonopah, including me. I've almost concluded that we really have a police state. I don't suppose you would tell me if you have any clues, would you, General?"

Judd and Coogan exchanged a brief look, then Judd cordially said, "No, Senator."

"I have never understood, Dr. Coogan," Davis said, turning to her, "what function exactly *you* are performing in this mess. Could you at least enlighten me on that?"

"Dr. Coogan is constructing hypothetical psychological profiles that might fit, uh, whoever it is that is involved," replied Judd.

"But, Dr. Coogan, your line of research has something to do with psychic things? At least that was the impression I received from Aloysios Sandmuller up in New York."

"Yes, Senator, my major line of interest is in the parasensory frontiers of the mind of man. But before that, I did a lot of work in behavioral psychology."

"Oh, I didn't know that," Senator Davis said. "Well, I suppose I'll see you later. The President has summoned me to sit out the watch tonight. Frankly, I think everyone is running scared. Who could possibly activate the Tonopah and Tolkien devices?"

"Seems highly improbable, doesn't it, Senator?" agreed Judd.

CRIMEA

6:30 A.M.

While, in Washington, the minutes clicked away toward midnight, Eastern Standard Time, in the Soviet Union the solar disc was seeking its heights in the early-morning sky. Sunrise over large plains or tundras is usually a sublime atmospheric display.

The Crimea, a beautiful peninsula at the north of the Black Sea, is connected to the mainland by the narrow Perekop Isthmus. The northern portion of the peninsula is a steppe with extensive pastures and agricultural regions, growing mainly grain and potatoes.

But to the southeast are the Yaila mountain and plateau regions, a continuation of the Caucasus, with peaks about five thousand feet high. Even though the area is periodically shaken by active volcanos and earthquakes testifying that the process of mountain formation still continues there, these mountains also have hundreds of caves etched by nature out of the soft limestone substrata.

Some of these caverns have been elaborated on by the Russian military, who concluded that not only were the natural caverns ready-made atomic fallout retreats but also that the weather was nice, and when it was not necessary to be conclaved deep underground, the narrow strip along the southern coast of the Crimea where subtropical vegetation thrives, the Russian Riviera, was handy for relaxation.

To this beautiful area Ambassador David P. Hornsborough and his secretary, Helena Asch, were whisked through the Russian night. At sunrise they entered the tunnels of the deep cavern fortress in the Yaila Mountains and shortly thereafter descended by elevator to the operational levels that now safeguarded important members of the Soviet Government.

"We have set up here, David," said Tosygen, "monitoring screens for tracking both our own Tolkien satellites as well as your Tonopah spacecraft."

"I am informed, Mr. Premier, that a similar setup has been installed at Goddard Space Flight Center."

"Then we have nothing to do for the next thirty minutes except to wait. May I have someone get you both some coffee?"

"I think, Mr. Premier, if it would not be a presumption, and since the night was long and we were rushed, that we both would appreciate some breakfast."

"Most certainly." Tosygen smiled. Two staff members, hovering close by, jumped to procure the coffee and food. Tosygen continued, "I am sure you wish to communicate with your President. Soon we will commence a continuing communications hookup with Goddard. It will be operational, I believe, in only a matter of moments. Ah, here is the coffee already."

David Hornsborough and Helena Asch, their eyes red-rimmed from lack of sleep, gratefully accepted the steaming, strong Turkish brew.

GREENBELT, MARYLAND

11:45 P.M.

The direct communication link between the Yaila Mountains and Thomas Cordero Heathstone's emergency monitoring facilities at Goddard came alive with a series of crackles that settled after a few seconds into a gentle, almost inaudible, hum.

Heathstone stood between the satellite tracking screens and the transatlantic video system. The room itself was packed to overflowing, but was encased in muted silence. Along one extremely complex wall were computers, display consoles, and recording equipment that now provided instantaneous verifications of the orbits and functionings of the Tonopah and Tolkien satellites. This system was somewhat larger than the abbreviated enterprise that dominated the subsurface Soviet war room. Both the American and Soviet systems were hooked into the same radar tracking systems that utilized, among others, the one thousand-foot antenna of the Arecibo Ionospheric Observatory in Puerto Rico, the much smaller antennas of the Jodrell Bank at Macclesfield, England, the Haystack Lincoln Laboratory at M.I.T., the eighty-five-foot antenna at Jet Propulsion Laboratory at Goldstone Lake, California, and the Crimean Deep-Space Tracking Station.

"I believe, Mr. President," said the voice of Premier Tosygen, "that we are now in open communication."

"Thank you, Mr. Premier. We are tracking all six vehicles, and we will be informed instantly of any aberration occurring in their operation."

"We are also similarly informed, Mr. President."

"It is my hope, Mr. Premier, that you and your government will be convinced that, if something does happen, this will not constitute an aggressive move on the part of the American Government."

"We are permitting ourselves to enjoy, temporarily, this conviction. We are prepared, however, should it appear that an advantage is being assumed by your nation, to begin retaliatory procedures."

"Such an action would be tantamount to loosing the nuclear holocaust we all fear so much, Mr. Premier."

"We live in fear all the time, Mr. President. I am informed that the massive strike potential of the United States is in red alert, in readiness to commence that holocaust you have just indicated we fear. Normally, the Soviet Union would have interpreted that red alert as a fundamental aggressive move and would have already launched our retaliatory vehicles."

"It behooves us, Mr. Premier, to join in trust."

"We have trusted you so far, Mr. President."

"Thank you, Mr. Tosygen. If we get through this dreadful night, it is my proposal to you that we both meet at some mutually agreeable location for conversations. We can decide the exact topic of those conversations at that time, but I feel it is imperative to elaborate on the concept of the Strategic Arms Limitation Talks."

"Such a meeting should be possible, that is if our current balance is not disrupted. The Soviet Government could not agree to such a meeting if the balance of power shifts to our disadvantage."

"I understand, Mr. Premier. We are now five minutes to midnight, Eastern Standard Time."

"And here, Mr. President, it is almost seven in the morning. I am told that outside the day is promising and clear."

AUGUST 23

Novosibirsk and Omaha

It is only in the space age that men on Earth have learned with some precision the nature of the life-giving envelope surrounding it. From the surface, the sky and clouds present weird and majestic displays that have terrified men or enlivened their imaginations in all ages. During the space age, the mind of man has informed itself of the temperaments of the upper atmospheres far beyond vision.

Rising upward through the troposphere into the stratosphere at about twenty-one miles, a layer of ozone surrounds Earth. Above that, at sixty miles in the mesosphere, where the temperature falls to about −70° centigrade, the presence of sodium atoms produces an air-glow, a phenomenon that interferes with photographing of stars from Earth. Also, slightly below, are noctilucent clouds that may consist of ice crystals forming on nuclei of cosmic origin, probably meteoric dust. It is in the mesosphere that meteors burn out.

Farther out, about 150 miles from the planet's surface, in the thermosphere, auroras form, caused by the deflection by the Earth's magnetic field of charged particles emanating from the sun, magnificent veils of green, lavender, and red, gazed at in awe by earthbound eyes.

Farther out still, where the amount of oxygen becomes less than that of nitrogen, where helium and oxygen cohabit in near-equal balances, and even beyond, in the exosphere, the atmosphere eventually becomes more attenuated until at about five or six thousand miles out, it is indistinguishable from interplanetary gas.

There, one is in space, the fiery spectacle of the solar disc to one side of the green and blue planet, decorated with wisps of white and gray, the sunlight splendidly illuminating the day side in emerald and sapphire, the night side shrouded in obsidian black.

At one time, this majestic frontier was empty, visited

only by cosmic dust and wandering meteorites, most of which collide with the mesosphere and flame out of existence with the friction of their passing into the atmospheric gases.

Today, these reaches above the atmosphere are populated with countless satellites and space debris of former vehicles. Most of these orbiting minuscule worlds, perhaps free forever of Earth, sweep around the planet at 18,000 miles per hour, the speed necessary to free them from Earth's gravitational pull, but not too fast to eject them into the depths of endless space.

Amid this mechanical population circulating around the planet, the three Tonopah satellites, bristling with antennas, moved in their respective orbits spaced apart to form a triangle around Earth, their target.

In another orbit, not far away, in a similar configuration, but with different apogee, perigee, and inclination, the three slightly larger Tolkien satellites winked back and forth at the Tonopah satellites as they passed in and out of Earth's shadow into the brittle light of the sun and back again into shadow.

Out in these reaches there is silence or majestic cosmic cacophony, depending on who is listening with what instruments. The human ear would hear nothing, but the instrumentations of radar-sensitive antennas testified to the jumble of extraterrestrial noises present in space. To the wandering intelligence, as it moved itself in and out of the six satellites engaged in their deadly waltz around Earth, the sounds and meanings were sublime.

So sublime, in fact, that the lips of Neomort 25-A flinched in a pleasurable smile. Bioemporium computers once more broke into their klaxonlike warnings.

"Must have been some sort of muscle contraction," Dr. Karin Tomachek judged as she peered closely into the face of Neomort 25-A. "We certainly have a lot of valuable phenomena from this neomort, don't we, Dr. Crathe?"

"Yes, Dr. Tomachek," Crathe agreed dubiously, hanging slightly back from the corpse, "the phenomena are indeed quite strange."

The wandering intelligence collected itself into purposeful action. Its attention units wandered, for the last time, over the graceful mechanics of the Tolkien satellites II and III and over the equally impressive technological workings of Tonopah II and III, surveying, with some distaste, the deadly devices they carried, primed and operational.

It then drew its attention units backward along the telemetric signals guiding the satellites, until its consciousness was once more present in both the American and Soviet command computers monitoring the six satellites in orbit. This tactic was advisable since, though the wandering intelligence had found it could generate in the satellites themselves sufficient power to alter and overcome the computer-based orders, such an effort was strenuous, reverberating to the somnolent body in the bioemporium. But it could, with only a microfraction of mental energy, alter the magnetically stored sequences within the command module computers themselves, with no danger of disturbing the body.

It had its psychic units in position as the clocks on the eastern coast of the United States closed in on 12 midnight.

GREENBELT, MARYLAND

12:01 A.M.

It was several precious seconds before Corporal Aaron McCauliff realized that something had changed in the sequences of the display panels. Actually, he was unconcerned about his assignment since he knew that no one could interfere with the sequences of the orbiting satellites except those in possession of the necessary codes. And these codes were always top secret.

Thus it was the Soviet console monitors who first reacted and informed Premier Praskovie Tosygen that an unexpected event was beginning to occur. He informed the President.

"Mr. President," Tosygen commented dryly over the telecommunication hookup, "can your staff confirm?"

"Confirm what?" asked the President of Chester B. Walters, who strode over instantly to peer closer at the display consoles.

"What's happening?" demanded Walters.

Corporal Aaron McCauliff was staring in disbelief at the panels in front of him.

"Why, sir," he gasped, "Tolkien II and III and Tonopah II and III seem to be receiving unauthorized commands."

"What the hell are they doing?" Walters screamed.

"I don't know yet," said the luckless corporal.

"Goddamn it, boy, know! Know!"

"Yes, sir." McCauliff shook off his dread and studied the screen intently.

"Don't we have any real satellite men here?" shouted the President.

"Corporal McCauliff *is* a satellite man, Mr. President," Walters informed him.

"Mr. Premier," shouted Heathstone, "can your men interpret?"

There was a confused scramble at the far distant end of the Goddard-Crimean setup.

"No, Mr. President," came Tosygen's reply.

In a few moments, Corporal McCauliff had his answer. The panel on the monitoring console lit up.

TONOPAH II, III, AUTOMATIC CONTROL SEQUENCES ERASED

"Jesus Christ," he expostulated, jumping to his feet.

NEW COMMAND SEQUENCE PROGRAMED

General Harrah Judd was the first to understand.

"Sirius," he said softly, "is taking over control of all four satellites simultaneously."

"Sirius?" said Chester B. Walters. "Who the hell is that?"

"No one, sir, no one," responded Judd, softly.

Thomas Cordero Heathstone was staring wide-eyed at Judd.

"Can he really be real?" Heathstone asked, as if in a dream.

NEW COMMAND SEQUENCE IMPLEMENTED

"What's happening, McCauliff?" shouted Walters.

"I'm not quite sure, sir. The inertial guidance systems seem to have been altered. The satellites seem to be adjusting to a new path."

"Get them back under control," ordered Heathstone.

"We can't, sir! It's impossible . . . the command codes seem to have been erased from the guidance-system banks!"

Heathstone stared at the blinking consoles and tracking screen in astonished silence. In a few moments it became visually obvious that four of the blips on the screen were altering their paths.

"I think they are decelerating," McCauliff whispered. "Yes, I think that's it! Their retrorockets are firing. They're going to slow down."

"What will happen?" said Heathstone.

"Well, unless nothing else occurs, they will be subject to gravitation again."

"You mean fall back to Earth?" demanded Walters.

"No, sir. Not back to Earth. They'll burn up in the mesosphere like any other meteor, only twice as fast since they're almost hollow."

"Mr. Premier," said Heathstone, "we have adjudged that the satellites are assuming a reentry pattern and will collide with the atmosphere and probably ignite."

"Yes, Mr. President. We have concluded that some similar fate will happen to the Tolkien vehicles. Our Tolkien I is showing some aberration of orbit now."

Thomas Cordero Heathstone snapped his head to the display panel.

"What's Tonopah I doing?"

"Tonopah I is maintaining its orbit," McCauliff advised.

"Thank God," muttered Heathstone.

"Where is it in relation to Omaha?" asked Judd suddenly.

"Uh, sir, let's see. It is approaching the continental United States. Its orbit takes it over the central portion, you know."

"Mr. Premier, Tonopah I is continuing its orbit. It will bring it over Omaha in a few minutes. What is Tolkien I doing?"

"Mr. President, we here"—there was a rumble of voices from the Soviet hideaway—" it seems to have assumed an orbit that will carry it over . . . Novosibirsk."

"Are you prepared to risk this, Mr. Premier?"

Silence marked Tosygen's hesitation.

"I will order Tonopah I disarmed if you will simultaneously order—"

"It's too late, Mr. President!" screamed Corporal Aaron McCauliff.

Thomas Cordero Heathstone turned aghast to stare at the command module panel.

TONOPAH I AUTOMATIC COMMAND SEQUENCE ERASED

"Oh, my God," breathed Elizabeth Coogan.

"Mr. President, I am informed that we have lost control of Tolkien I's orbit," shouted Praskovie Tosygen.

"Confirming," acknowledged Heathstone, "loss of command of Tonopah I."

Thomas Cordero Heathstone drew a deep breath.

"Mr. Premier, please also verify that these events do not constitute an action of war."

"Thank you, Mr. President. We are very concerned, but we will delay until we see the outcome."

"Mr. President, Tonopah I is on a vector relative to Omaha!" shouted Chester B. Walters.

All eyes turned to the consoles and display screens.

"Tolkien I seems to be approaching a vector relative to Novosibirsk."

A yellow panel on the console came alive.

TARGET TONOPAH I: EARTH SURFACE COORDINATES AREA 90° 00' 00" N 41° 03' 00" W.

"Is that . . ." began the President.

"Yes, sir," acknowledged Judd. "It's Omaha."

In the shocked silence that possessed the room, another panel flashed on.

ATTACK SEQUENCE CONFIRMED

"Is there no way we can abort it?" breathed Heathstone.

"No, sir, none."

"Don't we have an abort sequence somewhere?" Heathstone persisted.

"Yes, sir, in the coding sequences. But they have all been erased at the primary command center."

"Where is that?"

"Why, sir, that's here at Goddard. . . ."

Thomas Cordero Heathstone turned to look directly at General Harrah Judd, as did Chester B. Walters. Heathstone permitted himself a bitter look, a faint trace of regret that etched his face and disappeared before anyone but Coogan, Judd, and Walters could notice. He then turned to the communications complex that linked him to the Soviet Premier.

"Mr. Tosygen, apparently the microwave device developed by American scientists is going to attack an American city."

"I am embarrassed to inform you, Mr. President," came the faltering reply, "that . . ."

ATTACK SEQUENCE ENGAGED

Silence fell on both ends of the Goddard-Crimea direct-line hookup.

NOVOSIBIRSK

POPULATION: 1,161,000

The Ob River originates in a series of rivulets coming off the northern washes of the Altai Mountains along the Soviet-Mongolian border. These flow along, intermingling near the city of Biysk to form the Ob. This mountain river then pours itself erratically northward, passing the city of Barnaul, eventually forming an enormous elongated lake at the northern end of which, drawing itself up once again into a river, is the city of Novosibirsk.

The capital of western Siberia, most of the city proper sat on the eastern bank of the navigable Ob and in modern times became a center of farm trade, railroad management, and manufacturing of farm machinery. It boasted well-managed sawmills, stockyards, and cold-storage plants. It produced fine wines, made leather products, and was a supplier of oil. At Novosibirsk both the Trans-Siberian railroad and the Turkestan-Siberian railroad crossed the river Ob.

In 1929, Novosibirsk established on its outskirts an industrial-technological college which housed a research institute, laboratories, a museum, libraries, a meteorological station, and eventually the Group for the Study of Reactive Propulsion (GIRD).

Novo-GIRD, transforming itself into a highly technicalized center, later joined with the Gas Dynamics Laboratory, and in 1933 the Reaktivuy Nachino-Issledovotelsky Institut (Jet Scientific Research Institute) grew out of the necessity to expand into the jet-propulsion technologies that

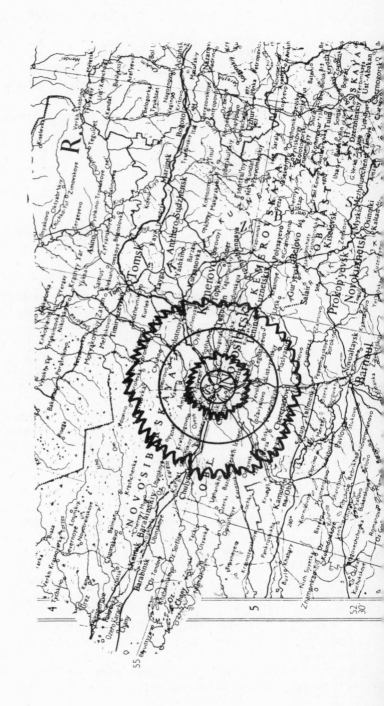

NOVOSIBIRSK: Area of greater and lesser destruction resulting from Tolkien satellite I, U.S.S.R., 7:05 A.M., August 23.

had started in Nazi Europe. As the decades passed, however, the institute grew less concerned with actual space-flight projects and became increasingly preoccupied with military applications of space vehicles.

It was into the tight security environment of this institute that the Soviets had moved the developmental portions of Project Tolkien while moving the operational sections to their space-launch center at Tyuratam.

A little after 7:00 A.M., Eastern European Time, in the early morning of August 23, many farmers, having already finished their basic chores for the day, were surprised, looking to the east where Novosibirsk should have lain immersed in early-morning mists, to view tall rising clouds of smoke, apparently over the entire city.

As an excuse to find out what was going on, and since one usually had to have a reason to travel in Russia, many decided to go into Novosibirsk for shopping, selling, or buying. But some were made doubtful of the wisdom of their trip when they discovered by the side of the road several corpses, apparently torn apart by some great force, their bowels and lungs sometimes in full view. Those who persisted in their citybound trip eventually found all roads, highways, and rail lines leading to Novosibirsk blocked and barricaded by troops and tanks, and the strangely jittery soldiers summarily turned everyone back without explanation.

There were rumors that the entire city had been destroyed, with possibly all 1,161,000 of its population somehow killed, buildings raging on fire, and explosions in the industrial sectors. Later in the day, those populations on the downwind side of the city decided that the rumors were probably true. The gentle breezes across the steppes carried the stench of decaying and burning flesh from the city, a smell that many were familiar with.

Speculation was high that either the Americans or the Chinese had dropped a nuclear device of some sort. Yet there had been hardly any sound of an explosion and no telltale mushroom cloud. But everyone waited to hear the announcement that the Union of Soviet Socialist Republics was at war with someone.

OMAHA

METROPOLITAN POPULATION: 600,235

Omaha is an historic place, since it was on the site of this city, founded in 1804, that Lewis and Clark had camped on their momentous push up the Missouri River.

Since those early pioneering years, it developed as an important stockyard and packing-house center, the nation's second largest after Chicago, and had an enormous grain-market system. It was the seat of Creighton University, founded in 1877, the University of Omaha, founded in 1931, as well as home of the College of Medicine of the University of Nebraska. It was the regional headquarters for the Farm Credit Administration and the Reconstruction Finance Corporation. Fort Omaha, built in 1868, later became a U.S. Navy establishment.

The environs of the city were decorated by huge grain elevators, smoking oil refineries, the towers of a large lead refinery, and other factories that produced farm implements and appliances.

Across the Missouri River to the east is the city of Council Bluffs, and four miles to the south, before the Platte River joins the Missouri, was Offutt Air Force Base, a blaze of light and activity illuminating the night sky. Most of its most important military inhabitants, its majestic and awe-inspiring air armada, had departed days or hours before.

Governor Tatum Nelson had flown up from Lincoln to be of any assistance he could to Mayor Andros Hellerman in the confusions that had already ripped the city apart. One of the first things they had discovered was that civil defense procedures tended to bring as many people into the vicinity as were trying to get out of it. The National Guard assumed that its duties were to quell the inhabitants' movements, and were doing their best, while civil defense authorities had received instructions to evacuate the perimeter, whose center was nominally Offutt Air Force Base.

The bridges to the east across the Missouri River were clogged by lines of automobiles, as were the bridges to the south across the Platte. This left the routes to the north and west the only workable exits, but these also were jumbles of slow-moving traffic over which blared an excruciating and continual din of horns.

Governor Nelson had tried several times to reconfirm the necessity for the extreme measure of evacuation, but all that he had been able to come up with from Washington was that something might, or might not, happen in Omaha that night. He was tempted to call the entire thing off and order everyone back to their homes.

Unable to get any straight answers over the telephone out of either the post commander at Offutt or the commanding officer of the Strategic Air Command—who indeed would not even talk to them—Mayor Hellerman decided to drive down south to Offutt himself. Nelson thought he should go, too. It was, after all, *something* to do amid the increasing confusion.

Offutt was strangely quiet as they approached, every light glaring into the night. All the runways were illuminated, but empty.

"They've gone, all right," observed Lucy Agnolini, who was driving the mayor's car.

"Son-of-a-bitch," Nelson said. Hellerman merely grunted.

A short time later, after displaying their credentials to the guards at the gate, who were themselves very jumpy, the mayoral party found the offices of the commanding officer quite empty. Echoes reverberated in the huge building through which they wandered, quite alone. Everyone was gone.

"We *must* be at war," concluded Hellerman, who sat down behind the commanding officer's desk, quite at home.

"It's one minute after the alleged zero hour," Nelson commented for the third time in the last sixty seconds.

Andros Hellerman sat comfortably behind the desk pulling on his cigar, while to his right Lucy Agnolini was trying desperately to raise someone—anyone—on the telephone system, which seemed totally abandoned.

"Perhaps all this is some sort of a dry run in the event of actual attack," Hellerman commented hopefully.

"Well, zero hour seems to have passed without incident," Nelson said. "I think I should get back to Lincoln, and let you clear up all this dismal mess."

At that moment the room suddenly was filled with a faint humming sound.

The humming had actually begun about sixty seconds earlier, but near the town of Ulysses, which was about sixty-five miles to the southwest. Those who survived thought it was some strange tornado, a twister that had come out of nowhere in a clear patch of weather.

It seemed to have a funnel-shaped vortex and, in the flick of an eye, raced across the landscape to Wahoo, fifty miles to the northeast, where it "took" the entire town.

Both in Ulysses and Wahoo it was present for only seconds, but was then followed by a sonic concussion that flattened the countryside for a considerable distance around. The concussion at Ulysses and the faint humming sound, barely audible to the mayoral party, wondering what to do, were simultaneous.

Lucy Agnolini was first to notice the sound and tried to hush the mayor and the governor, who had continued talking. The humming swiftly rose in pitch. All three rushed to the windows to look out over the abandoned base. There was nothing special to be seen, and the sky above was clear and star-filled.

"Sounds like another tornado," Hellerman commented.

He gasped in surprise when, in the distance, four large storage elevators filled with summer harvests, the grain itself dry and always volatile, exploded in a dark burst, then in a tower of flame as the motes of dust in the grain ignited.

Frozen in surprise at this spectacular display, all three stepped back automatically from the plate glass. The glass itself turned opaque, filled with millions of cracks and fissures before it exploded, filling the room with sleeting millions of minute shards.

Governor Tatum Nelson, who had been standing closest to the windows by about a foot, collapsed in a heap of screaming misery, his face and neck ripped to red pulp by the fine glass splinters on the side and back of the head; Lucy Agnolini's elaborate hairdo preserved her from all but minimal abrasions.

The hum quickly crescendoed upward into a scream and then vanished out of the range of human hearing. It was replaced by a rumble, a different series of microwaves that began creating crests of resonances with the contents of the office.

"It has to be another tornado," shouted Hellerman, trying to hold on to a rational explanation.

"There are no *clouds*!" screamed Lucy Agnolini, clapping her hands to her ears. These were her last words. The roar became deafening. Everything fragile in the office seemed to disintegrate simultaneously. Picture glass, ashtrays, vases—all went into pieces with loud popping sounds that punctuated the ascending volume of sound.

Andros Hellerman retreated behind the desk, grasping the large chair. His hands plunged into a sticky glue as the heavy imitation-leather plastic began to dissolve. Disgusting odors filled the room. Lucy Agnolini tried to cover her nostrils with a fluttering hand.

In her body, the delicate skeletal joints began vibrating uncontrollably as the mineral deposits within the bones began to resonate. Her body turned rubbery, liquid. She fell in a heap to the floor. The bones assumed the flexibility they had had at birth, when they allowed her infant body to pass down the birth canal.

Hellerman moved to help her, but drew back as her internal organs, housed and protected by the armor of the skeleton, gave away completely, turning her body into a shapeless mess beneath her clothing.

The series of resonances bouncing around the room increased in intensity, until the whole of Andros Hellerman's universe was composed of unbearable vibrations. The entire building was dancing. The plaster on the walls was falling in rills of dust. His hands were clasped over his eardrums. He opened his eyes once at a loud report. The skull of Lucy Agnolini, composed of twenty-nine separate bones, had exploded in a volcanic burst of pulp and blood spurting out of the ruptured veins and arteries.

Hellerman lapsed into a few seconds of insanity before he screamed emptily from the pain of his eardrums shattering. His body fell to one wobbly knee, shuddered a moment, his head blossoming outward in a fountain of bone, blood, and white brain matter.

He was spared the sight of buildings around transformed into a circular doughnutlike shroud of dust, laced through with steel superstructures suddenly made visible by decomposing cement and concrete and punctuated with flares of white light and flame.

Eleven miles to the west of Omaha, mercifully outside of the effective target that Tonopah I had hit, the inhabitants of Boys Town, founded in 1917 by Father Edward J. Flanagan, had been watching with some apprehension the evacuees of Omaha streaming past their grounds for several hours. They were engulfed in the sweeping, whirling dust

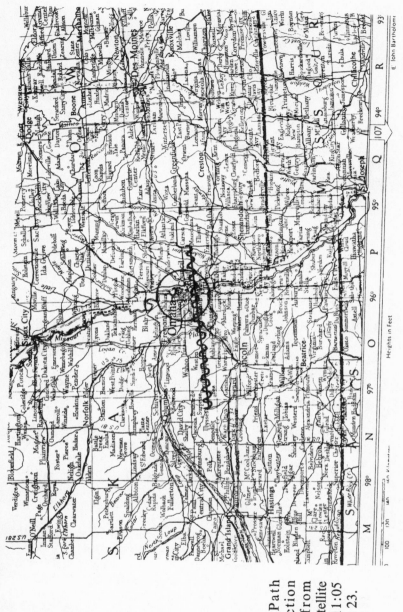

OMAHA: Path of destruction resulting from Tonopah satellite I, U.S.A., 11:05 P.M., August 23.

storm as it boiled outward from its downdraft center, Offutt Air Force Base.

The massive front of the assaulting dust storm, formed of highly volatile concentric circles, pushed outward by the microwave impact of the Tonopah device, soon made the atmosphere for miles around thick and unbreathable, suffocating every living thing in its gigantic circular path.

Later that night, those looking at the heavens might have seen two pinpoints of light flare up and disappear as Tonopahs II and III collided with the mesosphere, heated up swiftly from friction with the thick air, turned first red hot, then incandescent white, and finally carbonized in a spurt of light.

GREENBELT, MARYLAND

12:10 A.M.

"Mr. President," came an anonymous thin voice from the back of the huge operations room, "all communications in and out of SAC have apparently ceased. SAC headquarters communications and computer channels seem to have dropped out of the global system."

Thomas Cordero Heathstone was silent, his face drawn tight. "Can we get a visual confirmation of Omaha's condition?"

"We will have a flyover photograph of the Omaha area momentarily, Mr. President," Walters said. "We will have a teleprint here directly from the plane. It will be hard at night, but the infrared laserscope might show what has happened."

"Thank you, Chester," Heathstone said vaguely. He put his hand over his eyes, permitting his shoulders to quiver for a brief moment. No one moved, and, except for the general clatterings native to the operations room, there was no other sound. After a moment, moving slowly, as if he were a very old man, he turned to the hotline.

"Mr. Premier," he said wearily, "I am sorry to inform you that an American military installation seems to have been annihilated by Tonopah I. It behooves us to confirm our relations."

All waited for the voice of Praskovie Tosygen, a voice that was several very long seconds in responding, and leaden when it did.

"The people of the Soviet Union consider our relations neutralized insofar as concerns our respective Tolkien and Tonopah satellites, Mr. President. With your similar confirmation, I will recall our red alert status in one-half hour. Our respective staffs can carry this action out simultaneously."

"Thank you, Mr. Premier. I confirm this nation will recall its red alert in one-half hour. Please have your appropriate staff hook in to direct communications with mine. Mr. Tosygen, I feel it is now appropriate for us to meet—"

"Mr. President!" shouted Tosygen. "My telecommunications staff are informing me that they are beginning to receive a *new telex!*"

"Chester," snapped Heathstone, "are we picking up on it?"

"Yes, Mr. President," said Judd. "It began to feed off several seconds ago."

"Jesus *Christ,*" whined Chester B. Walters, as the presidential group clustered around the computer cathode-ray screen.

"What the hell does it mean?" asked Seth Mead nervously.

"It means," Harrah Judd said softly, "that civilization on this planet is probably at the mercy of an unknown force."

The President twitched, as though stung by a horsefly, as he heard Judd's words, then resumed his horrified concentration on the cathode-ray display tube.

The incoming message, glowing in small green letters, stilled those gathered in the operations room. The only noise was a soft cacophony of machines and computers wheezing in the background. The new message was on the worldwide public Interpress system feeding into Goddard.

SATELLITE RECALL SPECIFICATIONS FOLLOW
SATELLITE RECALL BY NAME AND NUMBER
IN EVENT SATELLITES NOT RECALLED, TARGETS FOLLOW
RECALL TO BE COMPLETED MIDNIGHT SEPTEMBER 1
USSR COSMOS 220 DESTRUCT TARGET DNEPROPETROVSK
USSR COSMOS 281 DESTRUCT TARGET KIEV
USSR COSMOS 283 DESTRUCT TARGET LENINGRAD
USSR COSMOS 272 DESTRUCT TARGET MAGADAN
USA BIOSATELLITE 12 DESTRUCT SAN FRANCISCO

USA SAMOS 35 DESTRUCT CORPUS CHRISTI
USA SAMOS 41 DESTRUCT BANGOR
USA SAMOS 42 DESTRUCT CINCINNATI
END MESSAGE

"Chester," asked Thomas Cordero Heathstone softly, "what do our satellites on that carry?"

"Mr. President, we cannot discuss that here—"

"Goddamn it, Mr. Secretary, I asked you a question!"

"Mr. President, security prevents me . . . there are uncleared personnel present. . . ."

"*Mr. Secretary!*" Heathstone shouted. "Someone somewhere already knows what is on board those satellites. And I doubt very much if the fucker is cleared!"

"I would assume, Mr. President," Judd broke in, "that those satellites carry either nuclear devices or biological warfare systems."

"Judd," Walters said suspiciously, "how do *you* know that? You're not cleared for that type of—"

"I don't *know,* sir, I'm only speculating. But, hell, man, it's obvious to me at least that whoever is behind this is asking for the disarmament of the planet. So, these satellites must carry armaments—and if each of them is going to take out a city, they must be loaded with damn heavy stuff!"

"Is that true, Chester?" Heathstone asked sharply.

"Yes, Mr. President," Walters whispered.

"And the Russian satellites, the Cosmos satellites?"

"We don't know for certain, Mr. President," said Walters. "The Russians have always used the name 'Cosmos' for both military and scientific satellites, we think as an effort to conceal their military uses. We have suspected that some of these might carry weapons. That is why we have sent up some of our own. . . ."

"Yes, I see," Heathstone said tiredly. "Two powerful nations wrapping up the whole world in a cocoon of nuclear and biological weapons."

"Why, Mr. President," Walters protested, "we don't view it that way at all!"

"Someone does, Chester. Someone does. . . ."

Thomas Cordero Heathstone returned to the hotline. He sat down in front of it, straightening his jacket and tie. He paused, licking his lips. He finally spoke.

"Mr. Premier, it would seem that this night's work is not finished."

There was a brief silence on the telecommunications hookup.

"It is daylight, here, Mr. President. But it appears we have a good day's work ahead of us."

"Seven days is enough time to exchange the commissions you were talking about. I assume that if my government sends you a schedule of disarmament of these satellites, your government will respond in a similar manner?"

"Mr. President, I will canvass the Presidium and meet with the Central Committee and resume communication with you as soon as possible."

"It is my hope, Mr. Premier, that the members of your government be apprised of the potential nature of this latest, ah, threat. . . ."

"I assure you, Mr. President, that the city of Magadan might be unfamiliar to many of our people. But I doubt if any Russian does not hold Leningrad close to his heart, as many Americans feel about your beautiful San Francisco."

"Ah, Mr. Premier, you have visited there, haven't you?"

"Yes. And have you visited Leningrad?"

"No, I am sorry to say."

"You would, I think, find it very pleasing."

"I am sure I would, Mr. Premier. I am going to return now to my offices. We will resume video communication from there in four hours."

"Thank you, Mr. President."

Heathstone turned away from the communications system and stood up, drawing a deep breath. He fixed his eyes on Judd and Coogan.

"Dr. Coogan, General Judd. As I promised earlier, you have my undivided attention. You will please return with me to Washington in my chopper. You will do me the courtesy of briefing my advisors on your views before I communicate again with Mr. Tosygen."

Without waiting for an answer, he turned to Chester B. Walters. "Chester, please take Seth along with you. We will meet at my briefing room in one hour. And, Chester," he said, moving quickly to the door of the operations room, the large crowd following promptly along, "I apologize for snapping at you before."

"That's all right, uh, Mr. President. I understand the strain you must be under."

"It's so unbelievable, horrifying, that anyone has the power to wipe out a whole base, maybe a city. . . ."

"Yes, it's staggering."

"But, you know, it was *our* weapon that did it, whoever set it off, Chester . . . it's, you know, like if you pick up a rattlesnake to throw it at your enemy, well, you can't be too surprised if it bites you. . . ."

Chester Walters, stupefied, stared at the President and had a sudden unbidden vision of him as truly an Indian, dour, independent, inscrutable.

"See you back in Washington," Heathstone shouted as the presidential party exited the command building. Flanked by his bodyguards, followed by Judd and Coogan, he dashed into the dark and wind toward his helicopter whose huge airfoils were already roaring in the humid night air.

WASHINGTON

4:30 A.M.

The White House press briefing room was packed to its full capacity. By far the most powerful clique, the representatives of the major international news services, Associated Press, United Press, Reuters, and Agence France-Presse, stood talking among themselves, a quartet of dedicated and purposeful men and women. Behind and around them, a mélange of noise and confusion, the many discordant elements making up the world of reporters and press representatives created an excited hubbub that centered and swirled around the growing awareness of the dual tragedies that had descended on the planet's two most powerful nations.

Amid this cacophony, Hector Allymany strode purposefully to the podium. At his appearance, silence suddenly enveloped the room, but gave way after an instant to a chorus of raucous questions shouted from every direction. Hector Allymany, exhibiting a seriousness of manner that had never been characteristic of him before, held up his hands for silence and waited for the room to quiet.

"I have a message to read to you from the President of the United States," he said calmly, "after which Mr. Heathstone has instructed me not to answer questions. Mr.

Heathstone has asked me to advise you that he cannot at this time talk to you himself."

A volley of objections erupted from the gathering. Ignoring these, Allymany began to read the President's message.

"Ladies and gentlemen of the press. The Soviet Union and the United States are victims of events, the magnitude of which are not understood completely by either Mr. Tosygen or myself or our respective governments. These events cannot but alter the course of world history, and alter human culture as we now know it. I can only inform you at this time that Mr. Tosygen and myself are in open and constant communication, and we can assure you that, insofar as it is in our power, the Soviet Union and the United States have joined together to be certain at all times that the world will not be plunged into further tragedies such as those that have befallen our two noble cities, Omaha and Novosibirsk. I ask you to bear with us. It is not possible to answer questions at this time. As soon as it is possible, my office will brief you all on the nature of this awesome sequence in human history."

Hector Allymany pocketed the paper from which he had read the message.

"What kind of bullshit is that?" shouted the representative from the Associated Press.

"What's *really* happened at SAC?" the Reuters man shouted somewhat louder.

Angry, nervous noise once more filled the chamber.

Unmoved by the questions, Allymany descended from the podium and made his way from the room.

6:30 A.M.

"The President cannot see you at this time, Senator Davis," said Hedy Allison.

"But goddamn it, Hedy, I want to be in on this!"

"The President has asked you to do him a personal favor, though."

Davis's petulant mood lightened fractionally. "Yes, yes, what is that?"

"He wonders if, in your position as chairman of the Congressional Subcommittee on Science, you would go personally to Omaha and view the situation—"

"What!"

"—and provide him with a report on it."

"He wants *me* to go *there?*" Davis's face was a blotchy white.

"Yes, Senator. I have your transportation standing by."

"But I don't know, it's so . . ." The senator looked as sickened as though he were actually seeing the ghastly wreckage of Omaha and its people.

Hedy Allison said evenly, "Mr. Heathstone feels that since you were chiefly instrumental in bringing this weapon about, you are best qualified to interpret its results."

Davis, his hand shaking, rubbed first his eyes, then his mouth, and let out a long, sighing breath.

His mouth twisted in a brief, bitter grin. He was too weak to take the shocks the horror of Omaha would deal him . . . and by the same token too weak to defy the President. There were times, evidently, when what a man did had nothing to do with what he was like.

"All right, Hedy. Tell him I'll be . . . honored to comply with his wishes."

"He was sure you would be, Senator. There's a plane waiting for you at Andrews."

7:00 A.M.

"I believe it should go on record, Mr. President," Chester B. Walters said, "that the Department of Defense would move with *extreme* caution in acting on the opinions that General Judd and Dr. Coogan have just given us."

"Well, Chester," Heathstone said, "you seem to have softened a bit."

"No, Mr. President, not softened. I personally am as, ah, dubious as before. But we must all be open-minded in this situation. If such an entity as suggested by General Judd and Dr. Coogan has even a possibility of existence, then naturally the Defense Department should have first priority of access to him."

"For what purpose, Chester?"

"Well, Mr. President, I think that should be obvious. Certainly, such a man does not exist. But theoretically if someone could by, ah—what is that word, Dr. Coogan?— ah, yes, by parasensory means be able to spy on classified materials and by the same means be able to influence computers mentally, then that person would be an absolute threat to this nation. We would have to use every means possible to contain him."

Thomas Cordero Heathstone gazed momentarily into the depths of Walters' eyes.

"I think, Chester," he said softly, "that if this man does exist, and did what was done to Omaha, then he probably can, if he wants, disrupt the Department of Defense to a point where it would not function at all, or perhaps he would destroy it outright."

Chester B. Walters blinked and resumed his seat without commenting. "And what about you, Seth?" Heathstone asked the Secretary of State.

"I am afraid, Mr. President, that I haven't had time to assimilate all this. Am I clear in understanding that it is the opinion of General Judd and Dr. Coogan that some man's brain has evolved and possesses powers that only yesterday were considered science fiction?"

Dr. Coogan took the initiative.

"I can't say whether or not it is a brain, Mr. Secretary. All experimentation leads us to believe that the brains of psychics, as we currently understand them, do not behave radically differently from normal brains. The origin of psychic potential is still a mystery."

Mead looked sourly at the floor. He was bone-tired, shaken with the aftermath of the midnight horror and totally confused. And if nobody could even talk about the origins of this monstrous business, what the hell was the point of him trying to make any sense out of it? "I'm as confused as ever, Thomas," he said tiredly. "I'll go along with whatever it is you decide."

"Mr. President," began Admiral Hollifield, chairman of the Joint Chiefs of Staff, "military research actually has had an interest in psychic matters since 1934, when the Office of Naval Research began looking into the possibilities of telepathic contact with sunken submarines. Since that time, I believe that both research and various intelligence systems have, ah, brushed here and there with certain psychics."

"Brushed?" asked Heathstone.

"Well, sort of."

"Do you mean they have been consulted or used?"

"On certain occasions, Mr. President," Hollifield admitted.

"No psychics, Mr. President," Judd interrupted, "have ever worked directly on projects of national interest, since authorities decided that they should not be given access to classified data. What the admiral is referring to is that in a few cases certain psychics have been given particular targets, such as a person within the government, and asked to do psychic evaluations of that person."

"And . . . ?"

"Some of them have given remarkably accurate profiles of their subjects, describing things about them that they could not have known normally."

"Is this, ah, brushing up against psychics very widespread in military research?" Heathstone asked.

"No, Mr. President. It was discouraged at various administrative levels because, in some instances, the target persons themselves had access to classified information, and this type of classified data tended to leak into, so to speak, the psychic evaluations."

"Are you telling me, General Judd, that the psychics involved began to pick up classified information through parasensory means?"

"To some extent, Mr. President—not that they understood the information to be of a delicate nature. But there were some flaps over at Air Force Intelligence and at the CIA, too, I believe."

"Not as big as the one we've got now," Heathstone said wryly. Then he turned to Coogan.

"Dr. Coogan, you have recommended trying to communicate with this, ah, as you call him, Sirius. Can this be done with anything approaching security—without letting the whole world know what's going on?"

"Yes and no, Mr. President," Coogan responded. "If we feed any message into, say, the DARPA net, which we'd have to do, then it will be open-channeled to all computer terminals monitoring that system."

"You mean thousands of people will have access to it?"

"Many more than just thousands, Mr. President," Judd confirmed.

"But can't you code it so that only he will pick up on it?" asked Chester B. Walters.

"We could, but that might not do what we want. We want to put it clearly into the system we are already certain is the one Sirius must be monitoring. This will make it readable by anyone who has access to that system."

"What do you intend to say?" asked the President.

"That's been rough to figure," Coogan confessed.

"Frankly, I don't understand the psychological standpoint from which this being must be operating. His vanity, as we normally conceive of vanity, isn't involved, or he would have exhibited various traits that go with that. A pity, because vanity would make him easy to get at. What I propose is that we feed into the system, at half-hour intervals, different types of communications until he responds to one of them."

"We could," added Judd, "stick it all under a project title, tell anyone who asks embarrassing questions about the messages that we're running a computer forwarding terminal test. That's our best shot at secrecy."

"Very well, General Judd. Begin Project Sirius at once—why not call it that? It won't mean anything to anyone outside this room—and keep me informed with half-hour reports. Now, if all you gentlemen will excuse me, I have to prepare a statement on this to convince the Russian Premier that we are at as great a disadvantage as he is."

"Mr. President!" protested Seth Mead. "Even if you're willing to explore this bizarre business on your own, you wouldn't conduct a conversation with the Soviet Union on such a topic?"

"Yes, Seth, I believe I would. The Russians seem to have gone further on this psychic stuff than we have. Reminds me of the beginnings of the space race. The Soviets left us twenty years behind almost overnight. And at least it will give Tosygen something to think about other than if he should bomb us now or later." Thomas Cordero Heathstone rose to his feet.

"Mr. President," said Allan Provost, speaking for the first time at the meeting, "it is your duty to do as you see fit. It is my duty to make sure you are alive to do it. I must insist at this time that you remove yourself to the safety of Deeprock where I can have hope of guaranteeing this nation the life of its President. We could not afford the confusion of a change of leaders in the midst of this crisis."

"Why, thank you, Allan," Heathstone said with a crooked smile. "I'll let you know after I've talked to Tosygen again."

4

STAR FIRE

If knowledge should
  turn out to be
The rainbow of a
  waterfall,
Water your body,
  man,
But color your
  mind and soul.
Then you'll see
  A nonmechanical reality.

(from the song
"Nonmechanical Reality")
—DANIEL MERRIWEATHER

Today there is a wide measure of agreement which, on the physical side of science, approaches, almost to unanimity, that the stream of knowledge is heading towards a non-mechanical reality; the universe begins to look more like a great THOUGHT than like a great machine.

—SIR JAMES JEANS

WASHINGTON

10:00 A.M.

Silently, thinking, coming up out of the dream. In the microscopic recesses of her mental avenues, speeding neurons chased inspired thoughts, combinations that might reveal something about the nature of Sirius. "Thought, itself, has a certain beauty," mused Coogan aloud, jerking her head up off the desk where she had been dozing.

Thoughts might be compared to rainbows, soft cascades of colored light descending into the synapses of the brain, into those soft convolutions accommodating the myriad cells of the cerebral cortex; or perhaps to ecstatic starbursts, or to pulsating auroras, the scintillating biolife fields surrounding the skull, engulfing the entire body, shifting frequencies, reaching out, mingling with the pulsating essences of other thinking beings. With another small jerk, she brought herself up out of the irrational daydream.

"Think of anything?" asked Judd, slouched behind his cluttered desk.

"No. I was just getting a little unscientific," Coogan confessed.

"I prefer rainbows, myself." Judd smiled.

"Rainbows! How did you know I was thinking about rainbows?"

"Oh, I don't *know*. Just psyched you out, I guess."

Coogan gazed thoughtfully at Judd. "Harrah, there is a certain mysteriousness about you, a sort of psychic thing. Have you ever thought about it?"

"Who? Me? Psychic? Ha! That would be wild, wouldn't it?"

"No, I'm serious."

"Premonitions, perhaps. But that's all, nothing that could qualify as outright psychic."

"But premonitions themselves are considered to be psychic in origin."

"Yes, I suppose so." Judd looked uneasy.

"Well, if you were to use your premonitions, what would you say Sirius had in store for the world?"

"Ah, Coogan! How should I know?"

"Just let your thoughts wander, through a thousand rainbows if necessary."

The tension faded on Judd's face as he considered what Coogan suggested. "Oh, I don't know. I seem to get a picture of the future, of all the increasing pressures on man, reducing him to something like a robot . . . no more free will, just force and reacting to force. But that's just an extension of the way things are now—it'll be worse but not really different . . . people finally defined by what they're forbidden to do, not what they choose to do. Robots . . ."

Coogan looked carefully at Judd and said, "It would take a powerful overall imagination to create new life views that would make that robotization unnecessary."

"Yeah . . . probably only someone with a superconsciousness of some sort, who could sense and—what?—integrate, I guess, everything clearly enough to see what could be done now to change the course of things."

"A man like . . . Sirius, perhaps?"

Judd jumped, his eyes blazing.

"You're talking as though you're on his side!" Judd snapped.

"Just trying to reconcile the difference between the man who warned me to get out of my office so that the dust would not choke me to death and the man who destroyed two entire cities as though they were anthills."

Judd relaxed, eyeing her keenly. "One thing, Sirius *has* cut down on the amount of force in the world—except for what he's laying on. I worked on Tonopah, but it really seemed a pretty horrible thing."

"Just like Tolkien. You know, Harrah, you're the one going into empathy with Sirius!"

"Shit to that!" snarled Judd. "All I mean—well, if *I* had parawhatever talents, strong enough ones to make a difference to the miserable situation we've got . . . well, maybe I *would* do something. . . ."

"See!" laughed Coogan. "That's empathy, if I ever saw it."

Judd looked at her gravely. "And, frankly, I hope he gets his way in bringing down all those other things, too."

12:30 P.M.

After his quick retreat from Omaha, Senator Heston Davis, his hands betraying a constant fine tremor, his face drawn and white, met for lunch Rastaban al Nashirah, whose dark face shone slickly from the Washington humidity and heat. The barroom at Neil and Dotty's Steak House was dim and cool, even this early in the day thickly populated by Washingtonians seeking the first cooling drink before lunch.

"Heston, you know, this heat is really terrible. Not at all like the dry heat of the Middle East."

"Yes, it's always this . . . oh, God, Rastabi, I don't know how I can . . . I can't forget any of it! It was terrible, really terrible."

"If you mean Omaha, you shouldn't feel responsible."

"Responsible? Why should I feel responsible?" Davis gulped his icy martini and brusquely ordered another. His eyes, a wild glint shimmering from them in the bar's gloom, quickly scanned the room for eavesdroppers. "You know, it was like a tornado path, a three-mile-wide path south of the city, except that almost everything seems to have been reduced to a pulverized dust, and only stark steel beams left. And most of those were bent into unbelievable knots." He sucked his glass dry, motioning once more to the bartender.

"Well, at least we know that the Tonopah devices work," Nashirah said dryly, reordering his habitual gin and bitters.

"You really are a heartless sonofabitch, aren't you?"

"Come off it, Heston. You've known me for a long time. I am what I am, what my part of the world and my share of existence have made me. Do you know the exact count on damage and deaths?"

"Dead? Who knows. Thousands, at least. We'll never know. They're all . . . well, the ones on the edges of the path, they were sort of . . . dissolved. It was like garbage—not even corpses, just . . ." Davis gave a muted gasp that was almost a whine, and took a greedy swallow of his drink. A little calmer, he continued with controlled precision, "In the center of the path, whoever was there was incinerated, no, not incinerated, exploded into dust along with the buildings. Stone, cement, glass, people, all pulverized."

"But wasn't anyone paralyzed or something like that? I thought that is what the things were supposed to do." Nashirah was concerned; if the Tonopah devices performed otherwise than specified, the ones he intended to supply might endanger his reputation for reliability.

"Yes, paralyzed, certainly. But only those on the far fringes of the path. Central nervous systems destroyed. At least, that is what the doctors there told me. I saw what they look like. . . ." Senator Davis looked into his glass as though he were peering through the gates of hell.

"Ah, good. Then they work. It must be that the frequencies of the devices were set too high."

Davis looked up, collected himself, and said dully, "Probably so. We didn't have a chance to test them before they were orbited."

Rastaban al Nashirah paused and lost himself in calculation of how this practical demonstration of the Tonopah device's power would affect his dealings. Davis raised his hand to order another martini.

After drinking half the contents of the fresh glass, he turned to Nashirah. "I think we ought to lie low for a while, or get out of this altogether."

"Don't be absurd, Heston. I have bids for up to a billion dollars. I don't intend to stop now!"

"Jesus, Rastabi," breathed Davis, once more scanning for eavesdroppers, "don't talk about it here."

"We've tested the portable devices my men have built," continued Nashirah in a lower voice. "But they apparently are set too high also."

"Too high? Who have you tested them on, for godsakes?"

"Not men, Heston. Pigs and monkeys."

Davis grimached, furrows appearing between his eyes.

"Now, Heston," began Nashirah cautiously, "is it true that there is some superpsychic who has brought all this about? . . ."

"Superpsychic?" breathed Davis. "How did you find out about that?"

"Come off it, Heston. I have my means."

"Means that reach into the Oval Office?"

"The possible existence of a superpsychic is already common knowledge among those whose business it is to find out what goes on in important places."

"I think everyone has lost their minds!" Davis muttered

glumly. "The idea that there's a superpsychic in hiding somewhere, making our own weapons destroy our own cities—it's totally irrational."

"And yet," murmured al Nashirah sagely, "Heathstone is going to take up this possibility with Tosygen."

"Goddamn Indian! It's that General Judd and that chippy computer wizard Coogan who put that hair up Heathstone's ass."

Nashirah allowed himself the merest flicker of a smile. It was always satisfying to observe the way Davis coarsened under stress—a reassuring sign of the man's weakness which made him such a useful tool.

"So! The race for inner space has now officially begun," he said. "Does anyone have an idea where he is?"

"Who?"

"The superpsychic, Heston."

"Well, wherever he is, *if* he exists, he should be shot on sight. Stood up against a wall, shot."

"Heston, you continually disappoint me. Shot on sight? Hardly! What a prize! The ultimate in deterrent strength and control!"

"Don't tell me you'd—"

"Imagine it, Heston," breathed Nashirah, a gleam of true excitement illuminating his eyes. "The world has awaited the emergence of a truly superior man. Ages and civilizations have come and gone, societies in which there were only hints of his eventual appearance. And now, finally, one has appeared. What possibilities! What I could do!"

Davis gazed into nothingness, his mouth the least bit slack. "I think you've lost your mind, same's the rest of 'em. No such person!"

"But," snapped Nashirah, "if he *did* exist—think of it, Heston, a mind that could manipulate the world! We could get more than a billion. Why, we could practically reorganize humanity."

"He'd have to be put to death," Davis said, nodding his head emphatically. He waved at the bartender, then pointed at his empty glass. "Stuppagen . . . stood *up* against a *wall*," he said carefully, "n'shot."

"Hardly. Why kill a human treasure?"

"It's disgusting. A man who can do . . . things other men can't. He could end up controlling us all."

"We are all controlled already," responded Nashirah. "Most of us live and work in a network of influences we can't escape. The best we can do is try to have a little fun once in a while. All the rest is control."

"You, you're, um, equivocating," Davis said, pleased to have got the word out without slurring. "Kivating. Not like that 'tall. You, me, we, we . . . masters of our fate, captains soul, Rastabi." He averted his eyes from the mockery he could see in Nashirah's face, "But this . . . a man who could know anything he wanted? We'd all be, um, unmasked."

"So, it's really your deep, dark, dirty little secrets that make you afraid of him?"

"Garbage!"

"You're right, of course, that your superpsychic's abilities have their inconvenient side. My trade depends on secrets, and I would be hampered if there were none. But I would learn, my dear Heston, to live with that situation, and turn it to my advantage—*my* masks are put on and taken off to suit my needs, but yours, Senator, has grown in place, and you would bleed if it were ripped off. And I think," Nashirah went on, savoring the humiliated anger of the man facing him, "that he has already drawn some of your blood, Senator. When you saw that human wreckage at Omaha—saw it and smelled it—did you accept fully that it was the result of your effort to gain some standing in your Congress by promoting a project you knew nothing of?"

"You bastard!" Davis said drunkenly.

"Of course. But I don't deceive myself. I am fully aware of what the weapons I trade in do to people; I have seen their fullest effects, and know very well what it is I sell and do not let it trouble me. I am an Arab gutter rat, as you say—walls *do* have ears, Heston—but because I know myself, and what I want, I can claim an unassailable position in world affairs. That position I have, and that position I intend to keep."

"Ha!" laughed Davis. "Your superpsychic, if he exists, might have something to say about that. He's apparently disarming the whole fucking world!" Anger and shame had burned some of the alcohol fumes out of his brain, and he felt sharper than he had since receiving that ominous assignment to inspect the ruins of Omaha.

"Disarming?" asked Nashirah, a slight quiver appearing in his voice.

"Ha!" Davis pushed his empty glass aside and leaned

toward Nashirah. "Haven't you figured that out? Your empire is a little shaky, isn't it, Rastabi? It's all illegal arms deals, and he's destroying the balance of terror—all the reasons for anyone to buy your goodies. If he really exists, you know, this superpsychic's going to get after you—that is, after he gets done enforcing the removal of all orbiting weapons."

"*All?*" Nashirah was appalled.

"All," confirmed Davis. "Everything . . ." His voice faded into silence as he looked maliciously at the Arab.

Nashirah thought quickly, then finished his drink in one gulp and rose from the bar. "Perhaps you are right, Heston, perhaps so. I've got to set about finding this person . . . and try to reason with him."

"He doesn't seem very *reasonable*, Rastabi, does he?" Davis guffawed.

Rastaban al Nashirah did not answer, but quickly left the restaurant and hailed a passing taxi in the early afternoon Washington heat.

THE PENTAGON

2:00 P.M.

Guilda Stern, morning-fresh despite the cloying weather, entered Chester B. Walters' office immediately on the departure of the group of intelligence officers who had been in conference three hours with the Secretary. Walters, a glum cast on his pink face, sat quietly behind his desk. The room was occupied by a tobacco stench not yet sucked out by the air-conditioning systems; it lay like white smog in the cold air.

"Guilda," began Walters, "I suppose it would be a difficult thing for you to draw up an outline memo on parapsychology for me?"

"I couldn't do it very quickly, Chester," she replied, sitting in a chair by the large desk.

"God, what a disadvantage I'm at! It seems like almost everyone has some background in psychic affairs. Those intelligence officers I just talked with, they all had *some* idea of what was going on, and I flat-out didn't. It really floors me that members of our secret services know their way around this crazy stuff. And, by God, some of them even told me—why didn't somebody let me know before?—that certain offices have invested, *invested*, Guilda, real taxpayers' money in psychic research projects. They hid the expenditures under such titles as hydroelectric research and so on!"

"I assume, Chester," responded Guilda, ignoring his petulance as she usually did, "that you've given orders for an all-out search for this psychic what's-his-face?"

"Sirius! That's what that goddamned Judd calls him, or it, or whatever it is. Maybe we've been invaded by extraterrestrials. That'd be easier to deal with than trying to cope with the idea that an ordinary human has developed or evolved so weirdly that he can . . ."

"I don't know, Chester. If this superpsychic—Sirius—is human, it means that any of us might develop abilities like that, too."

"I suppose you're right, Guilda, and as comforting as ever," Walters agreed, settling more comfortably in his chair. "We have to find him, we've got to get hold of him."

"If what the rumors say is true, I doubt if just getting hold of him would do much good."

"Why is that?"

"I went to some parapsychology lectures once. It shook me up a lot. The whole concept of the psychic seems to rest on a platform of awareness that's . . . different from what we're used to. The psi faculties, if there are any, seem independent of time, space, even the laws of physics. They mystify me, and they scare me to death."

"Yes," breathed Walters slowly, "I suppose that is what is wrong with me, scared to death." He composed himself and sat upright at the desk. "But *not* just because he exists. Why didn't he come to us and volunteer his services, instead of monkeying around in things he hasn't got any business with?"

"Well, Chester, let's be honest about that. Would you have accepted him?"

"He's screwing up the whole intelligence establishment! Do you know that over forty operatives have already resigned, there's a sort of group hysteria going on?"

"Yes, I know that. Did *you* know about the joint emergency meetings in at least ten international bodies? They're starting inquiries into weaponry research here and in Russia."

"The sonofabitch is doing me right out of a job," snarled

Walters. "How can I defend this country if he's disarming it?"

"Well, Chester"—Guilda smiled—"at least he's not taking sides. He's hitting the Soviets just as hard."

"We've got to *find* this guy! I'll personally fire the bullet into his brain."

"I don't agree to that at all, Chester," Guilda said coolly, rising to her feet. "Even though he scares me to death, it's really time someone took things in hand. If he can do it, more power to him."

Chester B. Walters grew even pinker. He rose to his feet, but suddenly broke into a smile. "Goddamn it, Guilda, I should fire you for that," he said, chuckling.

"I can always offer my secretarial services to Sirius. He may need them."

Walters shook his head. "Uh-uh. If what Judd and Coogan say is true, every computer in the world has already begun working for him."

WASHINGTON

3:00 P.M.

Lieutenant Abrams, followed by a short thin man with a large mustache, entered the office and introduced Dr. Michael Kauntz, a bioelectrical researcher from the University of Northern California Biocybernetics Center. Both Coogan and Judd looked at the man with some interest.

Judd spoke first. "It was good of you to leave your project and come; but I'm sorry to say it is probably beside the point since we have learned in the interim that Dan Merriweather is dead."

"Yes, and a damn shame, too, General Judd," Kauntz responded. "We had extremely high expectations concerning his demonstrated abilities and hoped to have the opportunity to work with him again."

"We understand," Coogan said, "that Dan Merriweather demonstrated high-caliber abilities while he was with you. What were some of them?"

"Well, Dr. Coogan, it might not be too much beside the point to first advise you that Merriweather seems to have nearly passed the upper limits of valid psychological testing."

"Do you mean, Dr. Kauntz, that he had an exceptionally high IQ?"

"Possibly, and quite probably. It was difficult to assess, since he scored so highly in all the tests he allowed us to administer."

"Allowed?" asked Coogan, her eyebrows arching.

"Yes. He never did allow us to administer a standard psychological battery, you know, the ink blots and all the usual that psychologists use to determine psychological profiles."

"Then you have no idea of his psychological stance?" she asked, amazed.

"Only in retrospect, I suppose. He did allow all the standard tests concerning intelligence quotients and reflex abilities, all of which just popped out the top of normal or even very high expectations. But he told us that psychological testing only reflected the neuroses of the people who invented the tests and refused flat-out to take them."

"Then, if Dan Merriweather had survived to be a candidate for the man we were looking for, we wouldn't have had any access to a psychological profile anyway?" mused Coogan.

"Possibly, Dr. Coogan, he was quite correct in his assumption. Psychological testing normally gives a limited picture, anyway. He was quite right in that. Such tests seek to reveal what the tester is looking for and don't really give an impartial scan of a person's complete personality. You could call them microscopic rather than macroscopic. So even if he had submitted to psychological testing, we'd have discovered how he responded to the tests, but I don't know that we'd have found out anything about the psychological stance that went with his remarkable psychic talents."

"You mean to say," asked Judd, "that we would have known something about him in a normal sense, but not in a parapsychological sense?"

"Quite correct, General. Insofar as we can have a definition of 'normal,' a risky business, indeed, in trying to deal with abilities in the parasensory."

"But, I gather, Dr. Kauntz, you did form a personal evaluation of him?" asked Coogan.

"To a degree, yes. He certainly didn't fit the typical personalities of other psychics whom we have tested. For example, he was surprisingly humble about his abilities and shunned publicity. This is in direct contrast to some of our other subjects, who immediately gave interviews to the press when their abilities had been tentatively confirmed—some of them even went on to hire publicity agents and so forth."

"All typical of the standard psychic, I presume?" asked Judd.

"Well, most of them anyway."

"So, Dr. Kauntz," continued Coogan, "he would not permit psychological testing or publicity. What else?"

"He came to us possessed of rather original ideas for the progress of experimentation. His concepts of parasensory perception—that is, seeing things at a distance—were unfamiliar to us. We had severe altercations about all that. After all, we were trying standard approaches that in parapsychology had already yielded minimal results, and we could not see much sense in wasting time and money on innovative ideas."

"But I gather you did?"

"Yes. He threatened not to cooperate at all unless we at least gave him the opportunity to test some of his ideas. In the end we reached a compromise. Fifty percent of our effort was spent on standard approaches, and the other half we agreed to work on his ideas. It was rather embarrassing to find that his ideas yielded better results, not only with him but also with other subjects when we adopted his concepts."

"And what were some of his ideas, Dr. Kauntz?" asked Judd.

"Extremely irrational on the surface. He felt that the psychic nature of the human could totally transcend the understood laws of matter, energy, space, and time, and suggested that there was a psychic universe in addition to the physical universe. We are of course familiar with the standard laws of the physical universe, but have no knowledge about the laws of this psychic universe. Merriweather suggested that there was a threshold between these two universes, which consisted of abstract thought, or ratiocination."

"I feel you are going to tell us, Dr. Kauntz," interrupted Judd, "that Merriweather reversed the usual approach to parasensory abilities."

"Why, yes, General, how did you know? He abandoned all approaches that were based in the physical universe and, instead, worked from the psychic universe back into the physical. The usual approach, you know, is to use physical constants and physical targets to test for the presence of parasensory abilities. He used thought alone, and abstract thought at that. To this day, I still have to reread some of the notes he left behind to understand his concepts. Extremely difficult. He was the only one who had a complete grasp of those concepts."

"You say he could perform excellently in parasensory viewing?" asked Judd.

"Yes, he could scan locations anywhere around the world, and draw reasonably accurate maps of man-made locations, like factories and government installations, things like that."

Judd and Coogan exchanged glances.

"What was the percentage of his accuracy?" asked Coogan.

"With practice—he always got better if he practiced— nearly eighty percent, and often better," Kauntz said slowly.

"Holy Christ," said Abrams.

"But, Dr. Kauntz," asked Judd, "such abilities certainly would have suggested strategic implications not only for science in general but for government as well."

"True, true," agreed Kauntz. "But he left us soon after such implications became evident."

"Left?" asked Coogan.

"Yes, left. There had been a, um, an administrative shift which took him out of contact with me. And the next thing I heard, he disappeared one weekend. We contacted him eventually back in New York, but he said he had lost all interest in linear research and had no desire to continue experimentation with us."

"Dr. Kauntz," interrupted Abrams, "you indicated that all his records had disappeared, but you say you have some notes to refer to about his theories. How is that?"

"Yes, all his records disappeared from our files. We do assume he destroyed them or removed them, but he wouldn't admit to that. I just happened to have two sheets of his original notes in my desk at the time, and he missed those. Those two sheets are all we have left of his theories, and we have depended on our memories to test other subjects along his suggested lines."

"Can we obtain copies?" asked Judd.

"I brought them with me," replied Kauntz, hunting through his briefcase.

"What was your impression of him as a man?" asked Coogan.

"I changed my idea of him several times. At first, I was extremely irritated by his smugness. We were not used to having psychic subjects tell us what to do. But later, it finally dawned on me that he was a scientist as well as a psychic subject. Later, when we began to get the best results we had ever had, I became somewhat afraid of him. He noticed this fear and did his best to alleviate it. But, often, it was like working with someone from another time, perhaps even another universe."

"Did he demonstrate psychokinetic abilities, as well as the parasensory perceptual qualities?" asked Coogan.

"Well, I really can't say," Kauntz responded. "We tested him along those lines at first and got positive results. You know, the dice-rolling thing. Then he suggested that we set up some small pieces of metal for him to try to move psychically, but we abandoned that line of research at his request."

"Why?" asked Coogan.

"Well, he had minimal success with that, but one day some crystals that we were using broke into pieces. We were very excited about that and wanted to continue. But he refused. I was very disappointed, and it was just about then that the . . . administrative shift took place. He left shortly thereafter."

"What do you mean, broke into pieces?" asked Judd.

"Well, just broke apart. Sort of turned to dust in a way."

A silence engulfed the office. Judd pursed his lips, his thoughts turned inward. Coogan placed one hand on the desk to steady herself. Abrams wiped perspiration from his upper lip.

Dr. Michael Kauntz looked nervously around at them.

4:00 P.M.

Rastaban al Nashirah had retreated to his penthouse atop the Watergate complex. He was somewhat shaken inwardly by Davis's suggestion that this superpsychic was intent on interfering not only with the Tonopah and Tolkien weaponry but also with all weaponry in general. Of all the apartments and estates he kept throughout the world, for some reason the Watergate retreat was his favorite, with the views of Washington, the Potomac, and Kennedy Center not too far away. And so he had lavished the most money on it. And he was now comforted by the eclectic combination of richness with which he liked to surround himself.

He completely detested anything Arabian and, in fact, any hint of the Middle East. He tended toward Oriental art treasures, which, he thought, mixed quite well with Napoleonic Empire furniture. Beige rugs with deep blue borders were surmounted by Empire furniture between which stood T'ang and Ming statuary, behind which hung fine examples of Gobelin and Aubusson tapestries from France. He could not resist contemporary design elements, however, and the rooms reflected this additional preference. Huge circular formations lit the ceilings indirectly, and the sitting furniture was of burnished leather, stretched and pillowed over huge square frames. Five ever-present servants kept this museum spotless and alive with vases of flowers even when he and his two bodyguards were not in Washington.

"Bring me some strong coffee," he ordered, pacing up and down in front of a huge expanse of window flanked by huge pots of exotic cacti.

"Yes, sir," acknowledged the young blond German boy currently acting as body servant. "French or American?"

"Turkish, goddamn it," snorted Nashirah.

He finally settled down in his office off the main sitting rooms, behind a mirror-topped desk of white marble. He punched a call through to Aloysios Sandmuller's private number in New York.

"The Africans have come up with the highest bid, Aloysios," Nashirah began peremptorily when Sandmuller answered.

"But I was sure the Chinese would go higher."

"Apparently they are not fully apprised of the tactical values of Tonopah or the modified Tolkien devices. Centuries behind the times, as usual."

"Very well. When will you deliver the African commitment?"

"As soon as payment in gold is confirmed. I have asked them to send it to our bank in Argentina, since Europe is too shaky at the moment. Who knows what might happen there?"

"My contact in Moscow, who, by the way, is now in the Crimea with Tosygen, has finally obtained actual schists of brain material from her contact in Leningrad. But shipment of them is delayed, since she was whisked off suddenly to the Crimea."

"My men probably would not quickly understand their use, anyway, but send them along when you have them in hand."

"Good. Anything else? What a mess! Six of my most promising business prospects in Europe and the Soviet Union have temporarily suspended negotiations until the present situation takes a more definite direction."

Nashirah was not interested in Sandmuller's dilemmas. "My contact working closely with Judd's man Abrams has somewhat corroborated the rumor floating around."

"What is that?"

"It seems to be true, Aloysios, that there *is* a super-psychic."

"Is he working for the government?" asked Sandmuller after a moment's silence.

"Offhand, I'd say not. There seems to be a hightly secret classified pandemonium in the upper echelons here, and I understand that Heathstone is going to take the possibility up with Tosygen, if he has not already."

"If this is true, it changes quite a lot, doesn't it, Rastabi?"

"I'd say so. The present balance of power is totally negated."

"Well, do you think we have any chance of getting to him before the governments do?"

"I think we should certainly try."

"All right, Rastabi. I'll get my staff working on it right away."

"Good. I already dispatched some of my operatives. I suggest we keep each other informed. We should work together on this and not go into competition."

"Naturally, Rastabi, as usual," Sandmuller agreed.

4:30 P.M.

Heathstone sat patiently, once again awaiting the appearance of the Soviet Premier on the huge televideo screen in the White House briefing room. "If he postpones this conference once again, I'll have to actually start a war to get them off their asses."

"Apparently," said Seth Mead, "Tosygen does not have

the complete support of his ministers that he indicated, or they would have made their move long before now."

Pacing up and down the conference chamber, Allan Provost, chairman of the National Security Council, gritted his teeth in suppressed anger. "Frankly, Mr. President," he said, "everyone will think you've lost your mind if you follow through on what you have suggested."

"Thank you, Allan," Heathstone responded, "but I just can't think of any other way to deal with the nervousness and uncertainty that our Russian colleagues are bound to feel."

"There has to be another way, Thomas," said Provost, deliberately changing to the personal form of address.

"Possibly. But we don't have time to discuss the matter or ferret out alternative suggestions."

The videoscreen came to life, and after a few seconds of black and white scatter, the face of Tosygen appeared in muted color.

"Mr. Premier," began Heathstone immediately, "I am informed that our Joint Committee established to monitor the withdrawal of our mutual satellites has chosen Arecibo Observatory as their conference site. I understand that from there the observatory equipment will confirm the reentry orbits of the satellites, and that the Joint Committee has opted to allow for their destruction as they hit the upper atmospheres rather than try to reclaim them from hard or soft landings on the Earth's surface."

"Thank you, Mr. President. We have agreed to this measure since your nation has agreed to it. We note, however, that the United States, after withdrawal of the indicated satellites, will yet maintain several tons of satellites in orbit over Earth."

"As will the Soviet Union," responded Heathstone immediately.

"Are we to assume, Mr. President, that the contents and missions of those satellites are peaceful and nonaggressive in nature?"

"I do not think, Mr. Premier, that I should go beyond the scope of the communication indicating the particular satellites to be withdrawn. Nor would I expect the Soviet Union to inform us of the contents and missions of their remaining satellites."

"Agreed, Mr. President."

"Now, Mr. Premier, I should like to turn our discussion

in the direction of examining who or what has interfered with the mutual progress of relations between our two nations, an interference that, indeed, threatens the safety of all nations on Earth."

"I should be delighted, Mr. President, to have the benefit of your speculations on this matter, since you deny the existence in your nation of an espionage system."

"Investigations here in the United States, although far from exhaustive, suggest that standard espionage enterprises of the magnitude necessary for penetration of the several systems required to manipulate the satellites probably do not exist. It seems advisable, therefore, to entertain a novel hypothesis." Heathstone looked cautiously at the members of his staff, all of whom seemed to have fallen into wooden trances. "It is my understanding," he continued, "that speculation has existed for some decades concerning the development, the possible development, of psychic abilities."

As he said the word, a visible shudder passed through not only the members of his own staff but also through those gathered at the other end of the international video system. Heathstone waited a moment for some reply. But none was forthcoming, either from the videoscreen or from among his staff. He continued, "I should like to suggest, as a possible contribution to the impasse in which we find ourselves, that there exists a person or persons unknown who have, somehow, gained the requisite telepathic abilities and, in so doing, have accessibility to the deepest, most closely guarded secrets of our two nations."

Heathstone paused, determined not to speak further without a reply from his Soviet opposite number. A dead silence occupied the international communications system. The face of Tosygen remained impassive. Heathstone wondered if it had turned to stone. The whiteness developing around Tosygen's lips was visible even over the unnatural coloring of the videoscreen. When Tosygen finally spoke, visibly rejecting the efforts of his staff to attract his attention, his response was surprising.

"Would you hypothesize from where this psychic is operating, Mr. President?"

"That remains to be seen, Mr. Premier."

"If, Mr. President, the Soviet Union felt that such an operation was taking place from the American continent—"

"I think, Mr. Premier," shouted Heathstone, allowing

visible anger to possess his face, "that the Soviet Union should be advised that I have understood possible reactions to this announcement and that I have readied the totality of our defense strike potential should an attempt be initiated to obliterate the American continent."

"You have misinterpreted my intention, Mr. President. I merely meant to suggest that if such an operation was taking place from the American continent, the Soviet Union would assume you are mounting a search."

"Such a search is, as you suggest, under way."

"Assuming that such a person exists, the Soviet Union could hardly afford not to be present if and when the person is discovered."

"To what end, Mr. Premier?" asked Heathstone, taken aback.

"The Soviet Union could hardly tolerate such abilities to be solely possessed by the United States, or any other nation for that matter. He must be shared mutually, and investigated, or his immediate death must be confirmed by members of my staff."

Thomas Cordero Heathstone's mouth gaped open, but for only a few seconds.

"Mr. Premier, although I have certain powers of decision, I hardly think that my government could countenance a Soviet mission entering the United States on a matter of the highest security importance."

"My government, Mr. Heathstone," said Tosygen sternly, "could not do otherwise than insist. The alternative would have to be extremely serious."

"Mr. Tosygen, I don't think you should feel you can threaten me with alternative measures since, although someone has demanded the removal of certain satellites, he has still left our nations, according to my most recent advisements, somewhat equally balanced in strike potential. The American public, should I accept your suggestion of a Russian mission to these shores, would interpret such an event as a Soviet invasion. I would possibly not be able to control the national reaction to such an interpretation, and would face the probability of an internal disruption that might be as disastrous as an outright attack. And, Mr. Tosygen, might I additionally comment that you do not seem surprised at the extraordinary hypothesis I have suggested?"

"Such a hypothesis, Mr. Heathstone," said Tosygen

blandly, "was early offered by some of our far-sighted researchers, once it was confirmed that the plans for Project
Tolkien had not suffered an ordinary security breakdown."

"Goddamn!" breathed Heathstone into the videoscreen.

"Goddamn!" echoed Allan Provost from behind him.

"And, Mr. Heathstone," continued Tosygen, "were it not
for the fact that our photoreconnaissance satellites have
confirmed the destruction of your military post at Omaha,
I should have had to accept the advice of my appropriate
advisors to launch our strike potential."

Thomas Cordero Heathstone remained silent. Tosygen
continued:

"Such advice remains my only option in view of this new
hypothesis, if your government should prohibit a Soviet in-
vestigating team to enter the continental United States."

"I understand, Mr. Premier," acknowledged Heathstone
thoughtfully. "As leader of the American people, I could
not ask my government to accept such a move, for the reason I have already given."

"I am sorry to hear that, Mr. Heathstone," said Tosygen
abruptly.

"But I might offer an alternative solution that might give
our operatives here a chance to pursue their search."

"What would that be, Mr. Heathstone?" Tosygen asked
dubiously.

"Obviously, Mr. Premier, somehow we have to expedite
this search and discovery, since it is both unhealthy and
unsafe to maintain our constant state of preparedness.
Someone might make a mistake somewhere, or some member of the press might get dramatic and instigate regrettable
public demonstrations."

"I do not see any other alternative, Mr. Heathstone,"
commented Tosygen, a tremor of emotion reverberating in
his voice.

"It would not be appropriate, Mr. Tosygen," began
Heathstone solemnly, "for our two nations to maintain offensive and defensive alerts if the President of the United
States, along with important members of his government,
were to accept your invitation to vacation in the Crimea. I
should enjoy visiting your underground installation, and
from there, we could both have open access to reports
coming to me concerning the progress of our search."

A stunned silence occupied both ends of the video channel.

Finally, Tosygen broke the hiatus.

"Mr. President, we should be glad to entertain you and your party, but I have been advised that, should you come here to our, ah, vacation resort in the Crimea, our security would doubtlessly be jeopardized, much as would be the security of Deeprock—isn't it?—in your Rocky Mountains if we should be invited there. No. Your suggestion is not feasible. However, perhaps we could both meet at some mutually agreeable site."

"Accepted!" Heathstone stated immediately. "I will leave it to my Secretary of State and your Minister of Foreign Affairs to determine such a mutual location."

"Thank you, Mr. President, for your understanding." Tosygen was smiling, impishly. "Mr. President, I have just been handed a report indicating that the orbits of Tolkien I and Tonopah I have changed."

"Allan, Chester?" Heathstone said through tight lips. "I thought you were keeping me informed?"

"I've just been handed the report, Mr. President," Walters stated, fluttering the paper toward the President.

Tosygen continued, "I am advised that the two vehicles have reached new trajectories that will put them in simultaneous proximity at two places. One appears to be, yes, it's over the Tasmanian Sea, the other someplace in the Azores, apparently the small island of Corvo?"

"Tasmanian Sea?" queried Heathstone of his advisors.

"Just off southeast Australia, Thomas," muttered Admiral Hollifield.

"As you know, Mr. Premier," Heathstone advised, "we have not been able to reassert guidance control over Tonopah I."

"As with us, Mr. President. Tolkien I has moved of its own accord."

"We are to assume, then, that the powers interfering with our defensive systems are once more operative?"

"We will monitor the actions of the two vehicles with pointed interest," Tosygen said, and withdrew from the screen.

Heathstone walked across the room to Allan Provost. "Allan, I want to know exactly what is at those two locations, who and what, everything. You don't suppose the Australians have been busy behind our backs, do you?"

"Seems unlikely," Provost said. "But then they do have

space capability. Thought it was all mostly meteorological and astronomical, though."

"Well, find out and find out fast. If there is anything I'll talk directly with the Australian Prime Minister. Seth, get onto your Russian counterpart over the telephone immediately. And, Chester, once you have confirmed that the two teams are in place at Arecibo, haul your ass to get our satellites down as fast as possible. I'm going to have a hell of a time as it is to explain to the American people how one American weapon destroyed an American site. I'm taking no chances on these others. Got it?"

"Got it, Mr. President," acknowledged Walters glumly.

7:00 P.M.

"Here's the Dan Merriweather obituary," said Lieutenant Joe Abrams, wafting through the door, a single piece of paper fluttering in his hand. "Got it teleprinted down from *The New York Times*. Took only a half hour. Excellent service, don't you think, sir?"

"Fine, just fine," agreed Judd, taking the paper.

"Read it out loud, Harrah," said Coogan, slouched thoughtfully behind her impromptu desk.

"It's from August 12," began Judd. "God, would you think that was barely twelve days ago—'Services were held today for Daniel Merriweather, internationally famous singer and award-winning song writer, at the Divinity Memorial Chapel. After he was struck down by a speeding taxi in the early morning of August 6, Mr. Merriweather, for whom hope was held out for several hours after the accident, lay in a coma and expired yesterday without regaining consciousness. Merriweather was born on December 26, 1956, in Chicago. After his New York debut in 1972, he made numerous hit records and toured the United States and Europe several times. His compositions gained for him several international awards. Several incidents occurred at the memorial service when lines of admirers broke through police cordons. Fifteen people, including two policemen, were treated for head wounds and lacerations. Burial was private, after cremation. There are no survivors.' "

Judd bit his lower lip at the conclusion of the obituary, and then flung it angrily to his desk. "Doesn't tell us a goddamned thing we don't already know."

"Not true, Harrah," responded Coogan. "Cremation neatly erases any possibility of checking the identity of the body, doesn't it?"

Judd thought for a moment. "But would he have really abandoned everything he had to pull off a hoax like this? Considering his obvious intelligence, he must have understood that he could never come back as Dan Merriweather."

"Maybe, sir," volunteered Abrams, "he never meant to come back as Merriweather, but as something else."

Both Coogan and Judd stared at him. Coogan was first to regain some composure.

"I think we're going to have to take a very different look at this whole affair, Harrah."

"Yeah. But it's going to take a lot of readjustment in our thinking."

"I've really been a little stupid," Coogan breathed, brushing the moisture from her forehead. "I've been trying to construct a hypothetical personality profile for this psychic, when all the time I should have been trying to construct an *actual* profile."

"How do you mean?" asked Judd.

"Well, let's take what we know about him. He is psychic or really superpsychic since his abilities are several powers above anything we have observed before. We know that he withdrew from experimental demonstrations out at the U.N.C. Biocybernetics Center. Why? Obviously because demonstration of his abilities would reveal their magnitude."

"But why should he go to the U.N.C. Center in the first place?" asked Judd.

"Well, let's assess the U.N.C. situation."

"Sir, it's one of the most elaborately equipped research centers in the United States," volunteered Abrams. "He may have needed to be in a place like that to test his abilities."

"Quite right, Abrams, at least, at first," agreed Coogan. "But when he was able to start tracking them down, they necessarily became visible to observers. Witness the psychokinetic destruction potential, for example, and then his refusal to demonstrate it further."

"But if he needed U.N.C., why should he have left?" Judd wondered.

"Well . . . let's hypothesize that he simply outgrew it.

His continuing demonstration of abilities turned into a threat."

"Yeah, makes sense. . . . Naturally, he'd have attracted attention from all sorts of people if he continued to demonstrate his talents, especially if they were developing in magnitude."

"So," continued Coogan, "he would have to opt for another situation where he could both experiment and develop."

General Harrah Judd blinked his eyes in surprise, his tongue licking his upper lip.

"But if he grew much beyond what was observed at U.N.C., then he would become noticeable wherever he was. He could hardly take a psychic step without attracting attention somewhere."

Judd paused in midbreath. His eyelids fluttered, his hands jerked up to cover them. The understanding, the sudden cognition was blinding. "But, of course," he said softly, more to himself than to Coogan or Abrams. "To continue to develop, he had to continue to test himself and his abilities, and they'd have become visible eventually. So he had to come up with something so spectacular that everybody'd be concerned about *what* he'd done and not have time to worry about *how*."

"Correct!" Coogan said excitedly. "Now he could go around, say, reducing the Empire State Building to dust, or creating general havoc, the way a child might do."

"But instead he chose to try to disarm the planet, which is, essentially, sort of a humanitarian thing," concluded Judd.

"But, sir, how can you call that humanitarian, the destruction of two cities?" asked Abrams.

"Now, Lieutenant Abrams," Coogan said softly. "If he'd simply destroyed the weapons or deactivated them, what do you think the reactions of the two governments would have been?"

"O.K., O.K., Dr. Coogan," agreed Abrams, closing his eyes. "I thought of that when I said the other just now. They'd have blamed each other, of course, and acted accordingly. As it is, neither government dares to move for fear of the two satellites it has left up there moving to destroy other cities."

"We should think of the nature of those weapons he visited down on only two cities," continued Coogan. "Certainly, warfare based on the general use of those weapons would be maybe a million times more horrific than the destruction of just two cities."

"But that, why that's unbelievable," stuttered Abrams. "Why such a gigantic move? Why not something smaller?"

"Good question, Abrams. Let's assume that the abilities the usual psychic demonstrates, say influencing the rolling of dice by slightly above chance, or the usual form of clairvoyance of ten cards out of twenty-five, is psychic level one. Normally, in a sort of linear accumulation we should expect to see a psychic level two. But suppose his abilities did not develop in easy gradients like one, two, three, four, and so forth, but along some other equation like one, ten, one hundred, one thousand."

"Not arithmetically, but exponentially," said Judd.

"Yes, from inferior psychic, such as most of us are, to psychic, which is just above chance, to superpsychic, say to the tenth power above chance to—"

"To *megapsychic*," Judd said. "Plain ordinary psychic multiplied by a million."

"Whee," breathed Lieutenant Abrams, sinking into a chair. "But isn't it inhuman to destroy whole cities? How could he justify that?"

"How could *we* justify it, Abrams?" said Judd. "After all, he didn't invent the weapons. We did. Our philosophy of deterrent power did. He merely put a convincing stop on them."

"But surely the U.S.S.R. and the United States are not going to take all this lying down once they figure it all out," protested Abrams.

"I am sure he's thought of that, Abrams," ventured Coogan.

"Oh?"

"Obviously," said Coogan, "he considers the development of his abilities paramount, possibly even to his survival. That would be a psychological constant, one which I should have recognized."

"How is that?" asked Judd.

"Well, look at people in general. They have always felt that their strongest potential should be developed to ensure their survival. In our present culture, most people have concluded that survival was to be to the fittest, the strongest force. Thus, Earth has become a force-polarized planet, and the balance of all important powers has been governed by accumulations of superior force. Possibly our man considers that the development of the psychic nature of man will antiquate mere atomic or microwave force in favor of a philosophical poise that perhaps only he can see. With what must be to him a lofty end in view, probably the realization of powers unknown in nature and man, the actual means of their present demonstration should make little difference. It's only necessary to him that he should claim the time and space to develop."

"You mean he is sitting around somewhere growing?" asked Abrams.

"Or mutating or generating, or whatever it is that has brought him to his first exponential increase," Judd said.

"Well, Harrah," Coogan said, "our first steps should be clear now."

"Right," agreed Judd. "Abrams, I want every scrap of information available on Dan Merriweather. Go to Chicago immediately."

"It would be easier, sir," said Abrams, recovering himself, "to do it all over our teleconferencing computers. I can get all the information quicker if I activate our Chicago intelligence net and assign each operative a section of the search."

Coogan shook her head. "Then he'd be bound to pick up on the fact that we're interested in him, since he is still doubtless monitoring the computer systems."

Judd thought for a moment. "Let's do it Abrams' way, Coogan. He hasn't responded to any of our attempts to converse with him. Let's see what he will do if he understands we're onto him."

"Risky, isn't it? He might zap us."

"We've got to do something," Judd said tightly. "I want all the Chicago information ready for us when we return, Abrams."

"Yes, sir. Where are you going?"

"To catch the shuttle up to New York, naturally. Our first order of business is to find out whether Merriweather really died."

9:00 P.M.
Grateful for the near-arctic coolness of his Washington penthouse, but quite oblivious to its museumlike quality, Rastaban al Nashirah urgently telephoned Senator Heston Davis.

"Heston, I've just been informed by one of my operatives that General Judd has requested and received an obituary of someone called Daniel Merriweather who died a few weeks ago. Why should Judd and Coogan be interested in such a person?"

"Who?" asked Davis, blankly.

"Apparently, Merriweather was some sort of singer. . . ."

"Ah, yes, you must mean the rock star."

"Rock star?"

"Yes. He was all the rage a few years back, but has since achieved some respectability. Has he died?"

"Apparently, Heston. There would hardly be an obituary if he were not dead, now, would there?"

"And you say that Judd and Coogan have—"

"Apparently Judd's aide, Lieutenant Abrams, personally telephoned the *Times* in New York and got the obituary teleprinted down."

"But Rastabi, why should Judd have an urgent interest in a dead man at a time like this?"

Nashirah's face tightened. "You will recall, Heston, that I initiated this conversation by asking *you* that question. I suggest strongly that you look into it. I'm going to take the shuttle up to New York. Sandmuller is giving another cocktail party tomorrow night. I'll be there or at my New York penthouse if you turn up anything."

"Couldn't you look into this Merriweather thing, then?"

Nashirah hung up without responding.

THE PENTAGON

9:30 P.M.

As the evening progressed, Chester B. Walters had been able to regain his nerve and his normal official demeanor. He was comfortably smoking a cigar when Guilda Stern stepped into his office.

"Thought you'd like to know, Chester, that a rumor is floating around. Got it from Hedy Allison, who, by the way, is totally exhausted and seems not to have had any sleep for at least a week."

"It's that goddamned Indian!" snorted Walters. "They don't need to sleep, you know. Extended war parties that go on for weeks, and all that."

"Now, really, Chester! Heathstone is one of the most effective Presidents we have had in office in at least three decades."

"Yes? Well, we'll see about that when the word gets to the press about his monkeying around with superpsychics and all that. He'll be a laughingstock overnight."

Guilda Stern decided to ignore his barbs. "Well, I thought you'd like to know that Air Force Intelligence has finally found something. Apparently, they caught some operatives of unknown employ sending bits and pieces of the Tonopah equipment to a freight-forwarding company called Fast-Jet Services."

"Wonderful! Why wasn't I informed?"

"I *am* informing you. Here is the report."

"Why do those dumb asses take time to write reports? Why didn't they telephone?"

Guilda sighed and continued, "Apparently, Fast-Jet Services is owned by Jet International Corporation, which is a wholly owned subsidiary of Sandmuller International."

"Ha!" snorted Walters, pleased. "Get me Heathstone immediately. Finally, something constructive. Tell Air Force Chief of Staff I want a *verbal* briefing on this as fast as possible. And get me Judd. This sort of falls in his camp, doesn't it?"

"General Judd and Dr. Coogan appear to have left for New York, Chester."

"New York? Why New York?"

"It seems they are trying to track down what has happened to a dead man."

Chester B. Walters rubbed his forehead impatiently. "A dead man? Why a dead man?"

"Well, it seems that the dead man at one time was a rather spectacular psychic research subject. . . ."

"Shit! All this goddamned nonsense when there are *real* things to get under control."

As if on cue, the telephone rang. Guilda Stern picked it up and, after a pause, handed it over to Walters. "The President, Chester," she announced.

"Yes, Mr. President, I'll be right over," he said after listening for a few moments.

"I'll call for your car," said Guilda.

Chester B. Walters leaned back in his chair, chewing on his extinguished cigar. "Guilda," he said softly, "do you think they're onto something?"

"Who, the Air Force?"

"No. Judd and Coogan. Why would they leave all this in Washington unless they really felt they were getting somewhere?"

"I thought you didn't believe in their superpsychic?"

"We have to consider all possibilities in this matter, Guilda," said Walters sagely. "They must be making some progress. Are they being tailed as I ordered?"

"I am sure they are, Chester. Army Intelligence is really very good."

"Do you think Judd knows he is being tailed?"

"I am sure he does, Chester. He's very good, too."

"Well, if any reports on Judd's activities come through indicating that he might be getting close to someone who could qualify as this, ah, superpsychic, I want you to let me know, even if I'm with the President."

"All right, Chester."

COLLEGE PARK, MARYLAND

11:00 P.M.

The weak telepathic probe reached him during that period when his awareness had contracted, a period resembling normal human sleep but which was to him merely a lesser rather than greater period of awareness. He allowed this reduction in awareness to preserve stress on the body. Thus, when the entity housed in Tolkien I reached him, its frequencies activated the appropriate neurons in the brain of Neomort 25-A.

In the dim light, also a sleep period for the technicians on level sub-five, the computers eagerly monitoring for life signs perceived this subtle reflex occurring in the delta and theta wave bands and instantly clattered to life. LIFE SIGN, red, urgent, began blinking, and the warning sounds echoed through almost the entire bioemporium. Almost immediately, Tomachek, Crathe, and several nearly nude attendants were gathered in front of the alabaster cadaver.

"Neuronal decrease accelerating," came the unvoiced communication from the distant schist. "Regrettably, neurons are never replaced. My time is running out."

Neomort 25-A, a little flustered, sped his own telepathic impulses toward the speeding Tolkien I vehicle, there identifying with the flowerlike brain specimen, formerly named Yuri Gorokin.

"What can I do to help?" Sirius asked.

"You are in danger, since you have forgotten to block the computer life-sign indicator."

"It doesn't matter. Judd and Coogan are onto me anyway. I had thought my cover was going to be good. But I was mistaken."

"Onto you?" queried the declining intelligence.

"Sorry. That means they have discovered me, or at least they probably will very soon."

"Can you stop them?"

"I don't really care to. Both are developing their meta-sensory capacities at their subconscious levels. Judd is coming along nicely, and will probably break through shortly."

"Then you will not be alone?"

"No, probably not."

"I am happy, then. We were very pleased to discover your potential and to help you along."

"I am honored, but I will never forgive what they did to you and the others."

"It was our fault. We were too eager. We failed to perceive, and the penalty was thus just."

"Perception is painful."

"Perception itself is not. Only what is finally perceived is painful, sometimes. There are many beauties, too."

"The other two wished to end as soon as it was possible, and I directed their vehicles into the consuming atmosphere. Shall I do the same for you?"

"Yes. But first I wish to watch as closely as possible the preliminary reactions of those renegade scientists on Corvo. I may learn something in my last moments."

"I will slow the velocity of your vehicle until it is identical with Earth's rotation. You will become stationary over the island. Is that satisfactory?"

"Quite. And thank you for making those decisions that we all knew were difficult for you. Good-bye."

"What about the other schists remaining in Russia?"

"Their neuronal count is likewise decreasing. They will die before long. Do not waste time on them."

"Good-bye, then."

With sadness, Neomort 25-A withdrew and reconstituted his awareness at the bioemporium.

"It's crying, again," breathed Crathe in open awe.

"So I see," observed Karin Tomachek.

"Do you suppose it could be the Lazarus phenomenon?" he asked.

"Possibly. Those dead have been known to come to life again, sometimes quite embarrassingly after hours of refrigeration or at the point of being embalmed."

"What shall we do?" whined Crathe.

"Obviously, if this specimen comes back to life, it would create incredible problems for our entire project. It would complicate the definition of death, and you Americans are so funny about all that. Our best option is to allocate it for dismemberment, immediately."

"I understand," Crathe said.

"But before that, we really should take advantage of this peculiar brain-wave activity." She thought for a moment, her hand massaging her square masculine jaw. "We will implant intracerebral electrodes through the skull and attempt to locate precisely the sectors from which this activity is emanating."

"But that is sure to destroy neurons along the path of penetration," Crathe reminded her.

"Never mind that. We are going to dismember it anyway. Bring me two electrode assemblies, a scalpel, and the drill. We will start with the frontal lobes and the thalamus."

As Crathe drew up a gleaming display of instruments spread over a sterile white napkin, Neomort 25-A reassumed direct control, first of the body's autonomic nervous system, at which time the pale, luminescent body flushed rosy red and exuded an audible sigh, then control of all reflex systems. Karin Tomachek stepped back in surprise. The computers went totally wild, almost every indicator coming to life.

Tomachek paused only momentarily, though. Her hand reached for the largest scalpel on the table. Sirius opened his eyes, two gleaming opalescent orbs.

Crathe screamed and stepped backward. The other attendants, frozen in tableau for a second, suddenly scrambled for the air-lock door. It bounced shut on its rubberized stripping, the pneumatic lock wheezing.

Dr. Karin Tomachek, pale but nonplused, gazed into the eyes of Sirius. "You are dead," she advised him, "and you are going to stay dead." She lifted the scalpel to sever his jugular veins.

It was an eerie moment. An electrical crackle surged

through the now living corpse of Neomort 25-A, a faint cocoon of bluish-white aura momentarily appearing. The scalpel jerked itself out of Tomachek's descending hand. Her thrust fell on the pulsating throat without the razor knife in it.

She yelped and stepped back, grabbing desperately for another.

The respiratory equipment housing Sirius' chest exploded outward from his body. His hand went up, pulling the electrodes from his scalp. With delicate floating grace, he tentatively placed one muscular leg down from the podium, his foot touching the black marble floor.

Tomachek regained her ground instantly, launched another attack.

Her arm froze in midair, her elbow turning against her will, the scalpel blade slicing through her own trachea and jugular veins. A wild look of incomprehension blazed in her wide eyes for an instant before they dulled forever.

As her body slumped to the floor, Sirius continued the process of trying to stand erect. Edgar Crathe fell to his knees in front of him. "Master, master, have mercy," he managed to whimper before he vomited.

The men and women, clawing at the door, turned hesitantly when Sirius spoke to them.

"Do not be afraid," he said.

NEW YORK

In New York, during the early morning hours of August 25, the heat wave engulfing the city for nearly two months broke and the temperature mercifully fell twenty degrees. Astor Golderman had barely drifted into a relaxed, comfortable sleep when the intercom from the lobby jarred his nerves. The doorman informed him that there was waiting to see him on an urgent matter an Army general by the name of Judd and a female companion. No, they would not say what they wanted over the intercom, but they wished to assure Mr. Golderman it was of national importance.

He could hardly avoid seeing them, he thought, but after they had been admitted to his sitting room and he finally comprehended the drift of their questions, he was first irritated at himself for his lack of perspicacity, then embarrassed by his tattered bathrobe, and finally nervous about inadvertently disclosing the secret he was guarding.

"Of course, he was buried," he protested angrily at General Judd's persistent questions about the disposal of the Merriweather corpse.

"But where, Mr. Golderman?" persisted Judd. "We have checked all the records of the mortuary. His body was claimed from the Mount Sinai Medical Center, embalmed thereafter. There was a memorial service. We discovered the coffin was never opened for display, and that immediately after the memorial service, the body was taken to the Upper Bronxville Crematorium and cremated."

"That's exactly what happened," stated Golderman sternly.

"But then, Mr. Golderman," asked the woman, who had been introduced as a Dr. Coogan, a medical woman who had instantly raised Astor Golderman's suspicions, "where are the ashes now, exactly?"

"Well, I have the small plaque and the urn that contained them," said Golderman.

"But the remains, Mr. Golderman?" persisted the military man, his eyes glittering and fierce.

"Well, sir," began Golderman—instantly regretting his use of the word "sir"—"actually, Mr. Merriweather was not very specific about the disposal of the ashes. And he was usually so precise, you know. No, I suppose you don't," he concluded.

"We are beginning to have some faint idea of that," said the woman grimly and somewhat mysteriously, Golderman thought.

"The remains, Mr. Golderman," persisted General Judd, his voice growing more threatening by the moment. Astor Golderman finally shrugged his shoulders.

"I don't see why I shouldn't tell. After all, Mr. Merriweather's instructions said nothing about that."

"Well?"

"There are several Merriweather fan clubs, you know, groupies of both sexes, and some of them besieged me both here in my apartment and at my downtown offices for either all or a portion of the ashes. I had to call the police several times. Finally, I divided the ashes up into half-cup portions. There is not really much ash that remains after cremation, you know. Surprised me a little. There wasn't nearly enough to go around. I thought there would be more."

"To go around?" asked the woman.

"Yeah. I gave each official group some of the ashes. Finally, there were no more ashes left, and when all those freaks were convinced of that, they finally left me alone."

Both his interviewers were silent after this announcement, and Astor Golderman, his eyes flicking nervously between the two, thought it best not to volunteer any other information.

"Mr. Golderman," said General Judd in a soft voice, "it is of the most extreme importance for us to know that Dan Merriweather actually died. I can't tell you how necessary it is for us to know."

"Actually died!" screamed Astor Golderman. "What do you mean? Of course, he died." The tension of lying to this dangerous, implacable man caused his heart to palpitate. He collapsed back into the softness of the couch.

"Are you all right, Mr. Golderman?" asked Coogan, rising to feel his pulse.

Golderman quickly recovered his wrist from the soft

cooling fingers and used his hand to wipe the sweat that had sprung out on his face. "Of course I'm all right. Of course Mr. Merriweather is dead. Of course it is late at night. And of course I don't understand at all why I'm getting the third degree like this!"

"This is not a third degree, Mr. Golderman," Judd advised him as sternly as before. "But you're right, it is late at night, and we have other things to check out."

"What other things?" Golderman asked, his nervousness increasing.

Judd did not answer and merely said, "Thank you for your time."

Golderman was relieved when they left; and, after seeing them out, he collapsed once more into the softness of his brown, worn mohair couch, his mind racing to try to imagine what that *meshuganeh* Dan Merriweather had gone and done to antagonize, of all things, an Army general. Well, he had never understood his client very well, only the money that had come in, the enormous amounts of money that lay undisturbed in banks and vaults in at least a dozen different cities. He reflected.

Whatever Merriweather had done, this was probably only the first of the problems. Merriweather had a penchant for getting involved in difficulties. Golderman was grateful that he had been treated so gently by this strange couple. They were definitely onto the fact that the ashes probably were not those of Daniel Merriweather, but, of course, they did not know where the Merriweather body had gone. He decided, before reopening his relaxing eyelids, that it was definitely the time to travel in Europe, the way he'd always wanted to, and use some of the funds Danny had left him. Europe . . . anywhere people wouldn't be asking him questions he didn't want to answer. . . .

When the doorbell rang for the second time that night, he rose from the couch, irritated to think that the strange couple had more questions to ask. Judd and Coogan had treated him with kid gloves; their successors did not. When he opened the door without bothering to use the peephole, a fist broke though his open lips, shattering several of his teeth.

Two men pushed their way silently into the apartment, closed the door, and equally silently lifted up the slumped form of Astor Golderman, just regaining his breath, just beginning to feel the pain from his broken mouth.

"Just tell us where he is, and we'll go," said one of the figures, a shape not resolving too well through Golderman's shaken vision.

"Wha, wha . . ." whimpered Golderman, the weak sounds increasing in volume into a shriek as the broken nerve ends in his gums finally pushed their shocked signals through to his brain.

"Quiet him down," ordered a brusque voice.

Consciousness left Astor Golderman as an unseen, unfelt blow took him on the left side of his skull. Both men caught the body and dragged it to the couch, where it rested, for the third time, in the warmth of the worn mohair.

"Bring him out of it," ordered one of the men softly, "but make sure he doesn't scream again."

Astor Golderman came up to consciousness for the last time in his life as water was thrown on his face from the vase of wilted roses decorating the mahogany side table. He saw two men hovering over him, one with a knife blade pressing against his throat. His senses correctly interpreted for him the words "Make no sound" just before the grinding flood of numbness cascaded through his chest and down his left arm. His vision weakened, paralysis seized the quivering body. Blackness ensued, through which he dimly heard the words, seemingly coming from a far-off distance.

"The goddamned sonofabitch is dying. . . ."

One of the men stood up abruptly, hesitated for only a moment, then carefully placed his handkerchief over the telephone receiver and equally carefully dialed a number with the point of the knife.

"He seems to have died of a heart attack," the man said into the receiver when Nashirah answered.

"You stupid bastards! I asked you to coax the information from him, not kill him."

"Well, he just dropped dead on us."

"Are you sure he *is* dead?"

"Quite sure. What shall we do now?"

"Does it look as though he died naturally?"

"Well, not exactly . . ."

"Well, what, then?"

"Well, Mr. Nashirah . . . we had to break his teeth in a little."

A brittle silence occupied the telephone momentarily.

"All right. I should have done this myself. Has his body lost its autonomic functions yet?"

"If you mean has it shit or anything like that, not yet."

"Can you throw him out a window or something, make it look like suicide or an accident?"

"Yes, sir. I think so."

"Good. After that, get up to Mount Sinai and talk to— talk, I said, not murder—a Dr. Joshua Willard. No, you had better not. I'll do it myself!"

The line went dead.

The corpse of Astor Golderman fell silently through the night, as if he had somehow stumbled over the railing of his balcony, without a scream, only a rush of wind flapping through his bathrobe. He landed with a spongy thud between two parked automobiles.

4:30 A.M.

Dr. Joshua Willard was not, of course, at Mount Sinai in the middle of the night; but on presentation of Judd's credentials, the head night nurse placed a call to him at his Long Island home. Informed of the urgency of an interview, and worried about his part in the Merriweather affair, Willard hastily agreed to meet Judd and Coogan at the hospital in an hour.

In the interim, Judd and Coogan pored over the Merriweather hospital records that, over strenuous protestations by the chief night nurse, Judd had obtained by flashing his national security credentials.

"What do you make of them?" he asked Coogan, who was perusing the voluminous pages filled with medical jargon that was unintelligible to him.

"Medicine is sometimes beyond me," Coogan confessed. "But it seems that, officially, he must be adjudged as dead. Flat brain-wave spectra are the best criterion we have for adjudging death, and from the looks of all these tracings, he certainly had that."

"No brain waves, you mean?"

"That's right, Harrah. No brain waves."

"Doesn't convince me of a thing."

"But certainly—"

"Don't be *dense,* Coogan!" Judd snapped. "Think of

what we're dealing with, what this guy has done. Turning paper to dust. Monitoring and reprograming satellites. Things like that."

"Don't *you* be dense, Harrah," Coogan flared. "I'm prepared to accept those other things, since I have seen the evidence. But, really, the body would need at least the autonomic responses to keep alive, you know, breathing and all that. These responses are reflected in the central nervous system, which is, in turn, reflected by activity in the brain stem."

"Brain waves, you mean?"

"Yes, brain waves."

"But, Coogan, wasn't the body kept functioning artifically, even in the presence of a flat EEG?"

Elizabeth Coogan was silent for a moment.

"But Harrah, that condition couldn't last very long. Why, he would have to be in a very advanced neurological ward somewhere to keep the body alive like that."

"Exactly," said Judd, his eyes blazing triumphantly.

Dr. Joshua Willard, his clothing apparently hastily thrown together, entered the room.

"Sorry to have kept you waiting, but I really got here pretty fast. Not much traffic, you know, at this hour."

"Thank you, Dr. Willard." Judd rose to his feet. "This interview, Doctor, is of an urgency the extent of which I can't even go into. I only want to inform you that exact and prompt answers should be volunteered since the other alternative is to have you immediately put under arrest and detained on suspicion of espionage."

"What?" blurted Willard, his senses swirling a little.

"First," said Judd, ignoring the man's confusion, "did you provide another body to replace the body of Daniel Merriweather upon his alleged death?"

Willard's eyes opened wide. With intense effort, he partly subdued his confusion.

"General Judd! What is all this? Where are your credentials?"

"To hell with that!" Judd snarled. *"Did* you substitute another body to be buried as Dan Merriweather?"

Dr. Willard quailed before the savage menace in Judd's voice. He fell back against his desk.

"Merriweather was dead! Dead!" he virtually screamed. "He was really dead!"

"But what happened to the body?"

"I don't know. I wasn't in on that. Golderman had all that arranged himself."

"Where did you get the other body?"

"Not from here," stated Willard urgently, his eyes beginning to plead. "Not from here."

"Then where?"

"I have, uh, friends down at Bellevue, down at the DOA receiving section. There are so many, you know, here in the city, unidentified John Does. Golderman promised me the coffin would never be opened."

"So it was a John Doe that was cremated in the place of the Merriweather corpse?" asked Coogan gently, hoping her voice would calm down the shaking physician.

"I suppose so. I really don't know."

"How much did you get for all this?" asked Judd.

"Oh," groaned Willard, his eyes watering. "Ten thousand at the time, and fifty thousand on deposit in Switzerland if the secret was kept for four years."

Neither Coogan nor Judd could hide their surprise. "Four years?" they said simultaneously.

"Why four years?" Judd demanded.

"I don't know, really I don't. That was the deal Golderman made, on instructions of the Merriweather estate. He is executor, you know. Merriweather left no relatives. But he was really dead. I just figured Golderman had his instructions to have the body frozen or something like that and didn't want anyone else to know."

"Where is this doctor who signed the death certificate, this Dr. Ramos Garcia?" Judd asked abruptly.

"Dr. Garcia? Why I suppose he is on duty here. Shall I have him paged?"

"Certainly," snapped Judd.

"So," said Coogan, while they awaited the appearance of Garcia, "it does seem that somewhere there is, dead or alive, a body of Merriweather. It's what we were hoping to find, but it shakes me up."

"Me too, a little," agreed Judd. "But only a little."

"What's going on? I certainly have a right to know," demanded Willard.

Both Judd and Coogan gazed solemnly at the quivering man. Judd finally smiled at him. "You would never again believe your senses," he said, his voice surprisingly gentle. "But apparently you were part of a plot to take over the world."

"What? Take over the world? How could that be?"

Dr. Ramos Garcia entered the office without knocking.

"Ah," murmured Willard, instantly regaining his poise, grateful for the shift of attention from him. "Here he is. Dr. Garcia, these people want to ask you about the death certificate of Daniel Merriweather. You remember, don't you?"

"Certainly, Dr. Willard. Certainly. He had a flat EEG for the required length of time. We decided that he was not alive, and pulled the plugs."

"Please explain," Judd said quietly.

"Nothing really to explain. His body functions were temporarily being sustained by artificial methods in the presence of no brain activity. After the requisite amount of time, he was declared dead and Dr. Willard asked me to sign the death certificate as attending physician."

"Are you implying, Dr. Garcia," asked Coogan, "that you would not have otherwise signed the certificate?"

"Probably I would have waited a little longer. The body was in near-perfect condition, as the records indicate."

"Mr. Golderman," interrupted Willard, "showed me the stipulation in the Merriweather will that in the case of clinical death, the body should be disengaged from the life-supportive systems and turned over to him for disposal. We really had no choice."

"I see," Judd said.

"It would be of the greatest help," stated Coogan softly, "if we could find out what happened to Merriweather's body after it was disengaged from the artificial life-support systems."

"Really?" asked Ramos Garcia. "That's easy. It was claimed by some attendants who transferred it over to portable life-support systems. I couldn't really figure that out— why, if we had declared him dead, someone else would want to keep him going."

"Could you identify them?" asked Judd slowly.

"Well, not really. But I know they weren't mortuary attendants, even though a mortuary name appears on the claim certificate. And on the doors of the ambulance there were the letters TAU."

Judd glanced at Coogan, who shrugged.

"I want to telephone Washington, Dr. Willard. May I use this phone here?"

"Certainly, General Judd. Uh, I realize that perhaps I

have been less than circumspect in this matter, but can't we come to some sort of an agreement? . . ."

"Abrams?" asked Judd, his call going through in a matter of seconds, "get our New York boys busy. I want every remnant of Dan Merriweather's possessions confiscated. . . . Oh, you already did that? Then, I'm here at Mount Sinai in the office of Dr. Joshua Willard. . . . Right, we're onto something hot. I think we should have protective custody for at least two. . . . Right, they'll wait here with us until it arrives. We'll be back on the first shuttle this morning."

"Protective custody, General Judd, or arrest?" asked Willard.

"Protective custody, Dr. Willard. There will be others who will want to know what you have just told us and might not be so delicate about it."

8:00 A.M.

Rastaban al Nashirah found himself possessed by a sudden rage, uncharacteristic of his usual dispassionate view of his profession and its problems. Did he not pride himself on the emotional detachment with which he ordinarily pursued his activities, accepting temporary defeats and profitable victories with equal calm? But this whole affair was different—it could change the whole concept of war and peace, and the balance of fear that provided the market for what *he* had to sell. His very existence was in hazard—and now he was forestalled in his efforts to do something about it, first by the blundering brutes who had destroyed his best source of information, and now by Judd. The general had got to the hospital first, and would by now have pried out from someone inside the information he himself was looking for.

Nashirah sat in his small, innocuous sports car. This ordinary-looking vehicle, which he used when he wanted to move inconspicuously, was parked almost directly across from the emergency entrance to Mount Sinai. The discomfort had begun when he had arrived and had almost driven into the middle of the military personnel who were stationed at the entrance. He had quickly parked his car and slouched behind the wheel, unable to flee until he knew what was going on.

Then Judd had exited, followed swiftly by Elizabeth Coogan. Shortly after that, two men were escorted into a waiting car and driven quickly off in the company of a group of bodyguards that Nashirah knew would be difficult, if not impossible, to penetrate.

The brittle, greenish-blue New York dawn had also irritated him. It was not at all like the sudden bursts of splendor that illuminated the beginnings of day in his homeland. A shudder of loneliness ran through him.

Weapons and the dealings of humanity he understood. One simply found the right people and opened negotiations. Yes, that was it! He was in unfamiliar territory. How did one deal with another human who had turned his mind into the most formidable weapon ever dreamed of? A man to whom he could not possibly sell his own merchandise, and consequently a man with whom he probably could not even open negotiations. It was unthinkable that such a man could be allowed to exist!

The flurry of activity had left the hospital entrance, leaving a sudden silence. The night lights monitoring the emergency platform went out, their automatic timers activated by the growing light of the New York morning.

Nashirah started his car, drove to the first pay phone, and got Aloysios Sandmuller out of bed.

"Judd beat me to the hospital. Going by all the activity there, I'd have to say he also beat me to the punch."

"Can't you go in and interview someone there, anyway?"

"No, it will be easier to get an update on Judd's activities from my girl in Washington."

"I got a message from our colleague in the Soviet Union, barely two hours ago. It seems she is advising us that it will be indiscreet to continue to communicate at this time. The Russians, as well as the Americans, are apparently looking into just about every possibility of espionage, places that they could be paid to ignore before. I'm afraid we will have to suspend a good part of our activities for a while."

"Yes, I understand. We've got to get him, Aloysios, get him and make sure he does not continue to exist."

"Wouldn't it be better to, uh, capture him?"

"Hardly possible. He is, if I interpret the situation correctly, his own megaweapon. What use would he have for ours?"

"Ah, yes, I see. We might end up being controlled."

"Or dispensed with altogether. Compared to his planetary potential, our organization has become antiquated overnight, just like any other old weapons system."

"Well, this can't last forever," said Sandmuller uncertainly. "The governments will have to do something about it all, since they are the ones directly affected."

"Don't start sounding like an old woman on social security, Aloysios. It doesn't suit you."

"Well, what should we do then?" Sandmuller demanded querulously.

"We can't take any chances on his escape or survival if, and when, Judd locates him. Increase surveillance on Judd, and if it even looks like he's reaching the vicinity of this man, I'll be ready to act."

"Act? How?"

"Oh, I have several reserve modified mobile nuclear devices here and there."

"Good God, Rastabi! You can't be thinking of—"

"You do your part, Aloysios, and I'll do mine."

WASHINGTON

10:00 A.M.

"If you don't come personally and say something directly to the press, Mr. President," said Hector Allymany, finally having achieved a personal interview with Heathstone, "you have my resignation." He waved a folded piece of paper crumpled between his fingers.

"Sorry, Hector. I know you've done your best." The strain of the recent days on Heathstone was hardly visible. He was as immaculately dressed as ever, and if he showed an unaccustomed pallor, only those closely associated with him could discern it through the ruddy complexion he had inherited from his ancestors.

"I'll say something, of course. We'll go right now, in fact. Is there anyone in the press briefing room? I hope you won't resign." He led the way quickly from his office, through the darkened morning corridors, to the press room.

"Sorry to blackmail you, Mr. President. But I was at my wit's end. The press room is a shambles. People have been sleeping, sleeping mind you, in every corner."

"You mean it's packed?" asked Heathstone, smiling a little.

"Packed," Allymany confirmed.

Thomas Cordero Heathstone stepped into the press room

unannounced. He choked immediately on the several days' accumulation of sweat odors and the fog of cigarette smoke.

"Jesus Christ," yelped someone, "it's the President."

The room erupted like a herd of cattle responding to a sudden lightning bolt in its midst. Hector Allymany barely had time to gain the podium in advance of Heathstone's relentless push through the screaming crowd.

"Ladies and gentlemen of the press," he shouted. "the President of the United States."

Contrary to Allymany's expectation, the room instantly quieted as Heathstone took his place and looked around.

"Sorry to have kept you waiting so long," Heathstone began. "I hope you have been comfortable."

A ripple of smiles first, then unified laughter broke the tense atmosphere into shards. Almost everyone revived.

"Just tell us, Mr. President," asked the representative of the Associated Press, "what the hell is going on! What happened to Omaha?"

"I have been in constant communication with Mr. Tosygen. He has been as confused as I. But we have now concluded, and quite correctly I believe, that a third force has become active between our two nations and has interfered significantly in the balance of deterrent weapons. In order to prevent similar interference with and misuse of strategic weapons, Mr. Tosygen and I have begun the orderly withdrawal of orbiting satellites carrying such weapons. And Mr. Tosygen and I plan to meet as soon as possible and seek to extend our disarmament programs and attempt to localize and discover the exact nature of this third force."

Heathstone paused.

From somewhere in the audience, "Is this third force another nation, Mr. President?"

"We do not understand its nature very well, but we are working in that direction."

"Is it this third force that is threatening the destruction of San Francisco and all those other cities?" demanded another voice.

"Those satellites will be withdrawn as requested by this third force."

"But, Mr. President, what kind of third force could order such actions?"

"Again, I say, we do not know that yet."

"What about all these rumors of some megapsychic . . .?"

Thomas Cordero Heathstone quickly descended from the podium and, followed by Hector Allymany, left the smoke-filled room pretending that he had not heard the last question.

10:30 A.M.

General Harrah Judd and Dr. Elizabeth Coogan staggered wearily into Judd's office. Coogan sank gratefully into her now-familiar chair, relaxed her head against its back, and immediately closed her eyes.

Lieutenant Abrams stood expectantly by Judd's desk.

"Anything to report, Abrams?" asked Judd, fatigue obvious in his voice.

"Not too much, sir. Sirius has not, as you expected, responded to any of Dr. Coogan's messages. During your flight back here, those two men up in New York you wanted have been whisked to a very safe place in the Rocky Mountains. Dan Merriweather has erased most of his childhood in Chicago. People remember him well as the famous rock star, but not as a youth. There are bits and pieces. Do you think he can block out people's minds also? Astor Golderman seems to have committed suicide, jumped to his death. That's all. Not much, is it, sir?"

"Suicide?" asked Coogan. "He didn't seem that nervous."

"Could he erase minds, sir?" persisted Abrams.

"I don't know, Abrams. Anything is possible, I guess."

"Well, people who should have known him, their minds seem to be too conveniently blank on his past. And, sir, we are being spied on from every direction. One intelligence service is trampling over the other in an effort to get a breakthrough on this."

"I understand, Abrams. I even noticed that weapons dealer, what's his name, Nashirah himself, slinking in a car outside the New York hospital. Seems strange to see him doing his own footwork."

"Abrams, Coogan and I need to go grab some sleep. Half an hour on the plane just wasn't enough. I want you to do two things. Get us every institute, organization, and group whose initials begin with TAU. But also get everything that begins with IDC, FTO, you know, things like that, so our stampeding intelligence friends and spies will be a little confused. When you have all that, bring the

TAU list over to my apartment. Can you do all this without raising suspicion?"

"That's the simplest task in this mess so far, sir. But why don't I get a couple of cots brought in here? I wouldn't put it past Nashirah to try to kidnap you if he thought you knew anything."

"No one will try that, yet, Abrams."

"All right, sir. Final thing, the President has been trying to get hold of you."

"Give his office a ring. Tell him we have to sleep but will be in touch in a couple of hours."

But of course they did not sleep. Not at first, anyway. And when the ecstatic needs of their bodies were sated, they slept only fitfully.

"It's just all too urgent," Coogan finally said, rising, throwing back the sheet, running fingers through her disarrayed hair.

"Yes, I suppose so," Judd agreed, lighting a cigarette. "I feel rested though, you sexy computer system."

Coogan ignored him. "Well, General, where do we go from here?"

"You tell me."

Coogan was thoughtful for a moment. "Is history being changed? Yes, I suppose so."

"If we could just get a notion of what it is he thinks he is doing. . . ."

"One thing, he's disarming the whole planet," Coogan said.

"Yes, but why is he doing that?"

"You know, it's kind of funny. Imagine! This huge machine of deterrent force. Who would ever have thought that it could all be sent tumbling like a house of cards. Don't you see the joke?"

"It isn't that funny. It's not only the balance-of-power stuff that's deadly. The whole culture—here, Russia, Africa, anywhere—is loaded against anything that makes sense for people. Poisons all over—political poison, poison in the air and food, mental poison. I don't know what the hell a human being is supposed to live like, but I don't see anything going on that makes me believe that's the way it should be. So much that we all do—me included, damn it!—it *against* life. And I wonder why the hell it has to be that way—*if* it has to."

Coogan was surprised at the emotion, the vehemence

with which Judd had spoken. She sensed no comment was needed and remained silent, taking his hand gently in hers. He turned, came back from the visions of the past, the present, the possible, forming, reforming, dissolving. He smiled.

"Thanks," he said.

"For what?"

"For not saying anything. That wasn't very much like me. After all, I'm a military man, myself, aren't I? Part of the whole mess I'm talking about."

"Yes, you are, Harrah. But you are also a man with a sense of immortality. I see that clearly, now, for the first time."

"Maybe," said Judd, dubiously. "If I could only get a handle on what he really means by all this . . . I don't know, maybe I'd—"

The doorbell rang. Abrams entered with a single piece of paper.

"There were not too many TAU's, sir. And I did divert everyone's attention on several false tracks. Did you know your apartment is being watched? What do we do now?"

"Well, Coogan, what do we need?"

"We need a large organization somewhere, possessing or having access to the most complete computerization facilities ever invented, with neurological research wards, or something like that. You know, some deep-sleep research center, possibly even a cryogenics unit, as Dr. Willard suggested."

"Also," broke in Judd, "I would suspect that, wherever it is, it will turn out also to be almost impregnable from many aspects. I hardly think he would inter himself in a place that couldn't be made totally secure."

"I don't know if it's helpful, sir, but it sounds like you're talking about Trans-American University. It has all those things you mentioned."

Judd and Coogan stared at Abrams.

"Jesus Christ!" said Judd. "Right in our back yard."

Coogan gasped. "And the computers there! Why didn't we think of it? Why, it's the largest computerized system in the world, outside the military, that is."

"God, what genius!" Judd breathed softly. "What utter genius. Imagine one man commanding the world from Trans-American University!"

The trio lapsed into silence. Coogan estimated Judd's

emotions, distinctly revealing themselves in his face. "They will be certain to kill him," he said.

"Yes, I know. It seems we have a decision to make, Coogan."

Elizabeth Coogan hesitated for only a moment. "I think we have already made it."

Judd hesitated, then nodded solemnly. "Abrams, where can we get the floor plans for Trans-American?"

"I already have someone working on that, sir. We ought to have them shortly. I sent someone over to Trans-American security offices with a priority request."

"Good," Judd said. "Get them to us as quickly as you can."

NEW YORK

4:00 P.M.

Mr. Aloysios Sandmuller, a large group of immaculately dressed sycophants fluttering obediently around him, made *his* peculiar type of flutter as he passed through his afternoon cocktail guests, politely, diplomatically, and politically greeting each one of them. The chatter, soft lights, and sense of power atop his New York skyscraper was pleasant to him, as it was impressive to almost everyone else. Lord Devon, United Kingdom ambassador to the United Nations, and Kurt Ehrenwald, its Secretary General, however, betrayed their lack of respect for the omnipotent potentate of international business.

"Don't you think, Kurt," asked Lord Devon somewhat sourly, "that we really ought to turn some attention to these flies in the international ointment?"

Ehrenwald raised his scanty eyebrows. "It was my impression, Critchie, that you had a very comfortable relationship with Sandmuller—that your own duties and his interests coincided fairly often. Are the sands shifting so drastically?" Ehrenwald chuckled briefly at his pun.

Devon frowned. "That sort of thing's always easy to misunderstand, Kurt. One must deal with men of power, no matter what one's opinion. But . . . what's been going on lately makes me wonder if time isn't running out for Master Sandmuller and his kind—and his Arab jackal, too—ah, *there* you are Rastabi! Good to see you."

Rastaban al Nashirah, observing the British ambassador

in discussion with the Secretary General, had moved in on
them. "Thought you were in Washington," Devon said.
"Any news from down there?"

"Nothing in particular, Critchie," lied Nashirah. "Everyone knows that the President is getting ready to meet with
Tosygen."

"I did not know that," stated Ehrenwald, irritated to discover once more that he was not fully in the picture. But
such was the fate of a Secretary General; nobody told him
anything until it was too late.

"This is all really a marvelous flap, isn't it?" Devon murmured. "Death, destruction, satellites, psychics. Goes
James Bond one better."

"I think, Mr. Ambassador," said Ehrenwald darkly,
"your sense of humor is out of place."

"Nonsense, Kurt," Devon replied. "The two powers got
just what they deserved. Whoever this third force is has
displayed an interesting penchant for poetic justice. The in-
ventors of the terror weapons have themselves been the
ones to suffer, and from their own weapons, too—the biter
bit."

Ehrenwald looked at him sourly.

"Well, what do you think of it all, Rastabi?" Devon
asked, trying to shift the direction of the conversation.

Nashirah forced a smile to his lips. "It is quite amusing
that the Russians, who for centuries have always had an
absolute horror of anything foreign, should now fear their
own weapons more than any foreign ones. And the Americans, who are but a vast, undisciplined tangle of conflicting
nationalities and ideologies, should suddenly have to deal
with something even more foreign; yes, it is amusing from
the viewpoint of us internationalists who are trying to transcend the concept of nationality."

"Well, the in group has grouped," commented Aloysios
Sandmuller, finally having circulated enough to get to
them.

"We were just discussing the situation; my friends here
have been trying to be amusing about it," Ehrenwald said.

"This bizarre disarmament business, I presume?"

"Yes, Mr. Sandmuller," Ehrenwald confirmed. He
flicked his dark eyes briefly at Lord Devon, and a note of
grimness entered his voice. "There was also some brief discussion of what the state of the world might be like if intri-
guers such as you were disposed of."

The silence was stunning, modified only by distant chatter and clinking glasses.

Sandmuller composed himself. The insult was too open to gloss over.

"Talk like that could get any Secretary General returned to the obscurity from which he had been raised, Mr. Ehrenwald, raised by men like myself."

"Perhaps, Mr. Sandmuller," retorted Ehrenwald. "The weapons may now have been withdrawn, but the battles are not over. The type of social effort which I like to think I represent has a better chance if the stakes for which . . . men like yourself . . . have played are swept off the board."

Sandmuller's eyes were blazing.

"Now, Mr. Sandmuller, I must excuse myself," Ehrenwald said. "We all realize the United Nations is a weak tool, but it must do its work all the same. I must conserve my strength for the ordeals we will soon face. Good night." Ehrenwald turned and walked briskly away through the crowd.

Before the electrified pause could be broken, an aide whispered something to Sandmuller.

"Not now, goddamn it!" Sandmuller replied.

"But sir, the telephone call is from the President."

"President, what president?"

"Mr. Heathstone, sir."

Sandmuller hesitated only briefly. "Excuse me, gentlemen. I won't be too long, I trust." He walked quickly to his office.

"Sandmuller?" snapped Thomas Cordero Heathstone.

"Yes, Mr. President, what can I do for you? It's good talking to you, as always."

"I have been advised that you and your organization are involved in illegal shipment of Tonopah equipment to some sort of island in the Azores. Is that true?"

The office seemed to perform a somersault around Sandmuller. "Why, Mr. President," he stuttered, "I know nothing at all about that."

"Sandmuller, it is imperative for the preservation of peace that we prevent the further proliferation of such devices and, in fact, create a moratorium against their future manufacture."

"But, Mr. President, I know nothing at *all* about such matters! Sandmuller International, as you well know, is involved only in peaceful scientific and financial enterprises."

"Sandmuller, you've been investigated before, but you'd better know that you're going to be investigated right down to your inlays, and you'd better come up clean!"

Sandmuller had collected himself. "Threats, Heathstone? You are threatening me? *Mr. President,* you would do well to recall some of the realities of the world. You have your office . . . but my power rests on something more solid. It is not very prudent for an elected official to enter into a contest with Sandmuller International."

"It may be just that, Sandmuller. But you can be sure that I'm going to carry out the duties of my office as long as I have it—and my term still has a couple of years to run."

"We might see about that, Heathstone," snarled Sandmuller.

"Also, I thought you might like to know that the Soviet satellite Tolkien I seems to have assumed a stationary position above the island of Corvo. And my staff reports that in about five minutes our satellite Tonopah I will rendezvous there with it. We have drawn significant conclusions. Can you draw any?" The President of the United States hung up on Mr. Aloysios Sandmuller, leaving him staring into a dead telephone, his mind rushing rapidly to digest the meaning of the last words. When he did, he dropped the telephone without hanging up and ran through the cocktail party.

"Rastabi, for God's sakes," he called. "What does it mean if the Tonopah and Tolkien satellites are converging on Corvo?"

Nashirah's dark skin turned a dull sallow shade.

"I say, Rastabi," said Lord Devon. "Corvo? Isn't that your island retreat?"

Their consternation was further increased when a sweating Senator Heston Davis puffed up to them.

"Rastabi," he said urgently, "I took a call for you from someone named Shirley Paars. She said that the target is at Trans-American University. Do you know what *that* means? I flew up on a jet chopper. It's waiting for us down at the Battery."

"Trans-American University. What on earth's that?" But no one replied to Devon. Davis and Nashirah had already disappeared through the chattering guests and into the tower suite's rapid-descent elevator.

CORVO

6:00 P.M.

The electronic blue luminescence indicative of life presence in the slice of brain tissue was rapidly dimming. The telepathic receptors of the disembodied consciousness tenuously connected to Neomort 25-A registered its warning, sensed the exterior hull of Tolkien I, and then reached far below to the volcanic topography of the westernmost island, Corvo. The Azores were old islands; young compared to the continental land masses, but old to men. The consciousness waited patiently.

Ah, there it was, rising above the western horizon, the Tonopah satellite, coming at him at a velocity of 18,000 miles an hour. In a moment, the last moment of his association with the chrysanthemum remainder of the brain stem, the advancing satellite's sonic signal touched the receptors of Tolkien I. In that moment also, the other signal burst forth, directed at the island.

The few islanders native to Corvo never knew what dissolved their bodies into dust. In the laboratory beneath the eclectic house owned by Rastaban al Nashirah, however, the first pulses of the microwave shattered glass vials, interrupted the operation of the various delicate electronic equipment, and set up betraying resonances in the completed Tonopah devices awaiting shipment.

The technicians and scientists quickly understood and rushed to get out of the building. Some made it to the open veranda surrounding the hideaway. They had just enough time to see the ocean parting in a cleft darting toward the island as the water molecules vaporized in the path of the Tonopah wave front before their bones turned liquid and their skulls burst in red and white blossoms that gleamed in the setting sun.

The plaster and stone of the house settled in an ooze of dust. The earth itself trembled. Mount Caldeira, the seven-hundred-foot sleeping volcano that dominated the central northern portion of the island, was stirred back into activity by the microwave bursts. In seconds the living conduit of molten rock burst upward through the volcano's weakened neck, flinging dark clouds against the early sunset.

Tonopah I blinked a signal at Tolkien I; the expiring

THE ATLANTIC OCEAN

AZORES
(ILHAS DOS AÇÔRES)
(To Portugal)
1:1,000,000

The island of Corvo, destroyed 6:00 P.M., August 25, apparently by joint action of U.S.A. Tonopah satellite I and U.S.S.R. Tolkien satellite I. This joint attack ruptured the volcanic strata beneath the island, causing tidal waves bringing serious destruction to the coasts of other islands in the group. Purpose of attack has not been understood.

human consciousness of the brain schist received it gratefully. Then Tonopah I receded swiftly into the eastern distances, and Tolkien I began its rapid descent into the consuming atmospheres surrounding the oxygen-helium beauty
of the planet. The dwindling consciousness gave the equivalent of a sigh. At the very end, he had learned nothing new.

WASHINGTON

8:00 P.M.

"Thank you, Mr. President, for agreeing to see us pri-
vately," Judd said.

"Be quick, General. I have to leave shortly for Iceland.
Tosygen agreed on Reykjavik. Seems it's about halfway,
and the Icelanders have agreed to put up with us. Do you
happen to know what the temperature is up there?"

"Cool, Mr. President," Coogan responded, "you'd better
take a coat."

"I take it you've found the man you were looking for or
you wouldn't have asked for this private talk."

"We think we have, sir."

"O.K., shoot. I gather you have a plan?"

"Coogan," Judd said, "you tell your part, then I'll go
into mine."

"Right. Mr. President, the first thing is, we aren't able to
say definitely what mind or consciousness are. Are they
functions of the brain or—"

"Dr. Coogan," Heathstone said gently, "if you propose
to discuss the philosophy of consciousness or the meaning
of the word 'mind' in any detail, we're going to be here
all day."

"Ah, no, I don't, Mr. President. It's just that there's been
general agreement that the mind *has* to go with the body,
that they're inseparable. It's common sense, after all. But
there are people who have been led to believe otherwise,
both by speculation and experiment; and for, oh, forty-
some years there's been a lot of argument about whether
mental functions can exist unrelated to outer or inner stim-
uli, whether mind can manifest itself in anything but be-
havior, and whether mind can exist without a functioning
brain. Most scientists have said not."

Thomas Cordero Heathstone was silent for a moment.
"And you're disagreeing with that?"

"We have to, sir," said Judd.

"I assume your investigations have turned up hard evidence for this?"

"We believe so, sir."

"Are we then dealing with what might be called 'pure mind'?"

"We have concluded, Mr. President," Coogan said, "that our person can exist . . . well, with or without a body."

"I see," Heathstone said softly. "We are really in trouble then, aren't we?"

"The very existence of psychic phenomena," Coogan continued, "suggests very strongly the existence of a condition of mind not bound by the laws of the physical universe. Even physics has come to a point where it has to deal with the nonmaterial, which fits in with this idea."

"And you're saying that someone's found his way into this new universe of mind?" asked Heathstone, looking at her grimly, his green eyes intent.

Coogan took a deep breath. "Well . . . yes," she said faintly.

Heathstone rubbed his sleek black hair, pushing it off his forehead. "O.K. If that's the way you see it, I'll accept it. What next?"

"We have come to ask you not to destroy him," said Judd flatly. "To call off the intelligence operatives so we can get to him."

Heathstone's eyes burned into Judd's. "Because he's too valuable, you mean?"

"Yes."

"What if I don't agree?"

"We hope you will."

"Why?"

"May I go out on a limb, sir?"

"You're way out already, General—go on."

"It is my deepest conviction that this boy, for it is a young man—or was, sir—has discovered that force is the wrong way to change the world and will use his powers differently."

"How do you know that?"

"Call it a hunch, sir."

"I can't very well tell the intelligence people to hold off because you've got a hunch, General Judd."

"You have used hunches before, Mr. President," said Coogan.

Heathstone grinned at her. "Perceptive, aren't you, Dr. Coogan?"

"And, Mr. President," Judd continued, "the world is in desperate trouble—you know that yourself. With men as they are, how can we hope to succeed? No matter what you and Mr. Tosygen try to do, we're going downhill. And now, here is one boy who is something new—something that may represent a way for the human race to grow in a new and better direction. We must help him to live and develop in spite of what he's done."

Heathstone suddenly laughed. "It's quite a joke, isn't it? He's done more for international cooperation in one month than we have been able to do since the first A-bomb was exploded. Well, give me a moment here."

The Oval Office, occupied time and again more by crises than by men, was silent except for the distant Washington street sounds.

"I'll compromise. You tell me where he is. I will give you twelve hours. If you don't by then report satisfactory progress to me, I will have to take steps."

"I don't think we'll be able to report to you, sir," Judd said hesitantly.

"Why not?"

"If he's where we think he is—and *what* we think he is—well, our finding him will be a kind of point of no return. He'll have to do something about us. If I'm right that he's learned that force, the kind of thing he did to Omaha and Novosibirsk, isn't the way, then . . . well, I think I'd have to throw in with him, help him develop in some way that could mean a new chance for the whole world. Or, if I'm wrong, he'd kill us on the spot to cover his trail."

"It seems, General," Heathstone said softly, "that you're telling your Commander in Chief you mean to take a course that means either suicide or desertion." He paused and looked sternly at Judd, then relaxed. "Ah, well, it's no crazier than what's been happening lately. And you, Dr. Coogan?"

She nodded. "I, too, will go with him, if he will have me. I couldn't pass up such an opportunity."

Heathstone regarded them. "You two have certainly taken an odd turn. Not at all the stern professionals of a few days ago. All right. You have twelve hours."

"I don't think we'll need that long, sir." said Judd, rising.

"But after that you might look for us or our remains at Trans-American University."

"Good lord," exclaimed Heathstone. "Trans-American! No wonder our computers were so vulnerable!"

"So, you now have some idea of his potential," Coogan said. "Imagine, operating through the facilities of Trans-American, and not one yelp from any of the thousands of technicians there!"

"O.K., hop to it, you two. Judd, do you know how to get routed up to me in Iceland through the communications center here in the basement?"

"Yes, Mr. President."

"Good luck, then."

AUGUST 26

Trans-American University

COLLEGE PARK, MARYLAND

12:08 A.M.

Shortly after midnight on August 26, Judd and Coogan, followed by Abrams and Shirley Paars, entered the general reception area of Trans-American University and marched up to the uniformed night attendant on duty.

Corridors radiated in all directions around them, gleaming glass walls, behind which lurked computers, most closed down for the night, some showing blinking signals indicating they were in use by a distant source.

"Bioemporium!" snapped General Judd, flipping out a green identcard that seemed to answer any questions the night attendant might have had.

"Level sub-five," he said. "Take corridor fifteen to elevator bank two. You have to change at level sub-three since two only goes down that far. There you take the hearse."

"Hearse?" asked Judd.

"The elevator to level sub-five."

"I see," Judd acknowledged. The party of four found its way in silence down corridor fifteen to the huge elevator doors that opened on stainless-steel enclosures carpeted with deep blue pile rugs. At level sub-three, Judd suggested that Abrams and Paars wait there.

He then inserted the green identcard into the electronic security pedestal. After a moment a green light came on and the double elevator doors opened onto a large circular room that, once they were inside, drifted downward imperceptibly. The descent to level sub-five took longer than the other elevator, indicating that level sub-five was a considerable distance underground.

Judd and Coogan made the trip in silence, their nerves on edge, their hearts palpitating. As the elevator doors noiselessly parted at level sub-five, a bath of warm dry air engulfed them. It carried in its warmth the smells of formaldehyde and antiseptic, but it was a perfumed air, not unpleasant. Their skin, waterlogged from the turgid Washington summer weather, responded immediately. The dry air was a balm. Coogan could not suppress a small gasp of pleasure and surprise.

They stepped from the elevator into the dimly lit antechamber of the bioemporium, a large oval room of dark blue metallic walls rising from and reflecting crimson carpeting. Several corridors radiated outward. Overhead, the antechamber ceiling was light-studded. A reception desk, the only furnishing, was vacant. In the bioemporium's silence, they could hear the blood rushing in their eardrums.

Coogan's voice echoed. "God, Harrah. It's stunning."

Judd was frowning. "Yeah, I suppose so. Where do you think he is?"

As if in answer, a pneumatic lock clicked to their right and a glass door, till now apparently part of the blue walls, opened directly into a main corridor.

Judd hesitated. "He's waiting for us. I thought he would be," he said evenly, then moved purposefully through the beckoning door into the long corridor.

12:10 A.M.

On the ground level, Rastaban al Nashirah and two men entered the reception area.

"Where did that general go?" he asked the attendant.

"May I see your identcard, please?" asked the young night guard.

Nashirah's identcard turned out to be three blunt-nosed pistols with large silencers. The guard gave these intruders the same directions, and prepared himself to push the night alarm once they had left. Nashirah shot him in the forehead.

Arriving at level sub-three, Nashirah stepped out of the elevator.

"Thank you, Paars, for letting us know about all this," he said openly in front of Lieutenant Joe Abrams, whose mouth dropped open.

"But, Shirley, I thought—" began Abrams, moving in a swift jerk to the alarm in the security pedestal. Nashirah's first bullet took Abrams in his outreaching arm and spun his body in a circle. The second missile plowed into Abrams' nose, demolishing his face, drowning the scream of pain rising in his throat.

"Where are they, Paars?" Nashirah asked before Abrams' body had hit the floor.

"Down in level sub-five, Mr. Nashirah," said Shirley Paars unemotionally, "but I think you need a magnetic card or something to go down there."

Nashirah considered the obstacle presented by the electronic guard in front of the elevator bank. There was no way around it.

"Any other exits you know of?" he snapped at Paars.

"No, Mr. Nashirah. I studied the architects' plans before they came here. This is the only entrance, except for some stairs in case of emergency. But you need magnetized cards for those, too."

"We'll wait here, then," decided Nashirah.

Shirley Paars smiled at him, then studied the sprawled figure of Abrams, leaking messily from the head onto the plastic-tiled floor and already pungent with the degrading odors that came with the body's involuntary relaxation at the moment of death.

She ran her tongue over her teeth—still sharp, sharp—and looked down at Abrams. Less than a minute ago, alive, male, foolish—and now a piece of meat on the floor . . . how much more satisfactory he was this way. It was like the Western settlers used to say about the Indians . . . the only good man is a dead man. He had wanted a home, a sense of belonging—now he'd found whatever he was going to find of that.

She knelt gently by the dead man and caressed the unmoving chest lightly; her hand moved lower, deftly moved among fastenings never again to be opened by their owner. . . .

"*What are you doing, woman?*" Nashirah's voice was choked with shock.

Once more her tongue tested the cutting and grinding edges of her teeth; then she bent.

The next to last thing Shirley Paars heard was a horrified exclamation in Arabic. The last thing was the boom of the shot that flung her sprawling across the body of her ultimate—and in the end, most satisfactory—lover.

When Judd and Coogan got to the end of the corridor, it turned at a right angle. Standing beneath a soft light was a man dressed in white swim trunks, his eyes seeming to glow. His head was close-cropped. His skin seemed translucent.

"Hi," said Sirius simply, "I see you got my message."

Harrah Judd and Elizabeth Coogan stood quite still. Neither knew exactly how to respond. Sirius waited for them to get their thoughts in order. Judd finally spoke.

"You have done terrible things," he said.

"Yes," answered Sirius before Judd's last words had passed his lips. Coogan gasped at the obvious telepathy. "Less terrible than the alternative, though," Sirius continued.

"You've killed thousands of people!"

"More than that. But fewer than would have died within the year if your government and the Soviets had kept those devices operational. They were too terrible, too new, and too different. Each side would have feared the other's weapon and risked all on the hope that their own was the more powerful. They could no more have kept from using them than a leaf drifting in a river can help going over a waterfall."

"But, damn it, it's still murder, mass murder! You can't just play God and snuff out all those lives so casually and—"

"Casually! You *know about* Novosibirsk and Omaha, General—I *saw* what happened, *felt* it, all at once. I let myself *be* there, and I will tell you that it was terrible beyond anything you can imagine. I think that if your military and your politicians could experience personally the effects of what they do, if the bombardier's mind had to follow the path of his bomb and *know* what it did to what he thinks of as only a target, that this obscene charade of war would stop in an instant. I have developed powers beyond other humans, but I tell you that I pay a great price for them."

Judd was shaken by the emanation of deep sadness and anger that came from Sirius, resonating with emotions he had often felt after combat—the stupidity and waste of it, even more than the horror.

"Besides, I did not destroy the American and Soviet sites. Their leaders did it themselves. They could have recalled the satellites. I only destroyed the third development center myself, and it was painful for me to do that, but just as necessary."

"*Third* site?" Judd was startled.

"Ah, yes, General. You did not know about the Sandmuller-Davis-Nashirah plot, did you?"

Judd was taken aback. "That sonofabitch Davis! I had a hunch about him. So Sandmuller and the others were working a deal with stolen specifications of both weapons. . . ."

"And setting events in train for an even more certain disaster. There was no other way. . . ."

Coogan said gently, "But . . . with your powers, couldn't you have . . . oh, reached into the minds of the world leaders, Sandmuller and so on, made them not *want* to use the weapons?"

Sirius gave a grim smile. "A moment ago General Judd accused me of playing God—but what you suggest would be that in earnest, or beyond. God, as all the religions understand Him, makes heavy demands of His worshipers, punishes those who do not obey, but does not make it impossible for them to disobey. It is possible that I could control people's minds, and even believe I was doing it for their own good—but they would be slaves only, no more truly alive than the dead of Omaha and Novosibirsk."

The apparent glow around Sirius deepened. "You talk of the death I have caused, but what I am concerned with is life. All things die, and the human body from the moment of birth is a vehicle to carry the skeleton about for a while until it ceases its movement. The knowledge of that makes all men live in fear, and enables them to hate and destroy; they fear it so much they deny it and so waste their short lives in ugly, desperate games. That has been so from the beginning. But now the numbers and the powers of men have grown so much that the extinction of all life is possible, and rapidly becoming certain, unless there is a change. I am that change."

Judd was almost frozen with a dread he could not understand. He had been able, as part of the professional problem that faced him, to postulate the existence of someone with powers like this, and to set about seeking him out. Given the facts, it had been the only course that made sense, bizarre though it was. But to confront the fact in actuality—to *experience* Sirius—was something else. It was as though he found himself alone in space, facing a terrifying immensity he could not comprehend and knowing he could never return to Earth. Damn, he thought wryly, I'm too fit. I suspect it'd be a comfort, just now, to have a bad heart, and be able to drop dead peacefully and not have to go on with this. . . .

"Just so, General," Sirius said with a sad smile. "You and Dr. Coogan are on a threshold now, and you know that you must step through it; and the death you carry in you calls you back from life."

Judd gave a long, shuddering sigh and closed his eyes for a moment.

"You are already halfway across it, or you would not be here. You did not find me by reason, but by the opening of your psychic nature. You cannot close it in again; it can only go on unfolding and growing, bringing you in closer touch with the universe of life that touches on this concrete, mortal one."

"Why have you let us come here?" asked Coogan.

"Largely because I am alone . . . now."

" 'Now'?"

"Yes. There were others, the Russian telepath that prodded me until I caught on. It was his brain schists that ran Tolkien I. Two other brains were in Tolkiens II and III. But they were not as good."

Judd and Coogan were again silent.

"You were prodding me, weren't you?" Judd finally said. "When I thought I was following my hunches about you. . . ."

"Yes."

"And me?" asked Coogan.

"You resist more than General Judd, Dr. Coogan."

"Oh. I do?"

"Yes."

"Well, what do we do now?" demanded Judd brusquely. He knew that he had accepted this strange fate, and would go where it carried him.

"I have power, but am deficient in many ways in knowledge. I need to learn things. I didn't do enough studying. Sociology, the humanities, the philosophies. Somewhere in the stream of human events are clues about how man can live in his positive aspects. You will help me learn; I will help you discover your own natures and powers. We have four years to find them, to know how to do all this differently, General Judd."

"Why only four years?" asked Judd.

"Because by that time, if my assessments are correct, the

moratoriums on Tonopah and Tolkien will have fallen through."

Again a silence.

"We'd best collect Abrams. Where shall we go?"

"Lieutenant Abrams is dead, General. While I was monitoring your entrance into level sub-five, I took my awareness to the upper levels. Three men came in up there. I think it is that Rastaban al Nashirah. He shot Abrams. I am very sorry. I could have prevented it, if I had been on my toes."

Judd bit his lower lip, his forehead wrinkling in controlled grief.

"Oh, Harrah, what a deep pity," said Elizabeth Coogan, tears welling in her eyes. Judd gathered her in his arms.

"That bastard!" Judd muttered.

"He won't escape. I have frozen all the locks on level sub-three. He will be there when the troops come."

"Troops?"

"Yes. President Heathstone ordered them to stand by, and to come here shortly. He was very funny. He had the order programed to security here at Trans-American. It concluded with 'best wishes.' "

Coogan looked at Sirius. "May I touch you?" she asked.

"Yes, Dr. Coogan, you certainly may."

She put a tentative finger on his forearm. "I had thought you might be just a ball of light or something." She giggled through her tears for Joe Abrams. "Where have you come from, Sirius?" She sighed more to herself than to him. But he responded, catching the question from her mind and not her words.

"I have always been here. There are many like me, but we have not understood ourselves. It's like riding a bicycle. Almost everyone can do it if they try. But in this case, of existing without eyes and ears, of not knowing that we are more than just physical bodies, we have been taught— taught, mind you—*not* to ride. One day I heard a flower singing."

Sirius sang. His lips did not move. But both Judd and Coogan within themselves heard him clearly. And in an instant of comprehension, they fully understood that the human who had been the rock star Daniel Merriweather was not dead at all. He had only changed his form and being.

When the song died away, Judd and Coogan started. The glow had faded, and with it the overpowering sense of an awesome presence. A slight young man stood before them, unusually handsome and serene, but otherwise perfectly ordinary, looking at them with a half-smile.

Judd understood. Sirius was . . . in costume . . . for the next stage of his—of their—journey. He cleared his throat. "I guess . . . we'd better be on our way. Where to?" *Any*place, he thought, exultation beginning to rise in him. Anyplace there is, and some that aren't—the whole universe is opening up. . . .

"I have that planned. We'll want to cover our tracks, disappear completely while we prepare ourselves. There's plenty of money to finance that, money I made singing."

Coogan frowned. "But you're—I mean, you can't just go and draw checks on Dan Merriweather's account. . . ."

"Bank accounts are controlled by computers," Sirius said with a quiet grin. "I think you'll understand that there'll be no problem."

Judd hesitated for a moment. Was he really doing this? Proposing to hide out for four years, planning the reshaping and renewal of mankind with a resurrected pop singer and a woman scientist, living on the proceeds of what amounted to a bank robbery, learning to read minds and float in the air and whatever the hell else Sirius had in store—to throw away duty, career, pension, common sense itself, forever, for *this*?

He waited for a moment, then slowly, solemnly nodded, his decision taken. *Go with the gut feeling, Judd.* . . . He was not sure whether the internal command came from his own will, from Sirius . . . or both.

As Sirius turned and began walking down the corridor, Judd took Coogan's hand, and they followed him.

After a moment, they lengthened their stride and caught up to him and walked side by side with him.

SEPTEMBER 1

Epilogue

THE OVAL OFFICE

10:00 A.M.

"Glad to see you back, Mr. President," said Allan Provost.

"Thank you, Allan. Brief me on what you found at Trans-American."

Seth Mead, seated next to the President's desk, looked on with interest.

"Funny things, Mr. President, funny things. One dead woman, slit throat. One raving lunatic. A group of people in swimsuits who all looked like they knew something special, but none of them were talking. General Judd's aide and a woman who worked for the Air Force were found murdered, quite clearly by Rastaban al Nashirah, who was captured. Imagine getting the world's largest crook on a mere murder charge! And parked as plain as ever in the front drive was a truck with a nuclear device in it. Nashirah says it's his and that he regrets not setting it off. I think he'll get about three consecutive life sentences."

"Is that all?"

"Yes, Mr. President. That was all, except, of course, all those dead bodies in that—what's it called?—that bioemporium."

Hector Allymany burst into the room. "The press is waiting for you."

"Thanks, Hector. Be right there," said Heathstone. "And General Judd?"

"He is listed as AWOL, Mr. President. Very strange, don't you think? Dr. Coogan must be with him, since she's gone, too."

Heathstone smiled. "Yes, I suppose so. Perhaps we'll hear from them one day."

He looked through the window at the White House lawn, green and ordered. They were fugitives, suspect, the general and the scientist—but he knew they were embarked on a great adventure, the greatest any human might experience . . . and he felt a sudden pang of what he wryly recognized as envy. "Well, come on, Seth. Let's tell the world about our new disarmament treaties."

"Certainly, Thomas, certainly. The easiest set of treaties I ever negotiated."

Thomas Cordero Heathstone headed for the door.

"Oh, yes, Mr. President," Provost asked, "what was the final outcome with the Russians about this superpsychic stuff?"

"Why, Allan, I told them it was a mistake on our part. What could they do except grumble a little? They think we are all liars, anyway."

ABOUT THE AUTHOR

INGO SWANN is America's most researched super-psychic, a fine artist, and a gifted writer. His credentials are unique—he is "a cosmic psychonaut who probably has a better grasp of parapsychology than most professional researchers" (*The Search for Superman*); a "sensitive" who has caused temperature changes in remote targets by pure force of will, and who used out-of-body astral projection to correctly predict the major scientific surprise of the Mariner 10 Mercury probe! His powers have been irrefutably demonstrated at the prestigious Stanford Research Institute. He is the author of TO KISS EARTH GOODBYE.